Follow me
Down the stream
Down to where the angels dream.
There we'll rest
Uncounted days
Sleeping silently beneath their gaze.
There, down beside the stream,
Down, down, down where the angels dream...

THE AUTHENTICITY INITIATIVE
Cari Lyn Jones
TOOK THE PLEDGE

Cari Lyn Jones

Where The Angels Dream

Lapis Moon Publishing

Where The Angels Dream

An Affinity for the Dead
Book one

Table of Contents

Table of Contents

VIII

PROLOGUE

Eyes He Could Not See

The wind blowing past him smelled of salt and wildness, that particular, sharp, clean scent that only comes from the sea. Somewhere, waves thundered against an unseen shore. Or was it the pounding of hooves on sand that he heard? But there was no horse. In fact, there was nothing around him but emptiness. He was alone beneath an endless gray sky, the horizon stretching out unbroken in front of him.

A blink.

A heartbeat.

The figure of a woman appeared from the nothingness, cleaving that line where the earth met the sky. Her night-dark hair writhed like a living thing around her as she stood there. The tall dune grasses between them bent like supplicants beneath the wind's merciless hand.

She turned towards him and the distance between them became no distance at all. Eyes he could not see captured and held him fast, as her lips spoke words he could not hear. The pounding of the waves crashed over him. It tugged at him, a tide that pulled him out into the waking world...

Devon woke with his heart racing. He was in his bed, the taste of salt from the sea wind still on his lips. A memory of its touch lingered gently on his skin as he watched the ceiling of his attic room lighten with the rising sun.

CHAPTER I

The Little White Cat

Sara's fingers tapped absently against each brick in the wall next to her as she passed by; tap… tap… tap… Overhead, on the top of the wall, the silent paws of a little white cat seemed to keep time with her as it trotted along.

She saw the white cat's rust-colored ears twitch once before it suddenly bounded ahead, coming to a stop in the shade of an old oak tree. Just below it stood a man, leaning against the rough brick that made up the wall she was walking along. Her step lightened as she recognized the familiar figure of her older brother, Devon.

"I am sorry that I am late," she smiled as she linked her free arm through his. They turned and started off down the street together.

"No need to apologize, pet," he smiled back at her from his lofty height. A lock of his dark hair escaped his cap and fell to cover one eye. It had grown long again. He might be ten years her senior, yet she knew she would have to badger him or he would never have it cut.

"How was school?" he asked, unaware of her woolgathering.

Her own smile faded at his question. She turned her gaze straight ahead to where the white cat was now walking in front of them, the tip of its tail flipping lazily back and forth. It turned its head to look back at her with big silver eyes.

"Mr. Hegdus asked me to stay after school," she confessed. "That is why I am late."

Her brother's arm stiffened beneath her hand. She could tell that he was trying to keep his voice perfectly neutral when he asked, "Should I go speak with him?"

"No, Devon! There is no reason to, really!" she insisted emphatically. "He was incredibly nice about it. He waited to talk to me until after everyone had left, even the two boys who were in detention. In fact, he made it look like I was staying to help him sort papers."

"What did he speak to you about?"

"He asked who I was talking to during recess," she told him, her heart quailing a little as she did so. She looked up into her brother's eyes. They always reminded her of the piles of autumn leaves back home, all shades of gold and bright copper. However, at that moment all she saw in them was worry. She had certainly not meant to make him worry. "I have been so careful, truly! And I was absolutely sure that no one could see me. It was just that Martha was so lonely and sad seeing all of the other children playing together. I could not, not talk to her," she insisted quietly.

"I know, pet. I know," Devon slipped his arm from hers so that he could put it around her shoulders. "What did you tell him?"

Sara looked down at her feet. The white cat was now walking alongside them. Its unblinking eyes looked up at her encouragingly.

"I told him I was talking to a make-believe friend. That it was only a game I was playing." The lie still bothered her. She hated telling untruths, even when she knew it was a better choice to do so. Devon gave her shoulders a slight squeeze. He also knew she hated to lie.

"What had he to say to that?"

The schoolmaster's answer had not been the one that she had expected.

"He said that everyone sees things a little differently in this world. But that it was important to be mindful of what kinds of friends I make. That having certain kinds of friends may make it hard to make others, which I thought was an odd thing for him to say."

"It was an odd thing for him to say," her brother agreed.

He said no more about it. He didn't have to. After all, this wasn't the first time such a question had been asked of her. Although, it was the most unusual reaction to her answer that she had ever received. That was for sure.

The long shadows of late afternoon chased them down Winding Street until they reached Mrs. O'Toole's boarding house, where they were staying. Devon pushed the ironwork gate open for her. The golden light of evening poured into the courtyard from over the brick wall. It gathered in honey-colored pools on the worn flagstones and dusted the cheeks of the bronze mermaid who sat combing her hair in the court-yard's small fountain.

The narrow steps of the boarding house waited just ahead and the white cat trotted up them without pause, disappearing through the front door. Only a few steps behind, Devon opened the door and held it for Sara. The smell of beef and fresh bread wrapped around her as she stepped into the foyer.

Setting her school things on a small table near the front stairs, she followed Devon into the dining room. He handed her a plate when she joined him, a little heap of buttery gold potatoes already on it. The rest of the food was spread out like a king's feast along the huge sideboard. Thinly sliced beef dressed in peppercorns and herbs sat next to a basket of crusty bread and a bowl of fresh tomatoes and lettuces that Mrs. O'Toole had grown in her garden. Which still seemed strange to Sara, given that it was already October, if only just.

Most magnificent of all were the thinly sliced onions that had been seasoned and fried to a crisp. A small vanity of Mrs. O'Toole's, who liked it to be said that her meals were of the same caliber as what one would expect to be served on Grand Avenue or at the Vue de la Mer Hotel. An absolute truth, Sara thought, as she happily added more than a few of the crunchy little strings to her plate.

She made her way over to the table where most of the other boarders were seated already. They greeted her politely when she sat down next to Devon.

At the other end of the table, Mr. Lawrence quickly returned to his reading of the newspaper's evening edition, having dispensed with the expected pleasantries. On the other hand, Miss Newkirk who was sitting across the table from Devon seemed determined to try drawing them into a prolonged conversation. Sara thought she was nice enough, except for the all-too-obvious interest in her brother. Sometimes she had the uncharitable thought that the young woman's only reason for speaking with her was to catch Devon's attention.

Sara watched as the white cat walked back and forth through Miss Newkirk's slender hands, making them tremble. The fork the woman was holding fell from her fingers, clattering loudly on her plate, much to her consternation. Sara guessed that the white cat did not like Miss Newkirk flirting with Devon either.

The quiet woman sitting next to Miss Newkirk patted the flustered woman's arm as she smiled across the table at Sara and asked how school had been. Mrs. Madison was a very gentle person. A retired school teacher, as Sara understood it, she often took the time to speak with her, offering Sara a kind word or to help with her homework. She had a smile for just about everyone, even though her eyes always seemed a little sad.

Sara was pretty sure that Mrs. Madison could not see the young man who often stood beside her stroking her hair, but she seemed to take comfort from it nonetheless. His name was Jeffery and he had been waiting a long time for her to be happy again. But she was still so sad that he stayed, and was content to stay as long as she needed him to.

He had once told Sara that he had been waiting for ten years. The dead were not always good with time though, and the thin streaks of silver in Mrs. Madison's dark hair told Sara that it had most likely been longer than that.

Sara smiled back at Mrs. Madison, doing her best to include the ghost standing next to the woman in her smile.

After dinner, Devon had gone out to sit on the bench beneath the red cedar tree, as he often did. The air was cool and the courtyard was quiet save for the watery trickle of the fountain and the wind sighing through the branches above. He could feel the damp chill of the seat beneath him, even through the sturdy material of his trousers. Still, it was not as chilly as it would have been at this time of year back home in the north.

He drew softly on his small pipe as he watched the evening shadows grow thicker. Tobacco was a luxury he used to rarely indulge in, mostly because of the expense. But circumstances had changed with his new job, and tonight seemed a good night for it.

The glow reflected from Sara's window above winked out, and the darkness folded in softly in its absence. He did not have long to wait before he felt a small body lean against his leg. A tail curled around his calf in a sort of hug before disappearing. The feel of small paws pressed against his shin was soon followed by the brush of whiskers across the back of the hand that he had draped over the ankle of his crossed leg.

He could not see the cat, of course. Sara was the only one in all their family that could see the spirits. He could touch them though, just as easily as he could anything made of flesh and bone.

"Is she already asleep, then?" he asked his companion and was answered by a deep contented purr. "Good. This afternoon could not have been an easy one for her."

The feeling of paws on his shin vanished only to reappear next to his collar. Whiskers tickled along his jaw as a weight settled on his chest. The cat's nose came to rest just below his ear where it continued to purr contentedly. He lifted his hand to stroke the phantom fur, having no need to worry if someone might see him in the darkness.

"It is not in her nature to lie," he confided softly to the apparition who was keeping him company. "It always makes her unhappy when she has to. But she does not want to upset the living you see, and she is unwilling to offend the dead."

The cat gave a little trill as if in agreement, before resuming its breathy purr.

"Do you know she has not even mentioned you to me? Though I've no doubt that you two are already well-acquainted with each other," he ruminated as he drew on the pipe he held in one hand, while his other continued to stroke the invisible fur of his companion. He blew the smoke out into the night, watching as it twisted and curled in on itself like a serpent. "And, that, my little cat, concerns me more than I care to admit."

That his sister might keep her own confidences did not bother him much, but that she might do so because she did not want to worry him, did. His sister may not like to lie, but she would make less of something if she thought it would ease the minds of those around her. Certainly, her reluctance this afternoon to tell him about her conversation with the schoolmaster had illustrated that.

The man's odd reaction to Sara's answer also set Devon to wondering. It may be a good idea to have a look at this Mr. Hegdus, he decided.

Eventually, the purring in his ear faded, as did the feel of the apparition's fur beneath his fingers. He took a final draw on his pipe before tapping it out on the side of his boot heel. He stood up and slipped the pipe into his trouser pocket before heading back through the courtyard and up the front steps.

He left his cap and coat on a hook at the front door. The house was dark and quiet, resting as its people slept, the sound of its ticking heartbeat coming from the grandfather clock in the hall. Devon turned left out of the foyer, making his way through the dining room to the silent kitchen beyond where the fragrant ghosts of dinners past twined with the scent of resting dough set aside for the breakfast yet to come.

His boots made little noise as he climbed the back stairs that led up from the kitchen to the floors above. The gentle glow of a gas lamp, turned down low for the evening, made the second-floor landing into a small island of light. It was soon left behind as he continued on towards the top and the two attic rooms he rented for his sister and himself.

He stepped off of the narrow landing into a shadow-filled hall. After a month of living at the boarding house, the darkness was not much of a hindrance, and he moved with surety towards the table that he knew stood just a little ways from the top of the stairs. Striking a match, he lit the candle that waited there. Beside it was a pad of paper and a pencil which he used to quickly write a note. He blew out the candle, folding the paper in half. Making his way to the door of the room on the right, he carefully slipped the note beneath it, then made towards his own door across the way. The doorknob gave a quiet snick as he turned it and another as he closed it behind him.

The street lamps outside turned the room's front window a soft gold but did little to light the room itself. Devon did not bother with a candle as he changed into his bedclothes, and soon he was stretched out across the clean sheets of his narrow bed. Whiskers brushed his cheek, letting him know that he was no longer alone. The feather pillow his head was resting on gave a little when the phantom cat curled up next to him. Its quiet purr soon settled into a steady rhythm, rising and falling like the rolling waves on an unseen shore. He let himself drift with the sound; knowing that when he closed his eyes, the now familiar figure of a dark-haired woman would be waiting for him, down at the edge of the sea.

CHAPTER II

Where the Angels Dream

When Sara had woken up that morning, she had found a note slipped under her door, asking her to wait before heading off to school. It turned out that she had not had to wait at all because by the time she had made it downstairs, Devon was already sitting on the porch waiting for her.

"Mrs. O'Toole asked for me to give this to you," she said, handing him the larger of the two lunch pails that had been entrusted to her on her way through the kitchen.

"Thank you, pet," he smiled, taking the pail in one hand while reaching out to tug at the end of her long braid with the other. "If your hair gets much longer, we'll have to find a tall tower to put you in," he teased as he stood up and offered her his arm. "Of course then I would have to watch for princes lurking about in the middle of the night, calling up to your window 'Seraphim, Seraphim, let down your golden hair!'."

She wrinkled her nose at his use of her full name. "I very much doubt there are many princes here in Ashwood, and even if there were, I see no reason for them to stand beneath my window," she pointed out, trying to sound properly grown up as she slid her arm through his, and instead feeling a blush warm her cheeks. That she blushed so easily had always been such a trial for her.

"That's just as well. What would you do with your prince once you were in Pine Hill?" he asked, holding open the gate for them to pass through. "And, princes are useless things, anyway. Better a knight, or given your age, a squire."

Despite her brother's teasing, Sara was unbelievably happy that he was walking with her to school. Even if the reason for him doing so was that he was feeling overly protective. She thought it a little silly that he felt that way just because a teacher had taken her aside to talk. She was thirteen (nearly fourteen), after all, and almost finished with primary school, with the possibility of secondary school and maybe even college before her. At that thought, she impulsively gave his arm a squeeze. Had it not been for him, she would not have been able to move down here in the first place. And then gone would have been her hopes of continuing her education. For that, and many other things besides, she was very grateful.

The sky grew brighter as they made their way down Winding Street. It was one of those perfect crisp mornings when the air was cold enough to make your cheeks tingle before the sun had a chance to kiss it away.

They turned onto Market Street, continuing on their way along one of the brick walks that ran beside it. The October trees above them had already put on their fall dresses, and the cool wind coming in off the water was having a grand time ruffling their hems. Their leaves fluttered down onto the bricks where they turned into vibrant islands of crimson and gold in an otherwise dull gray sea.

A flash of white caught Sara's eye. She glanced down, expecting to see that the little white cat had joined them, but was startled to find a large hound there instead.

"Is something wrong?" her brother asked, no doubt having noticed her jump a little in surprise.

"Not at all!" she assured him, conscious of the other people nearby. She slid her arm from the crook of his elbow and took his hand in hers, knowing that then he would be able to see what she could see. Then she looked back down at the white hound who was still walking beside her.

"Another new friend?" Devon asked as the hound turned its sleek head up towards them, rust-tipped ears standing at attention as it watched them with its bright silver eyes.

She glanced over at her brother sheepishly. His eyes danced as he chuckled, one corner of his mouth quirking up in that way he had.

"You should have learned by now that there's no sense in trying to keep secrets from your older and wiser brother."

She almost stuck her tongue out at him, remembering at the last moment that they were in public, and so chose for propriety's sake to keep it tucked safely behind her teeth. But she could tell by the twinkle in his eyes that he knew what she was thinking.

The white hound huffed at them both and trotted on ahead, disappearing in a ray of sunlight, between one shadow and the next.

Her brother let go of her hand. But his gaze remained intently fixed on the spot where the hound had vanished, a small line of worry creasing his brows. "Have you ever had a visitor like that one before we came here?"

"Do you mean one that was an animal rather than a human?" she asked. "No, I never have. But I have seen two now in just a few months."

They passed through the window of light in which their visitor had just vanished and a thought came to her. "Is it possible that they are not what we assume them to be, but rather something else entirely?"

"I don't know, pet. You have read more of father's library than I have. Perhaps one of us should mention it to him next time we write," he suggested. "Or we could ask Aunt Ruth when we visit again."

Their conversation stopped by unspoken agreement as they turned onto a narrow dirt road called Washboard Lane.

Sara could not stop herself from fidgeting when she saw the schoolhouse up ahead, its cedar siding practically glowing in the morning's golden light. Mr. Hegdus was standing in the deep recesses of its doorway, his dark coat blending with the shadows as though it was made of them. In her excitement, she could not help herself from pointing him out to her brother.

"There he is Devon, Mr. Hegdus, my schoolmaster."

Devon could not have said why he had expected the schoolmaster to be a nondescript man of a certain mien, but he had. He also found that he had been much mistaken.

For one, the cut of the man's coat was finer and more fashionable than he would have thought a simple primary school teacher could afford. It spoke of money and privilege that was much at odds with the man's chosen occupation. He was near enough in height to look Devon in the eye, though the man's build was much leaner. He also had a more affable countenance then Devon had expected.

Devon could tell his sister was more than a little excited to have him meet the schoolmaster because they had barely reached a distance for polite conversation when she began to introduce them.

"Good morning, Mr. Hegdus! May I introduce my brother to you?" The man was only just nodding his head as she continued on. "Mr. Hegdus, my brother Devon Amaris." Devon smiled at his sister's excitement, so different from the usual shyness she had when in a public setting.

"Please, call me Kristoph," the schoolmaster insisted, reaching out to shake Devon's hand warmly.

"Devon," he said, returning the schoolmaster's handshake.

"Devon, of course," the man continued affably. "A pleasure to meet you! Truth be told, your visit today is quite fortuitous, at least on my part. I have been hoping to have the opportunity for us to speak. Is there a convenient time I might call on you both?"

His sister was trembling, so much so that Devon thought she might jump right out of her skin from nerves. He tamed the grin that tugged at his lips when he glanced over at her shining face.

"We would be glad to make ourselves available to you this evening if you would like," Devon replied. "We are staying at O'Toole's boarding house on Winding Street."

"Splendid!" The schoolmaster's enthusiasm was evident as he reached out to shake Devon's hand a second time. "Would seven o'clock be convenient? Or would you rather earlier?"

"Seven o'clock would be perfect," Sara confirmed before Devon had a chance to draw breath. He nodded his agreement.

"We're agreed then, seven o'clock it is," said the schoolmaster. "I am very much looking forward to speaking with you this evening." The smile he gave Devon was a genuine one, but there was an expectation in the man's eyes that made him think their conversation tonight would be about more than Sara's schooling.

Devon took his leave of them then, continuing on down Washboard Lane for a little ways, before turning onto a narrow alley that ran between two rough walls made of piled limestone. That way led him down into the Flower Streets and what was considered the better section of the Bottoms. The houses he passed were somewhat older, but neatly kept. Their small yards lined with fences made of wood or short walls of coquina, a curious rock made up of tiny shells, which he had never seen before moving to Ashwood. Many of the garden plots still had growing vegetables, a testament to how much further south he was from where he was used to.

The lanes became smaller as he went along and the houses grew shabbier until he eventually stepped out onto Nightingale street. In contrast to the dirt lanes he had just been on, this one was nearly as broad and well maintained as the roads off of

High Street, paved with crushed shells and lined with a curb and brick walk as it was.

Most of the businesses at this end of the street were coffeehouses, pubs and the like. There was even a tobacconist. All of them were closed at this time in the morning, of course, and it left the street empty except for Devon. Or so it seemed, until a muzzle nosed up under his hand, followed by a narrow head pushing up against his palm. He could feel the hound's sleek body lean into his thigh. He did not bother to look. There would be no point since there would be nothing there for him to see. But he let his arm hang down, surreptitiously tailing his hand over the soft pointed ears as they walked down Nightingale. It seemed their visitor from this morning had chosen to follow him rather than stay at school with Sara.

Devon was just passing a large tidewater house, when a woman's velvet-wrapped voice called out to him.

"Good morning, love."

He stopped near where the house's broad steps swept up from the walk to the porch that stood well above street level. A woman, older but still lovely, was leaning over the balustrade there, a silk shawl draped artfully across her shoulders. Several younger women wrapped in brightly colored robes sat at tables scattered behind her. Their eyes blinked sleepily in the morning light as they sipped from mugs wreathed in steam.

"Good morning, Miss Rose," Devon returned the woman's greeting, touching the brim of his flat cap respectfully as he did so. "Ladies."

A brilliant smile lit the older woman's face. "Every day you walk past us and say good morning, but you never come past to say good night," she teased in a voice as decadent as chocolate, while the women behind her twittered and smiled warmly at him.

"Obligations, Miss Rose," he said politely. "My time is not my own."

"Of course, love, of course," she said. "But if you ever do find some time of your own, come see me and my doves. We'll make sure it is time well spent."

Devon smiled and nodded. Touching the brim of his cap again, he continued on his way, turning a deaf ear to the chorus of sleepy goodbyes and speculations that followed after him.

He was once again alone on the empty street, save for his companion who huffed softly as they left the brothel behind. Devon chuckled, "Don't think much of Miss Rose and her doves?"

His question was met with a dismissive snort.

"Ah, but they are the reason we are walking on a brick walk along such a well-kept road, even though we are down here in the Bottoms," he mused, keeping his voice low out of long habit, though there was no one around to hear him. "Most of her usual customers are ones who would prefer to not damage their carriages over ruts. So you see, even if I were inclined to visit one of Miss Rose's doves, it is doubtful I could afford to."

He felt a mouth close gently over his hand for a moment, then release it. He could only guess at what it was supposed to mean. Like Sara, he had never encountered the ghost of an animal before. Not because animals lacked souls, as so many people believed, but because animals did not fight against the natural order of things. And, the natural order said that when you died, you moved on. People seemed to be the only creatures to pit themselves against that order.

But now, in the space of a month, he had met two such apparitions, and they seemed to have taken an interest in his sister and himself. It should have troubled him more, but his gut feeling was that there was no maleficence about either one of them; quite the opposite actually. And he always trusted such feelings where the dead were concerned.

Not far past Miss Rose's, the gas street lamps and shell-packed road stopped, leaving downstreet Nightingale to go on as a much less gentrified version of itself. Rougher copies of the same businesses as the ones he had just passed lined either side of it until they eventually gave way to rows of little houses. Tenant houses for those people who worked for the Ascher family. Devon had been offered one, rent-free, when he had first accepted the job of caretaker for the Ascher's family cemetery.

It was a generous offer. The houses were small but well-kept. Many even had indoor plumbing. But he had decided that staying at Mrs. O'Toole's was a better choice since it was an easier walk to the school. And at twenty-five dollars a week, a phenomenal salary, he could afford it.

Devon had just about reached the cemetery when an elderly man hailed him from the porch of one of those tiny houses.

"Good morning, Mr. Amaris."

"Good morning, Mr. Henry," Devon called back with a smile and an amicable wave.

"Miss Eveline was a bit restless last night," Mr. Henry informed him, gesturing towards the cemetery. The amulets hanging from his porch clattered gently in the morning breeze as if in agreement. "Just thought you'd like to know."

"Thank you," Devon said, nodding his appreciation to the older man as he passed by.

Only a few yards past Old Henry's house, Devon came to the place where Nightingale Street met Fallow Road. There on the corner of that crossroads stood the great ironwork gate of the Ascher family cemetery.

Devon took out his keys and unlocked the gates. They swung open soundlessly, which was a vast improvement from a month ago when they had been nearly welded shut with rust. Now their imposing coquina pillars were clean and painted, and the briar of iron roses that made up the gate itself had been newly blackened.

He closed the gate behind him and made his way up the broad gravel path, now free of weeds. Oaks, thick-boled with age, rose like pillars throughout this part of the cemetery, their interlaced branches forming a domed ceiling as high as a cathedral's over the homes of the dead.

Not far in, he passed by the family chapel and continued on to an inconspicuous shed just beyond it where he kept his tools.

The windows, once fogged with grime, were now clear, and when he opened the door the smell of mold no longer assaulted his nose as it had before. The interior was dim, but there was still enough light for him to find what he needed easily. Shears, secateurs, and a machete joined the rake and small broom that were already in the wheelbarrow. He set a lantern and his lunch pail on top of it all, then grabbed up the handles and set out, locking the shed behind him.

He left the gravel path he had been walking on and made his way steadily between the crypts. Old brown leaves crunched under his feet and swirled in small wind devils as his companion followed in his wake. The undergrowth had not been too terrible here, but once he was out from beneath the trees' canopy, golden grasses grew tall around him. Errant breezes set the dry stalks to rattling on either side as he pushed his wheelbarrow along the path he had cleared a few days before.

Soon, he reached the tall iron fence, which by the look of it had been added some time ago to the old limestone wall that made up the cemetery's boundary. Just the other side of it ran the remains of Nightingale Street, now just an overgrown lane that led from the Bottoms up to the Ascher Estate. It was used mostly by those who worked for the family. Though, it was an old joke that the Ascher men had actually put the road there to make it easier to pursue their vices down in the Bottoms. And that the Ascher women had put the cemetery there so they didn't have to drag the men all the way back home.

Not that there was much of a family left now, to his understanding. The house had been empty of Aschers for years until recently, when the current head of the family had returned from abroad. If that were true, it certainly would explain the poor state of the cemetery, and why he had been engaged to rectify it.

Devon followed the fence a short ways until he reached the spot where he had stopped work the day before. A lone redbud tree stood there, its thin black branches covered in crimson leaves that glowed like little golden-veined hearts in the morning sun. He parked the wheelbarrow off to the side, and taking out his tools, began to carefully cut away the thick grass and weeds that grew beneath them.

Decades of neglect had made clearing the cemetery slow-going. He also had to take great care not to damage or bypass graves, many of which were lost beneath the accumulation of almost fifty years of debris. As he worked, he could hear the dead muttering around him. If he were to close his eyes, he would have thought himself on a busy street rather than in an empty cemetery. Empty of the living at least.

Until he and his sister had moved to Ashwood in September, it had been more than just the dead's voices in his ears to declare that he was not alone. He would often feel the occasional tug at his sleeve or brush against his shoulder. When he was younger, the dead would even pinch him sometimes, until they realized he could pinch them back. But since he had acquired his feline companion, fewer spirits seemed inclined to approach. And so far, the same seemed to be holding true for his newly acquired canine companion as well.

Devon worked diligently as the sun rose higher in the sky until his efforts finally revealed a beautiful bench next to a small grave. Like the bench, the headstone was made of white marble veined in the palest pink and silver. Ethereal and delicate, the picture of a rose just beginning to bloom had been carved in intricate detail at its top with the name, Lenora Ascher, engraved deeply beneath its timeless petals. She had only been ten years old when she died.

After clearing away the last of the weeds, he sat back on his heels. A deep sense of accomplishment settled over him as he surveyed his work. There was a tentative tap on the back of his hand. He turned his palm up and felt small fingers clasped his, he gently closed his own over them.

"Thank you," the voice of a young girl said, then she was gone in a swirl of grass cuttings and old leaves.

"You are welcome," he replied to the empty air.

Devon worked another hour or more before stopping for his noon day meal.

Sitting down beneath the redbud tree, he opened his lunch pail and pulled out the thermos of still warm coffee and the leftovers from dinner that Mrs. O'Toole had packed for him. As he ate, he felt a familiar feline head work its way underneath his hand.

"Well hello, sweetheart. Come back for a visit?" he said, scratching behind the unseen ears. "Is our friend, the hound, still here as well?" he asked.

The cat suddenly stopped rubbing its head against his fingers. Its tail, twined around his arm, twitched. A moment later, Devon thought he heard a carriage coming from the direction of the Ascher Estate. It was not long before he could see it as well. A black brougham drawn by a handsome, leggy bay gelding. The driver barely spared him a glance as he passed, but the same could not be said of the carriage's passenger.

All the spirits fell silent and the world seemed to freeze, gripped by an unnatural stillness. The silver gray of the occupant's suit and topper spectral against the dark of the carriage's interior as the gentleman's pale gaze regarded him. The moment stretched on and on, an eternity embedded in a heartbeat.

A low bark sounded from next to Devon, and time resumed its normal pace.

The gentleman touched the brim of his hat with his cane, nodding to Devon as the interior of the carriage moved out of view. The muttering of the spirits resumed.

Devon realized then that he was standing, but did not remember having done so. The lean muscular body pressed up against his thigh was certainly no longer feline, which begged the question where the little phantom cat had gone. Devon was also beginning to wonder if perhaps he might be going a little mad, because he was quite sure that the bark he had just heard had distinctly sounded like the word "mine".

Dinner had already finished by the time Devon returned to the boarding house that evening. He found his sister and Kristoph Hegdus drinking tea in Mrs. O'Toole's parlor. At the sight of him, the schoolmaster rose and shook his hand regardless of the grave dirt under Devon's fingernails.

"Mr. Amaris..." the schoolmaster began.

"Devon, please." Devon corrected him.

"Devon," the schoolmaster nodded, his eyes crinkling at the corners as he smiled good-naturedly. "Of course. Thank you both for agreeing to see me."

Sara had stayed seated, and greeted Devon in such a restrained fashion that he knew she was doing her best to appear mature and well-mannered. He smiled at her in return, resisting the urge to tease as he sat beside her on the sofa.

"Now as to the reason for my visit," the schoolmaster began, returning to the wing-backed chair which he had recently been occupying. "Sara has mentioned to me her desire to attend Pine Hill Secondary school after she has finished with primary. Perhaps even continuing on to college after that. There are a handful of other students in the school who have also expressed an interest in taking the entrance exams for Pine Hill. To that end, I felt it would be beneficial if I were to set up extra classes. They would be held after school, and would address subjects not covered by the school's regular curriculum, as well as give a more in-depth view of the ones that are." The man's angular face grew more animated as he visibly warmed to his subject. "I believe the classes will help to better prepare students for the entrance exams, and give them more of an understanding as to what they might study there. I was hoping that Sara would be allowed to attend these classes. Mrs. Lawson has said that she would be happy to make herself available if Sara were to join, so there is no need to worry about whether she would be properly chaperoned."

The schoolmaster's genuine enthusiasm about the prospective classes was almost palpable, and Devon already knew his sister's mind. She was fairly quivering with excitement where she sat next to him. He glanced over and found her soft gray-blue eyes staring hopefully up at his.

"If you wish to attend extra classes, I have no objections," he assured her. "I am, however, concerned with you walking home afterward. The days are getting shorter and I would prefer you not to have to walk home alone after dark."

A wash of emotions flitted across his sister's face, but they all said one thing, he was being overprotective. Which was absolutely true.

"A completely understandable concern," the schoolmaster agreed earnestly. "And I would be happy to escort Sara home when classes run late, if that is agreeable to you both."

"That would ease my mind," Devon admitted, surprised at how true those words were. Though he had some reservations as was natural when first meeting someone, it seemed that the schoolmaster's earnest disposition had struck a chord with him.

"So I can go?" Sara asked.

"Yes, you can go if you wish," he smiled at her.

"Oh thank you, Devon!" she exclaimed, abandoning all pretense of maturity and throwing her arms around his neck. The smile she gave him was as bright as the summer sun and as always, it melted his heart completely. The world had not always been kind to his sister, but her good nature never faltered.

Sara thanked the schoolmaster profusely. Devon stood as she excused herself and left the room, her feet fairly floating over the floor as she went.

Devon turned his attention back towards the schoolmaster who had also risen at Sara's departure. He could see that the unasked question he had noticed lurking in the man's eyes that morning was still there. It would be best for him to address that question now, rather than ignore it. Such things usually came back to haunt him, and always at the worst times.

"Mr. Hegdus..."

"Kristoph, please," the schoolmaster insisted, much as Devon had done earlier.

"Kristoph," he acknowledged. "I usually sit in the courtyard for a bit in the evening, if you would care to join me?"

"I would be glad to," Kristoph said. "If, it would not be too much of an intrusion."

"Not at all," Devon assured him.

He gestured for the schoolmaster to precede him as they left the parlor and made their way out the front door. Once they were on the porch, Devon led the way towards the small fountain with its bronze mermaid. He forwent his usual seat under the red cedar in favor of leaning against one of the courtyard's high brick walls. The schoolmaster unknowingly sat in the spot Devon normally would have occupied to smoke his pipe.

He did not give the man time to settle. "There seemed to be more that you wanted to speak to me about," he said, launching straight into the heart of the matter. A touch rude perhaps, but him giving the schoolmaster an opening to discuss his concerns would make the conversation easier in the end.

"Ah, yes. But I am not sure how to broach the question," the man admitted.

"Head on is usually best," Devon suggested, having a good idea of the nature of the question that the schoolmaster was about to ask.

Devon felt a weight settle on his shoulder, his feline companion coming to join him, as it often did in the evening.

The light coming from the boarding house lit one side of the schoolmaster's face. His lips were parted, in the process of asking his question no doubt, but he seemed to have stopped mid-thought. Then, a small, knowing smile stretched across his lips.

"Is your sister a medium?" he asked.

It was not the question Devon had been expecting, and it must have shown on his face because the schoolmaster immediately set about trying to mollify him.

"Peace, my friend, peace," the man said, holding up his hands in a placating gesture. "I mean no harm to you, or to

Sara. On my honor, I came to you only because I was concerned. I was sure your sister had the *sight,* but was not sure if you knew about such things. That changed of course when your guardian made an appearance."

"Can you see spirits than?" Devon asked cautiously, not addressing the man's speculations directly.

"No, no," his guest assured him, shaking his head. "But, my benefactress is an accomplished practitioner, and my family has served her household for a long time. We have become quite sensitive to many things, both seen and unseen."

While Kristoph Hegdus was talking, a whiskered cheek rubbed against Devon's jaw. He felt his companion leave his shoulder, then the man across from him fell silent and went very still. Devon noted that it was not the stillness of fear but rather the stillness that often comes just before the onset of action, which was interesting. The schoolmaster was looking down at his pant leg where the fabric appeared unnaturally stretched as if eight little claws were tugging at it. They disappeared and Devon could see a ripple in the man's hem, as if the phantom cat had brushed across the schoolmaster's shins. A warning and an endorsement? Devon did not know, but it unnerved him a little. He had never heard of a spirit before who was able to affect the mortal plane so strongly.

Devon raised his eyes up from the hem of Kristoph's trousers, meeting the schoolmaster's gaze. There was no fear there, just burning questions and a barely contained excitement.

"My friend, this is highly unexpected," he said. "I had assumed your guardian was a spirit. That maybe one of your ancestors had come to watch over you. What you have here... I'm not sure what it is, but it is strong! It might behoove you to speak to my benefactress. I am sure she could give you some insight into what it is that has attached itself to you."

There was no doubting the sincerity of the man's interest. His facial expressions and manner of speech became more and more animated as his excitement grew, just as it had in the parlor before when he had spoken of the extra classes.

"And I will admit to being very curious about it myself. Though I am not a practitioner, I have an intense scholarly interest in such things," the man paused, as if he were considering if what he was about to do was a good idea. "Devon… would you be amenable to me stopping by again in the future to visit?"

The question hung in the air as Devon considered his own answer, waiting a beat longer that was perhaps polite. Finally, he replied.

"As I mentioned before, I often come out here in the evening. You are welcome to stop in if you have a mind to, Kristoph."

A broad smile lit the schoolmaster's face. "Wonderful! I will take my leave then, before I drown you in questions," he said, standing up. "I hope you do not come to regret your invitation! Truth be told, my curiosity sometimes overrides my manners. Until next time, a good evening to you, Devon." With a parting nod, he left through the courtyard gate.

Devon watched the evening shadows swallow up the retreating figure of the schoolmaster. He would be the first to admit that he was not one who was inclined to seek out another's company, but he thought that Kristoph Hegdus might be a person whose company he would be inclined to keep. The man's gregarious nature was surprisingly comfortable to be around and his enthusiasm reminded Devon a great deal of Sara's and their father's. They also seemed to have that love of learning just for learning's sake. Something his mother was fond of pointing out. And there was nothing that made them happier than to share some bit of knowledge that they had just learned. The schoolmaster seemed much of the same mind.

In short, Devon liked the man. Time would tell whether that proved to be a mistake.

A familiar weight leaned against his calf, its tail wrapping itself around his knee as a close friend might slide an arm around one's waist in comfortable camaraderie.

"Still here," he said, bending over to pick up the little phantom cat by feel. The boarding house's mostly dark windows made it unlikely that someone might be up to see. He held it close and stroked its fur for a moment before placing it up on his shoulder. "Let's go see what Mrs. O'Toole left for me in the kitchen."

CHAPTER III

Dreams of Blackbirds

*B*lack *birds rose up from the golden field with a great whirring of wings. He watched the line of men as they walked along the narrow track. The bright sun on their shoulders did nothing to chase away the shadow twisting in their hearts. He could see it now where he could not before. It filled their eyes and stained their skin. They took no notice of him as he padded along beside them.*

Golden grass stretched out in front of him, an aurulent sea between the fence and the oaks' shadowy eaves. It rippled in the fitful wind, the darkened faces of the gravestones hidden there appearing and disappearing amidst the undulating waves in a peculiar game of peek-a-boo.

Devon had left his coat hanging over the wheelbarrow. His shoulders warmed under the autumn sun as he settled into the swinging rhythm of his scythe. The morning was quiet save for the shushing sound his blade made as it cut through the dry stalks and the ceaseless whisperings of the dead.

An errant gust of wind howled down from the north, pressing the grass flat and startling the blackbirds that hid there. They erupted from the golden field in an explosion of fluttering dark wings, filling the whole of his vision and calling to mind his dream from the night before.

It had been different. Not like the ones he had had nearly every night since coming to Ashwood. Not like the dreams of a woman standing alone beneath a gray sky with wind-tangled hair and eyes that haunted him. Eyes that he could never remember upon waking.

No, last night's dream had not been like those. It had had about it a sense of the inevitable, as if he were merely bearing witness. But bearing witness to what? He did not know, and that left him feeling disturbed and a little wrong-footed.

By noon, Devon had cleared nearly a quarter of the field back almost to the trees. He stopped there, sitting just at the edge of the shade to eat the lunch Mrs. O'Toole had packed for him. He listened to the murmured conversations of the dead as he watched the blackbirds pick their way across the newly shorn ground.

A hush descended, silencing even the rustlings and quiet cheeping of the birds. Devon looked over his shoulder into the dim beneath the oaks' branches. He saw a figure there, walking between the crypts, a shadow among shadows. He rolled to his feet and the blackbirds took flight behind him.

When he reached the spot where the shadow had been, there was nothing to see. Only a swirl of leaves dancing through the empty air between the crypts. The dead resumed their conversations and somewhere far off, Devon could hear a young girl's voice as it floated through the chill air, singing...

Follow me down the stream

Down to where the angels dream...

Sara sat at her desk in the quiet schoolhouse. Of the three boys who usually attended the special classes with her, only one had made it today. And he had left early to help his father. That meant it was only Mr. Hegdus and herself in the schoolhouse, with the occasional appearance of Mrs. Lawson for propriety's sake. So to Sara's mind, it was sort of like they were alone.

Her cheeks flushed a little at the thought. The schoolmaster was very handsome. Not at all crane-like, as the boys liked to say when they wanted to be mean. She thought he looked so refined with his large dark eyes and fine straight nose. He reminded her of a blood horse, like the ones that she saw pulling the carriages in front of the grand houses along High Street, all leanly muscled limbs and elegant grace.

Of course, she would never breathe a *word* of this to her brother! And she would be absolutely mortified if Mr. Hegdus ever found out. Her cheeks burned even hotter at the thought.

She glanced up through her lashes towards the front of the room where he sat at his desk, grading papers. The soft light of the oil lamp illuminated his face, leaving the rest of him lost in the gathering darkness.

It was then that she realized just how late it had gotten to be. She could barely see the book on the desk in front of her. It had been overcast all day, so she hadn't really noticed the light fading.

Sara stood and tucked her work into her bag. Then she headed toward the schoolmaster's desk.

"Mr. Hegdus, I have finished my work," she said.

He looked up from the papers that he had been grading, a smile on his handsome face. Sara watched as the smile drained away, replaced by a look of absolute horror. Before her mind understood what her eyes were seeing, he was up and out of his chair.

"Mistress!" he exclaimed, the pleasant amiable voice that Sara was used to now suddenly twisted with distress.

She turned to see what it was that had caused such a reaction in the usually genial schoolmaster. Standing just inside the doorway was a very fashionable woman wearing a dark red day dress and a stylish little hat. A veil was tucked neatly beneath her chin, covering her face despite the gloom that filled the schoolhouse.

The woman glided towards them, the gathering shadows following along like faithful hounds in her wake.

"Mistress," Mr. Hegdus said again, a note of panic still evident in his voice. "It is still..."

"Hush, Kristoph. There is no danger," she admonished.

Sara felt the woman's attention settle on her like a physical thing.

"Is this the promising new student you have told me of?" The question was obviously directed at Mr. Hegdus. "Will you introduce us?"

Her voice was polished and smooth, with the barest hint of an accent. Sara thought it made her sound cultured and exotic.

"Of course, Madame," Mr. Hegdus answered, seeming to have regained some of his normal composure. "Lady Anasztaizia Károlyi, my benefactress, Miss Sara Amaris, my newest and most promising student." The schoolmaster finished the introduction with a small bow.

"Aren't you lovely," the dark Lady breathed, seemingly unable to look away from Sara. "Even in the evening gloom, you shine like the sun."

The lace of the lady's veil did well in hiding her features from Sara, all except her eyes for some reason. Large eyes like bottomless pools that sucked her down into them. Sara knew it was rude to stare, but she could not seem to stop, she did not even feel embarrassed by her slip in manners.

Tiny garnet buttons winked a deep red as the lady's hand reached out towards her. Shapely fingers clad in black satin moved as though they would tilt Sara's chin up. All the while, Sara stood rooted to the spot as the night-dark pools that were the lady's eyes pulled her down, down, down...

A deep chuff sounded and Sara came back to herself with a giddy rush.

A familiar pale head with rust-colored ears had imposed itself between them, the hound's muzzle bumping the lady's hand away before her fingers could touch Sara. It took a moment for Sara's mind to register what it was it had just seen. The hound's muzzle had not passed through Lady Károlyi's hand. Her fingers had not jittered or shook like Miss Newkirk's had at the dinner table. It had been pushed back as though the hound's muzzle had actually made contact.

Lady Károlyi did not seem particularly startled. She did not gasp or exclaim aloud wondering what had touched her as someone else might. She only continued to stand there, motionless with her hand outstretched, as the hound watched her with its unblinking silver eyes.

"Ah, I see," the lady finally said, pulling her hand back. "Then she is yours. I suspect that it is better that way."

The lady looked back up at Sara, but her gaze no longer held the power it had before.

"Kristoph, please see the young lady home," she said, her eyes flickering up from Sara's face when her request was met with silence. "No need to look at me like that. Logan brought me and he is waiting outside. You can meet up with us later. Do not hurry, just take care that Miss Amaris gets home safely."

The schoolmaster stepped up beside Sara, offering her his arm. She took it a little self-consciously, flushing as she rested her hand in the crook of his elbow. He gave a small bow to his benefactress, and Sara, at a loss, bobbed an awkward curtsy. Her cheeks felt like they were on fire.

"It was very nice to meet you, Miss Seraphim Amaris. You may feel free to call on me if you have need, and my knight will protect you as he would me..." the Lady assured her, "though it seems unnecessary given the protector you have already. Take care, my dear."

Before Sara could think of what to say, Mr. Hegdus was leading her across the room and out the still open door of the schoolhouse. The white hound kept pace with them as they left.

Out front, practically on the doorstep, waited a beautiful carriage. The driver was standing beside it, busily lighting its lanterns. He nodded to them as they stepped out of the door.

"Don't scowl at me, Kris, 'twasn't my idea," the driver said speaking to Mr. Hegdus.

"I know, Logan, I know," her teacher replied. His warm hand covered Sara's where it rested on his arm. "I am off to escort Miss Amaris home. It will be a bit before I meet up with you."

"No fear. All is well," the driver assured him. "Here, you may need this," he said, handing him an umbrella. "Good evening, Miss."

"Good evening," Sara replied, as she was led quickly away.

The air cooled noticeably as soon as they turned onto Market Street. The gas lamps were already lit, the lamp lighters having made their rounds early because of the gloom. Their steady flames made little halos in the misty rain as the wind shifted it this way and that, like a path of will-o'-wisps leading them off into the growing dark.

This was the first time that Mr. Hegdus had escorted her home, and she felt as though her skin had been turned inside out, so that her nerves were on the outside of it rather than inside, where they belonged. It made her intensely aware of everything, of the cold mist prickling against her cheek. Of how the muscles of the schoolmaster's arm moved under the fine wool of his coat as he held the umbrella up over them both, and how he smelled of spices and fine tobacco. It was almost enough to distract her from the strangeness of what had just happened at the schoolhouse, but not quite.

It was not hard for Sara to credit the mesmerizing quality of Lady Károlyi's eyes to her own nervousness. However, the hound's white muzzle pushing away the lady's hand was not so easily dismissed, nor was her reaction. Unless Sara was completely mistaken, the lady had been speaking to the apparition when she had said what she had said after the encounter. And Sara was quite convinced that the lady had been able see the hound just as easily as Sara herself could. Or was she mistaken and it was all just an odd string of coincidences? It was so easy to doubt herself in these situations.

Sara's mind continued to run in nervous circles as the silence stretched on and on, and she began to feel as though she would shake to pieces if she did not break it.

"Mr. Hegdus..." she began, a little afraid he would hear the quiver of nerves in her voice, "your benefactress, is she a practitioner by chance?" Sara thought that she must have startled him, because she felt his arm flex a little beneath her fingers.

"Honestly Sara, that was not what I expected you to ask," the schoolmaster confessed, chuckling lightly. "To answer your question, yes, she is. Did your brother not tell you?"

"He did not," she admitted, feeling a tad hesitant.

That night a week ago when Mr. Hegdus had come by to speak to them about the extra classes, she had known that he had not left directly after she had gone upstairs. Sara had suspected that her brother and the schoolmaster had been out in the courtyard, talking, and had been afraid that the topic of conversation had been herself. That the schoolmaster had taken that opportunity to voice his concerns to Devon about how he had seen her talking to thin air at recess. Because of course, he would not have been able to see Martha like she could.

She had been so tempted then to open her window and eavesdrop, but in the end had been too afraid of what she might hear. Now that she had met Mr. Hegdus's benefactress, she wished that she had plucked up the courage and done so.

Mr. Hegdus, who had been waiting patiently as she had been busy woolgathering, finally broke the silence. "But you know about such things?" He prompted gently.

"Of course!" she brightened and her shyness eased as it often did when she thought of her family. "My father is a scholar, and well-known for his studies in the lost sciences and lesser-known mysteries. He has had practitioners from all over the world come to consult with him. And he is always studying something new. Mama says that he and I are just the same in that way."

"I see, so your mother is not a practitioner I take it," her teacher concluded sagely.

Sara felt a pang of homesickness and suddenly she was not sure if she could blame the blurriness of her vision entirely on the rain. She did not want to cry in front of the schoolmaster, so she kept her eyes focused on the white hound that ghosted along in front of them as she answered.

"Mama is…"

The hound looked back at her. It woofed once, catching her attention. Then its body began to ripple and shrink, leaving the white cat in its place. It winked at her and took off into the dark.

She must have stopped because Sara felt a tug at her arm as Mr. Hegdus continued on a step further before realizing that she was no longer moving.

"Sara? Are you okay?" The schoolmaster asked, concern coloring his voice. "Sara?"

But she could not find the words to answer him. She stood there, her mind trying to catch up to what her eyes had just seen. A figure materialized out of the misty gloom in nearly the same spot where the white cat had just disappeared. Said apparition rode unconcernedly on the figure's shoulder as though something completely untoward had not just happened.

"Sara?" the schoolmaster said her name a third time. "Is something wrong?"

"No, Mr. Hegdus. Everything is fine, thank you," she replied automatically. "Sorry to have worried you."

The schoolmaster's attention shifted, noticing the figure approaching them. "Ah Devon, it's good to see you. I apologize for our lateness."

Sara continued to stare at the cat sitting on her brother's shoulder. It squeezed its eyes shut, smiling at her as cats do, as though they shared a secret. Sara just wished she knew what exactly that secret was.

Devon watched his sister as she continued to stare at the spot on his shoulder where he had just felt the little cat's weight settle. "Are you okay pet?"

"Of course, Dev, I'm fine," she insisted, her eyes shifting to meet his.

The schoolmaster and Sara set off again in the direction in which they had already been walking, and Devon fell into step beside them. Sara was between himself and Kristoph, and the schoolmaster did his best to maneuver the umbrella he was carrying to cover all three of them with only moderate success. Devon silently offered to take the umbrella, since Sara's hand was still tucked in the crook of the schoolmaster's arm. The man gave it over with a nod of thanks.

"Sara was just telling me about your father and his fields of study," Kristoph informed him, trying to catch Devon's eye over the top of Sara's head. Clearly, he had noticed his sister's distraction, but was choosing not to speak of it. At least, not right at that moment. "She mentioned that his expertise is frequently sought after."

"It is," Devon admitted, caution making his voice sound cooler than he had intended.

"I told Mr. Hegdus that practitioners from all over the world often come to consult with father," Sara haltingly confessed. Devon did not know whether her hesitation was because of shyness, due to her obvious admiration of the schoolmaster, or because she was now unsure of her choice to share such a thing with a relative stranger.

"I would very much like to hear more about him," the schoolmaster insisted with an enthusiasm that Devon did not think was feigned. "As you might remember, I have an intense interest in such studies."

They turned onto Winding Street. Even though it was still early evening, the lamps had been lit there as well, and Devon could see the porch light at the boarding house flickering just ahead of them.

"In fact," Kristoph continued, "I am heading down to a coffeehouse, if you were of a mind to join me, Devon? It is not far."

They had reached the courtyard gate by then and Devon took a moment to consider. There were many practical reasons for him to accept Kristoph's offer, not the least of which was learning what it was the man already knew or suspected.

And if Devon was honest with himself, he had found the schoolmaster to be pleasant company the last time that he had called on them. It had been a unique experience for him to speak in a (mostly) unguarded manner. It had made the conversation easier.

But trust was slow to grow and he had a feeling that any conversation they had this evening would be of a more personal kind. Still, he reasoned that to put it off may only increase the man's curiosity, which could prove troublesome in the future.

Decision made, he turned to his sister. "What do you think, pet? Will you be okay if I head out for the evening?"

"I will be fine," she assured him, her eyes drifting up to his shoulder. "Perfectly fine," she insisted with more conviction and a brilliant smile.

"I would be happy to join you then," Devon said to Kristoph.

They walked Sara up to the porch where he took great pleasure in embarrassing her by giving her a kiss on the forehead, like he used to do when she was little. With flaming red cheeks, she went into the house. Devon felt the press of unseen paws slide down his chest and push off as his companion leapt from his shoulder.

He turned to face the schoolmaster. "Shall we?" he said, gesturing towards the courtyard gate.

"Of course," Kristoph replied, folding up his umbrella, which he had apparently only had open for Sara's sake.

They made their way out of the gate and back onto Winding Street. The moisture floating in the air around them made billowing curtains in the lamp light as it tried to decide whether it wanted to be rain or mist. For his part, the man walking next to him seemed unconcerned about the weather, and Devon certainly wasn't one to be bothered by a little rain, especially when it was as pleasant a rain as this.

"I am glad you decided to accompany me," Kristoph said as they crossed Market Street and continued on down Winding Street towards Nightingale. "Your sister, is all well with her?"

Devon knew the schoolmaster was hoping for an answer that addressed Sara's seemingly odd preoccupation, but Devon was disinclined to address it. In part because he didn't rightly know. "Yes, perfectly well. Where are we headed?"

"Gerard's. A coffee house just off of Nightingale, a block or so in from where it meets Winding Street. Do you know it?"

"I do, but it's usually shut when I walk past in the morning," Devon replied.

"Of course, Ascher cemetery is at the end of Nightingale," Kristoph nodded in understanding. "I had heard the position of caretaker was empty for some time before you accepted it?"

"It was."

"I imagine it was something of a mess you walked into then," the schoolmaster speculated.

"Truer words have never been spoken," Devon chuckled. "But I cannot complain. The job suits me and it pays well. More importantly, it has allowed us to move here so that Sara can continue her schooling."

"There were no opportunities for her to do so where you lived?" Devon could hear the puzzlement in the other man's voice.

"Not for the kind of education Sara wished to pursue," Devon said. "Our township is somewhat small. We had to take a ferry to the town on the other side of the narrows just to attend primary school. Most of the secondary schools closer to us only offered classes for girls whose goals were to find husbands."

"I see. And Sara's aspirations are a little higher, I am guessing. Is it safe to assume that "home" is some distance away, then?" the schoolmaster asked.

"Quite a fair distance away," Devon agreed.

"So you found a job and moved here so that your sister could pursue her education? That is a kind thing for you to have done."

"I want to see her happy," Devon said, glancing over at the man walking next to him. "Which reminds me, I do not believe I have thanked you yet for the kindness you showed Sara. It was very considerate of you to speak with her privately and not expose her to the others' ridicule."

Kristoph waved his hand dismissively. "I would never do that to any child, and certainly not someone like Sara. She has a lightness about her that few other people in this world have. Even the uninitiated would recognize that she is special."

"Ah, but not everyone treats such people kindly," Devon pointed out.

Kristoph nodded his head in agreement. "Sadly, that is true. I imagine that things are sometimes difficult for her."

"They can be," Devon admitted. "Though it is less so now than when she was younger and knew no better than to be perfectly open and honest about everything."

"So she can see spirits as well as speak to them?" The schoolmaster kept his voice even and mild although Devon could almost see his eyes were ablaze with curiosity. "You have never quite said."

There were fewer people walking on this side of Winding Street, but he still had an understandable reluctance to speak about such things openly. No doubt Kristoph noticed his hesitation.

"And there is no need for you to," the schoolmaster assured him as they turned onto Nightingale. "After all, I dragged you out to hear more about your father. From what Sara told me, his studies delve into the ancient mysteries and lost sciences. Is that true?"

"It is, but he has an interest in almost everything, from the occult to the mundane," Devon said. "The more obscure the subject the more likely it is that he has studied it."

"Ah, how unfortunate that he lives so far away! I would love the chance to speak with him," Kristoph lamented.

"Do you think he would be open to corresponding with me?"

"I am sure he would." Knowing his father, Devon had no doubt that he would be thrilled to correspond with another academic.

"Happy days!" the man beside him exclaimed, almost boyish in his excitement. "What is your father's name if I may ask?"

"Arthur Vandercroft," Devon answered as they reached the doorway of the coffeehouse.

"Vandercroft? Not Amaris? So, your family follows the matrilineal line. How interesting," the schoolmaster said as he held the door open for Devon. "That is a very old custom, and not one I often see used, even during this age of invention and enlightenment."

Devon stepped inside. He was surprised to find that the coffeehouse was much bigger than it appeared to be from the outside, and well-lit by numerous gas lamps. Tables and booths filled most of the space, arranged so that one could have a small intimate conversation or a large heated debate with equal ease.

Kristoph gestured to a man who was making his way across the room with a tray under his arm, holding up first one, then two fingers. The man nodded in acknowledgment as he continued on his way.

Devon followed Kristoph to a booth in a corner at the front of the room. It gave them a clear view out of the coffeehouse's small front window as well as a measure of space around them. They sat on the booth's overstuffed cushions to wait.

The man Kristoph had gestured to arrived practically on their heels. He set a plain white cup and saucer in front of each of them. A sugar bowl and creamer went in the center of the table next to a burning candle in a copper stand. Just behind him came another man with a large glass decanter of rich brown coffee. He expertly poured some into each of their cups, then set it on the stand with the candle. Their tasks completed, they left with instructions to ring the little brass bell at the end of the table should Kristoph or Devon need anything else.

"So, your family follows the old way of taking the mother's name," Kristoph resumed, picking the conversation up from where they had left off. He made an offer of cream and sugar to Devon who declined. The schoolmaster proceeded to add a generous amount of both to his own cup while asking, "Was that a product of your father's studies or has it always been so?"

"It has always been that way," Devon replied, relaxing back into the comfortable seat, coffee in hand. "In fact, there are a few families back home that follow that same tradition. It is not considered overly unusual."

"Your mother's family must be very old, then" Kristoph observed, taking a sip from his cup before adding a touch more cream.

"It is. My father's family came to this continent a little over two hundred years ago, and my mother's people were already here when they arrived."

"Really! I wonder if that is why they never felt the need to hide their name behind the male line's as was often done during the Burning Times. They must have been on this continent even before the Aschers," Kristoph pondered with a look that was so reminiscent of Devon's father's when he was deep in thought that Devon couldn't help but smile at the sight.

"I am afraid that you are talking to the wrong member of the family to answer that," Devon smiled. "I can tell you that both my mother and father are well respected in our community, though it is my mother they come to if there is a sickness, or someone is having a problem with their fields. It is really only the initiated that consult with my father. But the townspeople see a string of affluent ladies and gentlemen visiting and believe him well connected. Anything odd they see, they dismiss as the eccentricities of the rich."

Kristoph nodded his head and took another sip from his cup. "I suppose nowadays when every housewife can learn esoteric wisdom on a street corner and every well-to-do family has at least one Spiritualist who guests with them, there is less of a need to be so careful."

The uncharacteristic derision he heard in the schoolmaster's voice came as a surprise to Devon. "Why does it sound like you doubt that to be true?"

There was a long pause as the schoolmaster seemed to consider his words. "I have spoken to you of my benefactress in brief before. Where we come from, people have long looked to her and her family for guidance and protection. However, a few years ago, that all began to change. We are not even sure how it started, but unbeknownst to us an insidious rot had wormed its way into every belief we held, perverting long held traditions, twisting them until they were disgusting parodies of what they should have been. Good people began to do and say things that they never would have considered before. Until eventually we were driven from our homeland."

Devon listened without interruption, watching as the expression on the man's face hardened. It revealed a different side of the schoolmaster than the one that he had seen up until that point. It seemed that the intensity that his new friend had shown extended beyond his passion for scholarly pursuits. The man continued on, unaware or unconcerned with how much of his personality he was giving away.

"I have observed similar happenings in many of the places we have traveled to since, and have begun to wonder if it is this current trend of Spiritualism that may be at fault."

The irony of Kristoph's statement startled a bark of laughter from Devon. The schoolmaster looked at him flatly. "Forgive me, but considering the subject of most of our conversations, you cannot be surprised that I would find your current stance against such things amusing."

"Of course, you are right," the man across from him agreed, his good humor returning. "But there is a difference between those who have been introduced to the mysteries and those who have not. To expose the uninitiated only opens the door for charlatans and dabblers. Both of which are dangerous in their own separate ways."

"How can you be sure that my father is neither of those?" Devon challenged.

It was Kristoph who laughed then. "By everything you have told me and not told me. You reveal more than I think you realize, my friend. But only to those who know what puzzle pieces to look for."

That he might be giving away more than he thought did not sit well with Devon. His companion must have sensed as much because the conversation moved on to more mundane topics, safer topics to Devon's way of thinking. It turned out that he and the schoolmaster were of a like mind on many things. And once the schoolmaster waxed passionate on a subject, it seemed that there was very little input needed on Devon's part, which suited him just fine. All in all, it was a very agreeable way to spend the evening.

A clock chimed nine, and Devon finished his cup. "I understand why you enjoy this place," Devon said as he reached for his wallet. Kristoph waved him off.

"No need! Everything has been taken care of," he insisted. "And I need to be going as well. There are several obligations that I left to others which I should be getting back to."

They made their way to the front door and out into the much cooler night. The air was clear now; the misting rain had moved on, leaving behind a brilliantly dark sky and a damp chill.

A beautiful clarence pulled out from a side street across the way, as though it had been waiting for the schoolmaster.

"Thank you for the company," Kristoph said as he stepped out into the street. "I hope we'll speak again soon."

He watched the schoolmaster jump onto the carriage's running board as easily as a footman, his hand raised in farewell. Devon waved back as the carriage moved slowly past. For a moment, he saw the flash of a pale cheek through the fluttering curtains. An unexpected huff sounded next to him. He felt the hound's weight lean against his thigh, his companion having joined him at some point unbeknownst to him until now.

Devon watched as the carriage moved further downstreet, leaving the light behind. He realized that was twice now power had taken notice of him as it passed by. He was not sure he enjoyed the attention.

CHAPTER IV

The Infamous Mr. Ascher

The dirt of the road was dry beneath his feet, and the houses lining it were emptier than they had been when last he had visited. The few faces that looked out at him from the doorways were closed and unwelcoming. A darkness rode in their hearts that did not usually reside there. He passed through quickly when normally he would have stopped; his heart was pounding with a fear he could not place.

Across the fields and through the hedge he went, to the edge of where the wild places began. There a small hut stood on a path that did not lead back towards town. Inside was an old woman, her cheeks wrinkled and rosy as a dried apple. The drying herbs that hung from the ceiling brushed his hair as he stepped inside.

"Aisling, child, I told you not to come," the old woman said, not bothering to look up from the pot she had over the fire. "You never listen to me. I had hoped this time you would."

Though the voice that answered her came from his lips, it was not his own. "I do listen, but I tell you there is a wrongness in your village. A darkness in the heart of its people that I have not seen since that hellish night. But I see it again, here now. You need to come away with me. I tell you this place will not be safe for you much longer."

"Foolish girl," the old woman said, but concern shrouded her face. "I can't live in the wilds as you do. My gifts are strong, but not like yours."

"You are the one being foolish, I think I hear their feet on the road! There is no choice, it is leave now or let the fires eat you."

And then they were running. The old woman's weight no more than thistledown on his back. Hooves drummed across the fields. He heard the crack of the old woman's door as the townspeople broke it asunder. He ran on and on, his heart pounding, his nostrils blown wide as he pulled in as much air as his lungs could hold. Heather beat against his legs as he ran

Devon's heart was still pounding when he woke, arm thrown across his forehead, eyes still closed as he drew in great lungfuls of air.

A pair of hauntingly familiar eyes stared back at him from behind his own eyelids. He was not even sure at first if he was awake until a soft nose nudged him under his chin, purring.

He relaxed, reaching up to stroke the unseen fur. He had almost been able to see them, those eyes that never left him. This time, a ghost of that color remained. A pale gray, like a moonbeam captured in a jar. His eyes still closed, he tried to hold onto it, but the memory slipped away like water through his fingers.

Gone beyond remembering, he opened his eyes to find that the sky outside had just begun to lighten. Another adjustment that he had had to make now that he lived so far south. Back home at this time of year it would have still been dark for several more hours yet at least.

He got up and went to his door. There was a basin and a pitcher of warm water waiting on a small table just outside. The fresh herbal scent wafting up from it filled his nose as he brought it back into his room.

His mother would often use lavender or eucalyptus water for washing this time of year. She always said it kept the colds at bay. And so far, it seemed that Mrs. O'Toole held to the same tradition. It was like having a little bit of home with him.

He set the pitcher and basin down on the washstand in his room. Pulling off his bedclothes, he used the warm water and a cloth to wash away the sweat from the night before. The dream that had generated it still foremost in his thoughts. The smell of lavender coming from the water mingled with the smell of drying herbs, and his feet could not decide whether it was packed earth or braided rug beneath them. It was as if he stood in two places at once. He had never dreamed so vividly before coming to live in Ashwood. But this one in particular had felt so real, as though it were memory rather than a dream.

"Foolish girl..." It had not seemed odd then when the old woman had said it. But of course, it never did in dreams. For a moment, he remembered that she had called him something else. But what it was stayed stubbornly hidden from him, and like those mesmeric eyes, soon slipped away.

Another question for Aunt Ruth. The worlds between were something she was very familiar with. He hoped she could give him insight into these dreams that haunted him, following him even into the waking world.

Washed and shaved, he headed down to the kitchen, carrying the basin of dirty water with him. The other lodgers were not awake yet, so the biscuits, hot from the oven, still sat on the kitchen table along with his and Sara's lunch pails. He poured himself a cup of coffee from the pot on the stove and grabbed a biscuit, setting himself down at a smaller table in the corner.

He sipped his coffee and listened to the soft sound of his sister's feet as she came down from their rooms above, followed by the softer thump of dog paws on the wooden floor. When she appeared at the bottom of the stairs, she looked so grown up with her single braid of golden hair hanging heavily over her shoulder, his whole chest warmed with pride. He watched her come down that last step, her eyes turned down, as though she were looking at her feet. More likely, she was looking at the hound that he could hear, but not see.

He smiled fondly at his little sister. Her smoky gray-blue eyes, so like their father's, turned up to catch his, and she smiled back.

"I tried to stay up last night, but I must have fallen asleep," she confessed. "Were you out late? What did you and Mr. Hegdus talk about?"

"Not too late. And we talked about you, of course. How you need to study hard if you want to get accepted into Pine Hill. Though it may prove to be a hopeless case, given what a trouble-maker you are," he deadpanned.

At first, she looked horrified. But that look was soon replaced by a scowl that was very much like their mother's when she was annoyed with his father's tomfoolery. Devon laughed.

"I am teasing you. We spoke mostly about Papa. But we also talked about home, his and ours." He sobered, remembering the rest of what the schoolmaster had told him. "But we can talk about it later, if you want. Pet, you would tell me if anything strange happened, wouldn't you?"

"Of course," she assured him, glancing down at where he suspected the hound to be.

She grabbed a biscuit and her lunch pail, giving him a kiss on the cheek as she did so. "I will see you at dinner," she said as she hurried out the door, leaving Devon a little surprised at her abrupt exit. He had fully expected her to try to wheedle more information from him before she left.

Grabbing another biscuit and his lunch pail, he headed out to work.

Sara felt a little embarrassed about how quickly she had rushed out. But her reason for doing so was important! Or at least she believed it was. She had thought about it all night and had finally decided that she had to tell Devon what she had learned about their visitor, even though what she had witnessed had sort of felt like a secret. And, if you were going to tell someone's secret to another person, it was only right that you let them know before you do it. Which is why she was in such a rush this morning.

This early in the day, Winding Street was empty, which suited her just fine for the conversation she was about to have.

"You know I will have to tell him," she said, looking down at the hound walking beside her. It flicked a rust-colored ear back at her, but otherwise had nothing else to say. "I feel like it is sort of a secret, but I won't feel right not telling him."

Again the hound flicked its ear at her, seemingly unconcerned if she told her brother or not.

"Okay," Sara said. "Well, as long as you know. Are there any other secrets I should tell him?"

The hound snorted and walked ahead, its rust-tipped tail waving in front of her. Then from one sweep of tail to the next, it changed. Sara gave a start and must have called out in surprise, because a window opened in the house just next to her. A woman looked out to see what the commotion was about.

"Is everything okay?" she called down.

"So sorry!" Sara waved and smiled sheepishly. "Everything is fine."

Apparently satisfied, the woman disappeared back through the window.

When Sara turned to face the road in front of her again, she found that the rounded back end of a horse was still there. The tail, which looked as if someone had dipped it in rust-colored paint, flicked back and forth across her vision.

"You're a horse!" she exclaimed quietly, so that no one else would have occasion to peek out their windows. "What are you?" she asked because she knew in her soul that she was not looking at an ordinary spirit, animal or human.

The horse in front of her shimmered, and for a moment was merely a cloud of vapor hovering in the air. Something started to take shape at its heart, an indistinct figure that lengthened and flowed but never quite manifested. Sara felt a disquiet and frustration that was not her own. Then the mist shrank, folding down on itself into the now familiar shape of the white cat. Its tail flicked in annoyance. It glowered back over its shoulder at her in the classic look that all cats seemed to have when their wills had been thwarted. With another tail flick, it bounded away towards Market Street.

Sara followed along, her mind spinning in circles as she considered what she had just seen. She wished that she had her father's library to search through to see if she could find out more about their visitor. Or better yet, her father, who was a library unto himself. She felt a little bit wistful at the thought of home. Knowing that they were going to visit Aunt Ruth this Saturday was something of a consolation. She turned the corner just as a wind came whistling down Market Street from Edith Island and the sea beyond. She fancied that it carried with it the sound of glass chimes ringing.

Despite all of Sara's questions and speculations about their visitor, there was one thing she felt pretty confident about now; it was definitely a she.

Sara was already well down Market Street by the time Devon left through the courtyard gate of Mrs. O'Toole's.

It was a pleasant morning, but before he had even reached Old Henry's house, he heard the restless voices of the dead in Ascher cemetery.

They crowded him the moment he entered the gate, tugging at his sleeve or tapping his shoulders. One, an older woman by the feel of her papery soft skin, was even brave enough to pat him on the cheek. It was this forwardness more than anything else that told him that neither of his usual companions had accompanied him this morning.

Devon was not sure what it was that had stirred them up, but it made working hard, much harder than he had expected. So he did not even try. Instead, he listened to the spirits, who were only too happy to lead him to places he had yet to find in the acres and acres of overgrown cemetery. The map that he had first started drawing when he realized the size of the project ahead of him had several new places marked on it before the morning was half over.

He was looking for a fountain that a Miss Margaret Ascher insisted was hidden just up ahead, when the wind came howling down out of the north like a demon. Clouds followed close on its heels, swallowing up the sun, and he could hear the rain pounding on the ground as it raced towards him. It looked as though he was about to get a good soaking. He had just resigned himself to that fact when he felt a shapely hand slip into his.

"Come with me. I can show someplace dry to wait. Though it will mean that I will miss the chance to see what the rain would have done to your shirt and that lovely body you have hidden underneath it." The woman's sigh slid over his ear like a caress. "Such a shame!"

The hand tugged him into a run, not really giving him the opportunity to answer. He allowed it, seeing no reason not to follow. His guide led him down what might have once been a shell-rock path, now almost lost amongst the roses and azaleas that had been left to grow wild along it.

A structure appeared out of the growing gloom. Devon stepped through the open doorway just as the first drops of rain splattered on the ground behind him. He found himself in a crypt dimly lit by the thin light coming through its narrow windows.

"See, nice and dry. Just as I promised." Invisible hands glided across his shoulders and up his neck, gooseflesh chased after them across his skin. "Hmmm, it has been so long since I have been able to truly touch somebody," the voice crooned, fingertips brushing across his lips. "Can you imagine what we could do, with no one the wiser? The sweet mindlessness of unrestrained desire. The heady anticipation that comes with not knowing when you are going to be touched," the husky voice breathed, unseen hands stroking slowly down his chest. "Knowing that there is no one nearby to hear the sounds you would make. Those sounds that even the thought of anyone else knowing about would make you blush. It would be our delightful little secret."

Fingers slid teasingly over the taut muscles of his belly, continuing down past his waist. He reached out and grabbed the slender wrists with unerring accuracy, stopping their exploration.

"And what's even better, is that you can touch me," she purred as she brushed her own hands up her body, forcing his to follow. He stopped them before they reached their destinations, but it took more effort than he had expected it to. The spirit in front of him was a powerful one.

"Cali, my dear, leave the boy alone," a man's smooth voice admonished.

It drew Devon's eye towards the back of the crypt where the deepest shadows lay.

"Oh, but Serus, just look at him! He is delicious," the woman's voice sighed. A whisper of cold brushed across Devon cheek. "And best of all, he can touch me. It has been ages since someone has been able to touch me."

"But have you really thought about what that means, Calista?" The same voice asked in return.

Devon remained silent, still holding onto the wrists of the ghost in front of him. He felt the moment she tried to leave the mortal plane, heard the intake of a breath that she no longer needed when she fully realized the power he had over her.

"It means I can hold you, whether you want to be held or not," he informed her.

"He could even keep you here, my dear. Bind you to him and you would have no choice in the matter," the smooth voice continued. "Or force you to leave if he chose to."

Devon let go of the ghost's wrists and felt the wash of ether around him as she dematerialized, leaving the mortal plane.

"Ah Calista, always so impetuous." The owner of the voice finally revealed himself, stepping out into a shaft of thin, watery light. A well-dressed gentleman who gave Devon a polite smile and held out his hand. "Serus Ascher. It is nice to finally meet you, Mr. Amaris. Please allow me to apologize for my cousin's behavior."

Devon reached out to shake the offered hand, noting the scratches and smears of pencil lead on his own as he did so. Devon was sure the rest of him looked just as disheveled. The man's gray suit and silk topper on the other hand, were impeccable. A marvel given that they stood in a crypt strewn with cobwebs and dead leaves, at the heart of the most unkept part of the cemetery. Quite a marvel indeed.

"She is a powerful spirit," Devon said, releasing the man's hand as he took a half step back.

"So she is, in death as she was in life," Ascher agreed amicably. "Calista was an experienced practitioner when she walked among the living, extremely skilled in the art of sex magick. I am afraid the temptation of your being able to touch her was too great for her to ignore."

"Then I am surprised that it has taken her so long to approach me," Devon said, carefully considering the man across from him.

"You were unaccompanied today, so she seized the opportunity. No harm was meant," Ascher assured him. "And to be honest, I am sure it would have been an immensely pleasurable time for you, had you taken her up on her offer."

"There are complications that come with loving the dead," Devon contended.

"Quite true," the man acknowledged, the pale green of his eyes nearly luminous in the dim light. "Well, though my choice of welcome is quite different from my cousin's, I am still very glad that you have come to work for us."

"I am very happy for the job," Devon said. "It was lucky the position was open when it was, and that the city council offered it to me."

"Yes, lucky," Ascher said in a manner that had Devon wondering if luck had really played a part at all. "Though, I would be inclined to say you were the most qualified. Who better than a necromancer to uncover the homes of the dead."

"That is an old-fashioned and dangerous word," Devon warned, his wariness growing. "And one not to be used lightly. Besides, the truth of it is somewhat in question."

"I am an old-fashioned man," said Ascher. That he was also a dangerous man was something he did not have to tell Devon, despite his polite and affable nature so far. "And I would not use such a word lightly if we were not safe with only the spirits for company. As for the truth of the word, you commune with the dead and can bend them to your will without ritual or invocation. So one might argue that the word is truer for you than it would be for most."

Devon was at a loss. Outside of his own family, he had never had someone speak so frankly about such matters. Ascher continued to watch him, waiting to see his reaction, whether he would run, or fight, or stand steady.

"I certainly did not list it on my application to the city council," Devon pointed out after the silence had stretched on for several heartbeats.

"You did not," Ascher admitted, his smile broadening wolfishly, then he chuckled. "I suppose it is time I confess. Your father is very familiar to me, having corresponded with him many times over the years. So, when you wrote to the city council, it seemed a fine idea to suggest you for the position of groundskeeper for my family's cemetery. You have to agree, it is certainly in need of one."

"It is," Devon agreed. "I will admit that I had not expected it to be in such a state even though the council told me that it had been neglected for several years."

"Ah yes. Well as you can see 'several years' may have been an understatement. It seems that for the last few generations, my family have focused more on their vices rather than their obligations." He spoke with the authority of a much older man, though Devon would have said he was not yet forty, or perhaps only just. There was a frosting of silver in his hair, but his face was that of a man very much in his prime.

"Still," Ascher continued, "you have made admirable progress in the month or so that you have been here. And I have to thank you for uncovering little Lenore's grave. She is quite grateful."

"Did she mention it herself?" Devon asked. There was not a doubt in his mind that this man was a practitioner, and an accomplished one at that.

Ascher smiled at him. "Of course," he confirmed. "Everyone is quite happy to have you here, even with the company you keep. Which is unusually strong, I have to say. Did you bring it with you or summon it when you arrived? Or perhaps, did your father send it with you?"

All good questions, some of which Devon could answer. Some of which he couldn't, or wouldn't, even had he been able to.

"Summoning the dead is not something I often do," he replied neutrally. "And I don't believe conversing with beings on other planes is a gift I have."

"Though evading answers might be," Ascher deadpanned. "No matter. Your father is a man of unquestionable integrity and I have no doubts that his son is the same. It was very nice to have finally met you in the flesh, Mr. Amaris. However, since the rain has obliged me enough to stop, I do have to be on my way. Good day." He nodded to Devon before leaving through the crypt's only door.

A powerful man, in more ways than one, Devon thought to himself as he watched the rain-soaked foliage swallow Serus Ascher up.

When Devon arrived home after work, he found that Mrs. O'Toole had made a huge pot of chicken and dumplings. 'A dinner to combat the dreary day,' she had said, which sat perfectly well with Devon. The marvelous woman had also made hot cocoa, much to his sister's delight.

He took a cup outside with him after dinner and was surprised when Sara followed him out with hers. He did not head to his usual spot since the whole of the courtyard was wet. Instead, he stayed on the porch, eschewing the long bench that sat to the one side of the door in favor of the wicker settee in front of the parlor window. Sara settled down in one of the chairs at the table while Devon sat on the wide railing across from her. He leaned his shoulder against one of the posts.

"So pet, you decided to join me tonight." He left the statement hanging in the air, an open invitation for her to discuss whatever it was she had followed him out to discuss. He took a sip from the steaming mug in his hands as he watched her fidget with her own mug for a full minute before setting it down on the table in front of her. She seemed intent on the steam rising from it. Or more accurately, the little eddies that rippled through pale vapor. Which told him it was most likely the little phantom cat she was watching and not the steam at all.

"Is everything alright?" he asked after several more moments went by without his sister saying anything.

"Everything is fine." she insisted. "I just wanted to talk to you about something, and now I am not sure how to begin."

"At the beginning?" he teased, only to realize how truly bothered she was when she did not make a face at him. He moved to sit in the chair across from her, propping his elbows on the table as he continued to cradle the warm mug between his hands. "Don't worry about whether it makes sense pet, just say the words and we will figure it out from there."

A whiskered head brushed against his hand, making the cocoa ripple in the mug he was holding.

"Okay, but I am not sure I can find the words," she said, taking a sip from her own mug before continuing. "Do you remember last night when you met Mr. Hegdus and myself as we were walking home?" Another small pause, then everything poured out in a rush. "Well, the white hound was with us, but then just as I was telling him, Mr. Hegdus, about home, the hound woofed at me and suddenly it was the little white cat. And then this morning as we were walking to school, I told her (did I ever tell you that I think she is a her?) I told her that I was going to tell you what I had seen and asked if there was anything else she wanted to tell me about before I did. And then, she changed into a horse! A white horse with a rust-tipped tail standing right there in front of me. But when I asked if there was more she turned into this white cloud; you know, like how the penny dreadfuls always describe ghosts, but she only shifted back into a cat. And it seemed as though she was quite annoyed at something, but of course I have no idea what it could be..." Sara trailed off there looking up at him sheepishly.

"Well, so much for not being able to find the words," he smiled at her from over the rim of his mug. "So, if I am understanding you correctly, you saw our visitor change its shape from the hound you showed me the other day, to the little cat who first came to us when we arrived. You also saw her change her shape into that of a horse as well, and you are pretty sure she is a she."

Sara nodded her head. "And I can't say why, but I don't think she means us any harm. You don't, do you?" She asked the spot just below his chin where he could occasionally feel the flick of an ear against his jaw.

A deep purr and trill answered her question. He felt a furred body step over the crook of his elbow, a tail tracing under his jaw as it followed in its wake.

"Your schoolmaster calls her our guardian," Devon confessed, finding that he agreed with the man's assessment.

"Mr. Hegdus knows? I suppose that is not surprising, given who his benefactress is," she continued on without pausing to allow him to answer her question. She was much like their mother in that way when she was excited. "I met her yesterday. She was… well she was poised and elegant and very fashion-able. But, and this may sound odd, but you can tell when she *takes notice of you.*"

"Hmm, I understand your meaning," he said, thinking of the night before and the carriage that he had seen when he and Kristoph had stepped out of the coffeehouse.

"You know Devon, I am happy that she is here. Our guardian, I mean," Sara admitted softly, almost as if she was not sure she should feel that way. But he understood. They had an affinity for the dead, he and his sister, and they often found it easier to be in their company than that of the living.

'Unusually strong' Ascher had called their visitor. Devon reached out instinctually to scratch under the chin he could not see.

"So am I," he agreed. And he truly was glad their visitor was here, but that did not stop him from wanting to know why. Why had she chosen them?

CHAPTER V

Looking Through the Eyes of the Dead

S ara loved mornings like this.

An endless sky of the deepest, clearest blue stretched out overhead, while high, high up in it, clouds of pure white trailed by with long wispy tails. It was the kind of sky you only saw in the autumn time, and it made her feel immensely happy.

She and Devon had left very early that morning and had reached the ferry that went across to Edith Island even before the sun had risen. They had lucked into a ride on the back of a supply cart that was headed out to the barracks, so that even though it was now only mid-morning, they were already well on their way to Aunt Ruth's.

The sand was cool between her toes as they walked barefooted along the old dune road. All around them the tall sea oats bent and rustled in the wind. She turned her face into it and closed her eyes, smiling as it stroked her cheeks. It smelled of the sea and left behind a chill that the morning sun did its best to warm.

They crested a dune and she could finally see Aunt Ruth's house. It stood all alone just on the other side, nothing between its weathered walls and the ocean's crashing waves but a stretch of sea grass and sand. The road they were on continued past the house, curving down until it disappeared into a stand of red cedars. The tinkling sound of the glass wind chimes hanging

58

from the wrap-around porch called out to Sara on the breeze. She always thought they sounded so lonely; lonely, yet beautiful all the same.

She saw Aunt Ruth walking up the path that led from her house to the beach. The wind was having great fun as it twisted and tangled her unbound hair, sending the dark strands of it writhing around her head like a kraken's tentacles.

By the time she and Devon had reached the porch, Aunt Ruth was already waiting for them.

"You are early," she observed after a pause that was perhaps a heartbeat longer than was common.

"We were lucky enough to catch a ride on the way here," Devon told her as he walked up the porch steps to give the tall woman a hug. Sara did the same. She wondered if it was her imagination, or if her aunt's already spare frame really was leaner and harder than it had been on their last visit.

"Would you like me to make some coffee, Aunt Ruth?" Sara asked.

Aunt Ruth smiled knowingly at her, as if she guessed what Sara had been thinking. Which with Aunt Ruth, could be something of the truth.

"Thank you, dear. Hugh just stopped by, so there should be a few things in the larder if you're hungry," her aunt said in her usual, distracted way.

Sara left her brother and her aunt to follow while she made her way along the wide porch to the rear of the house. She passed the old ship's table that ran alongside the back railing, which faced out towards the sea. Just beyond was the end of the porch and a door. Sara opened it and went into the narrow galley kitchen which took up nearly all that side of the house. Warm light filled the room, courtesy of the morning sun streaming through the tall windows as it rose out of the waves.

The sun was much brighter and higher up in the sky than it would have been at home this time of year. A fact Sara was still getting used to, but one she found she really quite liked.

She made her way over to the stove and wasn't surprised to find it cold. The larder was full as Aunt Ruth had said it would be. But if Hugh had stopped by, it had not been as recently as her aunt had led her to believe.

It was going to take a while to heat the stove and get everything ready, but Sara did not mind. She had left the porch door propped open, so that she could hear Aunt Ruth and Devon's conversation as they sat at the long table. She listened with half an ear to the rise and fall of their voices. It was a pleasant sort of sound that went well with the shush of the waves on the sand and the whisper of the wind through the distant cedars. When the conversation eventually reached that topic she was most interested in, she began to listen in earnest.

"You have questions," she heard Aunt Ruth ask.

"There are things that are happening, and we could use your insight," Devon answered.

A long breath later, "… regarding your employer?"

Sara had not known that Devon had had any questions about his employer.

"He has said things that have made me wonder," Devon admitted, "but, no. We wanted to ask about an apparition, or what we believe is an apparition, that has attached itself to us."

"… A visitor. Powerful? Ah, but there are many powers in Ashwood now," Her aunt's words came slowly, as they always did, as though she were a half-step to the side from the world around her. "No need to speak of that at the moment. Tell me about the apparition. How it appears and when."

Sara was bringing out the toast when Devon answered, "Sara would be better able to tell you how it looks. Is the coffee on the stove?" he asked her as he stood up from his seat.

"It is," Sara replied.

"I'll be right back," he said, smiling at her as he passed by on his way into the kitchen.

Sara answered her aunt's question as she set the toast rack, filled with toast, on the table, placing the honey and jam she had found in the larder next to it. "I first saw her shortly after we arrived in Ashwood. She appeared as a little white cat with rust-colored ears, and the dead's silver eyes."

Devon rejoined them on the porch. "I also noticed her in early September, just after we first arrived," he added as he put the coffeepot and three mugs on the table. "But, did not think much of it at the time, even though I had never come across an apparition that was not human before. Then the hound appeared…"

"A hound?" Aunt Ruth asked.

"A hound," he confirmed as he headed back into the kitchen, leaving Sara to further describe their visitor.

"She is also white, with large rust-colored ears that stand straight up and a rust-tipped tail. I thought it interesting that both the hound and the cat had the same coloring and wondered if it had something to do with the spirits of animals in general, since I have never seen one before. Then one evening she changed shape right in front of me! That is when I realized that the cat and the hound were one and the same."

Devon returned from the kitchen with a small bowl of sugar and plates on a tray, along with butter and cream which he must have found in the ice box. "And we began to question whether we were dealing with a ghost at all."

"She can change her shape into other things as well," Sara offered as she passed out the plates and poured the coffee.

"…What other shapes?"

"I have seen her change into a horse," Sara answered. "And I feel she can change into more, but maybe she has forgotten how?" It was only as she said it that Sara realized that was the exact impression she had gotten from the shapeless figure that had appeared to her the other morning.

Sara spread butter and honey on two pieces of toast and put it in front of her aunt who did not seem to notice. She had picked up her coffee cup though.

"… Are you afraid of your visitor?" her aunt asked.

"Not at all," Sara replied. "In fact, I would say she almost feels protective." With that thought came a picture, of the hound inserting herself between Sara and Mr. Hegdus's benefactress.

"I have felt that on occasion as well," Devon agreed. "And I have had her labeled as my guardian more than once."

Aunt Ruth did not speak for a long while, her eyes drifting out towards the sea. Sara and Devon ate their toast and drank their coffee as she continued to sit there with her cup in her hand, the contents growing colder until Sara reached out to touch her arm. Aunt Ruth finally took a sip of her coffee, her attention shifting slowly back to them.

"So many shadows… I would be inclined to say that it could be a *servitor*, though the plane they exist on is a higher one than the one on which the earthbound dead walk. And that would bring with it the question of who does it serve and why would they set it over you?" she ruminated, her eyes losing focus as they often did when her thoughts turned inward. "But, there is something more here. A strangeness in how things appear to be and how they really are, hiding itself in plain sight. An obfuscation if you will. Did the apparition come with you today, even part of the way?"

"I have not seen her this morning," Sara admitted.

The conversation tapered off and a comfortable silence fell as they ate their breakfast. Sara looked out at the ocean, nibbling on her toast. The bright morning sun had turned the water into the most brilliant blue and tipped each wave with diamonds. A small white horse ambled along the shining shore. Sea ponies as she liked to call them. They sometimes drifted down from their grazing on the dunes.

Being at Aunt Ruth's was always a bit strange for her because the dead tended to avoid the house, by design. It was funny, but she had never felt that lack more keenly than she did right now.

A cool hand covered hers. She turned back to find her Aunt Ruth's nearly black eyes watching her warmly. "I am sure your visitor is close by."

Sara smiled back at her. "I am sure you are right," she agreed, realizing the white sea pony she had been watching had left no hoof prints behind in the sand.

Hugh had arrived just after breakfast and stayed to share an early supper with them. The sharp-jawed lighthouse keeper with his bright blue eyes was good company, and it heartened Devon to see the change in his aunt when she was in the man's presence.

He had left just before sunset. They had all walked down with him to the small dock on the northern side of the island where his boat was tied. Then stayed to watch as he rowed across the deep waters of Gerty Inlet, returning through the grove of wind-swept cedars only after the dying sun had already begun to paint their shaggy trunks in rose-gold.

Now with the evening full on, the house sat quietly in the dark. The only light came from the candle that shone from the minuscule attic window above where his sister lay in bed, reading. It cast a tiny golden square down to where the dune grass fluttered fitfully in the night wind below.

Devon walked out onto the porch. He found his Aunt Ruth exactly where he thought she would be, half sitting on the railing as she looked out across the silvered sand to where the moon was just rising from the black sea. A small stone bowl sat on the table next to her and to one side of it lay cards spread out across the wood.

He went over to where she was, but did not touch her. "What do you see?" he asked.

"Ripples in the deep," she answered in a voice that held the coldness of the grave. "Powers unseen; sly tentacles searching for a brilliant light. There are those already wrapped tightly in those tentacles, lost souls themselves. And there is a hunter waiting in the shallows; crafty and careful. A shape hidden in the corner of my eye."

She turned her gaze towards him. Her nearly black irises were awash in silver, which he knew meant that she was looking through the eyes of the dead. A sadness touched his heart.

He had been told that a seeress gave up a little bit of her own sight each time she tried to look beyond. It was the sacrifice she made for the power gained. He had always assumed that price was blindness, but he had come to suspect that it was not as simple as that. To lose sight of reality, well that would be a sacrifice as well, wouldn't it? For every ritual, a sacrifice has to be made, whether it is given from one's self or taken from someone else, or a bit of both; power must be paid for.

Except for those who were natural born of course, such as his mother, or Sara, or himself. However, he had his own thoughts on whether such gifts could truly be said to be without cost.

"You shouldn't have done a seeing for us," he said to her.

"There were good reasons to. Your worries paint your skin and power has touched you at least twice recently. Tell me."

"I met my employer," he confessed. The meeting in the Ascher family crypt standing out clearly in his mind. "He used a very old name for those like me, and he says that he knows my father. Does he know you?"

"He may, he may not. But I can see him. Pale, ancient power of earth and old bone. Protective, as is the second. Her power is darker though. More wild, driven by desire and unchecked passions. But she walks on the edge of the Middle Path. More I cannot see, for the dead will not look at her. To see her clearly, I would need to look through the eyes of the living, and I will, but not tonight. Not tonight."

The silver in her eyes now was only a reflection of the rising moon.

"Who is the second power that I saw?" she asked.

"The benefactress of Sara's schoolmaster is a powerful practitioner. He confessed as much when he came to see Sara and I at the boarding house. And I believe that she might have seen me just a few evenings ago, when I was leaving the coffeehouse with him."

"Powers unseen — Ashwood is near to bursting with them. Be careful that they do not swallow you up," his aunt warned. "But, I feel there is more you want to know."

"Yes," Devon admitted, thinking of the eyes that looked back at him whenever he closed his own. The ones he could never quite remember, but could never forget either. "Nearly every night since we arrived in Ashwood, I have been having dreams of a dark-haired woman. We are standing beneath a gray sky, on a dune at the edge of an ocean I cannot see. In the beginning, she is facing away from me, staring off in the distance. But then, it's as if she realizes I am there with her, and suddenly she is standing right there in front of me, filling up all of my vision. She haunts me even when I am awake, though I can't for the life of me tell you what she looks like."

"Does she speak to you?"

"Her lips move, but the only sound I hear are the waves crashing on the shore."

"And the dreams, they are always the same?"

"Near enough, until a few days ago when they changed. I was no longer on that gray shore, and it was as if I were someone else. There was one where an old woman called me by a name that was not mine." He could feel that name even now, hovering on his lips like a kiss. "But every time I go to say the name she called me, it slips away. I don't believe they are waking dreams, nor do I believe they are dreams like the ones my mother has. But they were so real! I could feel the wind on my skin, the weight of the old woman as I carried her on my back. The heather beating against my legs as I ran past it."

"These new dreams, you have had more than one?"

"Yes, two at least."

Several long minutes passed in which there was only the sound of the wind and the gentle hush of water on sand. But Devon was patient, knowing his aunt would only answer in her own time.

"It is true that sometimes your mother's dreams are prophetic; and sometimes they are waking dreams. But always her knowledge comes from living things. Yours would only come from the dead. When you say you are being haunted, you are more right than you know. You need to be careful. In dreams you are closer to their plane than to ours and the power you hold here may not carry over," she warned him, sharply and more lucidly than he could ever remember seeing her before.

"So even if I wanted to banish them, I couldn't?" he asked.

"Even if you could, you couldn't because you do not want to," his aunt answered. And he knew that she was right.

CHAPTER VI

The Dark-haired Boy

He stalked softly through the night, hunting those who thought themselves the hunters. They were not bold enough to move in the day yet, but if nothing was done, then that would soon change.

The dark figures surrounded the house, as they had other houses, as they had his own long ago, when he was young. They held their firestrikers and torches at the ready, too caught up in the fervor of their false prophet to care that more than the accused family lived in the house. Uncaring that babes slept quietly in their beds.

He felt a growl start low in his throat as he padded quietly up behind them. First one, then another and another. He took them down one by one, pulling the darkness from them like he would pull ticks from a dog. Then he hid and waited for them to wake, hoping this time they would lead him to the one he needed to find.

It was still dark when Devon opened his eyes. He heard the town clock as it began to chime in the quiet morning air. It appeared that it was not quite as early as the dark made it seem.

He could feel the hound stretched out next to him on the narrow bed, its head resting heavily on his belly. Had it been a living hound, he would have thought it asleep as he felt its jaw twitch. It made him wonder if spirits dreamed.

When he went down to the kitchen for breakfast, he found that Sara was already there helping Mrs. O'Toole to pack their lunches.

"You're up early," he said, pouring himself a cup of coffee from the pot on the stove and taking a biscuit from the tray. Mrs. O'Toole had put bacon and cheese in them this morning. They were delicious, as always. He could not deny that luck had been on his side when he had found this place for them to stay.

"I woke up and couldn't go back to sleep, so I thought I would come down and help," Sara said.

"And quite the help she has been," said Mrs. O'Toole from where she stood, chopping up the bacon left over from breakfast the day before and getting it ready to add to the next batch of biscuits. "But now she needs to eat. Here; leave that coffee there Sara. I'll pour it into the thermos for your brother. You go and sit. It's cold enough outside that you need something warm in your belly before you go."

While she was talking, Mrs. O'Toole put two biscuits on a plate and handed them to Sara at the same time as she was pouring coffee into the thermos next to the stove. Devon felt a fond smile pull at his lips. The broad-shouldered woman reminded him more than a little of his mother, in build and temperament. Though his mother was probably a head shorter. Not that that mattered; she could fill a room when she wanted. He wished his mother were here to speak to; she would understand the dreams best.

Thoughts of his mother reminded him that it had been some weeks since he had written a letter home. He resolved to remedy that.

"Are you thinking about home?" He looked up to find his father's gray-blue eyes looking back at him from his sister's face.

"Maybe," he said, smiling at her.

"I miss it too, sometimes," she confessed, her face nearly glowing with gratitude. "Thank you, Devon."

He didn't have to ask what she was thanking him for.

"You are very welcome, pet," he said, reaching out to tug lightly on her braid.

They headed out shortly after breakfast, parting ways when they reached the corner. Sara turned towards school, waving back at him from over her shoulder.

Devon crossed the wide expanse of Market Street to where Winding Street continued on. The sun was still low in the sky, it's light finding him only through the inbetween spaces of the buildings. The chill of the morning air was not enough to keep people indoors yet the streets were quiet as he made his way down them.

He turned at the corner where Nightingale met Winding Street. The coffeehouse, and the tobacconist's were all shuttered up tight. But there was steam coming up from the back of the laundry, and the doves on Miss Rose's porch waved to him sleepily as he passed by. He guessed himself to be alone since he did not hear the usual humph of his companion.

Most of the tenet houses were also quiet, their occupants either asleep or already at work, except for Old Henry of course, who was sitting on his porch. Devon waved as he went by.

He felt a weight land on his shoulder as he walked through the cemetery's iron gate, phantom whiskers brushing his cheek. Apparently he wasn't as alone as he had thought.

"And what did you dream of last night while I dreamt about chasing shadows?" he asked. He felt the paws on his shoulder flex, the tiny prick of nails on skin, before the weight once again disappeared. It seemed that his companion was in no mood to share.

The paths beneath the spreading oaks were chilly, even as the sun climbed towards noon. He made his way along those shaded avenues, noting which crypts needed repair. They were all much newer than the majority of the others he had uncovered, their dates falling within the last hundred years or so. The newest being Tam Ascher's, who had passed only a few years before. It was his passing that had left Ascher House empty, until its current master had arrived from parts unknown.

Devon listened to the spirits whisper and gossip as he cleared the land around their homes. The little swirls of dead leaves that skittered between the headstones told him his visitor was still there with him.

He had been half-joking when he had asked it (or 'her' as Sara had insisted) what dreams she had been dreaming. But those teasing words had caused other thoughts to fall like dominoes in his mind, beginning with last night. All his dreams, his aunt's visions, the visitor that was even now keeping him company as he worked, each thought seemed to lead to another, but he could not be sure of the connection or even if there truly was one.

It was as if he were looking through a million keyholes trying to figure out if they all led to the same room. It was both frustrating and intriguing, like the eyes he was forever trying to see. Like the name that danced on his lips, but that he could not say.

Sara had left school much earlier than was usual that afternoon. Normally, her preparatory classes would have just been about to begin, but for some reason Mr. Hegdus had not been in school that day. So, said classes had been canceled.

Left at a loose end, she had decided to pay a surprise visit to Devon instead. So, she had set off on a mission, confident she could find the Ascher cemetery even though she had only been there once before. There were plenty of ghosts around after all, if she needed to ask how to get there, as long as she was careful about it. The only problem with getting directions from spirits was that often things had changed after they died, but they did not always notice. They tended to see the world as they knew it, and not necessarily as it was in the present. But the cemetery was old, so she had felt she had a good chance of them being able to point her in the right direction.

She had turned down the same narrow lane she usually saw Devon turn on when she was looking out of the schoolhouse window. The houses she had passed at first were nice though a little older, with small gardens and chairs on their front porches. But a few blocks on, everything had started to look just a little bit shabbier, and she had been fairly confident that she was going the right way.

Now however, she was standing on a corner, unsure whether or not she had already missed the street she was supposed to have turned down. She thought it was the one just up ahead, but she could not be sure. She glanced down the narrow lane to her right and saw the ghost of a woman some distance away, standing beneath the nearly bare branches of a redbud tree. Despite the distance, Sara could see the apparition quite clearly. Especially her exquisite hair, which hung indecorously loose, flowing to her knees in a gold-etched river of molten copper.

Not giving it too much thought, Sara turned down the street with the vague idea of asking if this was the correct way to the cemetery. She had only gone a short distance when she saw the woman reach up and pluck one of the tree's blood-hued leaves.

The ghost's fingers did not pass through the leaf and cause it to shake loose. Nor had some stray wind come through and snatched it from its mooring. The woman had, in fact, reached out and plucked it herself.

Even as Sara continued to watch, the leaf sat like a heart-shaped wound in the palm of the woman's creamy white hand. And for some unfathomable reason, Sara could see it all in bizarre detail, as though she stood only a few feet from the woman rather than half a street away.

She felt her body begin to shake uncontrollably and she could not bring herself to move, not even an inch. An old feeling of dread that she had thought long gone bubbled up from deep inside her, the fear of not being able to tell the living from the dead. She fought to calm herself as she looked around to see if there was anyone near who could have noticed her odd behavior. But she saw no one, only ramshackle buildings with their gaping windows that stared back at her like empty eyes.

There was one exception to the shabbiness. On her left stood a lovely tidewater house, its lofty three stories looked out over a high-walled garden. But the sight of it, solid and somehow inviting, still did nothing to comfort her.

When she looked back at the redbud tree, the copper-haired woman was gone. Sara was sure she had only looked away for a moment, and there was no place that she could see nearby where the woman could have vanished to so quickly. Her uneasiness grew tenfold.

"Now why would a lovely girl like you be on a street like this?" a voice asked from off to her left.

Four boys stepped out from the shadow of the garden wall. They were all well-groomed and handsome, and their clothes were nice, very nice. There was no doubt in Sara's mind that they did not live in this neighborhood. If she were to guess, she would have said that they were from one of the well-off families that lived up on High Street. Or maybe even from Riverview where the very, very rich lived. This should have put her at ease, but it didn't. Not in the least.

"I have not seen you around here before," the tallest boy said, and Sara recognized his as the voice that had spoken a moment before. "Are you looking for something?"

She was not sure what to do. Despite the goosebumps on her arms, they had not said anything concerning, and she did not want to be rude. She thought to turn around and leave, but the idea of having them at her back made her feel uneasy. So, she kept walking forward and hoped that they would let her pass without too much trouble.

"Or maybe you are here looking for a job," he continued, stepping out into the middle of the lane.

"Is that it?" another boy asked, coming up to stand beside the taller boy. "Are you hoping to become one of Miss Rose's doves? You are certainly pretty enough. We could help you..."

"She might need training up a bit," said a third from over to her right.

"We can help with that too," the fourth added in from behind her.

Sara had no idea what the boys were talking about, but she was sure they were teasing her. It was something she was familiar with, and she had learned it was best just not to say anything in return. These boys though, their words had a nastier edge to them than she was used to.

She made to step past the tallest boy in front of her, but he moved to block her path. They were all around her now, and Sara was beginning to be very afraid. One of the boys tried to catch her braid, but she avoided him.

"So little dove, is that it? Do you want our help?" the first boy asked, taking a step closer to her.

She moved again to try to step past him, and that was when she saw a dark-haired boy walking down the street towards them. He had his hands in his pockets, and seemed in no hurry to be anywhere. But the same could not be said of the woman who was walking next to him. She was pulling frantically on his shirt, urging him to move faster. The boys surrounding Sara, intent on their game as they were, did not notice the newcomer. And even if they had, they certainly would not have seen the woman who was with him.

"Hey. Thomas. Why are you bothering that girl?" the dark-haired boy asked with all the confidence of someone used to getting answers when he asked questions. It did not seem to matter to him that the other boys were probably older or that there were more of them or that their clothes were nicer. In fact, a small part of Sara's brain thought it lucky that the boy was wearing suspenders and a belt or his pants would have fallen off entirely.

"None of your business, Liam," the tallest boy, Thomas apparently, said without looking over his shoulder. He reached forward to touch Sara, but she stepped back away from him, bumping into the boy behind her who took the opportunity to slip an arm around her waist.

The ghost who had up until then been urging the dark-haired boy to hurry, flew from his side with such a fierce look on her face that Sara flinched back. She avoided Sara while still passing through the boy holding her. It made his arm shudder and shake, allowing Sara to pull free.

The dark-haired boy, Liam, unaware of what his companion was doing, grabbed Thomas's shoulder. "Oh really? I think you're forgetting whose street you're on." He spun the taller boy around and landed a punch straight on his mouth.

And just like that, the fight was on! The other boys were quick to move in. When the one behind Sara made to rush past her, she stuck her foot out to trip him, which sent him sprawling face first onto the road.

He lifted his head from the dirt and looked up at her. Blood was running down his cheek, but the look he gave her wasn't anger. That she would have understood. But the malevolent hunger that twisted his face instead was terrifying. It made her feel like she desperately needed to go wash.

She stepped back and would have run away if it wasn't for the dark-haired boy who was still fighting. He looked to be holding his own against the two boys, at least, as far as she could tell. But she thought it would be a poor thing to do, abandoning someone who was in the process of saving her rather than leaving her to her own fate. Not that she had any idea how to help him. And, there were still the two other boys who were not yet in the fight.

Neither of them seemed to be paying any attention to the scuffle that was taking place. The one boy was still on the ground and his friend stood close by. They watched her, intent on every breath she took. Her mind screamed at her not to move, because if she did, they would snatch at her, pounce on her, devour her. The fear for herself and her would-be-rescuer grew. Her heart pounded in her chest as fast as a bird's and her ears were filled with a roaring, the sound of her own blood pumping through her veins.

Or was it? It seemed now like it was coming from behind her. A rushing sound like the rustle of leaves tumbling before the wind. It grew and grew, building towards a deafening crescendo, but she did not dare turn her head and look.

Then it was there, a frigid gale that howled past her, its icy breath buffeting them all. And on its tail, was the silver-eyed white cat.

The gale lashed at the two boys in front of her, scoring their flesh with thin red welts. The insatiable hunger in their eyes melted away, replaced by confusion and fear. The boy on the ground scrambled to his feet and bolted down the road as if the hounds of hell nipped at his heels. The second boy lost no time in doing the same.

The other two boys, who were still fighting Liam, did not seem to notice their friends' retreat. They kept on, trying unsuccessfully to pin the dark-haired boy between them as they exchanged blows. Not seeming to take notice even when the winds began to buffet them. Of course, they could not see the woman's ghost when she placed herself between the dark-haired boy and the oncoming gale, protecting him as best she could from its punishment.

"Leave him be!" the ghost woman shouted stridently at the uncaring maelstrom. "He's done nothing but try to protect her, same as you!"

Angry red welts appeared on the other two boys' skin, but the dark-haired Liam was left untouched. Still they kept fighting, until a strong gust sent one boy tumbling from his feet. He stood up shaking his head, and cringed from the stinging wind.

"Tom, come on let's go! We're not going to win this one," he called out to the taller boy.

"No," Thomas refused even as he threw another punch at Liam.

Sara watched her would-be rescuer duck effortlessly. At the same time, the white cat came sailing over his shoulder, its ears pinned flat against its skull as it landed with all four paws against the taller boy's chest. Thomas went sprawling on the ground, as if he had been kicked by a horse. The cat continued on, scratching the boy's face with its claws as it went. Thomas lay in the dirt, howling, his hand over the half of his face where the scratches appeared. The one eye that Sara could see was filled with pain and anger, but none of the darkness that she had seen before.

"That was too far Liam!" the other boy said as he came to help Thomas up. "How did you even do that?"

Liam threw out his hands.

"Not me!" he protested, a smile drawing up his lips despite a split in the bottom one. "But it's no more than you deserve. Maybe next time you'll keep in mind just whose streets these are."

Sara saw all this, but only paid it half-a-mind. Her attention remained fixed on the scratches marring Thomas's face, and the tiny drops of blood that welled up from them.

"That's going to bring trouble," the woman next to Sara said.

Still feeling stunned, Sara turned to look at the ghost beside her. She was uncommonly beautiful with hair as dark as Sara's rescuer, golden skin and a dusting of freckles across her nose and cheeks. Her eyes were silver, of course, as all the eyes of those on the other side were. But they sparkled warmly at Sara as the woman's full lips turned up in a brilliant smile.

"Don't worry yourself, *mon poussin*. It's nothing my son can't handle," the ghost reassured her, the accent of her French as rich as butter.

Sara blinked as Liam's face took the place of his mother's; a pair of green eyes replaced the silver ones that had been looking back at her.

"Are you okay?" the dark-haired boy asked, giving her the same warm, full-lipped smile that his mother had just been giving her. His eyes were the palest, clearest green she had ever seen. And they kept looking at her expectantly. She just stared back, unable to think of a thing to say.

Liam kept smiling at the girl in front of him. She in turn continued to stare at him, unblinkingly, with her gray-blue eyes. It was their color that grabbed at him, filling his head with a picture of little round birds flitting outside the window of a room he and his *maman* used to rent. *Gobemoucheron gris-bleu* she would call them and laugh as they twittered softly.

Maman, as strong-minded in death as she was in life. He had always felt that she was still with him, watching over him. And he was sure she was the reason that he had come down this street even though it was not the way he had meant to go. Even now he could almost hear her whispering in his ear, 'Watch over this one, *mon fils!*' His smile broadened at the fanciful thought.

"Are you alright?" he asked again, and the girl with the holly-blue eyes finally blinked at him.

"Are you alright?" she asked him back, staring at his lip. The sting of it told him it was probably split.

"Sure, right as rain," he said, sliding his hands into his pockets to hide his bruised knuckles.

"I am so sorry!"

"Nothing for you to be sorry about," he told her. "That bunch had no reason for being here in the first place. Just hanging around, trying to sneak a peek into Miss Rose's. Hoping for a glimpse at one of her 'doves', no doubt."

"Her doves?" the girl said, her brows drawing together. "One of the boys asked me something about becoming one of Miss Rose's doves, but he said I would need training up a bit. He offered to help me."

"Did he now?" His smile never faltered, but his hands clenched in his pockets. Train her up, huh. Well that wasn't going to be happening. But he could tell there were some lessons that needed to be handed out, and that was definitely going to happen.

"Well, I'm guessing he was wrong," he said, letting the matter drop. "You don't live around here though, do you?" It was not really a question because he was well aware of the answer.

"No, I was just..." the girl hesitated, her eyes flicking over his shoulder before she continued. "Just heading down to see my brother at his work."

"He works down here?" Liam asked. Curious, most people who worked down in the Bottoms, lived down in the Bottoms and Liam knew he had never seen her before.

"Yes, at the Ascher family cemetery," she replied.

Ah, Liam nodded knowingly. He had seen a man walking down Nightingale Street from time to time, and old Henry had called him the cemetery man.

"A tall man with dark hair?" he asked and she nodded. "I have seen him a time or two. Well, you turned one street short, but this one will take you to Fallow Road. The cemetery is just one block down it. Come on, I'll show you."

The girl paused for a long moment, her eyes flickering to the side again, then her face lit up with a dazzling smile.

"Thank you! I would like that very much."

Liam set off down the road, the girl following along beside him. The afternoon sun was warm, but the air was cool, nothing like that wind that had blown in during his fight with Thomas. That had been as cold as a crypt! Still, it was cool enough that now that he wasn't fighting, he had begun to feel it.

"So your brother is the caretaker for the old family's cemetery?" He had heard that there was an Ascher back in the big house again, but hadn't thought much on it.

"Yes!" she replied, and seemed to perk up a little. "He wrote to the city council looking for work, and lucky for us, they offered him the job right away. We were able to move down here in time for me to start school."

"School? Is that why you came to Ashwood? They didn't have schools where you come from?" he teased.

"They have schools," she insisted, flashing him a scowl that set him grinning despite the sting of his lower lip. "But I hope to go to Pine Hill Secondary in a year or so."

"Lofty goal," he said.

When she did not say anything return, he glanced over to find her chin set firmly and her eyes looking straight ahead.

"Nothing wrong with lofty goals," he added. Her chin lost its unexpected stubbornness.

Then suddenly she was no longer beside him. He turned his head to find that she had stopped in front of an old redbud tree. Her brows were knit together as she stared up quizzically at its bare branches.

She stood there for several seconds without saying anything, long enough that finally Liam asked, "Is there something wrong?"

"I thought I saw a lady," she answered, "before those boys showed up. She was standing right about here. She had long russet hair. Did you see her when you came past?"

"No, I didn't see a soul, only Thomas and his bunch bothering you. Was she someone you knew?"

"No... no, I guess I just... thought it was strange," she paused for a moment before continuing. "Strange that she just sort of disappeared when those boys started harassing me."

Liam was sure that wasn't what the girl had been going to say, or at least it hadn't been all of what she was going to say, but he would let it go for now. No need to push

"Not too strange," he said instead. "People around here tend to mind their own business."

"You didn't mind your own business," she pointed out.

"These streets are my business. All my customers live along them, so I have to keep them clear of the riff raff. Can't have people unwilling to give me jobs when I need them," he said, winking at her.

"That's not why you helped me," she declared guilelessly, looking him straight in the eye as she did so. "You did it because your *maman* would have been mad at you if you hadn't and because you hate when the lolli-boys come down here from uptown just so they can play at being t-to-tough..."

She stuttered to a stop, blushing hotly as he stared at her.

"True enough," he agreed after several long moments. "My *maman* would have been mad at me had I not helped someone like you. And I do hate when the lolli-boys come down here."

He said it casually, though his heart was pounding hard. He had often told his *maman* how he felt about the spoiled rich boys that came down to the Bottoms to slum it. But, never when she had been alive.

Liam started down the street again and the girl fell in step beside him. He couldn't stop himself from watching her out of the corner of his eye. Her cheeks were still bright pink and every once in a while, she shook her head ever so slightly.

It was not long before they came to the place where the narrow lane they were on emptied out onto Fallow Road. He could clearly see the cemetery just one block down from where they were.

"It's just down there," he told her, nodding his head in its direction.

"Thank you," she said, but she did not make a move towards the cemetery.

Liam watched her as she stood there uncertainly. He had seen a lot of girls, and not a few boys, react the same way after having been in a situation like the one she had just been in.

"Changed your mind?" he asked nonchalantly.

"I think so," she sighed, letting the words come out on the breath that she had obviously been holding onto. "I think it might be better to go back to the boarding house. I mean, Devon could be busy or maybe not even there." She looked around and he could see the moment it dawned on her that she had no idea how to get to where she wanted to go.

"I can walk you there," he offered, careful to keep his tone easy. "Or at least get you a bit closer, if you want."

She turned grateful eyes full on him. "Would you?" she asked, and the sun, as if it had been waiting for just that very moment, smiled full on the girl, wrapping her up in a halo of light.

La petite fée. Again, his *maman's* voice seemed to whisper in his ear. A little golden fairy straight out of the tales that she had loved so much. The ones she had often read to him when he was young.

"Of course," Liam smiled back at her. "Just tell me where we are going and I'll show you how to get there.

She told him and they headed back up the way they had come. He led her over to Nightingale Street, once they had passed Miss Rose's. All the while, he made a point of telling her the streets and landmarks as they passed them, so she could find her way again if she had to. It also served as an opportunity for people to see who she was walking with. Might save them all some trouble in the future.

They came out onto Winding Street, which they continued to follow until they had crossed over Market.

"There you are," he said, stopping at the corner.

She stopped as well, and turned to face him. "Thank you, for helping me." It looked to Liam as if she had more that she wanted to say. He waited, but she only thanked him again before starting off down the street towards the boarding house.

She had only made it a handful of steps before she paused and looked back at him. She was shaking her head ever so slightly and biting her lip, as though she was arguing with herself as to whether to say something or not. Finally, brows drawn together in what he thought might be resignation, she nodded.

"Your *maman* says that you were right to turn down Miss Rose, but that she hasn't given up on you, so be careful." She shook her head again. "I am not telling him that," she said, the blush on her cheeks blooming the brightest red yet. Then without another word, she hurried away, turning only once more to wave and call back her thanks one last time.

Liam stared after her, too stunned to move, until after she had already gone through the courtyard gate of the boarding house. Then, he turned and headed back the way he had come, hands still in his pockets. Others might have written such talk off as crazy, but he had always thought that there was more to the world than what a person could see.

"You taught me as much, didn't you *maman*?" he said to the empty air, not knowing if it was his imagination when he felt an icy touch on his cheek.

They hadn't spoken of the fight or the scratches that had appeared on Tom's face. And he wanted very much to know how she knew what she knew. But all that could wait; he was sure this would not be the last time he saw the little golden fairy with holly-blue eyes.

But that was something for the future. Right now, he had some ratbag, lolli-boys to find, and some extra lessons to give out.

CHAPTER VII

A New Friend

When Sara set off for school the next morning she had two cheese biscuits, hot from the oven, wrapped in her handkerchief. The air was downright chilly. Though not as cold as it would have been back home, she was glad for her coat and the warmth coming from the bundle in her hands.

She had just turned the corner onto Market Street when the hound's ears perked up and it wagged its tail once. A second or two later, the dark-haired boy she had met yesterday fell into step beside her, hands in his pockets.

"Good morning," he greeted her easily, as though they met there every morning.

"Good morning," she said back shyly as she unwrapped the handkerchief and handed him a biscuit.

"What's this?" he asked as he took the offered gift.

"A cheese biscuit," she replied, taking a bite of the other one in her hand. "Mrs. O'Toole makes really good ones."

The boy chuckled. "I can see it's a biscuit! Do you always bring two or did my *maman* tell you that I was coming?" He did not sound like he was teasing her.

"It was just a guess," she answered. Which was the truth, she had guessed she might see him this morning when she saw his mother waving at her from the courtyard gate.

Sara thought she heard a chuckle from the ghost following

behind them, and the hound walking next to her let out a soft snort by way of comment on her evasion. The boy, of course, could hear neither.

"A good guess, then," he said, "and I am certainly not too proud to turn down food when it's offered to me."

He took a bite of the biscuit he was holding. Sara couldn't help but notice his knuckles, which were bruised and scabbed over.

"Is that from yesterday?" she asked, and saw him follow her gaze back to his hand. Had they been that way the whole time he had walked her home? She wasn't sure, but she thought she remembered his hands being in his pockets most the way back.

"Bound to happen when you hit someone as hardheaded as Tom," he shrugged as he took another bite of his biscuit.

He said it so matter-of-factly that it didn't make Sara feel as if he were just acting tough or trying to show off like many of the other boys did. It truly seemed not to bother him at all, although he did put his hand back in his pocket as soon as he was done eating. Of course, that also could have been because the wind was a bit cool and his jacket was a bit thin.

"It's funny though," he continued. "Tom and his boys are usually pretty quick to back down. They're nothing but talk, like most of those lolli-boys."

Sara remembered the way they had watched her, the devouring hunger that looked out from their eyes. It made her stomach roil, and she found she could not finish her biscuit. She wrapped it back up in the handkerchief. Another image came to mind as she did so, the sight of Tom's face and the bleeding scratches that had appeared there. She wondered if it would bring trouble as Liam's mother had predicted. She hoped not.

"Do you think that Tom getting hurt will get you into trouble?" she asked, despite her reluctance to bring up anything that might call attention to just how strange the fight had been.

She glanced over to find Liam looking at her out of the corner of his eye, his lips quirked up in a ghost of a grin.

"Are you actually asking about Tom's eye?" he guessed. "That was a strange thing, don't you think?"

She looked down at the hound at her side, not sure what kind of answer she could give.

"You can trust him, *ma fée*," his mother reassured her.

Sara was pretty sure that had she been brave enough to look she would have found that the lovely woman had moved up to walk beside them. When she did finally pluck up the courage to glance over, it was into a pair of green eyes that glinted at her in good humor.

"Well, whatever it was, I was thankful for the help," he said.

Liam did not say much more after that, and they continued their walk in comfortable silence. A cold morning wind snuck up behind them from the sea. Its long fingers slid through their clothes like a pickpocket, looking for any gap it could find to steal away their warmth, stealing away their breath instead when it could not find one.

When they turned from Market Street onto Washboard Lane and the schoolhouse came into view, Sara tried her best to give Liam her handkerchief with its half-a-biscuit wrapped in it. He would not take it.

"Keep it, in case you're hungry later," he said, even though Sara had a whole lunch pail of food.

"You should ask him to meet you here after school," the ghost beside him suggested with an encouraging smile and mischievous twinkle in her eye. "He will most likely do it anyway. I can tell by the determined look of his chin."

Sara could not bring herself to say the words, but her hands had popped the kerchief-wrapped biscuit into his coat pocket before her mind had a chance to think about what it was she was doing.

"You can return the kerchief to me after school," she called back to him, waving as she hurried on towards the schoolhouse.

It was the bravest, boldest thing she had ever done in her life.

All day long Sara agonized over what she had said that morning. What if Liam thought she was being bossy and did not show up? He had certainly looked shocked when she had popped the biscuit into his pocket and told him to return the handkerchief after school. What if he had somewhere else he needed to be? It had been rude of her to assume that he had nothing better to do than walk her back home from school. And, she had not even thought to mention that she stayed late for extra classes. What if he *had* come but thought *she* wasn't coming when she did not come out with all the other students?

But despite her reservations, when Mr. Hegdus asked if she wanted him to walk home with her, she had assured him that there was no need. He had given her a wondering look, but had not questioned her, only wished her a good night and said that he would see her the next day.

When she stepped out of the schoolhouse, she found Liam there waiting. Without a word they fell into step next to each other as they made their way up Washboard Lane. He handed her handkerchief back to her, neatly folded and clean.

"Well done, *mon fils*," Sara heard a now familiar voice say from behind them.

She did not turn to look, instead she thanked Liam for returning it. Then because she was nervous and could think of nothing else to say, she began to tell him all about what she had learned in school that day.

He seemed happy enough to listen, so she continued until they had reached the intersection of Market and Winding Streets. There they parted ways. She waved as she turned towards Mrs. O'Toole's, and he waved in return as he headed in the opposite direction, down towards the Bottoms.

"Didn't I tell you?" His mother said as she leaned in, Sara felt an electric cold brush both of her cheeks as the ghost kissed them each in turn. "He will do good by you. *Bonne soiree, ma fée!*"

When Sara thought of the conversation she'd had after their

first fateful encounter, she found that for once she was very glad that the living could not always hear what the dead had to say.

Liam turned back once, waving to the golden-haired girl who was still standing on the other side of Market Street. Then he slid his hands into his pockets, and continued on his way towards the Bottoms.

He hadn't really made a decision that morning to meet her, his feet had just sort of carried him along until he found himself near Market Street about the same time Sara was turning onto it. Walking with her had cost him the morning's work, but he didn't mind. He hadn't really suffered for it, since she had shared her breakfast with him. Even if that had not been the case, he would have felt that the loss had been worth it.

The additional bruises on his knuckles had been worth it as well, and not just because a couple of High Street boys had gotten some much needed extra lessons. They had been less eager to fight when he had found them after their first run-in. Truth was, Tom, always the most cocksure of the bunch, had been almost contrite and the scratches hadn't looked as bad as Liam had expected them to look, given that Tom had been howling as though his eye had been torn from its socket.

Sara might have been concerned that he would get in trouble over that eye, but she certainly had not wanted to talk about it. And she hadn't wanted to talk about his *maman* either, not directly anyway. Though she was happy to talk about everything else. He couldn't deny that it had been strange hearing his own words said back to him, words he had only ever said to the empty air, as was hearing approval and advice from someone long dead.

"Strange but interesting," he said aloud. An icy wind brushed across his cheek and he smiled. He guessed his *maman* agreed with him.

He spent the rest of the evening as he often did, looking for small jobs on the east side of Nightingale, upstreet as those in the Bottoms called it, where the shops that catered to a better kind of customer were. They always needed someone to help get them ready for when they opened for business or switched over to their evening trade. His thoughts strayed back to the girl and her odd way of looking just to the side of him on occasion. It had him wondering if maybe the thought that his mother was still here watching over him might not just be the wishful thinking of an orphan.

It was well after the lamp lighters had made their rounds when he finished sweeping up in front of Gerard's coffeehouse. He was just bringing the broom back around to the kitchen door when he saw a man wearing a dark coat come out of the tobacconist's across the street. He was not sure at first why the man caught his eye, but something about him niggled at his brain. It did vaguely remind Liam of that dark-coated crow-of-a-figure that had been perched in the schoolhouse doorway watching as he met Sara to walk her home. He quickly lost sight of the man in the shadows of downstreet, the rougher west end of Nightingale. A frown tugged at his lips.

He collected his pay and followed after, heading towards Gertie's to see what she had for food tonight. He did not run into the man who might have been the schoolmaster again, though something in the corner of his eye kept catching his attention. Whatever it was, it was gone by the time he had turned to look at it.

Eventually Liam headed off towards the shed where he slept. Food in hand and a few pennies in his pocket, he contemplated whether he would be walking to school again the next morning. But he guessed since he had turned down the offer for the next morning's work that he already made up his mind.

CHAPTER VIII

A Night Out

Sara had been surprised when at Thursday's dinner Miss Newkirk had asked if she would like to attend a show with her the following evening at The Sands Theater. She had been doubly surprised when the expected offer for her brother to accompany them had not come directly afterwards. Devon had readily given her permission to go, though Sara had wondered more than once if he might have come to regret his choice. Mostly because he had had to endure her talking about nothing else since.

That had certainly been the case that morning when she had talked Liam's ear off the whole way to school. She had not been able to stop herself. Even in school, she had been unable to think of anything else the entire time she was there. And, she was still talking about it that afternoon as she walked home with Liam.

"So you think this Miss Newkirk has designs on your brother?" he asked, having patiently listened to her speculate for the hundredth time why Miss Newkirk had invited her and not her brother. He took a bite of an apple that had come from her lunch pail. She had been much too excited to eat it at lunchtime.

"I am sure of it," she replied. "So why didn't she ask him to go with us? To be honest, I'm not sure why she asked me to go, though it was nice of her to do so. I have never been to a vaudeville show. Well actually, I've never been to a theater, any theater. And now, I'm going to the Sands! I did walk past Grand Avenue once," she sighed as she remembered the graceful buildings with their sparkling windows. "The whole place looks like something you'd read about in a storybook. Everything is so beautiful! The ironwork balconies look like metal lace and the walls between them seem to have stone vines growing along their faces." She stopped, feeling her cheeks grow warm when she realized how odd her fanciful notions must sound. But when she glanced over, she found the boy next to her was smiling in a way that said he had seen them for himself. "You've already been there?"

"No, I haven't been there, and I've certainly never been to a show there. But I've walked past when I was looking for work down at the docks. And you are right, the buildings do sort of look like they were grown instead of built," he agreed. "Will you tell me all about it Monday morning?"

Sara could feel her smile stretch from ear to ear. "Of course!" she promised as they reached the corner of Winding Street.

She nearly ran the rest of the way to Mrs. O'Toole's after she and Liam parted company, not caring at that moment that she should be too old for such behavior. The question of why Miss Newkirk had asked her to go and not her brother did nag at her a bit, but the butterflies doing loop-the-loops in her stomach didn't care. They were just excited to be going to the show.

Mrs. Madison helped her get ready after dinner and even lent her a beautiful silk shawl to wear over her best dress. Sara felt a little self-conscious. But that feeling quickly faded away when she saw the pride in Devon's eyes as he kissed her forehead and told her to enjoy herself.

A carriage picked them up in front of the boarding house, much to Sara's delight. It carried them down Winding Street, past Town Square and the Green up to High Street with all its beautiful homes. Eventually they reached Fontaine Circle, where their carriage lined up with all the others that were delivering passengers to the newly built Grand Plaza by the Bay.

It took all the decorum that Sara could muster for her not to bounce on the seat like a toddler when the plaza came into view.

90

The buildings with their flowing lines and whiplash curves were even more magnificent at night. And the avenue which ran the whole length of the plaza, from Cafe on the Green to the Vue de la Mer Hotel, was full of people laughing merrily despite the cold, damp air.

When their turn came, Sara followed Miss Newkirk down from the carriage into that shining fairyland. The electric street lamps looked as though they had sprouted up from the cement sidewalks like beautiful iron flowers. Their radiant light made jewels of the colored glass windows. It gilded the graceful metalwork surrounding them and dusted gold on the faces of the nymphs that looked down on them from the stone leaves above. Even the most stubborn shadows melted away from their unwavering brilliance.

Sara could hear the click of the white hound's nails on the pavement. She was always curious why they made such sounds; breathing, footfalls and what not. After all, they didn't have to. Perhaps, they just thought they should, so the living would know they were there. She had never been able to bring herself to ask. It felt like too personal of a question.

There were few other spirits to be seen as Miss Newkirk led them down Grand Avenue, pointing out the places she had already been and recounting what it was that she had done there. The white hound behind them huffed her opinion loudly at each declaration. Even Sara had to admit that it sounded like Miss Newkirk was putting on airs, though it was uncharitable for her to think so.

They soon arrived at The Sands Theater. A line of people stretched down the sidewalk towards them. All were dressed in their gayest clothes; they laughed and smiled as they waited in anticipation for the front doors to open.

Sara felt almost giddy as they joined everyone else standing in line. It was warmer in the crowd, although little breezes still found a way to sneak in. They slipped between the buildings and along the curbs, ruffling hems with their frigid fingers and kissing cheeks with their cold lips. But the excitement was such that Sara doubted most people even noticed.

The brilliantly lit marquee above them announced "Herrmann Howard, Wonders of the World Vaudeville Show" in bold black letters. And all along the walls they were standing next to, playbills extolled the wonders that awaited them inside: *The Flying Stars, acrobat extraordinaires; The Dancing Fans of the FarEast; Madame Koshey, Mysterious Messenger of the Dead; The Lost Wife, an up-roarious comedy by Munroe and White;* and of course *Herrmann Howard, Master Illusionist,* the star of the show. The name of each act was spelled out in a variety of sizes and elaborate fonts.

Finally, the moment arrived! The huge glass doors opened and she was swept into the red carpeted lobby with the flood of people. Gold velvet ropes hung in neat paths, directing them where to go. They flowed past beautiful murals framed by gilded columns where bronze goddesses held up the electric bulbs that filled the lobby with light. Sara could easily believe a king's palace would have a hard time matching the opulence of The Sands Theater.

They were met at the end of their path by a young man dressed in a smart red coat with a pillbox hat to match. Miss Newkirk handed him their tickets. He in turn handed them to another young man dressed in a similar uniform.

"Ladies, if you would follow me," he said with a bright smile and a sharp little bow.

Their usher led them to a pair of seats right on the floor towards the end of a row, which Miss Newkirk seemed quite proud of. They were lovely seats padded in red velvet, with a clear view of the stage that was still hidden behind a closed curtain.

Sara was so excited that she found she was having a hard time concentrating on what Miss Newkirk was saying. The white hound who had come to sit in the walkway next to them yawned hugely however, as the young woman on the other side of Sara expounded on the acts she had already seen at this theater and others. Sara's eyes watched the stage intently where every sway and ripple in the curtain's heavy fabric hinted at the delights that were to come.

Finally, she forced herself to look away. Her gaze drifted up to the private boxes where smaller versions of the stage's glorious red curtain had been drawn aside. Elegantly dressed men and women milled about, the house lights sparkling on their jewels as they made their way to the plush seats that awaited them.

Something caught Sara's attention. She squinted and looked closer at the private boxes above. For a moment, she had thought she had seen a familiar figure in one of the ones closest to the stage, but she could not be sure. Perhaps it had been her imagination that had dreamed up Mr. Hegdus's tall dark-coated frame.

Just as the lights dimmed, one of the ubiquitous ushers came up to where they were sitting.

"Excuse me miss, could you and your companion please follow me," he said, keeping his voice low. It was hard to tell whether he was addressing Miss Newkirk or herself.

"What is the meaning of this?" Miss Newkirk demanded, her voice rife with indignation. "These seats have been paid for and we have every right to be here!"

"Please, miss. There is no need to be upset," he assured her in a placating tone. "The lady in box one offered for both of you to join her there."

Sara looked up at the box the usher had nodded to. Oddly enough, she could see Lady Károlyi sitting there, clear as day, despite the thick shadows that had gathered with the absence of the house lights. She nodded to Sara.

"Miss Newkirk, I believe that..." Sara began, turning towards the woman next to her, only to find that Miss Newkirk was already on her feet.

"Of course we would be happy to join her," the woman said, all the while chivvying Sara to stand up and crowding her out into the aisle like a mama duck herding a particularly slow duckling along.

The usher led the way with a small flashlight back along the rear corridor that ran behind the sea of seats. He brought them up a curving set of stairs to a wide hallway with three doors. Each going to its own private box, Sara supposed.

"Here we are then," he said, knocking on the door all the way at the end.

It was opened by Mr. Hegdus. "Good evening, Sara," he greeted her, gesturing for them to enter. "And good evening, Miss...?"

"Newkirk, Davina Newkirk," Miss Newkirk answered, handing him her card. Sara thought she sounded a little stunned and maybe even a bit breathless.

"We are very glad you both could join us," Mr. Hegdus said, with a small bow.

Sara stepped past him into the box. It was much larger than she had expected. There were five seats, but the only two people there were Mr. Hegdus and Lady Károlyi, who was sitting in a seat to one side where the view would be best.

"Miss Amaris, please join me," the lady said, placing her hand on the seat next to the one where she was sitting, only to have the white hound jump up instead.

"Yes, yes. I have not forgotten," the lady said, obviously addressing the apparition next to her. "There is no need for concern."

Sara made her way over. The hound jumped down from the seat so that she could sit in its place. She wanted desperately to ask the lady about being able to see the white hound (or at least she assumed that she saw her) but was keenly aware of Miss Newkirk only a short distance away. So, she only said "Thank you for inviting us to share your box, Lady Károlyi," as she sat politely.

"Call me Ana, please. And, I was very happy to, Miss Amaris," the lady smiled, and Sara realized that she was not wearing a veil.

'Stunning' was the only word that came to Sara's mind as she looked at Lady Ana's uncovered face. From her bow-shaped mouth to the up-swept brows that arched over her large dark eyes, Lady Ana was the very definition of beauty with just a hint of the exotic to make her truly unique. Yet, Sara did not feel awkward or self-conscious as she sat next to her, as can sometimes happen when in the company of someone so extraordinary. In fact, for a moment the lady inexplicably reminded Sara of her own mother. Which was nonsense since the statuesque woman next to her looked nothing like her mother. Nevertheless, there was a sense of comfortable familiarity that lingered.

Sara blushed hotly when she realized she had been staring.

"The contradictory nature of the effect can be most disconcerting for those who are sensitive. For everyone else, there is only the reaction, not the recognition. Pay it no mind," the lady insisted genially. "Tell me Miss Amaris, have you been to a vaudeville show before?"

"I have not," Sara admitted, looking at the hound who was sitting next to her feet, one rust-colored ear cocked back in their direction. "This is my first trip to a theater, to be honest."

"I would expect nothing less than honesty from you," the lady smiled. "Well, I can promise you will see and hear many a curiosity this evening."

The shadows around them deepened then, as the stage lights came up. Sara shifted forward in her seat, everything else forgotten as the curtain rose to reveal a snowy field beneath a painted starry sky. Across this landscape came a troupe of dancers; men and women dressed in spectacular costumes. They spun and leapt and threw each other impossibly high into the air. Sara gasped and clapped along with everyone else each time they did.

Then they were gone, chased into the shadowy wings by deafening applause. An expectant hush fell over the audience as one by one the lights snuffed out until the whole of the theater lay in complete darkness. The moment stretched on and on for an eternity until Sara felt her anticipation begin to shift to uneasiness. Then, with the suddenness of a thunderclap, a spotlight lanced down from above, illuminating a shrouded woman.

She sat enthroned on an elaborate chair of bleached bones, or so it had been made to look, with grinning skulls peering over her shoulders and resting beneath each hand. Chains snaked through their empty eye sockets, coming to an end at the shackles on the woman's wrists. She wore a diaphanous white gown, and a veil of white muslin lay draped over her head. What was most interesting though, at least to Sara's mind, was something the rest of the audience could not see. That was the dozen or so spirits that sat at the woman's feet.

It was clear to Sara that this was the Madame Koshey, Mysterious Messenger of the Dead, who had been listed on the playbill that she had noticed out front of the theater. She had been too excited to give it much thought then. And even if she had, she would not have been inclined to believe her a true medium. There were many who claimed to be able to speak to the dead, but few that actually could.

The fact that there were spirits waiting around her like well-mannered school children seemed to suggest that Madame Koshey might indeed be able to do as she claimed.

One of the spirits, a large big-bellied man, stood up. Sara watched as he sat right down in the already occupied chair. His body, seemingly solid to Sara's eyes, melted into that of the shrouded woman, the gauze veil billowing noticeably as the spirit took possession of her body.

A voice issued from behind Madame Koshey's veil which was clearly not her own. It called out to someone named Iris, reminding her to plant the roses like she'd promised. It also told her that she was well rid of that useless husband of hers, so there was no need for tears.

At this proclamation, a young woman stood up from the audience, crying out to her papa that she missed him and tearfully promising that she would do as he asked. Then the spirit emerged from the body that he had just taken possession of.

He was followed by another, then another. Each time, a different voice issued from behind the veil, and each time that voice was met by either tears of grief or cries of gratitude from someone in the audience. There was one lone heckler. But he was quickly disabused of his skepticism when his own mother spoke to him and revealed a secret he would have probably rather she hadn't.

There was an uneasiness that grew in Sara each time a spirit entered the shrouded woman's body, but she could not say why. After all, it was not like she was unfamiliar with channeling and mediumship. She had read a great deal about such things in her father's library and it was, in essence, much the same as what she herself could do. There were several religions where possession was a part of their rituals. Though she had never allowed herself to be completely taken over by a spirit before, the idea had never made her feel uneasy. But what she was witnessing now did, without a doubt.

The final spirit to come to the shrouded woman did not stand up from the group seated at her feet. Instead, he was pulled from out of the audience, somewhat reluctantly from what Sara could see.

If it had been odd watching the other spirits seemingly solid bodies sink willingly into the other solid body enthroned on its macabre chair, watching the reluctant spirit pulled in head first was a hundred times more so. The filmy dress the medium wore billowed out, enveloping the spirit, devouring it like an octopus would a struggling fish.

An ominous stillness settled over the shrouded figure, then she began to writhe, her back arched and her body contorted unnaturally. The veil covering the woman's face was sucked into her mouth as it opened in a silent scream. Then suddenly the figure was on its feet. The spirit that had been inside her now lay on the floor, curled up in a fetal position. Sara gasped and stood up from her own chair just as a voice from the stage cried out, "The dead have spoken!" And everything went dark.

Sara was still standing when the lights came back on to reveal an empty stage, its curtain lowered once again. Sara glanced around self-consciously. Miss Newkirk was absorbed in Mr. Hegdus, and seemed to not have noticed Sara's distress. The same could not be said for Lady Ana who Sara found was watching her with a knowing smile.

Sara apologized as she sat back down, but offered no explanation for her outburst. She was not sure how to explain it, even to Lady Ana who was a practitioner and no stranger to the unseen world. It was just not something she often talked about.

She jumped a little when Lady Ana asked in a neutral voice, "And what were your thoughts on Madame Koshey?"

"I will admit she made me feel very uneasy," Sara answered truthfully. "Though I cannot say exactly why."

The lady nodded her head once in accord. "Your feelings mirror mine, then," she confessed but offered no further opinion. Her attention returned back to the stage and the curtain that was once again rising.

Sara was grateful the lady did not press as to why she felt the way she did. But her thoughts were still all awhirl as she watched two women in brightly colored robes enter onto the stage in mincing steps. Their hair, smooth and black as silk, was caught up in an elaborate arrangement held together by ornaments of jade and gold. They knelt effortlessly on the ground. One woman plucked at a stringed instrument while the other began a slow sweeping dance. The sharply melodic notes conjured up visions of far-away lands. But the long trailing sleeves and graceful arcs of the dancer's fan only faded into the image of the shrouded woman with her billowing veil in Sara's mind. Her mouth opened in a silent scream. The glint of chains as she stood, arms upraised like a priest before an altar, the ghost a sacrificial offering at her feet.

Those images continued to rear their heads throughout the rest of the show. Even as the illusionist levitated his assistant from where she lay on his couch; even as a most marvelous machine projected moving pictures onto a silver screen, that prevailing sense of wrongness stayed with Sara.

When the house lights came on, everyone stood and Sara

stood with them. It felt a little like waking up. The soft darkness banished, leaving behind only a vague memory of disturbing dreams.

Once in the hall, Mr. Hegdus directed them to a private entrance, which led to a set of stairs, that eventually opened up onto the boardwalk. The cool air greeted them like an enthusiastic puppy as they left the theater, the low dark stretch of Edith Island on the other side of the bay doing little to stop the wind as it whipped in off the sea.

Sara was a touched surprised when Mr. Hegdus offered his arm to the obviously enamored Miss Newkirk rather than his benefactress. She was even more surprised when said lady linked arms with her, as though they were sisters or good friends out on a stroll. There was a moment of stillness as a speaking look passed between the white hound and the dark lady, but it soon passed with only a silent showing of teeth from the hound.

"Your guardian has her doubts about my motives. She knows the brightest lights often cast the darkest shadows." The lady looked over and chuckled warmly at the perplexed look that Sara was sure showed on her face. "Forgive me! Truly, I was not meaning to be cryptic. But you should know that despite what many would have you believe, those that walk in the darkness do not always run from the light. Rather they crave it, and are drawn to it like moths to a flame. Speaking of moths to flames, tell me if you would, did it seem to you as though the spirits that came to Madame Koshey did so willingly?"

"I would have said so, all but one that is," Sara replied, a little trepidatious. Given her experiences, she was almost positive that Lady Ana could see spirits as well as she herself could. "Did it look differently to you?"

"I suspect that I do not see them the same way as you do, Miss Amaris," the lady confided. "You said all but one?"

"Yes. The last spirit, the one who did not speak, he did not come willingly," she confirmed, the memory of the spirit being swallowed up in the dress's billowing folds springing vividly to mind.

"Interesting," Lady Ana nodded thoughtfully. "Yes, certainly a person to keep note of. And such a unique name she has chosen to give herself as well. Yes, very interesting indeed."

Unfortunately, whatever the lady had meant by her observations would remain a mystery to Sara because it was then that they arrived at the waiting carriage.

Mr. Hegdus helped Miss Newkirk up inside. He turned to Sara and she blushed as he helped her up into the carriage with the same care and deference as he had Miss Newkirk.

"Take care, Miss Amaris," he smiled at her warmly, but there was a concern in his eyes that was unexpected.

She wondered at that as the carriage pulled away and she watched the figures of the schoolmaster and his benefactress move off into the darkness.

"What an evening!" Miss Newkirk exclaimed, sighing as she sat back in her seat. "First, free tickets. Then being invited to sit in a private box by such a handsome gentleman! My star is surely on the rise."

In a somewhat uncharacteristic burst of negativism, Sara could not help but note that stars often shine brightest on the darkest nights.

CHAPTER IX

Rainy Afternoon Confessions

The following Monday morning, Liam was running late. He sped full tilt down Winding Street, passing by Sara's brother as he went. The man spared him no more than a glance, not that there was a reason for him to do so. It did make Liam wonder if his new friend had mentioned him to her brother or not.

He shot through the intersection of Market and Winding, just in time to fall into step with Sara as she turned onto the main thoroughfare.

"Good morning!" she exclaimed cheerfully as she held out a biscuit.

"Good morning," he grinned back at her as his fingers wrapped around the warm biscuit. He took a bite and nearly groaned. Work had been light yesterday, which meant so had his food. He took another bite as the golden fairy skipped along next to him near to bursting with excitement.

"Do you want to hear about the show?" she asked, apparently no longer able to contain herself.

"Of course I want to hear about the show! I was just afraid I wouldn't be able to over my stomach growling," he said as he finished the rest of his biscuit off in two bites.

He appreciated that she did not ask why he had not eaten breakfast. Not that it bothered him, not having money, but he was pretty sure that she would feel bad if she learned that he was not taking morning jobs so that he could walk with her to school.

"Here you can have mine, I'm too excited to eat it anyway," she said, handing him her biscuit which she had yet to take a bite of. "Don't worry," she continued when he did not take it from her immediately. "Mrs. O'Toole fed me eggs and toast before I left."

He accepted it, taking the time to savor the second flaky, buttery biscuit much more slowly. Mrs. O'Toole really did make the best biscuits.

As he was eating, he listened to Sara describe the show she had seen the Friday before in vivid detail. She told a good story. It wasn't hard at all for him to picture the acrobats twirling through the air or the master illusionist transforming his lovely assistant into a caged tiger. There was something though. Something that told him she was holding back. He just couldn't quite put his finger on what it was that made him think so.

"Did you ever find out why your Miss Newkirk invited you to go in the first place?"

"Yes, in a way... Oh! And I can't believe I forgot to mention who we met there! Anyway, as for the tickets, from what Miss Newkirk told me, the manager of the theater himself stopped by the boarding house and offered free tickets for one adult and one child. Miss Newkirk happened to be there, and she thought of me right away.

Liam kept his face neutral. It was not like the theater needed to drum up business, it was nearly packed every night from what he'd heard. So why hand out free tickets? He kept his skepticism to himself while Sara continued on.

"Now for the part I forgot to mention. While we were there, we came across Mr. Hegdus and his benefactress, Lady Károlyi. She invited Miss Newkirk and I to sit with them in her private box."

"Mr. Hegdus? Your schoolmaster?" Liam asked.

Sara nodded.

"And the tickets were free?" he frowned and glanced over at the girl walking next to him.

"I know, it is all a little convenient," Sara admitted, her enthusiasm dampening noticeably.

The question in Liam's mind was why, and to what end? But there were no answers to be had yet, so what he said instead was, "Well, whatever the circumstances, at least you enjoyed going to the theater." He was surprised by the moment's hesitation that followed his statement. He felt again as though there was something he was missing, a feeling he had felt more than once in the short five days he had known her. He wasn't one to push, but he couldn't deny his growing curiosity.

The schoolhouse came into view, and Liam could see the dark outline of the schoolmaster. His frown deepened. He was nearly positive that the figure he had seen the other night in the Bottoms was one and the same as the one that was standing in the schoolhouse doorway.

Liam finished up his biscuit and slid the crumb-filled kerchief in his pocket, along with his hands which were getting more than a little cold. He would have to see if he could make enough to buy gloves. Food was important, but so was his hands.

"See you after school?" he asked Sara.

She smiled back at him, nodding her head. "I will see you then!"

When Sara stepped out of the schoolhouse that afternoon, she was greeted by a gray blanketed sky and a cold wind that grew colder each time that it blew. Despite all that, Liam was waiting for her in the usual place. They headed off, walking a little closer together by unspoken agreement in a futile effort to keep warm. They had not made it even half-way to the boarding house when the first rain drops began to fall.

Liam grabbed her hand and they ran, ducking into a sheltered corner where two garden walls met. Cedar branches, heavy from the rain, drooped over the top making a nice little niche that kept most of the wet out. They huddled together shoulder to shoulder, and tried to stay dry as they watched the rain fall in a silver curtain just beyond the dark green needles. Liam had pulled his coat up to cover their heads in an effort to keep the stray drips from falling on them.

Sara realized that for the first time since she had met Liam, they were completely alone. There were none of the usual ghostly chaperons there to offer comments only she could hear. Even the vaguely Mr. Hegdus-shaped shadow that she had thought she had seen following them once or twice, was missing. They were the only ones tucked away in their little cave of greenery; a tiny island forgotten by the world around it. The circumstances almost begged a person to share secrets and make confessions. Not that she had any intention of doing either. Or so she told herself.

"There's something I have been wanting to talk to you about." Liam's warm breath gusted out, a plume of white in the cold air, as he seemed to search for words. "On that first day when we met, you told me my *maman* said that I had made the right choice when I turned down Miss Rose."

Sara could not look at him. For whatever reason, she had shared a lot of things when they had first met that she would have never normally shared. Things she was usually very, very careful about.

He must have noticed her unease because he quickly added, "It's okay. No reason to worry. I'm not about to ask you to jump off a cliff, or anything. I just wanted to know, did she tell you that herself? Did you actually talk to her, to my *maman*? Whatever your answer, I'll believe you. I've just… always wondered if she is still here with me, or if it's just my wishful thinking. So I wanted to ask since there is no one else around to hear… just us, or I think it's just us."

It *was* just the two of them, and that was sort of the problem. Because whether Liam knew it or not, he was asking her to jump off a cliff, in a way. And there was no Marguerite there to reassure her that he was trustworthy, and no Devon there to remind her that this was a bad idea.

Liam did not say anything else. He did not push or ask again. He just stood there quietly as the rain continued to fall, patiently waiting for her to make up her mind.

"Do you believe in such things?" she finally asked, her belly trembling with nerves. "Ghosts and spirits and whatnot?"

"I believe there are things that most of us can't see. And I have always believed my *maman* is still here. I can almost hear her sometimes," he confessed without a trace of self-consciousness. "On the day we met, I had no reason to turn down that particular street. That's just where I found myself, and right when Tom and his boys were giving you a hassle. I have no doubt that was her doing."

Sara's heart was in her mouth. She did not know how to answer. How many times had she trusted someone when they said they believed? How many times had she shared confidences only to come to regret those confessions later. And she had been trying to be so careful here.

A nudge against her shoulder drew her from the paralyzing spiral of her thoughts.

"You don't have to answer if you don't want," he reassured her. "But I can't deny being curious. Did she really say I 'was right to turn down Miss Rose, but that she hadn't given up on me'?"

Sara nodded her head once. "Yes," she said softly, then held her breath as she waited to see what he would say.

"I bet that was not all she said," he chuckled.

"It wasn't," she admitted on a sigh.

"Please tell me," and Sara thought she could feel him trembling as he asked. She wondered if he was nervous, or if it was just the cold.

She wasn't sure if she even could tell him. She was afraid that the embarrassment might be too much for her to even get the words out.

"She said, 'You are a good man, and a fine-looking man'," she confessed, but she had no plans on telling him what else his mother had said. Of course, her brain was quite happy to replay the whole of the memory for her.

"*You can trust him, mon poussin,*" she had told Sara after the fight with Thomas. "*He will lead you where you need to go safely, unlike those useless pigs. He hates when the lolli-boys come down from High Street to play at being tough.*

"*But my son, he is a good man. And a fine-looking man, no? Which is why Rose offered him a job. He was right to have turned her down, but she hasn't given up on him so he must be careful. There is no shame in doing what is needful, but that is not the life for him. He should find love and a family. Don't you agree, he would make a good husband in a few years? And he likes you, I can tell. You would make a beautiful couple and have beautiful babies when you are older. Oh, ce serait merveilleux! And he would always treat you well, ma cherie, always.*"

Sara's cheeks were almost burning she was blushing so hard.

"She also said that there was no shame in doing what is needful, but that was not the life for you. But I wasn't sure what it was she meant by that," Sara admitted. Her cheeks were still so hot she was surprised steam wasn't pouring off them.

"You're not sure but you're blushing like a house on fire? Now I am positive that was not all *maman* said," he chuckled softly. "But what she meant was that I made the right choice in not taking Miss Rose up on her offer for me to be one of her doves."

His explanation did not clarify a thing. So she stood there, cheeks burning with no idea what to say. To make matters worse, he had leaned in towards her, and was making a study of her face. She couldn't see anything but the pale green of his eyes, and for a moment her heart nearly stopped as the absurd notion that he was reading her mind popped into her head.

"You weren't lying. You don't know, do you?" he smiled at her. "Miss Rose's is a brothel, everyone working there is 'soiled dove', a prostitute."

"Oh," was all Sara could say. Suddenly, she understood exactly what Thomas and the boys with him had meant with their teasing. And with that came the crystal clear realization of just what kind of work Miss Rose had offered Liam. "Oh! Why would she offer you a job like that?" she asked.

He was very quiet, then his whole body started to shake. Sara was worried at first, until she realized he was laughing.

"What? You don't agree with maman that I have grown into a 'fine-looking man'?" He was teasing her now.

"That is not what I meant! I mean… I meant…" What did she mean? He had her all flustered now. "I mean why did she offer you a job at all?" she finished lamely. He was grinning at her like her brother often did when he knew she was flustered. She almost stuck her tongue out at him.

"I already do odd jobs for her, cleaning, fixing things, running errands and what not," he said. "She just wanted to see if I wanted to earn more. There's no shame in it, if that's what's needful to a keep a roof over your head and food on the table. But that is not the kind of job I want, even if the money's good."

He said it all matter-of-factly, without embarrassment. Unfortunately, she was having trouble listening to him without embarrassment, not because she really thought that there was anything wrong with that line of work. There were plenty of practitioners who practiced sex magick. But the fact that she was talking about it with a boy, and this boy in particular; she was surprised she hadn't burnt up into a cinder from blushing so hard. At this point, she almost wished he would ask about the scratches on Thomas's face. Trying to explain about the white cat and spirits would be preferable.

She was pretty sure that Devon would have told her that what she was about to do was a very, very bad idea.

"Your mother is very beautiful," she finally said, biting her lip to keep it from trembling. When she glanced up at Liam, she found the softest expression on his face.

"You can see her then?" he asked.

She nodded her head, not quite brave enough to say the words out loud.

"Yes, she was very beautiful," he smiled softly.

"How long ago did she die?" It was a question she rarely asked. It seemed a little rude to do so when the spirit was standing right there next to you.

"I was about six, I guess, and I'm going to be fifteen, so almost nine years ago now?" he said.

"Six years old!" she exclaimed. She was trying to picture a young Liam, alone with no one to look after him. Suddenly she wanted very much to give him a hug, or maybe it was the young Liam in her head that she wanted to hug and tell him it would be okay. But had it been okay? "Who did you live with?"

"Myself," he said. "We have no relations here that I know of."

"Yourself? Where did you stay?"

"For the first couple years I stayed in Miss Rose's attic. *Maman* was one of her doves, and had been since I can remember. Not that we ever lived there. We always had a separate place, just for us. But Miss Rose was fond of my mother, so she let me stay and fed me. She is also a shrewd woman, and she knew having a young boy around to do chores was cheaper, and safer, than hiring a man to do it."

"But where did you live after that?" Sara asked.

"Anywhere I could," he said. "There was always some dry place I could hole up in for a while."

Sara's heart hurt. "Where do you live now?" She asked anxious to know if he was still having to live in such a way.

"I've been staying in an empty shed for a while now, a couple streets over from Nightingale. I think it might be a left over from when they were building the bridges across the river. At least,

I've never heard of anyone owning it. It's not half bad. It stays dry and is cool in the summer, so I can't complain."

Sara noticed he didn't say anything about the winter though. The winters this far south were mild, but still. She felt her eyes begin to burn. She was NOT going to cry! How would she explain to the boy next to her that she was crying for him and not sound even stranger than he probably already thought she was?

Instead, she gave in to the urge and hugged him. It was a quick, awkward hug, but it made her feel better. He jumped and the coat slipped a little before he pulled it back up over their heads. She glanced over and was surprised to see that his cheeks were a little pink. Serves him right for all the times he had made her blush! At least he didn't look like a fire engine when he blushed, not like she did.

"What was that for?" he asked.

"I guess, because your *maman* can't, and I think that she would have wanted to," she replied.

The blush disappeared from his cheeks. "Thank you," he said and the smile he gave her was bright enough to chase away the rain.

It was edging on towards evening when the rain finally let up. Liam slipped his coat back on and they left their little cave of greenery. It was pretty cold now, and the dampness of the air allowed it to seep through to the bone.

She and Liam resumed their interrupted journey down Market Street. They parted ways where they always did, with Liam waving back at her as he headed off towards the Bottoms. He did not give her the chance to ask about his wet coat, or if he would be warm enough tonight. Sara reminded herself that he had been doing fine on his own for more than half his life, thank you very much, and probably wouldn't appreciate her trying to mother him. But that did not stop her from worrying, all the same.

CHAPTER X

Silent Graves

The sun had not shone its face all day, and the fitful wind was cool and damp. Even so, Devon stood in only his shirt sleeves, his coat off to the side, as he cut at the tangled branches. He had been working steadily on clearing the way to the old crypt where, only a couple weeks earlier, he had met the infamous Mr. Ascher for the first time.

His progress had been good, despite last week's rain, which had given everything a good soaking. The roses and winter-bare azaleas no longer overhung the wide shell-rock path that he could now clearly see did not end at the crypt, as he had once thought. The path continued on for quite a ways beyond it, in fact. At its end, Devon found a pair of quiet graves resting amidst a grove of red cedar. The same red cedar whose branches he was even now working on thinning.

The dates engraved on the headstones proclaimed them to be nearly three hundred years old, the oldest he had found so far. The stonework itself, however, looked to have been put in place more recently than that. Not by much though, since time and the weather had still taken their toll on the names that had been carved there.

But the silent angel that watched over them was conspicuously free of the creepers that had overgrown much of the rest of the cemetery, as was the ironwork fence that guarded them. At his touch, its gate had opened easily on quiet hinges. Any brush or grass that might have hidden those lonely headstones had been cleared away, and not long ago by Devon's estimation.

Arms full of branches, he stopped to look at the silent graves. There was something more than distance that separated them from the others he cared for, and he had just realized what it was. They felt empty.

In any other part of the cemetery, the dead made enough noise that he could easily believe himself standing on a busy street, if he were to close his eyes that is. As far as he could tell, nearly every other grave he had come across had a spirit that lived there. But there were no voices here, only the sighing of the wind through the cedar branches.

He read aloud the names engraved in the pale marble. "Nora Ascher, gentle wife and loving mother. Hannah Ascher, beloved daughter. Angels sing thee to thy rest, my little bird."

He stood there for the longest time puzzling over those two graves and who might have been caring for them.

"There are no spirits here to speak with, caretaker." A voice said from behind him.

"You are here," Devon pointed out. He did not bother to turn around, since he knew there would be nothing there for him to see.

"So I am. But this is not where I sleep."

If Devon were to guess, he would have said the voice was that of an old, old woman. It was a pleasant voice, the kind that sets one at ease.

"Would you like to show me where you do sleep?" he asked as he added the branches he was carrying to the growing pile in the wheelbarrow.

He felt a thin arm link through his and a hand came to rest on his forearm. The skin of that hand felt thin and soft, like a cotton shirt that had seen many, many washings.

"I would love to," she chuckled as her other hand patted his bicep. "It has been forever since I brought a nice young man home."

He followed the subtle tug and pull on his arm as the old woman's ghost led him away from the grove of cedars and its quiet graves. The hammock beyond was filled with oak and had a healthy bit of shrub underneath. The rest of his tools were behind in his wheelbarrow, but his machete was still hanging from his belt.

"Why are no spirits there for me to speak with?" he asked, clearing the way along what might have been a narrow path quite a bit of time ago. His guide, who had let go his arm so that he could work his machete, answered from just ahead.

"Because they were already gone long before this place became what it now is," she informed him. "Before we who are still here made the choices we made."

"And what choices would those be?" he asked, his interest piqued.

"Necessary ones, I would say," the ghost contended, her words underscored by the shing of the machete cutting through the undergrowth. "How much do you know about the Ascher Family?"

"Very little," Devon said as he stepped out from the shade of the trees into a more open section of land. It looked as though it had once been cultivated, but nature had long since started to reclaim it. "I know that the Aschers are one of the oldest families in the region and that they founded Ashwood. Am I heading in the right direction?" he asked his guide.

"Yes, it is just up ahead, near the orange grove." The ghost once again took his arm. "Is that truly all that you have heard?"

"I just recently learned that the Ascher family has been in decline for several generations. And that after Tam Ascher passed, the place stood empty for years until the most recent Ascher returned from parts unknown."

"It is true. The family has been in decline for some time now," his guide confirmed. Her voice, if anything, sounded disappointed rather than sad. "Despite their tendency towards good constitutions and long lives. How could we have known that such a blessing would eventually lead our family to excess and vice?

112

"It wasn't always so," she continued. "The good health that is. When we first came here it seemed like we lost people every other day."

"'When you first came here?'" Devon asked.

A dry chuckle sounded from beside him. "Yes, we were the first to arrive here. Well, not right here. My father and most of the settlement set up nearer Gerty Inlet. It was my cousin, who was a good twenty years older than me, who continued on through the bay until he found the mouth of the Blue Sedge River.

"He and his wife, with their little girl, built themselves a house not far from here. My brother and I would come up the river whenever a ship came in, to bring supplies and visit. His wife Nora was a bit delicate, but she could cook the most amazing meals from almost nothing at all. And their daughter was a beautiful little thing. We always called her Little Bird because she would sing and sing. Her voice could make the angels weep. We lost them very early on. First Nora, then Hannah a year later."

"That must have been hard," Devon sympathized.

"It was, especially Hannah. She was the sweetest, most caring little girl. I was only twelve, but I had come to stay with my cousin after Nora died to help with Hannah. She came down with a fever almost a year to the day after her mother had gone.

"I remember that morning so well. We had nursed her all through the night, but lost her just as the sun was rising. My cousin scooped her body up into his arms and carried her out of the house. The light pouring in through the doorway made it look like he was carrying her straight into heaven, to the waiting arms of the angels.

"He laid her to rest next to her mother, in the cedar grove where they all loved to picnic. When he came back, he packed me off home, locked the door to the house and walked off into the woods."

"He walked off into the wilderness? Just disappeared?" Devon asked. For some reason that did not sound like the end of the story.

"No, not entirely. He would visit our settlement occasionally, each time looking more and more like a wild savage. A far cry from the neat, scholarly man we had known up 'til then.

"Then a few years later, our settlement was raided by pirates. They killed my father and a good half of the people with us. It was still a mess two days later when my cousin came walking out of the woods. He put things back in order, gathered up the people that were left and brought us back here. He took my older brother and I in and helped everyone else build their lives anew. And that was really the beginnings of Ashwood, or Ascher's Wood as it was called then. Our cousin seemed to once again become the well-read, genteel man my brother and I had grown up with. And if the times weren't exactly happy ones, we were so busy we didn't notice."

"Was your cousin unkind?"

"No, not at all. In fact, he was very good to us, caring as well. No, it was that we kept losing people. To disease, or hunger or lack of medicine.

"To tell you the truth, most of us who came here were from aristocratic or well-to-do merchant families. We did not really have the knowledge or constitution for what we had set out to do. We had determination though. But that is not always enough."

"So then this must have been before your family began to enjoy uncommon good health?" Devon theorized.

"Hmm, yes. That came a bit later actually, when I was nineteen or so. After I had just had my first child. It was a hard birth. I was not recovering, and the babe was not thriving. My cousin came in, took one look at us and left.

"I asked my husband where my cousin had gone, but he could only tell me that he had walked off into the woods. After that I was too delirious with fever to care. I kept hearing wolves howling outside our windows every night. But on the morning of the fourth day, I woke feeling fine and Jeremiah, my son, was as healthy as you could wish a newborn to be. My cousin returned no more than an hour after that, looking as he always did."

Devon stopped a moment as understanding began to take shape.

The soft wrinkled hand patted his forearm, urging him to continue. "Just this way."

He saw then that he was standing at the edge of a grove of winter-thin orange trees. Their old branches, untidy and broken, stuck out at odd angles and the ground at their feet was littered with the leftovers of seasons past.

The line of trees eventually led him to a short limestone wall that ran parallel to them. Within its protective embrace, gravestones leaned crookedly against each other for support, like lost, forlorn children.

He followed the wall along the grove's edge, careful to avoid the trees' spiny fingers as he went. His guide led him over to a shaded corner where one of the orange trees grew nearly right up to the wall. Since there was no entrance in sight, Devon hopped over and found himself in front of an alabaster crypt. It shone softly in the day's dim light. The name Elizabeth Ascher-Fontaine was etched deep in the gleaming stone. He looked at the dates.

"One hundred and twelve years is a long life to live," he said.

"It was," she agreed. "Do you understand how such a thing could happen?"

"I understand that there are ways to bring such a thing about," he replied. "Is that the reason your spirits stay on this plane?"

"Yes, in part."

"Is it a willing sacrifice?" he asked.

"The choice was ours, although that part of the sacrifice did not come about till decades later," she told him.

"My cousin had left when Jeremiah was only five, and he did not return until I was a great grandmother. My brother had passed only the year before, so one else knew him of course, but I did. He came through the door one spring, looking just the same as he had when he had left. He married again and had several children, all healthy and strong. By then, the Burning times were almost two hundred years in the past and we were moving into an age of enlightenment. So, when I asked him how such a thing was possible, he told me. Then he taught my children and my grandchildren, even my great-great-granddaughter Calista about the rules of sacrifice and magick. He taught me as well, so when it was time for me to leave this world, my cousin and I had already talked a great deal about how the family could continue to protect our own."

A small whirlwind of leaves swirled across the top of the crypt. The ghost, Elizabeth, let out a great sigh, and Devon smiled. He was always amused that the spirits still felt the need to do those little things that were obviously meant for the living.

"I was the first to stay," she continued. "For all the good it did, I suppose. You cannot protect fools from themselves. Neglect, vice and just plain poor judgment will kill you off just as easily as disease and starvation. And of course, misfortune can play a hand in things as well. Like what happened to little Lenore, poor child. So here we are, once again down to the last of our line, and the first. I wonder if he will start again, or give up on the family altogether."

"Your cousin?" Devon concluded.

"Of course," she said, patting his hand again.

"What is your cousin's name?" he asked though his suspicions had been growing since the very beginning of their conversation.

"Don't you know it already?" she chuckled.

He was quite sure that he did.

A short time later, Devon went back for the wheelbarrow and tools he had left behind. He spent the rest of the day clearing the small plot all the while Elizabeth, or Liza as she preferred to be called, continued to entertain him with stories of Ashwood in the early days. The sky above stayed blanketed in a wash of grays with only the occasional phantom ray of sunlight that disappeared so quickly, it was easy to question whether it had been there at all. At one point during his work, he felt a feline head brush against his shins and a tail wrap itself around his calf, before leaving, off on its own business again.

By the time he was finished, he had uncovered around two dozen graves, many older than Liza's. Like the two in the cedar grove, these housed only old bones and no spirits at all. But there were a few that had ghosts of their own. One of which was Liza's son, Jeremiah, who it turned out had built the lighthouse on the other side of Gerty Inlet and the garrison house on Edith Island, and who had lived nearly as long as his mother.

The dim light of the day grew dimmer as the sun began to set. Devon lit the lantern he had brought with him and hung it from a pole that was attached to the wheelbarrow for just that purpose. He pulled out the old leather case that held his ever-growing map of the cemetery, and carefully added the location of Nora and Hannah's graves as well as Liza's small plot. Unseen fingers patted his forearm.

"Just the other side of the orange grove is the first Ascher house, if you want to see it," Liza told him. "Something interesting to add to your map."

"Thank you," he said as he blew on the ink to dry it. He carefully rolled the map back up, and put it in its case. "For the suggestion and the stories."

"Thank you for finding us," Liza replied, patting his hand again.

A weight settled on his shoulder as he picked up the wheelbarrow's handles and a familiar whiskered cheek brushed against his as he headed off into the falling gloom.

He found the house just where Liza had said he would, its white plastered walls materializing from the evening shade. Arches gaped in its face like mournful mouths, making sad vacant eyes of its windows.

It was much larger than Devon had expected. But he guessed that stood to reason, since it had housed generations of Aschers. Generations that had left their mark as the house grew with them. Now it sat abandoned, empty of even ghosts as far as he could tell.

He felt the cat's tail give a hard twitch against his shoulder. Seconds later, a figure stepped out from the dark into the golden circle of light cast by Devon's lantern.

"You are here late, Mr. Amaris," Ascher said drolly, as if a chance meeting at night in a cemetery was only to be expected.

"The dark comes on quickly this time of year," Devon noted.

"So it does," Ascher agreed. He turned to face the house. "I always thought it a shame when the latter generations decided to leave this place in favor of building a new, better one. Only to tear that one down to build an even newer one. And now the buildings still stand but there is no one left to fill them."

"Except yourself, of course," Devon pointed out.

"Ah yes, except myself," Ascher assented. "Good evening, Mr. Amaris." He said and left, disappearing into the darkness that had cast him in the first place.

Devon had heard the clock tower bells chime seven as he was locking the iron gate to the cemetery, so he wasn't surprised to see Kristoph through the window of the coffeehouse. The schoolmaster looked up just as Devon drew even with the window. The man waved for Devon to come in and join him.

Dirty and sweaty from the day's work, he was about to wave the schoolmaster his regrets, when Kristoph abruptly stepped out of the door in front of him.

"Come on in, man. I have already ordered another cup for you," Kristoph insisted, gesturing for Devon to follow him through the door. "Have you eaten? I was just considering a light supper..."

"Thank you, but honestly Kristoph, I should be heading home," Devon insisted.

"Nonsense, come in," the schoolmaster urged.

Devon gestured to the scratches and dirt that covered him.

"Ah, I see your point. Well, perhaps we could meet here again, say tomorrow?" The schoolmaster suggested. "There was something I wished to speak with you about."

"I'll be happy to meet with you tomorrow. I'll just remember to bring a clean shirt with me."

"Fantastic! Till tomorrow then," said Kristoph. He clapped Devon on the shoulder once, then retreated back into the coffeehouse as Devon resumed his trek towards Mrs. O'Toole's.

He was a fair ways down the road before his tired brain thought to wonder what in particular it was that Kristoph had wanted to speak with him about.

Liam was on the other side of the street, sweeping the front walk of the tobacconist's when he saw Sara's brother and the black-coated schoolmaster meet at the door of Gerard's. He watched them as they spoke for a minute or two more before parting ways. Sara's brother moved off, heading towards Winding Street most like, while the schoolmaster retreated back into the coffeehouse.

Not even a half-hour later, Liam saw him leave again. It looked as if the man was headed towards Miss Rose's, but then for no reason Liam could see, he stopped and leaned against a fence just short of the bordello. Liam continued to sweep, but kept half-an-eye on him as he went along.

A familiar clarence pulled by matching bays passed between them. It was headed downstreet to the dark side of Nightingale, when most of the other carriages that had come to drop off the rich folk seeking their vices tended to head back upstreet to wait, back to where the light from the gas lamps kept the shadows at bay.

Liam saw the schoolmaster's head turn to follow the carriage's progress. The man seemed to relax even more against the fence. He pulled what looked like a thin black cigarette from out of his coat pocket. A match flared and the smell of fine tobacco and cloves drifted across the street to where Liam was working. He snorted the smell from his nose.

The schoolmaster wasn't the only man loitering about. In fact, the streets were starting to fill up, as they always did, and would become even busier as the night went on. Men drifted past Liam into the tobacconist's shop or down the dimmer alley towards the smoking rooms in the back, where they might also do a bit of gambling if they were of a mind. Liam watched them from the corner of his eye, recognizing most everyone who walked past, from the regulars down from High Street who had come slumming it, to the sailors and docker workers that were there most every night they were in port. Everything seemed just as it always was. Still, Liam's gut kept telling him something was not right in the Bottoms. Perhaps it was only the ghost of his *maman* whispering in his ear, reminding him to be careful.

The schoolmaster had just crushed the ember of his cigarette out beneath the toe of his shoe, when a woman stepped from the gate of Miss Rose's. The dress she wore was not one any person in the Bottoms could afford, and though it was full dark, her veil was pulled down over her face and tucked primly beneath her chin. There was a man on her arm; the modest coat he was wearing said quite clearly that he was not from the same part of town as the woman he was with. And neither of them were from the Bottoms, that was for sure.

Liam had seen other such women before. They came down to Nightingale Street for the same reason as the men, to find a bit of something they couldn't find at home. A tumble the way they wanted it. No harm as far as Liam was concerned, what was good for the gander was certainly good for the goose. What he did take notice of was the schoolmaster's sudden desire to stroll down the street in a direction which mirrored the couple's.

The woman and her companion left the last street lamp behind, not missing a step as they moved into the darkness beyond it. Liam continued to mark their progress as they passed by the lit windows of the buildings downstreet. He wasn't terribly surprised when they stopped at Molly's and made their way up the stairs that ran along the side of the saloon to a door on the second floor. Molly rented rooms up there by the half hour, which was more time than they would ever need as far as Molly was concerned. The schoolmaster walked by the stairs, continuing on into the building's bottom floor where the saloon was. That was a bit of a surprise. Molly's was a rough place and Liam was having a hard time picturing a man like that sitting at Molly's stained bar, drinking cheap whiskey and rubbing elbows with the field hands and river rats who liked to drink there.

By the time Liam had finished his work, given old Berk, the owner, his broom back and picked up his pay, the schoolmaster was back out in front of Miss Rose's. He was not standing in quite the same place as he had been before and he was holding something wrapped in paper. Little specters of steam rose up from it into the cold night air. Liam knew what was in that paper bag and it reminded him that he hadn't eaten yet. So, he took his pay and went to old Gertie's.

The front windows of the place were wide open. Gertie herself was handing bags of fried cracklin' bread out through them while her daughter collected the money. When Gertie saw that it was him, she added two extra pieces to the bag she handed him and told him to come back later if he wanted to earn more. He thanked her and went off to sit at the end of her porch, out of the way of other customers.

The wall there was warmer, so he leaned against it and loitered with a half dozen other men who were also leaning against that side of the house. Liam could see a good part of the street from where he sat. The well-dressed woman from before was strolling down the street again, this time with a different man on her arm. And just like earlier, the schoolmaster-shaped shadow followed at a discrete distance behind them. The couple continued past Molly's, but hers wasn't the only place downstreet that rented rooms for convenience.

Sure enough, a short time later the lady drifted back up the street, alone save for her shadow. What was the schoolmaster to this woman, Liam wondered. A jealous lover? An obsessed admirer? A servant?

Liam watched the same scene playout several more times as the night went on, and always with a different man. Sometimes they stopped at Molly's, sometimes they continued on. Liam never saw the men she brought in with her come out, except for once. There were two men then, both dressed like they were from one of the estates on Riverview Row. They made even the men that came from High Street look like poor country relations.

When the two men came down the stairs, they were alone, and not as put-together as they had been when they had gone up. Neither man would look at the other; they just went their separate ways without a word. Liam was a little concerned at first, wondering if something had happened to the woman who had gone up with them. But the lady in question came down the stairs only a few minutes later, perfectly poised with not a button out of place. This time the schoolmaster met her at the bottom of the stairs. They spoke for a moment, then the woman gestured and the schoolmaster bowed, turned and went striding off down the street.

After he left, the lady turned back upstreet, looking as though she were headed back to Miss Rose's. She hadn't even made it past the alley next to Molly's before Big Ken crossed the street and stepped into her path.

Liam frowned, and wondered where this would lead to. It wasn't like Big Ken to take a chance with softer sport. Truth be told, even some working girls wouldn't take him on. Not that he was cruel, but he was big, as he liked to brag, and he liked things rough.

The lady did not seem bothered though, she let the big man take her hand and lead her into the darkness beneath the stairs. Their writhing shadows soon left no doubt as to what they were doing there.

Liam was no stranger to such things, but for some reason, this time he was feeling uneasy about it. He kept an ear open, in case it turned out the lady had gotten in over her head.

Even though they were a ways away and on the other side of the street, Liam swore he could hear every rustle of skirt, every jagged breath. Even the creak of the wooden wall as their bodies pounded against it. He was no voyeur, but his gaze still drifted in that direction of its own accord. He blinked and recoiled, sure that he had seen a pair of eyes staring back at him from the undulating void beneath the stairs.

The clarence from earlier pulled up just then, its lanterns flickering in the darkness but doing little to dispel it. It passed by Molly's before stopping a half block up the road. The driver remained in his seat, but Liam saw the schoolmaster step down from the footboard. The man headed towards the corner of the narrow alley where the woman and Big Ken were. The lady emerged from the shadows, stepping into the meager lantern light at the foot of the stairs where the schoolmaster waited. She rested her hand on his proffered arm, and allowed him to escort her to the waiting clarence.

As Liam watched the carriage pull away, he remembered the conversation that he and Sara had had just that past Monday. So that was the schoolmaster's benefactress? Well, now he knew that this wasn't her first time down to the Bottoms. She seemed none the worse for wear from what Liam could see, not even mussed in fact. Liam chuckled to himself; that wouldn't do Big Ken's reputation any good should someone notice.

It was then that he realized he hadn't seen Big Ken come out from beneath the stairs. Frowning, he rolled up what was left of his bag of cracklin bread and put it in his pocket.

"Hey Gertie, I'm going to borrow this," he said, grabbing a lantern from the hook where it was hanging.

"Bring it back when you're finished!" Gertie hollered after him.

He crossed the street, lantern in hand, but stopped at the edge of the alley. He had never been afraid of the dark before, but the memory of something looking back at him from beneath the stairs froze his feet in place. He should not have been able to see those calculating, hungry eyes. Should not have been able to hear the sounds that came from those shadows; the panting grunts, the creak of the wall as they pounded up against it, the rustle of skirts and the sound of cloth as it slid along the wood's rough surface. He swore he could still hear them. It dawned on him then that what he was hearing was not in his imagination.

Liam hesitated. He knew he had seen the lady leave. Was there someone else back there with Big Ken? If there was, Liam wanted no part of that. He made to turn away, then he heard the sound of something in pain. He shifted direction and stepped fully into the shadows beneath the stairs.

For an instant he was sure he saw two people up against the wall. But when he lifted the lantern, he found only the big man leaning there, pants open, grunting as he mindlessly pumped the empty air. The whole front of him was a sticky mess. Light from the lantern Liam held up illuminated the big man's face. It fell on the tears that poured from his wide staring eyes, making them into little shining rivers as they flowed down over his unshaven cheeks. The whimpering sounds that came from his twisted lips unnerved Liam.

He should go on about his own business, but the man was obviously in a bad way. Liam didn't know what to do. Ken was twice the size of Sara's brother, who was a big man himself. There was nothing he would be able to do on his own; he would need help. Turning his back to the alley, Liam looked out towards the street to see who was about. His skin suddenly tightened to the point of pain as an icy chill shot up his spine.

Liam spun back around to face the alley. Something was there in the darkness, watching him. It was worse than before; its desire to devour him crawled over his skin like worms. Irrationally, he wanted to throw the lantern at it, to hit it, to chase it down and beat it into the ground. He had never been so afraid.

He jumped when a voice called out from the street behind him. Liam looked back over his shoulder and found the Tighe brothers standing at the mouth of the alley.

"Hey Liam, what are you about there?" Silas, the eldest of the two brothers, asked.

"Something's wrong with Big Ken," Liam replied. He stepped further down the alley and held his lantern up higher for them to see.

"What the devil is the matter with him?" exclaimed Sean, the younger of the two Tighes.

"Ah, he's just drunk," Silas replied. "Come man, cover that up, and let's get you to the pump down the way. We'll get you cleaned up and back home."

Liam held the lantern for them, as the two brothers, who were not small men themselves, went to put Big Ken to rights.

"This is more than the drink," Sean said. "Hey Liam, how'd you know he was back here?"

"Leave the boy be, Sean," said Silas. "This is none of his doing. The stupid git probably got himself into something he shouldn't have, the fool. Come on, get his other arm. We'll take him out back before Molly sets up a ruckus. They've all been in a mood lately."

Silas slipped Big Ken's arm over his shoulder while his brother did the same with the other.

"Get yourself home, Liam," Silas said as they started off with the big man between them. "The devil's in the air tonight, better that you were out of it."

Liam didn't argue. He left the brothers to it and headed straight away towards the shed where he was staying. He didn't even bring the lantern back to Gertie. She would give him what for tomorrow, but at that moment, he didn't care. He would buy her a new candle in the morning, and that should set it right. Of course, that meant he would probably have to do without breakfast, but it wouldn't be the first time.

The whole of his life, it had never bothered him to walk around in the night. These were his streets after all, but there was no denying that he felt better once he was in the shed with the door jammed shut. There was no lock of course, but a brick and a wedge worked well enough to secure it.

Liam left the lantern on the floor and pulled his bedding down from where he kept it on top of a crate. He stretched it out on the ground and lay down, doing his best not to think about the darkness under the stairs while he did so. Instead, he watched the flickering candle and thought about the golden-haired girl he would meet in the morning.

He twitched and frowned as he drifted off, watching the darkness close in on the little light.

CHAPTER XI

Dreams of Fire

Devon watched the pile of brush burn in the late afternoon sun. The air had turned from crisp to cold as the day had gone on. He threw a few of the larger logs on the fire and realized it would be a while before they burned down.

No matter. He set himself on the ground a little ways away, and leaned back against the side of a nearby crypt. The stone was still warm from the sun. He felt the weight of the hound's head settle across his knees; a contented huff followed soon after.

The familiar scent of wood smoke turned his thoughts towards home. Tonight was All Hallow's Eve, a busy time in their small town. He wondered who his mother had found to help her hang the lanterns in the wild grove that grew out just beyond the orchard. It would be ablaze with light as soon as the evening fell. The glowing faces of jack 'o lanterns grinning out into the darkness while their toasted seeds waited in bowls, ready for eating.

He leaned his head back and closed his eyes, his body relaxing into the memory of heat that radiated from the stone behind him. His hand came to rest on the hound's head, as he thought of home.

Right now, they would be filling tables throughout the wild wood with food. And in the field just beyond the trees, a man-sized pile of brush and deadfall would already be standing at the ready, waiting for the bonfire to be lit… *He could see the line of torches as they wound their way through the growing darkness. Their greedy tongues licking at the dry wood. The flames stretching higher and higher as the murmur of voices, both living and dead, filled the night. A figure writhed helplessly in the fire's scorching arms. The house burning with his mother inside. The faces above him covered in a shadow no one else could see, making them into twisted masks of unnatural glee. He ran, bounding away as a sea fog crept over the sand and up the shore's broken rocks. The clinging cold surrounding him, hiding him, clutching at him...*

Devon's eyes snapped open to darkness. A creeping fog slid past the crypts and swirled around the headstones. Its damp fingers slipped across his skin and over the fire's now dead embers.

Cold panic sank its claws into his belly as the memory of his mother burning burrowed deep under skin. The voices of the dead rose up in a desperate keen, his affinity to them ensuring that they shared in his terror. Mindlessly, he leapt to his feet and bolted out into the night, leaving the wheelbarrow and his tools behind him. The pounding of his feet on the ground reverberated through the air like the hoof beats in his dreams, relentless as they fled from the malignancy that hungered to consume everything. Like the flames that had consumed his mother while those who once loved her fed the fires.

A desperate need to know his mother was safe warred with the certain knowledge that she was dead as he ran down a familiar dark street made strange by the nightmare that still rode him. The faces of the people he passed leered after him. Their baleful countenances made demonic by laughter, mocking him as his mind replayed the image of his mother burning, burning...

"Devon!" One of the grinning devils called out to him. He ignored it.

"*Devon!*" it called again, stepping into his path. Its almost-familiar face distorted further with surprise as Devon picked the creature up and tossed it aside for its trouble.

A strong hand grabbed his arm, forcing him to pause in his headlong rush.

"For heaven's sake man, what is the *matter*?" The familiar voice implored him, breaking through the panic that fogged his brain. He blinked and found himself looking into the very concerned eyes of Kristoph Hegdus.

They were standing out in front of Miss Rose's. The passersby eyed him warily as they circled wide to avoid the spot where he and Kristoph were standing. The schoolmaster, whose hands had somehow ended up on Devon's shoulders, let go and took a step back.

"Come, have a drink and tell me what all this is about," Kristoph suggested, gesturing over to the well-lit front porch of the bordello.

Devon shook his head. The blind panic may have been gone, but it had left behind a shivery unease in his belly. He could feel that there was something deeply wrong, some corruption that stalked through the night.

He wanted to find somewhere that had a telephone. His mind was clear enough now to know that what he had seen had only been a dream, but he still had a driving need to hear his mother's voice. He must have spoken out loud because Kristoph answered.

"Well, you are in luck. There is one right in there," the school-master gestured once again at the brothel. "And I have no doubt Miss Rose would be happy to let us use it."

Devon was headed up the front steps almost before Kristoph had finished speaking. The doorman looked over Devon's shoulder to Kristoph behind him and nodding politely, opened the door for them as they approached. It seemed the schoolmaster was no stranger to Miss Rose's.

The room beyond was filled with people. Mostly gentlemen seated on couches where lovely women listened to them attentively and served them drinks.

Miss Rose was the first to notice them enter. A smile lit her carefully beautiful face as she left where she was standing on the other side of the room and glided with studied grace in their direction. Devon saw Kristoph step hurriedly past him, smoothly intercepting her before she had gone very far. He could not hear what was said between the schoolmaster and the proprietress, but it was obvious that his words were enough to convey a certain urgency. Her smile lost some of its brightness, but she waved for Devon to follow her.

She led him to a short hall with a nondescript door at the end of it. The door opened up on a diminutive private room just off the main one, only big enough for a chair and the small table where a lamp and telephone sat.

Kristoph thanked the woman as Devon headed for the phone with a single-mindedness that pushed all sense of propriety from his thoughts. He lifted the phone's receiver and was surprised at how steady his voice sounded as he asked the operator to connect him to his parents' home. It was in sharp contrast to the roiling tightness in his belly. He waited an eternity for his mother's voice to come over the line. All the while, endless scenarios, each one more horrifying than the one before it, bubbled up like hot tar in his mind.

"Devon!" his mother's voice exploded over the line. "Is everything alright? My heart has been trying to pound its way out of my chest for the past half hour! I was sure you told me that your boarding house had a telephone there, but when I had the operator try to connect, no one answered. Has something happened?"

Relief sluiced through him at the sound of his mother's voice, lessening the feeling of panic that still squirmed in his belly. Her rapid-fire questions told him just how worried she had been.

"Mama, give me a moment and I can give you an answer," he said. His mother's strong presence, almost palpable even over the phone, grounded him. He took a breath and steadied himself. "Everything is fine, better now that I have heard your voice. And the boarding house does have a telephone. Most likely the reason no one answered is because they are all down at the town square for the bonfire and social."

"The fact that I feel an irrational need to thrash someone says that everything is not fine," his mother insisted. How hard it must have been for her, he thought, knowing that something was not right with her children but being too far away to do anything about it.

"I had a dream," Devon confessed, lowering his voice. The image of a figure twisting in the flames surfaced behind his eyes. "I needed to know you were safe."

To anyone else, this admission might have sounded odd and childish coming from a full-grown man of three and twenty. But that was not the case in his family.

"Ah," there was a wealth of understanding in his mother's voice. "We are all well here. Is this the first one you have had?"

"No," Devon said carefully, very much aware that he was not alone.

"Tell me about them," his mother said.

"It would be difficult to explain over the telephone." It was a poor idea to talk so openly about such things, especially when you were on a device where others could be a party to your conversation. "And I cannot stay on this line for long."

"You are not at the boarding house now?"

"I am not," he confirmed.

An exasperated sigh gusted over the phone at this revelation. "I won't lie sweetheart; I hate not being able to speak to you when I need to."

He felt his mother's words keenly, and never had he felt more homesick than at that moment. Before moving to Ashwood, neither he nor Sara had ever been away from home for more than a few days.

"It is not something I am happy about either," Devon admitted. "Unfortunately, it is not possible for me to be by a telephone every minute of the day. But I will ring you tomorrow evening, around 7:00…" He trailed off as a small piece of paper slid across the table towards him.

He hastily read the note that was neatly written on it. 'If you have need…' and at the bottom was listed a name and a room.

He looked up at the dark figure standing just the other side of the table from him, understanding the offer for what it was, but not sure if he should accept it.

"Mama," he continued, "There is a place you can reach by telephone that could bring a message to me if you feel the need is urgent." He read what was written on the little piece of paper off to her.

"Lady Anasztaizia Károlyi, The Imperial Suite at the Vue de la Mer Hotel?" He could hear the wariness in her voice. "Who is she and why would she be willing to send you a message from us?"

"She is the benefactress of Sara's schoolmaster, Mr. Hegdus. It was he who offered, in case you had a need to reach me quickly."

"And are you at this hotel now?"

"No."

"Where are you then?" His mother sounded downright suspicious.

"A place where I cannot continue to occupy their telephone, unfortunately," Devon insisted. There was a great deal more he wanted to tell her, but couldn't. Not at that moment, anyways. "I just needed to know that you are well. The rest will have to wait until my next letter, I'm afraid."

"Which you will be writing soon."

"Which I will be writing soon," he promised.

His mother's harrumph let him know that there would be no quarter if he did not follow through on that promise. She assured him once again that everything was well there, and cautioned him to be careful.

After promising that he would pass along his parents' love to his sister, Devon replaced the handset on the cradle. He turned towards the schoolmaster who had retreated the few steps back to the doorway.

"I apologize," Kristoph said as he opened the door that would lead them back out into the main room. "It was not my intention to eavesdrop, and I hope you will forgive me for intruding like that.

But I hoped to give you and your family peace of mind. All the guest rooms in the hotel have a phone, and there is always someone there. It would be an easy thing to send a runner to find you or your sister if there was need."

"There was no intrusion. I appreciate your offer," Devon insisted. "But are you sure your benefactress won't mind?"

"Not at all!" Kristoph assured him as they made their way back through the main room. Miss Rose was nowhere to be seen, which suited Devon fine. As much as he wanted to thank the woman, he had no wish to become embroiled in a conversation.

Kristoph must have recognized Devon's desire not to linger because he headed directly for the exit. He only stopped a moment for a quiet word with the doorman while Devon continued down the stairs. He caught up to Devon in short order.

"I could tell you had no wish to stay there, but how about you join me for a coffee?" the schoolmaster suggested, clapping him on the shoulder as they stepped out onto the street.

"Thank you, but no." Devon shook his head as he turned in the direction of upstreet. "There is something not right in the air tonight, and I feel like I should check on Sara."

"Yes, Sara. That was what I wanted to talk to you about the other day," Kristoph began as he fell into step beside Devon. "The boy you have walking home with her, what do you know about him?"

Devon stopped and looked over at the schoolmaster. "What boy?"

"The boy that walks her to and from school every day. I was under the impression you knew… Devon. Devon!"

He did not wait for the schoolmaster to continue his explanation. Once again, he was off, running full-bore down the street. But this time it wasn't blind panic that spurred him on, it was a vicious need to know that his sister was safe.

He came down Winding Street like a hurricane with the schoolmaster only a half-step behind him.

CHAPTER XII

The Devil's in the Air

Liam's dreams the night before had been anything but restful, so it had been an easy thing for him to get an early start. It meant that he had been able to find a candle for Gertie before meeting Sara that morning.

Unfortunately, that had been the last bit of luck for the day. Work had been hard to come by, and the same bad feeling from the night before kept gnawing at him.

He almost mentioned it to Sara on their walk home, but didn't for some reason, even after she had said that she didn't plan on attending the bonfire on the Green. Instead, he set off like usual to try to find himself some work for that evening. He did manage to find some, but couldn't seem to settle into it.

So, after he picked up the few pennies he had earned, he turned his restless feet in the direction of a certain boarding house on Winding Street.

The night was heavy. The familiar streets didn't feel as familiar as they should. Jack o' lanterns sat in the windows and on the porches of houses he passed by. Their pumpkin faces leered at him. Or maybe it was the figures that lurked in the shadows that they were watching. The ones plotting mischief with their flour bombs and string at the ready.

Of course, no one bothered him. In fact, more than a few whispered out a hello or an invitation to join them in their fun. He waved them all away having left that sort of nonsense behind a long time ago.

He found himself standing outside Mrs. O'Toole's courtyard gate not long after the streetlamps had been lit. The whole house was dark, except for a single light shining from a garret window. Everything looked quiet, but he couldn't seem to bring himself to leave. He couldn't bring himself to walk up and knock on the door either. So, he walked around to the narrow alley that ran next to Mrs. O'Toole's and found a niche in her neighbor's garden wall that looked a likely spot where he could keep an eye on things.

The thought crossed his mind that if he had seen someone else doing what he was doing, he would have thought him a creep. But a niggling worry kept him where he was, half hidden in the wall's shadow. He watched the people as they strolled down Winding Street. A night parade of witches, devils, angels and the like, moving beneath the flickering lamps and the cold fog that rolled in off the sea. Occasionally he glanced up at the square of golden light across the way where he would sometimes see the flicker of a silhouette ghost across the room's ceiling.

The alley was mostly quiet, though there were a few passersby who used it as a way to get to Winding Street from the neighborhood that was behind Mrs. O'Toole's. All walked by the spot where he stood with nary a glance in his direction.

Most continued on their way without stopping. But one, a woman, halted just a little ways down the alley from him. She stood beneath an old oak tree that grew there; its huge trunk slowly swallowing Mrs. O'Toole's iron fence as it leaned over the garden, like a nosy neighbor peeking into the boarding house's windows.

The woman stood there for a good long while, her hair shining like copper pennies even in the gloom. Her face was turned up towards the same garret window that had also been the focus of Liam's interest all evening. The hair on the back of his neck stood on end, and had he been a dog, he would have growled. Why was she standing just there? He had had a thought to go find out. But when he went to leave the spot where he had been loitering, he found he could not move, not even an inch. The air around him had turned icy cold.

A figure stepped into the alley just then, a dapper gentleman in a tall silk topper. The woman did not look back over her shoulder at him, but she did move away from the place where she had been standing, drifting off as though she had never stopped at all.

The gentleman did not seem to take any notice of the woman when she passed by him, just continued on towards the spot where Liam stood frozen. The light from the gas lamps on Winding Street made him into a thing of quicksilver and ebony. He glanced straight over at Liam as if the darkness was of no hindrance at all. His eyes shone uncannily from the shadows of his topper, as his lips quirked up in a wry smile. He touched his cane to the brim of his hat in acknowledgment, a larger dog taking notice of an overly ambitious pup. Anger burned away the cold and Liam thought he might have actually growled then because the man's smile broadened as he passed by. Liam watched the man's retreating back until it had disappeared around the corner.

His eyes returned to the golden square of light above him. They followed the branches nearest to it all the way back to the oak which the woman had been under. Its trunk leaned so far over that it was nearly parallel with the ground as it stretched across the garden. Liam left his niche next to the neighboring wall and went over to stand beneath the tree. It looked like an easy climb, so after a quick glance around, he slipped off his shoes. Tying the laces together, he threw them over his shoulder and began to climb up the trunk. It was as easy as it had looked. In fact, he could barely call it a climb at all because just a couple of feet off the ground he was practically able to walk along the trunk. He made it almost all the way over to the porch roof before having to climb again. There was a nice thick branch just a little ways above his head that would put him nearly across from the garret window, which was open to the night air. He could not see Sara, but he could hear her talking to someone. He stopped climbing, and started to rethink his admittedly harebrained idea. As a result, he found himself inadvertently eavesdropping on Sara's conversation.

"I agree, there is something in the air tonight and it is chilling me right down to my bones." He heard her say. "That's why I didn't go with Mrs. Madison and Mrs. O'Toole to the bonfire. Though I sorely wanted to."

He could not hear what the other person said, but he heard Sara's answer easy enough.

"I am worried about my brother. And your son as well. I hope he's not gotten mixed up into anything." At this, Liam froze. "I... I couldn't have done that!" He heard her stammer loudly, then quickly lower her voice. "What would he have thought about me inviting him over just after I told him everyone else was going to the social?"

There was a pause.

"No! I don't think he would have done anything untoward," she continued.

There was a much shorter pause during which Liam wondered if he should start back down the tree.

"No! I don't wish he would do anything of the sort! Stop teasing me! I have no doubt he has other things he'd rather be doing tonight..." Sara stopped speaking as though someone had cut her off, then continued with a squeak. "What do you mean he is outside my window?"

Before his brain had the chance to fully register that statement, a pair of gray-blue eyes were looking down at him from the open window above, framed by a golden halo of hair.

"Liam! What are you doing there?" Sara exclaimed.

The ridiculousness of his situation hit him full force then, and he grinned up at the golden fairy above him as he replied, "Well apparently I thought it a good idea to climb this tree so that I could check on you."

"Why in heaven's name didn't you just knock on the door?" she asked. "Oh, of course, everyone else is out and I may not have heard it anyway. Yes, that makes sense." She spoke as though she were answering someone else. "But what would you have done if it was not me who was up here?"

"I would have quietly climbed back down," he remarked. "But I knew it was you when I heard you talking."

"Oh," she said, then went very quiet. Most likely trying to figure out what it was that he might have overheard.

The way the light fell, he couldn't quite see her expression. But knowing her as well as he did now, if he were to guess, he would have said that she was probably blushing. He took the opportunity to swing up to the sturdy branch that he had been eyeing earlier. From there he could see that she was kneeling on a cushioned seat just inside the window. She blinked at him for a few moments and he wondered if she was trying to figure out what he was doing or if she was listening to a conversation that he could not hear.

"Are you staying?" she asked a couple of seconds later.

"Unless you don't want me to?" he offered.

"Don't be silly, of course I want you to! But I am not going to yell out of my window just to talk to you," she insisted. "Come down and I will let you in the front door."

"No need," he said, swinging off the branch he had been sitting on. He clambered back down the tree to the place where it came closest to the porch, then leapt over and soft-footed it across the roof to where Sara leaned out of her window.

"You best come in," she said, moving out of the way so that he could climb up.

He swung the glass pane in a little more. The casement was much deeper than it had looked from down below. He easily hopped up and sat on the wide sill.

"You don't have to sit in the window," Sara said.

"I'm comfortable here," he insisted. He didn't worry too much about himself, but it wouldn't do her reputation any good if someone were to come in and find them all alone in her room. No reason to give people fuel for gossip.

"It's not like we would be alone," she pointed out, as if reading his mind.

Any doubt as to who she might have been speaking to earlier vanished. "Unfortunately, I doubt anyone would count the spirit of my *maman* as a chaperone. No offense, *maman*." He found that he liked the fact that he could say such things out loud and not have to worry about the person he was with thinking him crazy.

"That is true," she sighed and sat next to him on the window seat she had vacated just the moment before.

"What are you reading," he asked, leaning forward to look at the cover of the book she was holding.

"This? It's a history of Ashwood, or Ascher's Wood as it was originally called, written by Jeremiah Fontaine. He was the son of Elizabeth Ascher-Fontaine who was the daughter of one of the first settlers. She was later adopted by her cousin into the Ascher family after her father was killed. Jeremiah was the one who built the lighthouse and the garrison." She barely paused to draw breath. "Mr. Hegdus gave it to me for my extra classes."

Liam glanced over at the girl next to him from the corner of his eye. Her face beamed with excitement. He wondered if it was for the book itself or the one who had given it to her. The latter thought did not sit well in his belly.

Unaware of his thoughts, Sara had already opened the book back up and was happily turning the pages as she showed him what was inside. He recognized a map of Gerty Inlet, and the Blue Sedge River, but that was pretty much it. None of the words that he saw were ones he recognized, which was too bad. He always liked listening to Sara when she talked about her school lessons and he wouldn't have minded if he could learn more things on his own. She stopped suddenly. He looked up from the book to find her blushing.

"I'm sorry, I didn't realize you couldn't read," Sara apologized.

"Is my *maman* telling tales again?" he asked, and smiled at how bright red her face had become. "It's true. She could read, but never had the chance to teach me."

"Do you want to learn?" Sara asked shyly.

"Sure, just never found anyone to teach me," he said. Most people in the Bottoms couldn't read. They could do sums well enough though. After all, no one wants to get cheated out of money owed them.

"I meant… would you like me to teach you?" she reiterated, and he could tell she was afraid of offending him. He smiled reassuringly at her.

"If you want to. But… I think that book there might be a little much to start on," he admitted.

"That's okay! I have another." She jumped up and went over to a small shelf in the corner. She brought back another, much thinner book. Her cheeks were still pink as she sat down again next to him. "I kept this because I liked the illustrations so much." She opened to the first page and read, "This is the letter *A. A* stands for Ariel, who in the night on a bat's back, wings his wonderful flight…"

The time passed as Sara continued to read, stopping on occasion to quiz him on the letters as she went. Perched on the sill as he was, it was easy to lean over and see the pages she was showing him. By the time they had reached the letter "M", the uneasiness that had led him there was all but gone.

They had just reached the letter "Q" when he heard a crash downstairs. He was through the window in a heartbeat and had himself between Sara and the door just as it flew open. A moment later he was up against the wall dangling by his collar, his feet nowhere near the ground. The body of the man who held him was pressed close enough that Liam couldn't get a kick in or really move much at all. The air in the room grew suddenly frigid. He could see his breath panting out in front of him as he looked down into the angry face of Sara's brother.

"Devon!" he heard Sara plead frantically, but the man holding him didn't say a word.

The black-coated schoolmaster did though, having come in on the heels of Sara's brother. "You little sneak," he snarled over the bigger man's shoulder.

As far as Liam was concerned, Sara's brother, having just found him alone in the room with his sister, had every right to want to beat him. The schoolmaster however…

"Who are you to talk," Liam snarled back, the horror from the night before bubbling up as anger. "Following your mistress around as she plays at being a whore."

For a moment, Liam thought he saw his death in the schoolmaster's eyes. Then there was a blast of bone-aching cold and he was falling.

When his vision cleared, Sara was standing in front of him with her brother several steps beyond her. The schoolmaster was just picking himself up from the floor. The room's walls and ceiling were glazed with ice. Even the air itself felt like it was full of frozen needles.

"*Damn it, Devon!* I said he was my friend!" Sara screamed, and that stopped everyone in the room.

Her brother's surprise was plain, and the corner of Liam's mind that was not still reeling from getting slammed up against a wall wondered if this was the first time he had ever seen his sister angry. Or, if he had just never heard her use such language before. Most likely it was both.

"Then why haven't you mentioned him before?" her brother demanded, though in a much gentler tone than Liam would have expected. That alone told him a great deal about Sara's brother. "And friend or not, what are you doing in my sister's room?" The last was obviously directed at Liam, and the tone was not gentle at all.

"I was outside of it until I heard the door slam downstairs," Liam informed the man as he picked himself up from the floor.

"It's true, he was only sitting on the windowsill until then," Sara confirmed.

"There's not much difference between the two," her brother pointed out, his face dark as thunder.

"I am the one who told him he could sit there," Sara insisted, which was a half-truth really because she had actually told him to come inside.

"You trust too easily, Sara," the schoolmaster admonished, but not harshly. "As I have said before."

That was rich, Liam thought. "But she should trust you?" he snapped, stepping up to stand beside Sara. "After you and yours left Big Ken in the dark, f…" he remembered the company he was keeping, "the way you did."

"You should be careful of the assumptions you make," the schoolmaster warned softly.

"There are no assumptions about what I saw," Liam shot back.

"But you would prefer me not to make assumptions about what I saw," this came from Sara's brother. The anger seemed to be gone from his face, but there was no softness in it. "I am going to ask you again, why are you here?"

Liam pressed his lips together. He had no idea how to explain, and saying that 'he had had a bad feeling' didn't seem like it would be enough even though it was the honest truth. He felt Sara's warm hand on his shoulder.

"Whatever you say, they won't think it strange," she promised him.

It had not been lost on him that no one had yet mentioned the ice-glazed walls or the fact that something had thrown the schoolmaster up against them.

He took a deep breath, then another, willing the words to come out of his mouth no matter how idiotic they sounded in his head. "Something hasn't been right, down in the Bottoms," he was finally able to say as he cast a sharp glance over at the schoolmaster.

"So you wandered over here and knocked on the door?" Derision dripped from the schoolmaster's words

"Well actually, he climbed the tree outside," Sara corrected.

Given the look in her brother's eyes, Liam doubted that addition had helped his case.

"I hadn't actually planned to come up at all," Liam added. "I just wanted to check that no one was causing any trouble here, being that it is Halloween and the mischief makers are out and about. The house was dark when I arrived, except for Sara's window. I couldn't quite bring myself to leave, so I tucked myself into a corner of the wall on the other side of the alley."

Sara's brother gave him a measuring look. "That doesn't explain why you decided to climb a tree to my sister's window."

The memory of a dark silhouette walking down the alley instantly sprang to Liam's mind. "There was a man… a Riverview man, judging by his silk topper and cane. He was…" He remembered the shine of the man's eyes in the dark, "dangerous," Liam finished lamely.

That had not been the only thing, he was sure. But, when he opened his mouth to say as much, whatever it was slipped away, leaving behind a vague sense that there was something he should remember, but couldn't. "There was someone else before him, I think. Someone who shouldn't have been stopping to stare up at Sara's window…" The uneasy feeling that had first led him to the boarding house returned. He found that he had clenched his fists as gooseflesh raced over his skin.

The two men in front of him didn't scoff at his inane explanation. They didn't exactly relax afterwards, but they settled a little bit. Their hostility shifting focus from him to somewhere else. He thought Sara had been right; they did not find what he had said strange. Whether they believed him or not, he couldn't say, but he got the notion that they understood what it was he was trying to explain.

"Oh Dev! Look at the room!" Sara exclaimed, and all the men present started a little.

Liam looked over to see little runnels of water rolling down the walls from the melting ice. The sight shook him a good bit, but his only coherent thought was that it was a good thing the walls were painted not papered.

They all spent the next half hour with towels and a mop doing their best to dry up the water. Liam noticed again that no one seemed surprised by the fact that there was water puddling on the floor, or that it had come from walls that had, only a few minutes before, been coated with ice. It gave him some insight as to what Sara's brother knew. But overall, it left him with more questions than answers. Had it been his *maman* that had caused such a thing to happen? Had it been Sara? It wasn't a question he was sure how to ask.

Liam was following Sara's brother down the back stairs when he heard the front door open. By the time he had reached the sink with the wet cloths, a large woman with her hat still pinned to her head was already in the kitchen.

"Ah there you are, Sara!" she said her eyes looking past to the girl who was just a few steps behind him. "Anna, she is in here! Mrs. Madison and I picked up a couple of things we thought you might like since you couldn't join us… Lord above, what happened?" she demanded, seeming to have just noticed what they were carrying.

"Just a bit of a spill, Mrs. O'Toole," Sara's brother answered smoothly.

Devon felt a little guilty having left Sara to do most of the explaining about the "spilled wash basin" to Mrs. O'Toole. He could still see the slightly panicked look Sara had given him when he had said that he needed to head out because he had left a few things undone at the cemetery.

Kristoph was the first to step out of the courtyard. The young man, Liam, followed just after, and Devon brought up the rear, closing the gate softly behind him. He had expected Liam to bolt as soon as he was clear, but he didn't. Instead, he turned and squared off with Kristoph. He gave himself plenty of room to move though, so at least the boy wasn't a fool.

"What *did* your mistress do to Big Ken?" The young man's voice was steady as he demanded an explanation from Kristoph.

"Nothing that he did not want, I can assure you," the schoolmaster replied, his usual affable nature nowhere in evidence.

"I doubt that. No man wants to be made blind with fear. Nor does he want to have to be carried off by his friends and cleaned up," the young man retorted.

"You would be surprised what some people want," Kristoph deadpanned. It was apparent that he understood what Liam was talking about and just as clear that he was dismissive of whatever conclusions the boy had made. "Devon?"

The question he was asking was clearly implied, did Devon need him any longer?

"All is well," Devon assured him. "Thank you, for your help."

"Of course, think nothing of it," Kristoph said, sounding more in the manner of what Devon was used to. "Will you be free tomorrow evening?"

"Yes, I'll be here," Devon replied.

"I will see you then. Good evening."

The schoolmaster nodded to Devon and headed up Winding Street. It was then Devon noticed that the man was hatless. He was sure that had not been the case when they had left the brothel, which meant it must have been lost in their headlong rush back to the boarding house. Hats were expensive. In Devon's opinion, it said something of the man's character that he had never stopped to retrieve it. However, it was evident that the young man beside him did not share in his growing trust of the schoolmaster.

Devon started off down the street, in the opposite direction from the one that Kristoph had gone. He was surprised once again when Liam fell into step beside him. He looked over at the young man. "Did you have something you wanted to ask?"

"No. It's more that I thought you'd have questions for me," the young man replied.

Devon felt his eyebrows leap in surprise. "I do," he admitted, though he had planned to ask Sara to explain everything to him when he returned to the boarding house. Still, it didn't hurt to see what story he would hear here first. "Do you go to school with Sara?"

"No."

"But you walk with her to school?"

"Yes."

"And you know the schoolmaster."

"I don't know him," Liam stressed. "But I've seen him down in the Bottoms."

"You didn't see my sister down in the Bottoms," Devon pointed out.

Liam was suspiciously silent.

"Where did you meet my sister?" Devon asked as they turned onto Nightingale Street. He was beginning to suspect that Liam was having second thoughts about offering to answer his questions. He wondered how much of it had to do with the boy being worried that he would cause trouble for Sara.

"How did you meet?" Devon pressed.

"I think you should ask Sara," Liam responded. At the same time another voice, a woman's voice, was saying. "They met when he rescued her from some High Street rich boys who were set on bothering her!"

Devon was almost positive that the voice making this strident declaration on Liam's behalf was the same voice he had heard in Sara's room; the one had been screaming obscenities at him in French. Devon wondered if Liam knew about the spirit.

"Why did you start walking to school with her then?" He asked Liam, ignoring the ghost's previous statement.

"It was the right thing to do," Liam answered simply.

"Because he is a good man," declared the spirit who seemed intent on being his advocate.

For someone who was there to answer Devon's questions, there didn't seem to be many answers forthcoming. But he stayed in step with Devon as they continued down the street, making Devon wonder if Liam was going to follow him all the way to the cemetery. He glanced over, but noticed Liam's attention was focused on two men who were standing just outside one of the shops, flirting with a girl. By the cut of the men's coats, they were not from the Bottoms, but Devon was certain the girl was. For her part, she did not seem to mind the attention, but it was obvious something about the whole thing bothered Liam.

Beside him the woman's voice scoffed. "Silly girl's going to get herself in trouble." Devon said nothing about the prediction, but he had a feeling the ghost was right.

The tenet houses were dark when he and Liam walked past. Their occupants tucked safely inside behind the charms — of which there seemed to be more of than usual — that hung over the doors and between the porch posts.

When they reached the cemetery gates, Devon saw they were wide open, just as he had left them, he suspected. Though to be honest, he had no recollection one way or the other.

"Oh, not in there, *mon fils*," the woman said from behind them. It was plain from her voice that she was unhappy. "I can't follow you there."

Devon fished around in his pocket for a match. Finding one, he lit the lantern that hung from a hook on one of the gate posts. Liam followed him through without hesitation, obviously oblivious to his advocate's protestations.

Devon said nothing as Liam again fell in step beside him. He continued to bide his time, sure the boy had something else to say.

He headed back in the direction of where he had left his tools with his wheelbarrow. The wind moaned as it swirled past them through the crypts, but the spirits were uncommonly quiet. Especially given that it was Halloween, and the veil between the worlds was as thin as tissue paper. Devon had expected them to be even more lively than usual but they remained stubbornly silent. He could feel them though, gathering around them, their interest piqued. But by what, he wasn't sure.

Finally, he reached the spot where the fire had been. The smell of wet ashes and old smoke was still strong. Its heavy scent made Devon pause, the memory of his dream like the soft prick of claws on skin. The young man next to him remained as quiet as the dead around them.

"Here, hold this," Devon said, handing the lantern over to Liam. "Hold it up as high as you can."

Liam did as he asked, and Devon used the light to gather his tools and load them up into the wheelbarrow.

"Sara's offered to teach me to read." Liam blurted out, finally breaking his long silence.

So there it was, the thing that Liam had been wanting to tell him. Devon's response was painfully neutral. "Did she?"

"Yes, and I plan to take her up on the offer," the boy informed him, all quiet determination, but without any of the unnecessary defiance some young men feel the need to show.

"And do you still plan on walking with her to and from school?" Devon asked, knowing the answer already.

"Yes, I do," said Liam.

Devon quietly gathered up the handles of his wheelbarrow and started off towards the shed. He remained silent the whole way back. Liam for his part did not crack under the pressure of that silence, which to Devon's mind spoke to the young man's character.

They reached the shed with Liam still carrying the lantern. Devon had made no comment on the young man's declaration, only asking him to hold the light up higher as he put away his tools. Once he was finished, he took back the lantern and locked the shed. He led the way back down the broad gravel path.

"Do you need the lantern to walk home with?" he asked Liam, once they had reached the cemetery gates.

"No, I'm fine," the young man assured him.

Devon nodded. He blew out the flame and hung the lantern back on its hook. Pulling the gate shut, he locked it behind them. Liam was still there. Well, if he was determined to stick around, Devon reasoned that it would make sense to keep him as close as possible.

"If you want a job, be here tomorrow after you walk Sara to school," Devon said without preamble.

The smile on Liam's face was bright enough to see in the dark.

"I'll see you in the morning then," Liam nodded, and sliding his hands into his pockets, he turned and walked away down Fallow Road.

Devon watched him go. Now that that was all taken care of, all that was left was to go back and face his sister's wrath.

CHAPTER XIII

Afterwards

As soon as Devon left, Mrs. O'Toole unpinned her hat and set it aside. She began to help, despite Sara's protests. Mrs. Madison, who had come into the kitchen after having heard that Sara was there, also set to helping.

They talked about the social while they wrung out cloths. Both women seemed to think it a good idea that Sara had not accompanied them there. Not that they said that in so many words, but it was clear that they were uneasy about something. It was evident by the fact that beyond Mrs. O'Toole's initial question, no one asked about the wet cloths or Mr. Hegdus or Liam.

After everything was all wrung out and hung up on the back porch, Mrs. O'Toole pulled out the tremendous toffee apple she had brought back for Sara.

Mrs. Madison had also brought her back a gift. A perfectly grown-up shawl, knitted from the softest lavender-blue yarn. Sara nearly burst into tears. To be fair, her overly sensitive reaction may have had more to do with the emotional evening she'd already had than the extreme generosity of the two women. Either way, the whole thing left her feeling as raw as a newly-peeled potato.

Devon was still not home by the time the two women had bade her a good evening. So Sara finished her toffee apple, then wrapped her new shawl around her shoulders and went out into the courtyard to wait.

150

The white cat kept her company, laying on the bench beside her, paws tucked beneath itself and tail held close like a loaf of bread. It made Sara smile until she thought again about the whole kerfuffle that had happened upstairs in her room. It was probably the first time in her whole life that she had ever felt truly angry.

Of course, Devon had been angry too. Angrier than she had ever seen him before. He wasn't one to get angry easily or stay angry for long. He was like Papa that way, the complete opposite of Mama. Their mother was like a force of nature when she was angry, truly angry. Maybe that was why the rest of the family was so mild-tempered. Mama got angry enough for everyone, usually when she was feeling protective of those she loved.

Perhaps it was how all mothers were? Marguerite had certainly been livid when Devon had Liam pinned against the wall. That thought sent a white-hot stab of anger into her chest.

Could it have been Marguerite's anger that she had been feeling and not her own at all? There were times when a spirit's emotions would press in on hers. But she did not think that was the case this time. This time, it was definitely her own anger that she had felt. At that moment, she had been incandescent with it. But it had burned out quickly enough afterwards and now she just felt empty and worried.

Marguerite had gone when the others had. That had left Sara to wonder if the ghost was still mad. Maybe mad enough to not want anything to do with her any more? Which of course made her wonder about Liam and how he felt about all this. He probably wanted nothing more to do with her either. Her heart squeezed tight in her chest.

"He is the only friend I've made since we moved here," she said to the white cat sitting next to her.

The white cat looked up at her with big silver eyes and blinked once, slowly.

"Oh, I'm sorry! Of course, you've been a friend to me," she said, smiling at the apparition. "But…" She trailed off. It would be rude for her to say that it was not the same. It had been so nice to talk to someone and not have to worry that other people would think she was only talking to herself. Her eyes felt a little achy, like she might cry again.

The cat next to her began to purr. She had never been able to touch their visitor, but at that moment, Sara wished very much that she could pet the soft fur. The cat's ear twitched just before Sara heard the soft scrape of the courtyard gate. She looked over and saw the familiar silhouette of her brother walking unerringly in her direction. Without a word, he sat down next to her on the bench, on the opposite side of the phantom cat who had been keeping her company.

"Are you still mad?" he asked her.

"No," she replied, not sure if she was being entirely truthful.

"Good. But I guess we have some things to talk about," he said, taking up her hand in his.

"I guess we do," she said.

The white cat sniffed in the direction of their linked hands, then climbed up into her lap. She stroked the fur with her free hand, only able to do so because of Devon. It wasn't quite like real fur at all. It was cool to the touch and her fingers tingled as they passed through it. It felt more like she was petting thunderclouds than fur. Her brother reached over to stroke one rust-colored ear. She realized then that she wasn't angry with Devon anymore.

"Why didn't you mention Liam before?" he asked and she could tell he was trying very hard to keep his words from sounding accusatory.

Why hadn't she mentioned Liam before? It wasn't like she had been trying to hide him from her brother.

"I don't know," she admitted. "We have both been so busy. And the times when we were together, there was always something else going on. What with my new classes and all, it had truly never even crossed my mind. I promise Dev, I was not trying to hide Liam from you."

"I didn't think you were, pet. Not on purpose anyway." He squeezed her hand. "How did you two meet?"

"He didn't tell you?" she asked.

Devon chuckled. "No. He said to ask you."

At least she knew why she hadn't told Dev about this part. The rapacious look in the boys' eyes still haunted her, popping up in her thoughts when she least expected. Even now, her mind shied away from thinking on it too hard. As if thought alone would make it more real and she would be consumed by that hunger. But now that her brother had asked, she knew she should have mentioned it a long time ago. Things like that did not just go away, after all.

"One afternoon Mr. Hegdus was not at school, so there were no extra classes. I thought to come visit you at the cemetery, but I must have turned the wrong way, and…" she trailed off, not sure how to continue. That whole afternoon seemed a jumble. "A few boys saw me and started to tease me," she continued after a moment. "It was more than teasing actually. More even than them just being mean…" She bit her lip as she tried to come up with the right words. "This is going to sound silly, but I felt like I was a… umm…" She sighed, then said all in a rush, "like I was a cake that they were greedy to eat down to the last bit." She didn't tell him how soiled that made her feel, not sure how to put that into words and feeling incredibly awkward talking about it to her brother. Something she had never really felt before.

She looked up at Devon's face, the porch light was just bright enough for her to see the teasing smile that underlined her brother's worried eyes.

"A cake?" he said. She knew that look from past experience; he was trying to cheer her up.

"Stop, I'm being serious," she admonished, but the familiarity of his teasing did make her feel much better. She did not know what she would have done had he reacted any other way, probably melted into the ground right there on the spot. "Truly, it is not a comfortable thing to feel like someone wants to eat you."

"I can imagine. Is that when Liam came to your rescue?"

"I thought… ah, Marguerite told you, didn't she?"

"I suppose that must be who it was. Is she his mother?" he asked.

"Yes. She was why he was on that particular street at all that afternoon. When he saw what was happening, he stepped in."

"And by "stepping in" you mean…"

"He told them to stop and when they didn't, he punched the one boy," she clarified.

Devon's eyebrows disappeared beneath his forelock of hair, which still needed to be cut, Sara noted. "How many boys were there?" he asked.

"Four."

"Four? And he beat all four?" Her brother sounded impressed.

"Not exactly," she admitted. "He was holding his own against two of them though. We might have been in trouble if the white cat had not shown up." The apparition in question looked up at her with half-lidded eyes, closing them tight for a brief moment in a cat smile. "Thank you by the way," she said to the cat in her lap. "I am not sure how you did what you did, but I am grateful."

"What did she do?"

Sara did her best to describe the scene as it had happened; the biting wind, the raised welts on the boys, the scratches on Thomas's face. All the while she continued to stroke the cat's icy fur, her fingers tingling. She was afraid her words were not enough to do the whole thing justice.

This time Devon did not tease her, but listened gravely without interrupting.

"Curious and concerning," he said to the white cat, scratching under its chin. "You seemed to have adopted us. Are you going to make us regret that, I wonder?"

The white cat worked her head up under Devon's hand, nuzzling into his palm. "Words would be more helpful, you know."

At that, the white cat sneezed. She stood up, stretched, then jumped down from Sara's lap. Sara felt her brother's hand slip from hers as he leaned back on the bench.

"How long ago did this all happen?" he asked.

Sara counted back the days to herself. "Around two weeks ago," she said. Had it only been two weeks? It felt like she had known Liam forever. Again the worry that he may no longer be her friend pounced on her.

"What else can you tell me about him?" her brother asked.

"He is almost fifteen and lives in the Bottoms. He has been on his own since he was six years old. He seems to do a lot of different jobs for the people down there and at the docks. In fact, I think he just does whatever jobs he can, except… well there are some jobs he doesn't do," Sara really hoped that it was too dark for her brother to see what she was sure was her very red face. "But he still finds time every morning and every afternoon to walk with me. Ever since that one afternoon that is…" Sara trailed off, chewing on her lip as she tried to get out the one question she was afraid to ask. Finally screwing up her courage she said, "Devon, does Liam not want anything to do with me now?"

"What? Not at all pet," Devon reassured her. "In fact, he told me in no uncertain terms that he still had every intention of walking with you to school. He also said that he planned on taking you up on your offer to teach him to read."

"He did! That's wonderful!" She felt all the worry she had been holding on to drain away.

"But those lessons will not be happening in your bedroom window!" Her brother admonished and Sara blushed a little.

"Of course not!"

Devon stayed in the courtyard after Sara had gone up to bed. The weight on his shoulder and the occasional eddy in his pipe smoke told him that the white cat had stayed to keep him company.

He listened to the spirits whisper, more and more gathering as the hour grew later. The sounds of mortal devilry intruded occasionally as troublemakers sought to play tricks on those unfortunate enough to still be out.

Finally, he was able to allow himself to think about the dream that had set off the chaotic whirlwind that had been this evening's events. The burning figure twisting in the flames was still there every time he closed his eyes. He wondered if there was a connection to the other dreams he had been having. This one felt deeper, more like the dream he had had of the herb woman. More like a memory than a dream.

He could feel the connections, like spiderwebs all around him, but he could not quite see the pattern yet. Certainly, his dreams and their visitor had something to do with it. The sense of wrongness that Liam had spoken of, and Aunt Ruth's seeing, were they part of it too? Or were they something separate?

"I guess we'll have to wait and see, won't we?" he said softly to himself. Phantom whiskers brushed against his cheek.

Later when Devon settled into his own bed and closed his eyes he was met by the sound of the sea and the now familiar figure that was waiting for him there.

CHAPTER XIV

First Day on the Job

It was not that Sara hadn't believed what her brother had told her the night before. It was more that she hadn't believed that Liam would have still wanted to be friends after everything that had happened. Even when Marguerite had appeared in her room that morning, telling her that all was well, she hadn't quite believed it. So when on her way to school Liam fell into step beside her as he always did, her nerves were such that she nearly burst out in tears.

"I told you *mon poussin* that there was nothing to fear," the ghost next to him said reassuringly. The white cat, who was walking in front of them twitched its ear once as if to say; *See, you were being silly.*

"You didn't think I would come, did you?" Liam asked her.

"I wouldn't have blamed you." Her reply was choked with unshed tears.

"And I can't blame your brother for feeling protective," Liam shrugged. "Plus, I can't complain on how things turned out, you offering to teach me to read and your brother offering me a job; it seems like I landed on my feet just fine."

A warmth grew in her chest at hearing this. "Devon offered you a job? That's wonderful! Are you going to take it?"

"Probably. It's steady work, and I can still pick up side jobs for extra money when I need to."

The ghost on the other side of him sighed gustily. "I should be happy, but I'm not so sure I am."

"Why?" Sara asked before she thought better of it.

"Because I cannot follow him into the cemetery," answered Marguerite.

"Why? Why would I still want to pick up side jobs?" Liam asked at the same time.

Sara didn't know what to say. It happened sometimes, answering when she shouldn't, especially if she wasn't careful. It was hard being a part of more than one conversation when one of the other participants didn't know there was more than one going on.

"Ah, it wasn't me you were answering, was it?" Liam realized.

She looked over in surprise when she felt his warm hand take hers.

"Sorry *ma fée*, I didn't mean to make things awkward." Marguerite apologized. But rather than sounding contrite, the ghost seemed delighted.

"Sorry *ma fée*, I didn't mean to put you on the spot" Liam unknowingly echoed his mother, though at least he sounded remorseful.

It was odd to hear nearly the same sentence being said at the same time, but in two entirely different tones. She could not help but laugh.

"Your mother said nearly the same thing just now," she informed him. His face lit up with a brilliant smile. "Does it make you happy knowing that?"

"Yes," he said, green eyes sparkling. "Though it makes me curious about what else she might be saying," he admitted, winking at her. She felt her cheeks warm right up. She was starting to suspect he teased her because he liked to make her blush! Worse yet, his mother was laughing right along with him as her cheeks grew hotter.

"Oh tell him little bird, before your cheeks burst into flames! He is his own man and can make up his own mind,"

Marguerite chuckled. "You would not want him to draw the wrong conclusion about what was said, or at least what was said in this conversation."

Sara huffed at both of them. "Well in this case, she is worried about you working in the cemetery because she cannot follow you in there."

"Huh, Why can't she follow me?" His smile dimmed as his brows lowered with the weight of the question.

"Because it is consecrated ground. Many times, that means only those spirits whose bodies are buried in that ground are allowed to walk the earth there," Sara explained.

"I see. Sorry *maman*," he said quietly.

Sara watched as sadness and old anger chased each other across Liam's face. So much meaning hidden behind such simple words.

"I understand, *mon fils*," his mother replied, though he could not hear her.

"She understands," Sara told Liam, though she was not sure she understood, and it seemed so personal that she couldn't bring herself to ask.

It was nice to have someone who did not look at her strangely when she spoke for the dead, someone other than her family that is. She almost felt giddy and a little like she was flying. Which made her a little scared because when you're up that high it hurts more when you fall.

The quiet stretched out between them as they turned onto Washboard Lane. It was not necessarily an uncomfortable silence, but Sara was uncomfortable with it.

"Did you know that Washboard Lane got its name because people used to use it to go down to the river to wash their clothes?" she asked, remembering the book she had been reading the night before, prior to Liam climbing up to her window. "I was just reading about it last night in the history book Mr. Hegdus gave to me."

"I did not," Liam replied, seeming happy to be diverted from his thoughts. "Though I shouldn't be surprised. I know a good number of people still use it to go down and wash their clothes even now."

The schoolhouse had just come into view, and Sara could already make out the dark form of Mr. Hegdus standing in the doorway.

"Be careful of that one," Liam said, and when she looked over at him, she found he had the same stony expression he had been wearing the night before when facing off with the schoolmaster.

She also remembered the fierce look on Mr. Hegdus's face when he had come charging in behind her brother, so different from the affable one she was used to. The energetic, urbane schoolmaster she was acquainted with had been nowhere in evidence, replaced instead by someone powerful and capable as her brother. It had been a shocking difference, but it had not bothered her as much as it had obviously bothered Liam. Sara had not missed the fact that Liam had changed what he had been about to say last night when the accusations had been flying around her room like bullets. Whatever it was, he had not wanted to say it in front of her.

Unlike most mornings, Liam walked right up to the school-house door with her. It was the affable Mr. Hegdus that she was most familiar with who greeted her there. His smiling face looked as it always did except for his eyes, which were a little cooler and flashed a warning she did not think was meant for her.

Sara felt Liam relax, apparently unfazed by the look directed at him. He smiled at her. "I'll see you this afternoon, and tell you all about my first day at work." Sliding his hands into his coat pockets, he continued on down the lane.

"Good luck!" she waved after him. It was only then that she noticed that her hand felt empty. Liam had held it the entire way and she hadn't even realized.

A touch on her shoulder caused her to jump, and she found that she had stopped right in the middle of the doorway.

"Are you okay, Miss Amaris?" the schoolmaster asked.

Sara was not sure how to answer.

Devon had been penning the promised letter to his parents when Sara had left for school that morning. So he had just arrived and was unlocking the cemetery gate when he saw Liam jogging in his direction from down Nightingale Street. He waited for the young man to reach him.

"Morning," Liam called out as he came up.

"Good morning," Devon replied, eyeing the young man in front of him. "So, are you interested in the job?"

"I am. What kind of job are you offering?"

"About what you would expect," said Devon. "Helping me clear away the overgrowth in the cemetery, and fixing anything that needs to be repaired: grave markers, fences, structures and the like. It isn't easy work and it can't be rushed, but the money is steady."

"Regular work would be good," Liam said. "Mostly I do odd jobs here and there, but I've picked up a few useful skills."

Devon opened the gate and went through, the young man followed in on his heels without hesitation.

"What kind of work have you done?" Devon asked as he led them down the broad gravel path that ran past the family chapel.

"I've done a bit of work down on the docks. Cleaning and mending things mostly, but I have picked up a bit of carpentry as well. I've worked some at the stables and with the black-smith, when they're down a boy or have a lot of work," Liam said. "My usual jobs come from down here in the Bottoms though, whatever work the people or shop owners need to get done."

"Like taking care of 'High Street rich-boys'?" Devon prompted, thinking of what the ghost of the boy's mother had said the night before.

Liam laughed. "Sometimes," he admitted.

When they reached the caretaker's shed, Devon unlocked it and gestured for Liam to follow him in. It took no time at all to show him where all the tools were. Then they loaded up the wheelbarrow and headed out to get started on the day's work.

They soon reached an older part of the cemetery where ranks of angels, eternal in their beauty, stood in constant vigil, their sightless eyes judging the world as they looked out upon it with compassion or despair. The morning light broke through the barricade of branches to fall on them, wrapping their shoulders in cloaks of gold.

Devon set to work, explaining to Liam as he went what it was that he was doing. For his part, Liam started to help straight away, bringing tools and dragging away brush without Devon ever having to ask.

They worked together that way for a good long while. Devon found the young man's company easy to be in. He didn't seem to feel the need to fill silences. Of which there were quite a few that morning, even for Devon; the spirits being unusually quiet with only vague whisperings here and there. He wondered at this until he saw a figure in an aubergine coat moving just beyond the silent angels, appearing and disappearing like an apparition behind a screen of nearly leafless azaleas.

The sight of Serus Ascher walking through his family cemetery came as no surprise to Devon. He had seen him there a handful of times in the weeks since their first rainy day encounter. This time though, Ascher did not stop to speak with him, only nodded and touched the brim of his homburg by way of greeting as he walked past a break in the hedge. Devon raised his hand in acknowledgment.

When he glanced over at Liam, Devon found that his assistant had stopped working. The boy's face was closed up tight as he watched Ascher's retreating figure disappear from sight.

Liam was certain sure that the man who had just passed was the same man he had seen last night in the alley next to Mrs. O'Toole's. And now it wasn't hard to guess who the man was.

"That was Mr. Ascher, I take it," he said to Devon.

"It was," Devon confirmed.

"Does he know you've hired me?" Liam asked. Sara's brother hadn't quite come out and said he was hired, but he hadn't said he wasn't either. Devon chuckled, having caught Liam's assumption.

"He does now," the man replied matter-of-factly.

Liam turned back to his work, but the memory from the night before still bothered him. He also thought it a bit odd to see a man walking through his own cemetery at this time of the morning with no funeral to go to. Odder still that he was heading into, not out of, the cemetery.

He followed Devon back to the shed around noon to sharpen the tools and eat lunch. They sat on a short coquina wall just outside the shed, and Devon handed him a package from out of his own lunch pail.

Liam raised his eyebrows.

"Yes, for you," Devon replied, answering his unspoken question.

Liam took the offered parcel. "Thank you," he said as he opened it up. He found an orange, three hoecakes and a shortbread. For a long moment, Liam just stared at the spread before him. He couldn't say it was the most food he had ever seen, but it was certainly more than he was used to.

He looked up to find Devon watching him.

"Does this come out of my pay?" he asked the man who was already eating his own lunch.

"No," Devon assured him as he took a bite of a hoecake. "The work is hard. You can't keep up with me if you're hungry."

It sounded like charity to Liam. But even if that was what it was, he certainly wasn't so high-minded as to not accept it.

Being prideful didn't put food in your belly, so he had always aimed for being practical instead.

He nodded his head in thanks, and set about eating his lunch. Unfortunately, he was really only able to finish about half of it before his stomach started to feel overfull.

"Keep it for later," Devon told him as he stood up, dusting crumbs from his trousers. The man stopped mid-swipe and turned toward the direction of the gate. Liam looked that way as well, wondering what it was that had caught Devon's attention. Then he heard it too. It sounded like a young girl.

"Mr. Amaris! Mr. Amaris!," her panicked voice shouted. "Sir, come quick! Please!"

Liam jumped up and followed Devon as he took off in the direction of the shout. Liam was quick, but the man's long legs still outdistanced him in short order. When he finally caught up, he found a young girl, no more than seven years old, talking to Devon.

"She's down that way," the young girl was saying, pointing up the lane that led to the Ascher house. "I was bringing Da his lunch when I saw her. Old Henry said I should get you. Please come quick!"

To his credit, Devon did not quiz the girl or drag his heels, just told her to lead the way. Liam closed the gate, and followed, catching up quickly.

The girl did not take them far up the lane before she turned off of it, leading them over to an old, old drainage ditch some twenty feet away. Its grassy banks were lined with full-grown laurel oaks on either side.

"She's just down there," the girl pointed towards the ditch, though she would not go a step closer to it.

Liam followed Devon as he slid down over the edge. The ditch was wide, but only about as deep as Liam was tall. He could see someone at the bottom, a woman as far as Liam could tell, and she wasn't dead. Her body shook fitfully, twitching and jerking. It looked as though she had tried to drag herself to the water but had stopped a foot or so short of it, unable to make it all the way.

Devon knelt down beside the woman without hesitation. He did not touch her, just watched her for several minutes before he called Liam over to join him.

"Help me move her," Devon said, "but be gentle about it. I don't see any injuries, but I'm not sure if she's hurt somewhere we can't see."

He knelt down on the other side of the woman and helped Devon gently roll her over and away from the water. It took Liam a minute to realize that he knew the girl. Her hair, caked with mud and spittle, covered a good part of her face, but he still recognized her. He had seen her just last night, talking to two lolli-boys over in front of Berk's.

"Her name's Marie," he told Devon, finding it hard to look away from her eyes which were rolled back in her head so that only the whites were showing. The muscles of her face twitched endlessly, contorting it until she didn't even look like herself, before smoothing back out, only to do it all again. Her jaw was clenched so hard that Liam thought she'd break her teeth. The dried blood in the corners of her lips told him she had most likely bitten her tongue or cheek a while ago.

"I see now," Devon said, leaning a little over the girl. "You had enough sense to try to get to running water, but didn't quite make it, did you?"

To Liam's surprise, Devon gently pulled Marie towards the sluggish water until both of them were all the way in. He knelt there, water up to his waist, holding her shoulders as she floated in front of him.

"Liam, go up and tell Edie to find her Da. Tell her to have him bring a cart down here and some blankets," Devon directed.

Liam did as Devon asked, sending the young girl, Edie, running up the lane. As soon as she was off, he slid back down into the ditch where Devon still held Marie in the water. She had stopped twitching and her face had relaxed enough so that she almost looked like herself again.

He was about to ask Devon how he could help, when he noticed Marie's dress move in a way that had nothing to do with the fact she was floating in water. Odd little dimples appeared and disappeared in the fabric, like a cat walking on a blanket. As though something invisible was moving up Marie's belly towards her head. Well, invisible to him at least.

"So you're here," Liam heard Devon say softly. "I think Ascher should know about this… Liam," he said the last bit a little louder, turning to look over at the spot where Liam was standing. "Can you climb up and make sure that Samuel sees where we are when he brings the cart? He may not bring his daughter back with him. I know I wouldn't bring mine back if it was me."

"Will do," Liam said.

After one last glance at the very paw-like depressions in Marie's dress, he climbed up to the top of the bank so that he could be seen from the road.

But Liam had always had sharp ears, so he could still hear Devon when he said "Can you find Ascher and bring him back here?"

Liam almost answered before he caught himself, realizing the question had not been for him. It seemed that Sara wasn't the only one in her family that was familiar with things that others could not see. Perversely enough, it made Liam feel even more comfortable with the man who was now his boss.

It was only a few minutes later that he heard the pounding of hooves. They weren't coming from the direction of the house, but rather from down Fallow Road way. Liam turned to see a heavy-maned bay galloping full tilt in his direction. He recognized the rider on its back easily enough, having just seen him in the cemetery that morning.

The man slid down practically before the horse had even had a chance to stop. He was hatless, but besides that, he looked as neatly dressed as he had when Liam had last seen him. Ascher stopped in his headlong rush to take a hard look at Liam before continuing on.

"Take care of him," Ascher called back over his shoulder as he slid over the edge of the ditch without a care for his trousers. "And when Samuel arrives, have him stay up there unless I call for him."

Great gusts of hot air blew against Liam's neck as a soft nose nudged him, hard. He looked up into a pair of large brown eyes nearly hidden beneath a thick black forelock.

"As demanding as your master, I see," Liam said as he took up the reins and began to walk the blowing horse cool. He had some experience with horses, having sometimes picked up jobs at the stables and with the carters down at the docks. Though he had never known anything as grand as this animal, for sure.

As he was walking the horse out, he caught glimpses of where the two men were down with Marie, but the angle was such that he could not see what it was that they did.

It was only a short while later that Liam saw a cart coming down the lane at a good pace. Devon had been right, the man driving it was alone. The little girl, Edie, was nowhere to be seen, and there was a hard look on the man's long face.

"Mr. Amaris?" the long-faced man called out as the cart drew up next to Liam.

"He's down there," Liam nodded in the direction of the ditch. "Mr. Ascher is with him. He asked for you to wait here until they come up."

The rangy man climbed down from the driver's seat just as Ascher stepped up onto the bank. His fine trousers were muddy but he didn't seem to notice as he turned back to take Marie from the arms of Devon who was lifting her up to him.

"Mr. Ascher!" the man exclaimed, rushing over as though he would take Marie from the gentleman's arms.

"I have her Samuel," Ascher insisted. "Just get the blankets stretched out in the back."

Samuel did as he was asked to. When Ascher reached the cart, he lifted Marie up over the side, wet clothes and all, with hardly any effort on his part as far as Liam could tell. He laid her down gently on the blankets that were there.

"Samuel, take Briza back up to the stables. Tell Jonas to prepare a room for purification, he will understand what that means. And have Mabel meet us at the back of the house. We will follow along in the cart," Ascher said, taking the reins back from Liam and handing them off to the long-faced Samuel who was looking a bit dumbfounded. "Mr. Amaris, will you ride in the cart with me?"

Devon, who had climbed the rest of the way up the bank while Ascher was putting Marie in the cart, nodded then turned to Liam. "Do you think you could put the tools away in the shed before you go to meet Sara? You remember where I put the keys?"

Liam nodded, "I do." Part of him felt that he should go with Devon and help where he could, but the other part of him was just as happy not to have to.

"Then I will see you later. Good job today." Devon clapped him on the shoulder. Liam fought down a bubble of laughter at those words, while his mind stumbled over all that had happened that day.

"Be careful on your way home," Devon added. But Liam knew what he really meant was, 'take care of my sister'.

"I will," he promised.

He watched as the two men stepped up into the cart and started off down the lane towards Ascher House. The long-faced Samuel set a pace ahead of them that would put him at the house well before they arrived.

Liam turned and headed back down the lane. Ascher had not seemed to have given him a second look since handing him the reins, but for some reason Liam still felt as if the man had been scrutinizing him down to his bones. Something about Ascher set his teeth on edge. Which was odd, because it wasn't in Liam's nature to pick fights that he didn't think he could win. Or to pick fights at all really, though he was happy to finish them if need be. Good sense dictated that it was a poor idea to butt heads with a powerful man, and his employer's employer to boot. And yet, each time he had seen the head of the Ascher family, that was exactly what he had felt like doing.

It also hadn't been lost on him that Ascher himself had been out and about that morning.

He went back to where they had left the tools and the wheelbarrow. The morning had been pleasant, but the sky was solid gray now, and the wind stole the breath right of his lungs as he finished putting the tools in the shed. It seemed that the sun had run away the moment they slid down into that ditch and found Marie. Locking the gate behind him, he pocketed the key and set out to meet Sara.

Purification

The gardener had swung up on the horse and was now well ahead of them while the cart Devon rode in with Ascher followed behind at a slower pace. Ascher drove up the old servants' road with a careful hand so as to not bounce the girl in the back around too badly.

Devon had watched the shadow-writing writhe under the girl's skin as he had waited for Ascher. He knew next to nothing about ritual magick save what he had picked up from overheard conversations while growing up, but he was sure that it had been a part of whatever had been done to her. From Ascher's reaction when he had arrived, it looked as though Devon had guessed correctly.

"You were smart, Mr. Amaris, to pull her into the water as you did," Ascher said. "It helped to cleanse some of whatever it was that still had a hold of her. Though, I suspect it will take more than that to free her completely. There will still be some research necessary before I am sure, and I am afraid that you will not be able to help me in that aspect of the endeavor. Unless I am mistaken, and you also share your father's scholarly interests."

"You are not mistaken, I would be of little help to you there," Devon agreed. "So, why then did you ask me to come with you?"

"Just because your knowledge of the arcane is limited does not mean that you would be of no help at all," Ascher informed him. "But you would be correct in thinking that there is an entirely different matter on which I wished to speak to you. That young man who was with you, how well do you know him?"

"Not well," Devon answered honestly. "I have only just met him, but he has been an acquaintance of my sister's for some time now."

"I see. And since I saw him working in the cemetery with you this morning, I feel safe in assuming that you have taken him on?" Ascher concluded.

"I have," Devon confirmed. He glanced back to check on the woman who lay in the back of the cart. Her eyes were now closed and her face, though slack, was relatively peaceful compared to how it had been earlier. He turned his eyes back to Ascher.

"He also walks with my sister to and from school every day," Devon volunteered, curious as to where Ascher's line of questioning was leading.

"Does he now? So, I gather that you trust him." It was less of a question and more of a statement.

"I do. And so does the 'company I keep' as you have called her," Devon informed him, remembering the ice glazed walls from the night before, and how the schoolmaster had flown up against them. It seemed that though Kristoph might have their companion's approval, it was Liam who was held in a higher regard.

"That was a wise choice by the by, sending your companion to fetch me as you did," Ascher said. "And if the boy comes with such shining references, I can understand why you would choose to trust him. Though I suspect his friendship with your sister may also have something to do with your desire to keep him close."

Devon did not bother to refute the man's observation. There was more than a little truth to it after all.

Ascher smiled knowingly at his silence. "What is his name?"

"Liam," Devon answered.

"And his surname?"

"I have not heard one."

"Hmm," Ascher hummed thoughtfully. "Do you know who or where his family is?"

"I do not." Devon replied with the simplest truth, though it was not all he knew. He felt it wasn't for him to share the rest of what Sara had told him, little as it was.

Ascher was silent for a long time after that. The woman behind them still lay unresponsive, and it made for a quiet ride as they continued up the lane towards Ascher House.

Unlike what Devon was used to seeing back home, the land in and around Ashwood was fairly flat. The sand dunes were the closest thing to hills this area had. And yet, Ascher House sat up high, atop a rise in the land made by the discarded shells of a long dead people.

The house itself was not that old though, at least to Devon's understanding. It had been built a little more than five years ago, only a short time before Tam Ascher, the previous head of the family, had died. It stood a good three stories high and looked more like a miniature castle than anything else, with its towers and turrets and gabled roofs. A fairytale house wrapped in porches, dressed with gingerbread trim and leaded glass.

"What do you think of the house?" The man next to him asked as they came closer.

"It makes quite a picture," Devon answered truthfully.

"So it does," Ascher agreed. "A useless picture and a colossal waste of money when there is no family to fill it. Such grand ambitions, but that fool Tam still could not be bothered to let go of his vices and mind his obligations. The houses you tend are much fuller than the one I do."

Devon considered all that Liza had told him about the family's history and thought Ascher might be entitled to a little bitterness.

The lane split and Ascher nudged the cart along the right fork which soon brought them to the back of the house. Two people were waiting for them there, a tall pale man and a much shorter, darker woman. There might have been a huge difference in their heights, but Devon would have bet a nickel their shoulders measured nearly the same width.

As Ascher pulled the cart to a stop, the man, who looked to be a head taller even than Devon, no mean feat, came and took hold of the horse's reins.

"Jonas. Is everything ready?"" Ascher asked as he stepped down from the driver's seat.

It was the woman standing at the back door who answered though. "It is, sir."

"Good, thank you Mabel."

A third man came from around the corner of the house. He made his way to the side of the cart and reached over as though he were about to pick up the girl who was lying there.

"No Nathan!" Ascher barked and the man's hands nearly flew away from the girl. "For now, no one else should touch her save myself or Mr. Amaris."

Devon, understanding the statement for the veiled suggestion that it was, swung down from the cart. He gathered Marie up as gently as he could and lifted her over the side.

"Well you know your business," Mabel said, but her lips said otherwise, pressed tightly together as they were, as though she might be having trouble keeping her opinions from escaping them.

"I do. And I respect the concerns you have kept to yourself," Ascher said agreeably. "You can come with us if you want, as long as you feel you have the nerve for it." He turned to look over at Devon. "Mr. Amaris, follow me please."

The young woman was limp in Devon's arms as he followed Ascher up the steps and across the wide back porch. Mabel led them through the back door and up a set of stairs to a large bathroom on the second floor. Mirrors hung from every wall, and when Devon looked up at the ceiling above, he found little images of himself looking back down at him from the tiny mirrors suspended amidst the stained glass. The air was thick with steam and incense.

"Put her into the bath, Mr. Amaris, just as she is," Ascher instructed as he stripped off his own soiled jacket. "Be prepared to hold on."

Devon lowered the girl with her mud-covered clothes into the bathtub as directed. She had been quiet since they had taken her from the ditch, but as soon as she touched the water she began to shriek and thrash wildly. Beneath her skin, the shadows of words rippled in languages that hurt to look at.

This was no doubt ritual magick and beyond his ken. He narrowed his focus down to the girl he was trying to keep in the bath and let the rest of the world devolve into flashes reflected in the mirrors surrounding them; Mabel across the room, her mahogany cheeks growing paler by the moment. Jonas silently helping his master. The violent thrashing of the water and the calm face of Serus Ascher.

The moment stretched on for an eternity until Ascher's voice cut through it like a knife.

"Close your eyes, Mabel. You as well, Mr. Amaris," Ascher instructed. "Keep them closed. Even without them open, you may see things you wish you had not. Do not allow yourself to be drawn in by them. Let them slide away. They are only mist, with no substance."

He could hear when Ascher began to incant the ritual, but if there were words they slid off of Devon's ears. He heard Mabel gasp, then growl something about such shadows not being welcome. But for his part, all he saw in the land behind his eyelids was the familiar figure of a dark-haired woman standing on an unseen shore, the sky stretching out forever behind her in shades of pewter and silver.

A pressure built in the room around them. The thrashing of the girl he held became wilder and he worried that she would hurt herself. But his worries were distant things, not connected to him or the place where he stood. The sound of wind and waves filled his ears, growing louder and louder…

Silence crashed down on him like a sack of flour. The girl

beneath his hands went still. He almost opened his eyes, but Ascher's voice stopped him before he could.

"Just a moment more," it promised.

Devon heard the rustling of cloth for a good long while, before Ascher told them it was safe to open their eyes. When he did, Devon found that all the mirrors in the room had been covered with sheets. Mabel was still standing where she had been, sweating freely, but steadfast.

"Best to keep your gaze focused down for now," Ascher told them. "Mabel, please take this young lady to the guest washroom and give her a proper bath. Do not worry, she is free of the taint for now, but she will most likely be unresponsive for a while yet."

Mabel came from where she was standing and helped Devon coax the glassy-eyed Marie out of the tub. As soon as the girl was steady on her feet, the woman insisted that they all turn around as she stripped the girl to her skin. Marie was wrapped in a large robe by the time they were told they could look again.

"Add this to the bathwater, Mabel," Ascher said, holding out a small wooden box for her to take as she passed him. "All of it, and don't worry about any of this," he waved at the room, "Jonas and I will take care of it."

"I'd hope so," the woman muttered none-too-softly as she led the docile girl through the door. "You'll be lucky to get me to ever step foot in this room again."

Devon could not fault her for that.

"I will be a bit longer here. Jonas, please take Mr. Amaris some place where he can clean up," Ascher instructed as he began to unbutton his own shirt, pulling it free from his waistband. "I will meet you in the library in about an hour. And Jonas, all of this will have to be burned."

"Of course," the fair-haired man said, speaking for the first time since they had arrived. His voice took Devon by surprise. It was higher and much more melodic than he had expected from such a big man.

Jonas opened the door, gesturing for Devon to proceed him out into the hall.

"Mr. Amaris…" Ascher's voice stopped him mid-step.

He turned and was surprised to find the man standing close behind him. He had not heard him move but there he was, shirtless and more powerfully built than Devon had expected. Gone was the urbane dapper gentleman. The veneer of humanity had been stripped away somehow, and in its place stood something primal and even more dangerous than Devon had guessed upon their first meeting.

The man's eyes locked on his, acknowledging the recognition he saw there. "…would you join me in the library later?"

Devon nodded his assent, then followed Jonas out into the hall. He heard the lock in the door snick after it closed behind them.

Jonas led him to another bathroom. There he left Devon with the promise of a change of clothes to come as he took his old ones away to be burned.

Stripped to his skin, Devon was looking around for a washcloth when there was a knock. The voice of a young woman called in to him from the other side.

"Sorry to be buggin' ya Mr. Amaris, but the master asked me to letcha know the bath is waiting for ya, just on the other side of that screen. He also asked me to bring ya this. I'll just leave it right here on the little table next to the door."

Having nothing to wrap around himself, Devon was careful when he opened the door, but he needn't have worried; the hallway was empty. He found a porcelain box had been left on a table nearby, within easy reach, just as the young woman had said. Inside was a folded piece of paper perched atop a bed of salt. He unfolded it and found a set of instructions. Devon had no idea when Ascher would have had the time to write them, but they were clear enough. Soak in the tub with the salts and don't spare the hot water, taking care to submerge himself completely at least three times.

Devon was happy to follow them. Hot running water, especially in volume, was a luxury, and his muscles were starting to realize just how much he had asked of them.

The bath was behind the large painted screen that stood on the other side of the room, just as he had been told. He emptied the entire contents of the box into the water as instructed. The salt dissolved quickly, leaving behind the smell of the sea.

He slipped into the steaming water, sliding in until it closed over his head. The warmth and silence embraced him and held him close, softening the sharp-edged memories that came now that the crisis had passed.

But the reality of the situation broke over him as his face broke the water's surface. The crisis may have passed, but whatever had caused it was still out there. He slid beneath the surface again.

Ripples in the deep. Powers unseen; sly tentacles searching for a brilliant light. Aunt Ruth's words came back to him.

He surfaced again, pushing himself up just far enough so that his head could rest on the back of the tub. He closed his eyes and felt a whiskered nose brush over his cheek.

"And who are you in all of this?" He asked the apparition as he reached over blindly to brush a finger along the furred cheek. The ghost offered no answer.

...a hunter waiting in the shallows; crafty and careful. A shape hidden in the corner of my eye.

Devon stepped out of the bathroom just as the clock chimed three. His borrowed clothes were surprisingly loose in the shoulders and unsurprisingly a touch short in the leg. But all in all, they fit well enough. The quality of the fabric, if nothing else, told him they most likely belonged to his host, which was unexpected.

Nathan, the steward, met him in the hall. "If you will follow me, I will show you the way to the library."

Devon followed the older man to a room on the first floor. It was a tall room, but not as big as Devon had expected. Although his family's house was much smaller than this one, his father's library took up nearly half of the second floor. This room, however, looked like it was made more for comfort than for study and research. There were two windows and a large glass-paned door that opened up to a patio overlooking the garden. From where he stood, Devon could see a column of smoke billowing up from just beyond the ordered greenery, the dirty gray of it merging with the slate-colored clouds above.

Mabel came in shortly thereafter with a pot of coffee and a tray full of mugs. She set it down on a small table in the corner.

"Here," she said as she poured a mug full and added cream and sugar to it. She held it out to Devon. "You need this more than anybody."

Devon took the proffered cup, smiling his thanks to the woman who had offered it, and wisely keeping the fact that he drank it black to himself. His first sip told him that more than cream and sugar had been added to his coffee.

Ascher stepped into the room then, impeccably dressed and cutting a much more familiar figure.

"You might as well pour one of those for yourself, Mabel," Ascher said as he made his way to a reading desk.

"Don't worry sir, mine's in the kitchen," she replied. Devon was sure there was no coffee to dilute whatever it was that was waiting for her back in the kitchen. "I put the girl in the small guest room and Lucy is watching over her."

"Has she said anything?" Ascher asked, accepting the coffee she handed to him.

"Not a word," the woman answered. "I don't think she even knows where she is."

"That is to be expected," he nodded and took a sip of his coffee. "Tell me again Mr. Amaris, how did all this come about?"

Devon spent the next quarter of an hour explaining to Ascher

178

the happenings of that afternoon. There were a few things he did not elaborate on. In part because he did not know how much Mabel or Nathan knew about magick or the hidden sciences. In part because the retelling was not pleasant. Even with those omissions, the hard look on Mabel's face made him glad that he was not the person who had put the girl in that state.

"And you do not know her?" Ascher asked him, after he had finished describing the day's events.

Devon shook his head.

"I know her, sir," Nathan spoke up from where he stood near the fireplace. "Her name is Marie and I have seen her down in the Bottoms often enough, usually looking for her poor-excuse-for-a-father. He works on the river boats, when he works at all."

"Do you know if she has any other family? Is there someone who will miss her?" Ascher said.

"None that I know of," the older steward answered.

"I'll ask about," Mabel offered. "I'm sure someone will know where her people are."

"Good," Ascher said. His attention was drawn to one of the windows.

Through it, Devon could see the tall pale figure of Jonas as he made his way up to the house.

Ascher took another sip from his cup, his gaze still fixed outside.

"Thank you Mabel, for your help this afternoon. Take the rest of the day off if you wish. You as well Nathan. Jonas will see to my needs and answer any of Lucy's questions regarding our guest."

Both made to leave, but Mabel stopped just short of the door. "What will happen to the girl?" she asked, her question obviously meant for Ascher.

"For now, she will stay here," he replied. "At least until I find a way to contact her people. After that, if she still needs help, I have an acquaintance, a doctor, who is well versed in matters of the mind. She has a prickly, no-nonsense personality that some find hard to work with. However, I suspect you two would most likely get on famously," he told Mabel drolly. She pressed her lips together, and gave a little snort which Ascher ignored. "While the girl is with us, feel free to bring on an extra person to help, if you have need."

Both servants nodded their heads at their master's clear dismissal, and slipped out the door. Devon made to follow them.

"A moment more of your time Mr. Amaris," Ascher said, as he walked over to pour himself another cup of coffee. As soon as the door to the library was shut, Ascher turned to face Devon.

"Am I right in assuming that you could see the malevolence that was trying to inhabit that girl?" he asked.

"I could see the shadow script running under her skin," Devon said.

Ascher nodded. "That would be part of it. Was there anything else that you saw or heard?"

Devon shook his head. "Do you have an idea of what happened to her?"

"An inkling; I will need to look into it further. However, I suspect that she was being prepared as a vessel for possession."

"Possession by what?" Devon asked.

"A spirit, a demon, a traveler from another plane, I am not sure," Ascher admitted. "But I would ask that you please notify me if you see anything else, or if something draws your friend's particular interest. I am not keen to have fools practicing such arts in my home. Also, there is no need for you to pay for your assistant out of your own pocket, Mr. Amaris. I had stated before that you could bring on help, when and if you needed."

"I remember. But I was under the impression when you told me that you didn't expect anyone to take me up on my offer," Devon deadpanned.

Ascher shot him a sharp tooth grin. "You are absolutely correct, of course. But it is a large job. If this young man has impressed you and has enough backbone to work in the cemetery, then there is no reason I should object to him doing so." The glass paned door from the garden opened, and Jonas stepped through. "Now, if you will excuse me." Ascher turned to his valet. "Is it done?"

Devon took that opportunity to show himself out of the library. He made his way to the empty kitchen where he rinsed and left his cup near the sink before stepping out of the back door into the now gray day.

The lane was quiet as he walked along, save for the moaning wind. The fine fabric of his borrowed shirt did little to protect against its cold breath. The little phantom cat rode quietly on his shoulder, her tail only giving a hard twitch as they passed the spot where they had found Marie.

The cemetery gates looked to be locked when he passed by, but he stopped and checked to be sure. He could hear the ghosts on the other side of them, as restless as the wind was. He left them behind and headed up Nightingale, coatless and bare-headed. His mind circled back through the day's events to the last words Ascher had said. It came to him then, that when the man said he was unhappy with fools practicing such arts in his home, he was including all of Ashwood in what he considered his. Devon felt that would be a detail he would do best to remember.

CHAPTER XVI

Revelations and Fine Tobacco

It was early evening by the time Devon made it home. He stepped into the parlor to find Sara and Liam sitting on the settee, shoulder to shoulder, a book held between the two of them. They were so intent on their lesson they never even noticed when he came in the door. Mrs. Madison was also in the parlor, sitting in a chair near the window. She had a book in her hand as well, though Devon doubted that she was reading it. It seemed that she was more intent on watching Sara and Liam, her face set in a soft expression that spoke of happy memories. She looked over and smiled at him. He smiled back, and quietly left Liam and Sara to their lesson.

His next stop was the kitchen which was blessedly warm, a welcome contrast to the increasingly dirty weather outside. Mrs. O'Toole was there, putting biscuits in the oven. An enormous pot of what smelled like beef stew simmered on the stove top.

"Good evening, Mr. Amaris. That must have been some bitter weather to have had to walk through," Mrs. O'Toole commented as she bustled by. "Would you like a cup of coffee?"

"I would love one, Mrs. O'Toole," he said.

She reached overhead to the blue and white mugs that hung

from hooks there. Pulling one down, she filled it from the pot on the stove.

"Cream's over there, if you'd like," she said as she handed the cup to Devon.

He thanked her and took a sip from the cup, not bothering with the cream. Then he had a thought. "Mrs. O'Toole, is there enough supper to set an extra plate this evening?" he asked. "In fact, I would like to adjust our board to include at least two extra meals a day if I could, for my assistant."

"That'll be no problem," the woman answered. "And we can take it out in trade if you want. It'll be cheaper for me to feed an extra mouth than to hire someone for the repairs around here. If you and the young man are agreeable to that?"

"Perfectly agreeable," Devon replied.

He took his coffee to a small sitting room where the boarding house's telephone was to make good on his promise to call his mother.

The conversation was not as long as he had expected it to be. Unfortunately, it suffered from the same difficulties as his phone conversation from the night before. There was only so much that Devon could say openly over the phone. Operators were not supposed to listen to conversations, but that did not guarantee they didn't.

Many of the things he wished to speak about, the dreams and the apparition that had attached herself to him and Sara, he could only hint at, and it was frustrating in the extreme.

Still, there were a few things he could share safely. He was able to explain to them more about who Lady Anasztaizia Károlyi was and what she was to himself and Sara. He was also able to tell them about Kristoph Hegdus and the very strong possibility that a letter from him might arrive there any day now, if it had not already. He also mentioned Liam and the reading lessons which were even now taking place in the parlor down the hall.

He did not tell them about Marie, or the events that followed the finding of her. He had yet to post the letter he had written that morning, so there was still time to add another page.

It was good to hear the voices of his mother and father, and he found his mood lighter by the time he had hung up the line.

When he finally walked back into the parlor, he found two sets of eyes on him, one green and the other gray-blue.

"Devon, you're home!" his sister cried.

"I've been home for a while, pet" he chuckled. The nightmares of the day vanished for good in the light of his sister's smile and the general feeling of homecoming that was steeped in the very wood of Mrs. O'Toole's. "You were just too busy to notice."

A range of emotions crossed her face, including the one that told him she wanted to stick her tongue out at him. But in the end, it was pride that won out.

"Come see how far we've gotten!" she exclaimed, her cheeks pink with her excitement.

"Actually, I believe that it is time you came to dinner," he said. "You as well Liam, if you want."

Sara beamed at him. She closed the book and set it to the side and turned to Liam. "You will eat with us, won't you?" she asked.

Liam's stomach rumbled loud enough for even Devon to hear. "I don't think his stomach would let him say no, even if he was of a mind to," he observed.

"I think you're right," Liam agreed.

The three of them made their way to the dining room and served themselves from the sideboard. Afterwards, they took their plates and sat at one end of the table with Sara sitting in between himself and Liam. Devon noticed that Liam watched them closely as they ate. It dawned on him then that the boy might not have ever sat down to a dinner. He also noticed that Liam had been practical in how much he had served himself, not overloading his plate. Devon felt it was more than Liam trying not to be greedy, and it revealed a great deal about the boy's true circumstances.

184

Their association may have had a stormy start, but in the just under twenty-four hours that Devon had known Liam, he had been impressed by the boy's practicality and level-headedness. Especially under the extraordinary circumstances that he had been thrust into that afternoon. Though that stoicism begged the question, how much had Sara shared with him already?

After dinner, Devon went upstairs for his pipe and his coat, which Liam had apparently brought back with him from the cemetery where Devon had left it.

When he came back down, he went out onto the porch. Liam and Sara followed on his heels. The weather still left something to be desired, but at least the rain had let up. No one else joined them, which was a good thing since the conversation that they were about to have was not one for all ears.

"How is Marie?" Liam asked as soon as he and Sara were settled in on one of the porch's long benches.

"She was better than she was, last I saw her," Devon answered. "Though it seems she will be staying up at Ascher House for a bit. Nathan, Ascher's steward, told us that she only has a father, who apparently isn't much of one, to speak for her. Do you know anyone else who might know her? Friends or acquaintances?"

"I think she has an aunt who lives on one of the flower streets," Liam replied. "She also works for a widow up on High Street sometimes, but I don't know the widow's name. I can't think of anyone else off-hand. Did she tell you what happened to her?"

"She hasn't spoken yet that I know of," Devon answered.

"So you don't know what happened?"

There was no trace of accusation in Liam's question, but there was a definite concern. Devon took his pipe out of his pocket. He studied the young man across from him as he packed the bowl with tobacco, and contemplated what to tell him. The truth for sure. But how much of it? Now, that was the question. That question joined the other one on Devon's mind, of just how much had his sister already shared with Liam.

"We don't," Devon said. It was the only safe answer to give, and it was true, Ascher's speculations about possession aside.

Sara spoke up. "Liam told me some of what happened on the way home from school. He mentioned that he had seen her talking with two High Street men last night as you were both walking to the cemetery."

"Was that odd?" Devon asked Liam.

"Odd enough to catch my eye," Liam replied. "Marie isn't a working girl. Though she isn't above a bit of flirting, if she thinks it might get her something."

Devon struck a match and lit his pipe. Now that Liam had mentioned it, he remembered seeing him take notice of the girl and the two men that were with her. Unfortunately, their faces had been in shadow, so he wouldn't know them even if he were to meet them again.

"There was more to it than just a girl being taken advantage of, wasn't there?" Sara asked.

"There was," he admitted. "A good bit more. Though we know nothing for certain."

The two sitting across from him did not say anything else, but their expressions did. Sara looked as though she wanted to ask him a lot more questions, but was not sure she should. While Liam's face said he had come to some conclusions that he was being careful to keep to himself. Neither seemed to want to share what it was they were thinking. To be fair, Devon had not been entirely forthcoming either, had he?

"Well, I'm supposed to be at Berk's now, sweeping up," Liam said, standing up from his seat. "Thank you for the lesson and the food. I'll see you in the morning?"

"Definitely!" Sara answered.

"What about me?" Devon asked. "Will I be seeing you in the morning?"

Liam grinned at him. "Well, you've hired me, haven't you?"

Devon grinned back. He had not been sure if Liam would return

186

after all that had happened. He was even more surprised that the boy was heading out to another job. But he supposed even with the prospect of a steady income, money was hard to turn down. And Liam certainly looked like he was in need of a steady income, of food if nothing else. Which reminded him…

"Can you be here a little early tomorrow?"

"How early?" Liam asked.

"About an hour or so," Devon said.

"I can be here."

"Good, and here," Devon took off his own coat and handed it to Liam. "It's going to rain again. You can bring it back with you in the morning."

Liam hesitated.

"Take it, *mon fils*," a familiar voice said from thin air. Devon now had a name to put to that voice, Marguerite. "Pride won't keep you warm."

"Go ahead, Liam. Pride won't keep you warm," Sara echoed, touching the boy's hand as she did so. Devon felt his eyebrows jump up into his hairline, though neither his sister nor Liam seemed to notice.

It was obvious that what Sara had said struck a chord with Liam. He reached out and accepted the coat from Devon.

"Thank you," he said as he slipped the coat on overtop of the one he was already wearing.

"That was kindly done," said Marguerite. "*Merci*."

"I'll see you early tomorrow," Devon reminded the boy as he started off down the steps, ignoring the ghost's offer of gratitude.

"See you tomorrow," Sara echoed.

Liam waved as he stepped down off the porch, but he noted how quickly those hands went back into the coat's pockets. Devon watched as his sister's eyes followed Liam out of sight, and his earlier thoughts returned to him.

"Pet, how much have you told Liam?" he asked. She glanced over at him sheepishly and he laughed.

"That much?" he said, doing his best to keep his tone light and free of the concern that this new revelation had brought with it.

"Dev, I know it seems foolish, but… oh I don't know! It isn't like I have explained everything to him. But he does know I can see Marguerite and that I can hear her," his sister admitted. "She wanted me to pass on a message and it was just after Liam had stepped in for me with Thomas. It seemed rude to not do so. Especially since, in a manner of speaking, she was the one who had brought him to my rescue."

Devon went over to sit next to her. His sister was such a good egg. He put his arm around her shoulder and kissed her on the top of her head.

"Don't worry pet. If he fails you, I will bury him in the orange grove," he promised her.

"You will do no such thing!" she declared and pinched him for good measure. He laughed, and assured her he was joking. Which was the truth, mostly.

Sara headed inside to study shortly thereafter. Devon searched around in his pocket for another match as he watched a dark-coated figure slip in through the courtyard gate.

"Is it too late?" Kristoph asked as he stepped up onto the porch.

"Not at all," Devon replied, finally finding a match. He struck it against his shoe. The flame flared brightly in the dark as he relit his pipe, which had gone cold.

Kristoph went over to lean on the nearest porch post, in the very same spot that Devon had vacated only a short time before. He seemed much more somber than Devon had come to expect.

"So, I guess that boy gave you satisfactory answers last night, since he is still walking around and not buried somewhere in Ascher's cemetery," the schoolmaster observed, taking out a thin cigarette from his pocket. He leaned forward to take advantage of Devon's still lit match. "I saw him on my way here."

"He did," Devon agreed, drawing on his own pipe. The air filled with the fragrant smell of pipe tobacco and the sweet-sharp scent of Kristoph's cigarette. "What's more, I offered him a job."

"Whatever for?" Kristoph exclaimed.

"At first, because it seemed a good way to keep track of him," Devon admitted honestly. "It is obvious that he and Sara have already formed some sort of friendship. That is not an easy thing for her to do, as I am sure you have guessed. Not with the living at least. That is one reason I am reluctant to interfere."

"That is understandable," the man reasoned, though he sounded a little dubious of Devon's logic. "But is he trustworthy?"

"I can tell that you have doubts," Devon consented. "Any I might have had have since disappeared. Especially after seeing him handle himself today."

"Did something happen today?" Kristoph asked on an exhalation of spice and tobacco.

So Devon told the schoolmaster everything that had happened from when they had found Marie in the ditch to him leaving Ascher house. And since Kristoph was already familiar with such things, he didn't have to hold anything back or couch it in mundane terms. It was a refreshing change.

"And the boy was there for all of it?" Kristoph asked.

"No, not all of it," Devon confessed. "But he was cool-headed for what he was there for."

"A thin reason to give him such high regard," Kristoph quipped.

"Does your dislike for him stem from the fact that he had something to say about your mistress, Kristoph, or is there another reason I don't know about?" Devon asked, deciding to put the schoolmaster on the spot and see what happened.

The man scoffed merrily. "Well if you are going to admonish me like that, you might as well call me Kris," he said. "And I can't deny that there is something to what you say. The uninitiated rarely understand what it is they are witnessing. So, they make erroneous assumptions that often cause trouble for themselves or others."

"Is that what he has done then, drawn the wrong conclusion?" Devon asked. "Do you know what it was that he saw, or thinks he saw?"

"No, I am not entirely sure what it was that he thinks he saw," Kristoph admitted. "I don't know the man he is talking about. It could be that my benefactress was involved in some fashion. She often goes to the Bottoms to find willing partners."

"Should I assume that when you say 'partners' you are not strictly speaking about bed partners?" Devon surmised.

Kristoph nodded. "You are correct. I have mentioned before that she is a powerful practitioner. That power comes from others' desires. The deeper, more secret the desire, the more that comes from its fulfillment. She removes their inhibitions, excites them to act on those desires. But I promise you she is careful to make sure that all parties are willing."

"That sounds like it has the possibility of bringing trouble after the fact," Devon guessed.

"It could," Kristoph agreed. "But the power she gains allows her to influence the mind. To the people involved, the events are never quite real, more like waking dreams or fantasies. Later, when all is said and done, they only remember them in flashes or moments of déjà vu."

"So no harm is done to them physically?" Devon asked.

"Oh, I am sure some are a little sore," Kristoph said, a grin playing about his lips. "But there is never any lasting physical harm, and their minds are intact, save for the vagueness of those memories. There has even been some debate in certain academic circles that helping to alleviate such repressed emotions can be beneficial to a person."

The man paused to take a long, thoughtful draw off his cigarette, filling the air again with the smell of cloves, exotic spices and fine tobacco. When he exhaled, all his wry amusement from the moment before had gone.

"My questioning of that young man's intentions aside, I have to say I find the story you have just told me extremely concerning.

The girl you mentioned, do you know what happened to put her in such a state?"

"Ascher suspects it was a possession, or an attempted one at least," Devon replied, sharing with the schoolmaster the suspicions that he had been unwilling to share with Sara and Liam. "But I am not very knowledgeable when it comes to ritual magick. I am fairly certain that it was not a willing sacrifice."

Devon knew that there were those who willingly summoned creatures from other planes, making bargains with them in the hopes of gaining knowledge or power. According to his father, it was a risky, foolhardy business at best. At worst, it was disastrous.

"So you feel that it was not of her own doing?" Kristoph concluded. "I am afraid of what that might mean. And you don't feel that Ascher could have been involved? Perhaps cleaning up a failed ritual of his own?"

The idea had never occurred to Devon. But now that the question had been put to him, he was fairly confident of his answer.

"I don't believe so," he said. "If anything, I was of the impression that he took it as an intrusion." More than a simple intrusion, if Devon were to guess. The man had been angry, deeply angry as a matter of fact. "Have you met him? Ascher, I mean."

"No, though he and my benefactress move in the same circles, they have had little interaction with each other. Personally, I have only seen him at a distance," admitted Kristoph. "He seems a bit of a peacock to me."

Devon found Kristoph's statement amusing. "Does that factor into your regard for him?" he asked, completely willing to believe that it might, given the schoolmaster's own propensity towards neat but understated attire.

"Maybe," the schoolmaster answered in all seriousness. "He dresses in the latest fashion, but it seems an afterthought. Something done because it is expected rather than a natural inclination. It makes him appear frivolous when he is not. It makes me wonder why he would take the pains to appear so."

191

"For having only seen him at a distance, you have made a bit of a study of him," Devon pointed out.

"I have often found that it is important to note such things," Kristoph said.

That statement among others the schoolmaster had made in the past had Devon questioning exactly what role Kristoph fulfilled in his benefactress's household. It also made him question Kristoph's motivations. How much of what he did was driven by his own wishes, and how much by those of Lady Károlyi?

As for the lady herself, Devon felt sure he now knew who the darker power driven by desire in Aunt Ruth's seeing was.

He took a long draw on his pipe. One thing was for sure, he was glad he had not had time yet to post the letter he had written that morning because it looked as though it was about to get a great deal longer.

Sara woke early the next morning. Her eyes refused to close again, and if she was honest with herself, that probably had a lot to do with the prospect of Liam's arriving early. She was fairly certain that she knew the reason why Devon had asked him to, but of course she was not absolutely sure that she was correct. Her stomach would not stop doing cartwheels while she washed and dressed, which was silly. It was only Liam, after all.

Gathering up her things for school, she made her way down the stairs. She found Mrs. Madison waiting for her on the first landing with a candle in hand and a bundle sitting at her feet. Jeffery was at her side, as always. To Sara's eyes, he was the brightest thing there, undimmed by the shadows around them.

Mrs. Madison greeted her in a quiet voice. "Good morning. Do you have a moment to spare?"

"Of course," Sara replied, taking care to keep her voice low as well, so as to not disturb the other lodgers.

"I don't really have a need for these anymore," the woman said, the meager light from her candle softening the sadness in her kind eyes. "I thought that perhaps the young man who walks you to school could use them."

Sara looked down at the lumpy bundle at Mrs. Madison's feet. It was of a good-size and looked to be held together by a blanket.

"They are just some old clothes of mine that she hasn't yet been able to bring herself to give away," said the ghost of the young man standing beside her. His eyes looked sad as well, but it was an old sadness. And perhaps it was just wishful thinking, but Sara thought she now saw a bit of hope there as well. "It was hard for her, but it will be better now."

"Thank you! That is very kind of you… I am sure he will be glad of them," Sara finished, almost having said 'very kind of you both'. The near slip came because she wanted so much to tell Mrs. Madison that she was not alone. But Sara knew things wouldn't end well if she did. It had always been a bad choice when she had done so in the past. Even with Liam, she often questioned whether she should have told him all that she had, and sometimes wondered if he truly believed her. Sara looked searchingly at Mrs. Madison's face. "Are you sure?"

"Yes," the woman said decisively, her face lightening as some of the sadness faded away. "He reminds me a bit of my Jefferey. In fact, the two of you often remind me of us when we were young."

"That is the first time she has spoken of me in years," the ghost said. A tiny wind tugged at Mrs. Madison's shawl as he put his arm around her.

Sara gave Mrs. Madison a hug, reaching out further than she needed to so that her hands passed through Jefferey. Unlike her brother, she could not touch spirits. But, she could, on occasion, allow them to touch the living through her.

She did not do it often; the dead almost always had a hard time letting go again. But she was willing to take a chance for Mrs. Madison and Jeffery's sake, and for the sake of the kindness they had both shown to her and Liam. So, for the first time in a very, very long while, Jefferey could hug his wife, even if it was only for a moment.

Sara stepped back. The sadness was gone from Mrs. Madison's face, and there was a peace in her eyes that hadn't been there before. The ghost beside her was a little fainter, but he smiled at Sara with such a look of gratitude that she nearly hugged them again.

"Thank you," she said. Putting her school things on top, she picked up the bundle and continued on down the back stairs.

When she reached the kitchen, she found Liam and Devon already sitting at the small breakfast table that stood at one end of the long room, a bowl of rice porridge in front of each of them. She smiled at her brother, very happy that her speculations had proven correct.

"Good morning, pet," Devon said in between sips of coffee. "What do you have there?"

"Good morning! They're for you, Liam. Mrs. Madison thought you might be able to use them," she said, placing the bundle in a corner, out of the way.

"Here you go, dear." Mrs. O'Toole handed her a small bowl filled with warm porridge.

Sara went over and sat down next to Devon, just as Liam was finishing up. She ate a spoonful of her breakfast as she watched Liam go over to where she had left the bundle. She gave a little hum of appreciation for the food. Mrs. O'Toole made her rice porridge sweet, with raisins and cinnamon. It was a lot like mama's rice pudding, only hot.

"Are you sure she wanted me to have all this?" Liam asked as he looked into the now open bundle. Sara nodded, her mouth full.

"If there is a sweater in there, you should probably put it on before we head out this morning," her brother said as he finished off his coffee. "The air is damp and the wind is colder for it."

Liam took off his jacket. His shirt seemed a lot thinner than Sara remembered. He pulled a sweater from the bundle and put it on over his shirt. She felt immensely better seeing him with warmer clothes. He pulled a jacket out of the bundle and a scarf as well. They were a touch too large and looked a little worn, but over all, they still had plenty of wear left in them. The scarf however, looked new and was of a very similar color to the shawl that Mrs. Madison had given her only two days ago. Sara felt her cheeks warm. It seemed that Marguerite wasn't the only one playing matchmaker. She glanced over at her brother and found him smirking at her from behind his coffee cup. She stuck her tongue out at him before she could stop herself.

His eyes sparkled mischievously as he asked, "Aren't you going to be late to school?"

A Letter from Home

A man stood on a stage above the people, telling them of wonders while their shining faces turned towards him like flowers to the sun. They called him a great man, a voice for all that was good and divine.

Not her though; she stood at the edge of the crowd, just another hound searching for scraps, watching as the face of the man on the stage folded in on itself again and again; a sickening kaleidoscope of darkness made flesh. But the people to whom the great man spoke could not see it. They cheered and clapped as he fed them sugared poison.

A small group of people stayed after all the others had left. They were the best of those who had come to see him, those with the noblest of intentions. They listened in rapture as the twisted malevolence spoke through the great man's mouth, appealing to their best natures. The sweet-sounding words he used dressed up the horrors they would do in the trappings of goodness. She knew the darkness would soon take root in their golden hearts. And all the while, the abomination squatted inside the great man like a toad, gaining power from each unwilling sacrifice, leaving the soul of the man whose body it inhabited to suffer the destruction that came with such sacrifices.

She laid her head down on her paws. She was a patient hunter, she would bring this creature to an end, even if she had to follow it down through the ages.

Devon woke to a quiet rapping on his door.

"Dev, are you feeling unwell?" Sara's concerned voice asked from the other side.

"Everything is fine, pet," he reassured her. Glancing over at the nickel alarm clock on his nightstand, he suddenly understood why Sara was concerned. "I just overslept. Could you tell Liam that I'll be along a little later? He knows where everything is and what needs to be done."

"Of course, Dev." She answered, then gave a mischievous giggle. "It serves you right for staying out so late last night!"

Devon listened to his sister's footsteps retreat down the hall. He felt the hound's head disappear from where it had been resting on his belly, no doubt to follow Sara.

He had met Kristoph at Gerard's last night, and they had ended up staying out much later than was his usual. But he did not think that was the reason for this morning's laziness.

Last night's dream had held him close, closer than any of the others. He had been her and she had been him. They were her memories, not his. He understood that with the instant clarity that always comes when waking from a dream. That perfect understanding that fades even as one scrabbles to hold on to it. Even as it was now slipping away from him with the brightening morning sun.

There was a letter waiting for Devon when he returned home that Friday evening. The long-awaited reply to the one he had posted to his parents a little over two weeks ago. He washed up, then took it into the parlor to read while he waited for dinner. The now familiar sight of Sara and Liam, their heads tucked in together over the top of a book, greeted him.

Devon nodded to Mrs. Madison who sat with her tatting in the corner. He made his way over to the large wing-back chair nearest to the wall sconce. Turning the flame up slightly, he sat down and opened the letter.

It was an extremely long missive, but a fairly innocuous letter as letters went. His father had written about the harvest and how things were with only himself and their mother rattling around in the house. Of how much they missed him and Sara, and hoped that they were well. All the things one would expect in a letter sent from a loving father to the children who were far away and whom he missed. All of which was true beyond a shadow of a doubt.

But if one knew how to read between the lines, quite literally in some cases, they would have read a different letter entirely.

Dear son,

Yes, of course I am familiar with Serus Ascher. We have corresponded many times over the years.

As to your question, there are a few details that I am unwilling to share about his nature unless things are truly dire, out of respect for his privacy. But I feel comfortable in telling you that he walks the path of the Úlfhéðnar. That is the old Norse name for it. In Old Frankish it is wariwulf, and in Old English werwulf. Although there are some differences in nuance, they all share certain key aspects. He is a strong practitioner. In fact, I would even go so far as to call him an adept. I have consulted with him about ancestral magick and necromancy many times. In both areas, his knowledge often exceeds my own.

One word of caution, he is dedicated to the protection of that which he feels is his to protect, namely family and the town which you are in. That motivation, to some extent, will always be forefront in his mind in whatever decisions he makes. And I can't say whether you and Sara would fall within what he considers his to protect or not. That does not make him an uncaring man, nor a cruel one, but do not doubt that it will always be his own goals which drive him.

I am curious to know more about this benefactress of the schoolmaster's. Magick that feeds on the desires of others sounds like a form of vampirism. A word of caution, and I only say this because of the dreams you have mentioned, many of the tales of succubi grew from practitioners of such arts using dreams to grow their power. It is still a willing sacrifice on the part of the dreamer, but can lead to addiction which some practitioners argue is an unwilling sacrifice.

However, your mother is of the mind that your dreams may be memories and is something akin to if Sara were to channel the dead directly. In short, she agrees with your Aunt Ruth that you are being haunted. Her fears here are less than my sister's though. She says to remind you that on any plane, your power over the dead is undiminished.

Now about this apparition you mentioned, your guardian as you call it. This is a complete enigma to me. I have never come across anything in my studies to date that matches all that you have told me about it. Your Aunt Ruth's suggestion that it might be a servitor or some other such creature from a different plane is an interesting one. However, given yours and Sara's interactions with it, there is a strong argument that it, at the very least, touches the same plane as the dead. Unless I am mistaken, neither you nor your sister have ever seen angels or demons or fairies or any of the other creatures that come from the different planes. However, that may be because of a lack of opportunity, so I am not completely discounting the possibility.

From all that you have shared with me about the friends both you and Sara have made, (and by the way, I have had a letter from Kristoph Hegdus) I can understand your reluctance to leave Ashwood. But your mother and I are very concerned after what you shared with us about that girl's near possession (although on my part, I will admit to there being some curiosity as well). I will be reaching out to Serus with many of my own questions and promised your mother I would seek his reassurance of yours and Sara's safety in the same missive.

Despite that promise, I have still had a devil of a time trying to convince her that there is no need yet for us to go harrying off to Ashwood on the next train. I know you to be a practical man and we trust in your judgment. But keep in mind son, you can always come home and those that are important to you or your sister will be welcome here as well, always.

Take care, and give our love to Sara.

Fondest regards,

Your father

Devon leaned back in the chair, his hands and the letter they held coming to rest in his lap. The last part, both hidden and plain, had been the same. And it was not hard for him to picture his mother packing her trunks, fully intent on being on the next train south while his father calmly stated all the reasons why it would be best to wait.

A chill tightened his belly at the thought of his parents coming to Ashwood. As much as Devon would love to see them, he felt better knowing they were back home, safe.

CHAPTER XVIII

Rumors

The gentle scratch of the broom on the floorboards was the only sound to be heard that early on a Sunday morning. Liam steadily swept the front porch of Miss Rose's as his warm breath steamed out like smoke into the air around him. The night before had been too cold to stay in the shed. So, he had offered to do some work around the brothel in exchange for a warm spot to sleep, which Miss Rose was perfectly amiable to.

It was still finger-achingly cold an hour or so later when Miss Rose's doves started to drift down, sleepy eyed and yawning. Priscilla walked over to where he now knelt, polishing the railing with lemon oil and beeswax, and bent over to kiss him on the top of his head.

"Good morning, love," she said, as she went to sit at one of the tables, a steaming cup of coffee in hand.

Rachel had come out on her heels, also cradling a warm cup in her hands. "Joy of joys, our working man has come to keep us company," she quipped, stopping to ruffle his hair as she walked past.

Most of Miss Rose's doves had known him since he was young. But Priscilla and Rachel had been good friends of his mother, and had known him his whole life.

The other doves drifted by, murmuring sleepy good mornings. They settled into chairs and around small tables, steam wreathing their faces as they gently blew at their cups. Simon and Simone were the last ones to come out, Simone had two cups in her hands.

"Did you stay warm last night?" she asked, setting one of the cups down next to him.

"Of course he did," Simon groused as his twin came to sit next to him. "Took up nearly half the bed, didn't he?"

Liam had also known the twins since he was young. He would have bet money that Miss Rose had had him bunk with Simon in the hopes that he would reconsider taking her up on her offer to do more than odd jobs. Her plan might have backfired on her there. Simon was as beautiful and exotic as his sister and he had made it clear last night that Liam had better keep his job with the cemetery man however he could, because working with the dead beat working with the living any day. Life had not been easy for Simon.

"I don't know why you're complaining, you took all the covers," Liam reminded him. He stood up from where he had been working. Taking his coffee, he went over to lean against the porch railing across from where everyone was sitting.

"You wouldn't have needed covers if you had stayed with me," Charlotte, one of the newer girls, smiled wickedly over at him. Rachel reached out and smacked her in the back of the head.

"Our young man is respectable now! And I would have thought you had your hands full enough with your "Mr. Saturday" last night."

Charlotte's carefully plucked eyebrows drew together. "Maybe I needed someone 'respectable' to follow after him," she shivered, pulling her robe closer.

"I thought you liked him? Didn't you say he was good to you?" The concern in Priscilla's voice was clear to Liam.

"He was! Always a gentleman, till it was time not to be," Charlotte giggled, then sobered. "But he's not been the same lately."

"He's not the only one," Simone commented into her coffee while many of the others nodded their heads in agreement.

"And it's not just here, either," one of the other new girls, Dolly, pointed out.

"What do you mean?" Liam asked, finally speaking up from where he stood.

"I was talking to some of the girls downstreet, and they were telling me that a lot more of the upstreet men have been coming down their way. Some of our own regulars, even."

"Bragging, were they?" Simon grimaced. "That won't make Miss Rose happy."

"They weren't bragging. They were scared," Dolly corrected. "We all have some that likes it different, that's why they come to us instead of eating at home, right? But lately their games have got more of an edge of mean to them. At least here, Miss Rose only allows things to go so far. But you know how it is down-street, anything goes as long as they pay for any damage they do. Well, lately there has been a lot of damage. And I've even heard some of the girls have been paid for and taken."

"I've heard something about that too," Priscilla admitted. "When I was over at the tobacconist's to pick up our order. Nancy, one of the girls who works there, was telling me that they found a girl behind their shop. She was gibbering and fitting, then suddenly she stopped and just stared at them slack-jawed. I hear one of the rich ladies offered charity and they put her in one of those houses for troubled women."

Liam didn't let it show, but a sinking feeling had begun in the pit of his stomach. The memory of Marie's face when they first found her thrust itself into his mind in vivid detail.

"You say there's been a lot more High Street men down here? Have any of you seen or heard if one of them was from the old family?" He asked, thinking of Ascher walking past the silent angels in his aubergine coat.

"There's only one Ascher in town now," Rachel pointed out, "and you work for him."

"Really?" Charlotte said, and Liam could see the tell-tale gleam in her eye. The aspirations of a working girl who hoped to get to know a rich and powerful man. "What does he look like?"

"Dark hair, pale green eyes," Liam described, bristling a little at the memory of those eyes shining at him from the shadows of a hat brim.

Simon laughed. "You describing him or yourself? Should we start calling you Mr. Ascher now?"

That set all the others, even Priscilla, to teasing him. Which he took without minding much, but something about it all sent goosebumps across his skin. Maybe it was just his *maman* telling him it was time to go, since Miss Rose had come out and was eyeing him speculatively. He began to gather up the rags and broom he had been using to clean.

"You have another job to go to?" Simon asked, giving him the excuse he needed to leave.

"I do," he said, which was half-true as he could probably find more work today if he wanted to.

"If you need to stay here again tonight, love, you are more than welcome to," Miss Rose told him.

"Thank you," he said, giving her cheek a kiss as he walked past on his way to bring the rags back to the kitchen. He decided right then and there that it would be a bad idea to come back here and sleep, no matter how cold it got tonight.

"Liam," Priscilla called after him. He stopped to look back at her. "You be careful too," she said and he could tell she was worried. "It's not only girls who have gone missing."

He left soon after that, tucking his hands into the pockets of the new coat Sara had given to him from Mrs. Madison. He was glad he had it. Whatever bit of sunshine that had been out that morning was gone and he could feel the rain coming in off the ocean. It would be a cold rain when it fell.

It would also be another cold night, he thought. And it might be worth him using a little of the money he had been paid to actually rent a warm place to stay. He had been working with Devon for two weeks now, as well as doing odd jobs here and there. And, he had been getting a lot of his meals at the boarding house, so he had a little money set to the side. Miss Rose had always been good to him, but the calculation he had seen in her eyes this morning wasn't something that was safe to ignore.

He turned and headed towards the cemetery. His clothes and things he kept in the shed where he usually slept, but his money he left in a safer place.

When he reached the gates, he fished out the key that Devon had given him. The well-oiled lock turned easily enough. But when he made to push them open, the wind, in a fit of pique, tried to snatch it from his hands. The shriek the hinges gave made his heart jump, but he carefully kept hold of the gate as he went through.

The wind settled a little once he was inside and headed towards the caretaker's shed. It was still gusty enough to send the dead oak leaves skittering across his path and shake the branches overhead ominously.

Unsurprisingly, he saw no one in the time it took him to reach the shed. Not that he felt like he was alone. That was one thing he'd had to get used to, working in the old family's cemetery. No matter what his eyes told him, his gut insisted that he was not the only one here.

When he reached the shed, he used the same key to open the door there. He kept his money in a box just under the sill where they kept the sharpening kit for the tools. Devon knew it was there, of course. But Liam wasn't worried about that, he trusted Devon. Moreover, he found it was a bad choice to put too much stock in money. Those who had it always lost it, and it seemed that those who worried about it lost it even faster. He couldn't deny it was a good thing to have at the moment, though.

Liam carefully counted out about half the coins he had in there. Leaving the rest where they were, he slid the box back into place under the sill, glancing up through the window out of habit. As fate would have it, that was the exact moment when Ascher was walking by. Liam did not know how the man could have seen him through the shed's tiny window, but he must have, because he was looking straight at Liam when he nodded his head in greeting.

The man was uncanny. Always seeming to know where Liam was no matter what, just like on Halloween. It got Liam's back up then, the same way it was doing now. But why it did was a mystery to him. Such things didn't usually bother him, but something about Ascher got his hackles up.

The man might have noticed him, but apparently, he wasn't concerned enough to come over and see what Liam was doing in the cemetery on a Sunday because he continued on his way without breaking stride.

Liam turned his mind back to the task that had brought him there. He tucked the money he was taking away in his pocket, then left the shed, locking up behind him. When he stepped out onto the path, he looked back in the direction from which Ascher had come. Curiosity pricked at him, and he had an urge to follow those steps back to where they had started. But, the creak of the branches in the rising wind and the gray sky above were enough to convince him it would be a poor choice on his part. That didn't mean he wasn't still curious.

Leaving the mystery for later, he made his way out of the cemetery, and locked the gate behind him.

He had only gone a short ways down Nightingale when the skies opened up. Over the lash of the storm, he heard someone call out his name. Looking around, he saw old Henry on his porch waving him over.

"Come on up here and get out of the rain before you get yourself sick," the old man called out from where he was sitting.

Liam was quick to follow his advice, taking the wooden steps onto the porch two at a time.

"Thank you, Mr. Henry," he said, carefully shaking the rain off his coat.

"I didn't think that you worked on Sunday," the old man said, eyeing him up and down. "A man can't work every day of the week,

206

you know, and I wouldn't think Mr. Amaris one to expect it."

"Mr. Amaris?" Liam smiled wryly. "That sounds like you're talking about some High Street man."

"Well, he owns it more than any High Street man I've ever met," the old man argued. "That one has power, no mistake in that. Mr. Ascher made a smart choice when he hired him to care for the old family's cemetery."

A strong gust of wind blew through just then, setting the metal charms that hung from the roof to clattering. The mist that came in onto the porch from the blowing rain settled like dew on the tightly curled cap of silver hair on old Henry's head.

"What do you mean, he has power?" Liam asked the old man curiously.

"I mean you can tell when someone's got the magick. The dead mind him, don't they? Nowadays it is safer in the cemetery then outside of it." The old man levered himself up out of the chair. "Let's get out of this wet. Come on in, and get dry. Too cold out here for my old bones anyway."

Liam followed him inside the door, through the sitting room and into the kitchen. No one could say anything about the tenet houses the Ascher family provided. They all had a stove and running water with an outhouse around the back. Which was more than could be said for many of the homes in the Bottoms.

"Hang your coat over there to dry. There's still some coffee in the pot on the stove if you want it," Henry said as he went to sit down in a chair at the kitchen table. "Did you hear about Silas Tighe disappearing?"

Liam shook his head as he took old Henry up on his offer, gesturing to the pot to see if his host wanted coffee as well.

"Sure, pour me one. Thank you," Henry said as he took the proffered cup. "Yep, Silas was gone for a good long while and everyone just thought he'd gone off on a bend, as he has in the past. His youngest brother was left caring for their old mother on his own. Then after about a week he up and comes back. But he's different. Doesn't speak a word now and he'll do whatever you tell him but no more. And you know that wasn't how he was before."

Liam nodded. He did know how the Tighe brothers were. Molly would hire them to keep the peace at her place sometimes. They were hard, but not bad men, though you wouldn't want to cross them if you could help it. Much like Big Ken. That brought to mind when he had last seen all three of them. Big Ken, propped up against a wall, eyes glazed with fear as he pumped empty air.

"And there's been more," old Henry continued. "Men and women just disappearing. Then coming back changed. There's bad things going on around here, shadow men and angry ghosts. You need to be careful. Where you sleeping nowadays?"

"I've been staying in that shed down near the river, just off Fallow Road. But last night I stayed at Miss Rose's."

Henry clucked his tongue in disapproval. "You're getting a little bit too old to be staying there if you don't want Madame Rose to start getting ideas," he worried.

"She already made me an offer," Liam said, taking a sip from the warm cup in his hands. "Just before I started working at the cemetery. I turned her down."

"Things being as they are, you turning her down may not be enough. She's better than most, but there's more Riverview and High Street men coming down here all the time. The things they're looking for ain't always the things that people are wanting to sell, but they have the money to get them anyway. Could be at some point that the offer is too good for her to pass up."

Given what he had heard this morning, Liam was inclined to give what old Henry had said more weight.

Seeing that Liam was taking his words to heart, the old man nodded his head in approval. "Tell you what, my niece Mabel comes most nights to make sure I'm taking care of myself. If you are interested, could be that she has a room to rent for a night or two. She works for the family as well, up at the Ascher House."

"She does?" Liam said. "You worked for them as well, didn't you, Mr. Henry?"

"Yep, for close to fifty years, up until the summer before last," the old man nodded. "They may be filled with vices, but they're good masters. I still have this place, and five dollars a week till I die."

"That is something," Liam said. "But you never worked for the current Ascher, did you?"

"No, no. In fact, the old Ascher, Tam Ascher, was gone for nearly three years before this one came last fall. I was surprised, I can tell you. Didn't think that there were any Aschers living outside of Ashwood. Family's always been here, and not often inclined to move anywhere else for very long."

"So where did this one come from, do you think?" Liam asked.

"Abroad is all anyone will say," Henry replied. "He brought his own valet with him when he came, which was a good thing since most of the staff there were long gone. There is only Nathan, who is steward up there, and my niece Mabel, who is the cook. Samuel takes care of the gardens, but that was it for the longest time. I hear they took on a young girl a couple of months back. How things change! Was a time when everyone down here in the Bottoms worked for the family."

Liam could hear the rain slowing down. "Thank you for the coffee, Mr. Henry. When should I come back if I want to ask Mabel about the room?"

"Around 6:30 this evening," Henry said. "If you're not here, I'll still let her know that you might be interested."

"I would greatly appreciate it," Liam said as he set his cup near the sink and took his coat down. "I'll see you then. Thank you, Mr. Henry."

Putting his coat on, Liam left the old man sitting in his kitchen, and made his way back through the small living room to the front door. When he stepped out onto the porch the sharp wind nearly took his breath away, but the rain had stopped just as he had thought. He pulled the collar of his coat up as he went down the steps. Walking along through the sandy mud of downstreet, he vowed that his next big purchase would be a sturdy pair of boots.

The day's weather had not improved much by the time Liam stepped up onto old Henry's porch at 6:30 p.m. sharp. He knocked on the door. When it opened, he found a broad-shouldered, female version of old Mr. Henry looking back at him.

"Are you Liam?" she asked, then continued on without waiting for an answer. "Come on in, Uncle Henry said you'd be coming by."

Liam followed her in, closing the door behind him.

"If you're hungry, there's plenty of leftover soup I brought down from the big house. Help yourself," she said, gesturing over to the pot on the stove while she brought a bowl over to the table where old Henry was sitting.

"Thank you for the offer, but I'm just stopping by on my way to Berk's," Liam said regretfully, though he could feel his stomach arguing with his backbone.

"Nonsense, you have time for a bowl before you go. No one's going to be out early in this dirty weather. Besides, aren't you working with the new caretaker now? I'd think that was plenty of work for you," she commented, brows drawing together to reflect her opinion on the matter as she ladled out a bowl of soup. Apparently, she did not plan on waiting for Liam to take her advice and serve himself.

"Now Mabel, leave the boy be," old Henry said between spoon-fuls of soup. "He's smart to not put all his eggs in one basket."

Mabel snorted softly as she sat down at the table herself. Liam dutifully sat down in front of the bowl she had put there for him. Clearly, the formidable woman had no plans on talking about renting him a room until he sat down to eat, and there was certainly no reason to turn food down twice.

"Uncle Henry says you're looking for a room," she said, lifting a spoon full of soup up from her own bowl.

"For a day or two, yes. Just while the weather is so cold," Liam replied, taking up his own spoon. It was a thin soup, but nearly too rich for him to eat nonetheless.

"My William has a job building that railroad they have coming down from up north," Mabel's skin flushed darker with pride. "So I have a room I can let you while he's away, thirty cents a day. Uncle Henry tells me you aren't one for trouble-making, but I feel the need to tell you all the same, no guests and no drinking in the room. And if you come in late, use the back door. Better yet, send someone round with a message so I know. I wouldn't want to brain you with a frying pan thinking you were a burglar. I get up early since I have to be up at the big house in time to have breakfast ready, so keep that in mind."

"I will," Liam promised, taking another spoonful of soup. "Ms. Mabel, how is Marie doing, if you don't mind me asking?"

The woman's brown cheeks paled as much as they could. "You heard about that did you?"

"I was with Devon when he found her," Liam explained.

"An evil business! But I can't fault Mr. Ascher for his treatment of her. Nothing improper about it, that I can promise you. He goes in and speaks to her in a language I don't want to understand and gives her things to hold, which seem to calm her some…" Mabel paused, and old Henry spoke up.

"So this Ascher's a magick man?" he asked. "It's been a long time since they've had one of those."

Even if Liam had been inclined to ask, he wouldn't have had a chance before Mabel had picked her tale back up.

"He certainly has some sort of hoodoo and I'd be perfectly happy to have no part of it ever again," Mabel nodded sharply. "But you asked how the girl was? She can feed and care for herself, but she don't unless you tell her. Mostly, she sits in a chair in the corner, watching the shadows on the walls, still as can be, like a mouse hoping the cat won't see it. It's plain creepy, though I don't hold anything against her for it."

"So she's staying there?" Liam asked.

"I asked Mr. Ascher the same thing," Mabel replied. "And he told me she'd be there for a little bit more yet, but that he knew a woman with an estate on the other side of the Blue Sedge River. She is a doctor who helps troubled women, if'n you'd believe it. Here, let me take that bowl," she said, reaching across to take Liam's now empty bowl. "I've been locking my doors with all the strange things going on down here, but I'll leave the back door open for you until midnight."

Her dismissal was clear, apparently believing all their business was done, thank you very much. Liam felt a smile tug at his lips despite feeling like a cat who had just been put out for the night.

CHAPTER XIX

Down at the Shallows

The ship tossed wildly on the raging sea. The waves rose higher than mountains, determined to break the ship to pieces in the troughs between them. There was a groan, then a shriek when the timbers finally gave way. The wood screamed out as it was torn loose from its fastenings...

Sara glanced up from the book she had been reading. She had thought for a moment that she had heard someone crying. But when she looked around the schoolyard, there was nothing amiss. None of the younger children appeared to be having any trouble or to be upset in any way. And Martha was playing happily right alongside them, although none of the other children knew it.

Her breath misted out in front of her and she shivered a little. The cloudless sky above was a clear, hard blue, and the air was brittle with cold. But the sun shone brightly, so it had been easy enough for her to find a warm spot in which to read during recess. No one else had come to sit near her, but that was not unusual.

She looked around again, frowning. It could have been her imagination, she supposed. Her attention turned back to the book in her lap and the overfull lunch pail next to her.

The night before, Mrs. O'Toole had cooked enough dinner for an army, even though most of the boarders had been away visiting family. And Mrs. Madison had surprised Sara by gifting her the book she was currently reading. It was an adventure story with pirates and shipwrecks, and Sara could not wait to add it to her reading lessons with Liam.

The sharp ringing of the bell called an end to recess. Sara packed up her new book and mostly untouched lunch, and headed back inside.

She thought she heard the crying again, just as she was settling into her afternoon work. But again, when she looked around, there was no one near her who seemed at all upset. Not even Martha, who had followed them in from recess and was now sitting in the one empty desk at the back of the room, wistfully watching the class as she sometimes did. Sara tried to turn her mind back to her work, but the sadness of it kept plucking at her ears like a child trying to get someone's attention. It was such a hopeless sound, not the same as someone would make if they had just skinned their knee. It was more like someone who was alone, lost and not sure how to find their way home. Everything else seemed to fade away, except the loneliness of that sound.

"Sara?"

She looked up with a start at her name, and was surprised to find Mr. Hegdus standing beside her desk.

"Is everything alright?" he asked.

Her cheeks were burning with embarrassment. She could not remember a single thing about the lesson that the schoolmaster had been teaching.

"I'm sorry Mr. Hegdus. I seemed to have missed the last part of what you were showing us on the board."

He looked down at her papers. "It appears you have missed a little more than that."

She saw then that she was the only one left in the room.

"Oh," she said bewildered, realizing she had lost the whole of the afternoon.

He did not admonish her for daydreaming as many others had before him, but he did look at her with concern. "Is there something amiss?" and she knew he was asking after more than her general well-being. "I can walk you home if you would like."

It was too bad that Liam and Mr. Hegdus so obviously did not get along. It left her a little out of sorts with how to answer and not offend or annoy someone. As she struggled with what to say, she was saved by Mrs. Lawrence's plea for help with a certain troublemaker caught in the act of vandalizing the school's fence.

With a quick farewell delivered to a distracted Mr. Hegdus, she slipped out of the schoolhouse. She saw Liam and Marguerite waiting for her in the lane.

"*Bonjour*," the ghost greeted her at the same time as her son said "afternoon."

The heartbreaking sound of soft weeping that had filled her day returned with a vengeance as Sara's feet turned towards home. The sound tugged at her, drawing her attention down Washboard Lane.

"Liam, I think I need to go this way," she said, turning to find that Marguerite was still standing next to her.

Liam looked back at her with a quizzical expression, but he immediately fell into step beside her as she started off down the dirt lane in the opposite direction from the way they usually went.

"So, why are we heading this way," he asked, once they had left the schoolhouse behind.

"I don't know!" she exclaimed, a little exasperated. "I know this road leads down to the river, but what is there?

"A lot of the factories are further down, the cattle yards and cartier are in that area as well. And the flower streets back up to the east side of the lane," Liam replied. "Are you looking for some place in particular?"

Sara shook her head. "I really don't know." She hesitated then plunged on, hoping against hope that she was not about to end her friendship by sharing more than she should. "All day I've heard what sounds like someone crying, but I don't know where it is coming from. Then, as soon as I stepped out onto the lane, my feet wanted to go in this direction."

Liam nodded his head at her explanation but said nothing. She did not know whether he was being supportive or thought her daft, and she was too afraid to ask.

It was not long before they reached the area where most of the factories and businesses were. The people there in the work yards went about their noisy business, mostly ignoring Sara and Liam as they walked along.

They passed the last drive leading up to the canners. The lane narrowed down considerably after that, becoming little more than a sandy path just wide enough for three people to walk abreast of each other. The noise of the factories died down quickly before they had gone much further, muffled by the woods lining the path.

Beneath the canopy of oak and pine everything quieted, even the sound of crying that had drawn Sara there. The hush was broken only by the soft strains of a song that the wind carried back to her. The haunting melody wept as the voice of Marguerite caressed its somber words.

"Follow me

Down the stream

Down to where the angels dream

There we'll rest

Uncounted days

Sleeping silently beneath their gaze.

There, down beside the stream,

Down, down, down where the angels dream…"

A shimmering through the trees heralded the end of the path they were on. Sara could see why it was called the shallows. The bed of white sand lay only a couple of feet below the aqua blue water that flowed over it. Marguerite stood there at the river's edge, looking out towards the bank of an island on the other side. The words of her song echoed softly beside Sara as Liam unknowingly sang a duet with his mother.

He too was looking out over the water towards the tree-covered island. Her gaze followed theirs to the lone figure of an angel. Wings up-swept and head bowed, it stood in silent vigil amongst the dark trunks of the trees.

A hand reached out and took hers, strong calloused fingers which trembled ever so slightly.

"Was this the place you needed to go?" Liam asked. His voice steady as always, though perhaps a little rougher than usual.

Sara felt the pull at her feet, urging her to the right, along the river bank. "No, I don't think so," she replied. "Why? What is on that island?"

Liam's lips were set in a grim line when he answered. "It's where the poor come to bury their dead when the churchyard won't have them."

"It's where my bones lie," Marguerite said from where she stood, still at the water's edge. "But don't tell him I told you so. It would be best if he thought you did not know his shame. He feels it too strongly."

Sara bit her lip to stop herself from asking what shame and why. Liam had turned his face away from her and she thought for a moment that he was crying. But when he turned back toward her, his eyes were dry.

"So which way?" he asked.

The tug at her feet grew stronger. She turned to the right where she saw a footpath running along the river bank. "I think, this is the way we need to go," she said, pointing in that direction.

"Then that's the way we go," Liam smiled over at her.

She gave in to the urge and started down the path. Her hand, still linked with Liam's, pulled him along with her.

"Do you know where this path leads?" she asked.

Liam shook his head. "I've always been a little too busy to go exploring this way." Though Sara wondered if that lack had more to do with avoiding the sight of the dark island in the middle of the river than a lack of time.

The woods were sparse on the one side, with only the occasional tree between them and the water. On the other side of the path, it was a different story. The branches of the live oaks there were as thick as the trunks of most trees. Their fissured bark was bearded in Spanish moss and little ferns. Palmetto and wax myrtle filled in the space beneath them.

An ominous weight pressed down on Sara, and she shivered. Her good sense was telling her to leave this place. But the crying was just up ahead, and her feet weren't listening to her good sense.

The path came to an end at a set of stairs. They led up to the porch of a house built atop oyster shell pilings and tucked back beneath the oaks. Gray tendrils of Spanish moss reached down to brush across the cypress shingles of its roof. Its windows were black pits staring out from its rotting walls. It might have been a pleasant house once, but it was dead now; just like the little girl sitting on its steps.

Sara would have gone over to her, despite the feeling that clung to the house, if Marguerite had not placed herself in her path, arms outstretched. She stopped short of the ghost, unwilling to be so rude as to walk through her on purpose.

"*Non, non ma Cherie,* there is a wrongness to that place. You should not go anywhere near it."

The warm hand holding hers also seemed to become firmer, anchoring her to the spot at the end of the path.

"I don't think you should go there," Liam said, echoing his mother's good sense.

"Listen to him," Marguerite urged, and Sara could hear the fear in her voice.

It was hard, because the little girl was crying and Sara felt a need to go over and comfort her. But she could not deny the odd sense of unease underlying that desire to console. Part of it came from the fact that the ghost never once looked in Sara's direction. Usually, the dead were quick to notice her. But it seemed as if this one did not even know she was here, and that was extremely unnerving.

"Is someone there?" Liam asked.

Sara nodded. "But I think there is something wrong. She doesn't seem to see me."

The girl's crying slowed to a sniffle. She lifted her head up and looked around; her silver eyes brilliant against the ebony skin of her face.

"Is someone there?" she called out softly, as though she wasn't sure if she wanted someone to answer.

"We're here," Sara replied, quelling the urge to step closer.

"Where? I can't see you in the darkness."

Sara stayed mum. She didn't want to frighten the girl by asking what darkness because it was obvious the ghost was seeing something she herself couldn't.

"Are you still there?" The little girl called out.

"We are. Can you leave this place? Just stand up and walk towards my voice." Sara asked, hoping against hope.

"No! I'm stuck like a lizard on tar paper."

"Did something happen to you here?" Sara asked. She had heard spirits could get stuck in a place, if their ties to it were strong enough.

"No, this place means nothing to me," the girl hiccupped. "But it won't let me go!"

"Sara, I can't hear but half this conversation," Liam whispered softly next to her. "But maybe it would be a good idea to get your brother."

"Yes! That is a fine suggestion, *mon fils*," Marguerite agreed.

"I don't want to leave her," Sara protested, keeping her voice low as well.

"I will stay," Marguerite said, then turned to face the little girl on the steps. "Now, now, *ma belle*. There is no need for tears. My son and his sweetheart are going to find someone to help you, and I will stay to talk with you. *Que dis-tu?*"

It was a measure of how upset Sara was that she did not even blush at Marguerite's proclamation.

"Your mother offered to stay," she told Liam, turning quickly and practically pulling him back down the path. "I agree with you, we should get Dev. Do you know the way to Ascher cemetery from here?"

"Sure, Fallow Road runs right into Washboard Lane. That'll take us straight to the cemetery."

Once they reached the spot where the two roads met, they picked up their heels and ran.

Devon stood in front of the forgotten cracker house, hand in hand with his sister. He could plainly see the little girl who sat there. At his feet, the white cat waited, alert and bushy tailed.

"It's fine, pet. You won't need to go any closer with me," he said.

"I don't mind Devon," Sara insisted.

Liam's frown and his mother's disembodied voice saying an emphatic "Absolutely not" would have made Devon laugh had the situation been different. But he could feel the sucking pull of the place, and he did not want his sister anywhere near it.

"I know," he said, squeezing her hand gently before letting go.

Devon felt the familiar weight of the white cat settle on his shoulder as he walked up to the porch steps. He stopped in front of where he had seen the young girl sitting, empty though it now was to his sight. Even without being able to see her, he could feel she was there, like when you close your eyes but you still know when someone walks close to you.

"I'm told a darkness is making it hard for you to see, but can you see me enough to take my hand?" he asked, holding out his hand.

"How can I not see you! You're bright as the sun," the little girl answered, and Devon felt her hand come to rest in his. "Are you the Reaper come to take me away?"

"I'm not the Reaper, but I'll take you from this place if you want to go."

"I want to, but I don't think I can," the little girl's voice shook.

"I'll help you then." Devon bent down and felt little stick-like arms come up around his neck. He lifted her and immediately felt the pull of the place enveloped him, unrelenting as a riptide dragging them out to sea.

He stood up against the current, refusing to give. A growl of warning sounded near his ear, but he knew it was not meant for him. The familiar weight sitting on his shoulder grew a hundredfold, but it did not bring him to his knees. Instead, strength settled on him like a cloak, and his first step landed on the earth, unyielding and solid as a mountain. He took another step, then another. The sucking darkness clutched at them, pulling like hot tar as they moved down the path.

The way stretched out for an eternity it seemed, but finally they came to the place where the crystal water flowed freely over the pure white sand. Gently, he unwrapped the child's arms from around his neck and set her on the ground at the very edge of the water. She kept a tight hold on his hand, and he did not need to be able to see her to know she was afraid.

"Step into the water," he said. The little hand in his trembled. "Don't be afraid. Step into the water; let it wash away the darkness. Let it carry you beyond its reach to where the light waits."

He felt his sister's warm fingers wrap around his other hand so that he could once again see the apparition. The little girl's silver eyes looked up into his, unsure, her fingers clutching tightly to his. He smiled down at her, content to wait until she was comfortable enough to let go.

Though it was getting on to evening, the sun still shone brightly on the water, coating it in diamonds and gold. The girl took a deep breath she did not need and stepped in; first one foot, then the other. A wonder filled her face and she let go of his hand. The power of the water slowly washed away the taint that had been fastened onto her like a leech. He watched her ghost fade as it left the mortal plane, moving beyond that of the dead, till it passed through to the unknowable that awaited all souls. The world settled into a quiet peace. Then it blurred and shifted as Devon fell.

"Steady, steady. Give yourself a minute."

Devon woke to three pairs of eyes staring down at him, one green, one gray-blue and one nearly black. The last was unexpected though they were set in a familiar angular face.

"Kristoph, why are you here?" Devon asked, thick-tongued, as he slowly sat up.

"Would you believe me if I told you I just happened by?" The schoolmaster asked as he held his hand out to Devon.

"No," Devon said, taking the proffered hand. He needed more help standing than he had anticipated.

"Well, the truth of the matter is I followed you here. I had gone to the boarding house to check on Sara. And when I found that she was not there, I headed towards the cemetery to find you and arrived just in time to see the three of you disappearing down Fallow Road."

Devon's head swam. He reached out and blindly grabbed onto Kristoph's shoulder to steady himself. "Possibly a bit of luck for me," Devon admitted.

In the end, they walked back up Washboard Lane, Devon swaying like a drunkard most of the way. Eventually, he sent Liam and Sara on ahead to the boarding house so that neither would miss dinner. Thankfully, one or the other of them had the good sense to send a hired carriage back for him.

Still, dinner was long done by the time he and Kristoph had arrived at Mrs. O'Toole's. He had the cabbie drop them off in the alley rather than on Winding Street. Kristoph followed him through the side gate and onto the back porch, rescuing

222

the whole line of washing that was there when Devon swayed and nearly pulled it down.

The back door was open and the kitchen thankfully empty when they went in, saving Devon the embarrassment of having someone see Kristoph helping him up the backstairs. He had barely made it past the last step when the whole world went black.

He woke to a pounding head and a soft knock on the door.

"Devon…" he heard his sister call out softly.

He heard quiet steps move across the room, then the door opened. There was a soft exchange of words before it closed again.

"Your sister was worried," a familiar voice said from out of the darkness. "There is water on the nightstand next to you, if you think you are up for it. Would you like me to light the lamp?"

Devon saw the man's tall, thin silhouette perch on the windowsill. The soft glow from the street lamps outside lit his profile, but even that small amount of light was too much for Devon's eyes. He groaned.

"Absolutely not," he replied.

His declaration was met by a sympathetic chuckle from across the room. "How did you manage to get yourself in such a state?"

Devon turned to his side and slowly sat up; the pounding in his head receded slightly. "I really couldn't tell you."

"Well it certainly wasn't from overindulgence!" Kristoph commented. "Did your collapsing on the riverbank have anything to do with why Sara was so distracted all of today?"

"She was distracted?" Devon's mind was having a hard time spinning all the threads together from the past several hours.

"Yes, noticeably so. Which was why I went to the boarding house after school to check on her, only to find she was not there."

"So then you came to find me at the cemetery…"

"And saw you already rushing down Fallow Road, yes. I told you all this earlier, don't you remember?"

"Vaguely," Devon replied. "Sara did not explain?"

"I can assume that she was a bit worried, and my hands were quite literally full," Kristoph pointed out. "In addition, you sent her and that boy off before we reached Market Street."

"I suppose I did," Devon said, his mind slowly clearing. "To answer your question, yes; the reason she was distracted today could have very well been the same reason that we were down at the river. There is a house down there. Did you know of it?"

"That is not an area I would have reason to frequent," Kristoph said.

"Me neither, but Sara was drawn there," Devon said, and went on to describe the malevolent sucking feel of the house and the ghost of the little girl who had been trapped there.

"Hmm, there are places that develop something of a presence of their own. If terrible things were done there, it may draw dark things to it. But from what you have just told me, there was nothing dark about the apparition you met. And why did this sucking vortex, as you described it, not draw her in?" The schoolmaster paused for a moment. "Now there is a disturbing thought. What if she had been left in that manner on purpose? As a lure. But a lure for what?"

All the while Kristoph speculated, an incessant scratching noise grated at Devon's ears. He felt blindly for the matches on the table next to him, and braving the light, struck one. The glare pierced his eyes, but settled as he lit the lamp next to the bed.

"Oh, perfect, that makes things much easier," the schoolmaster said as the scratching resumed. "I'm glad you are able to handle the light now."

Devon squinted over to where Kristoph was still sitting in the window, head bent over something. "Are you taking notes?"

"Of course I am taking notes. So, Sara came to find you… to do what?"

At that moment, Devon's muddled head began trying to sift through all the past conversations he had had with the schoolmaster, but he could not remember how much he had already shared with him. He had thought he had left him to guess most of what he knew rather than verify, but he realized he had long since ceased to be as careful around the man.

"Devon?" The scratching of the schoolmaster's pencil stopped. A note of concern returned to his voice.

"She came to me hoping I could help the little girl leave that place," Devon said.

"And did you?"

"Yes."

Silence spun out between them for a good long while. Finally, the man sitting in his window gave an amused snort.

"You, my friend, can be quite annoying at times, did you know that? Not that I blame you for playing your cards close to your chest, but still…" Kristoph sighed. "Let us just assume that I have figured some things out. You can confirm or deny what I say as you see fit.

"Like your sister, you have an affinity for the dead. And, given your detailed description, I would speculate that you also have the *sight*. But there must be something more or else why would she have gone to find you? Can you actually draw them to you? Is that what you did then, draw the ghost to you? If the maleficence you spoke of was as strong as you say, then no wonder you were knocked flat on your back!"

Devon let out a soft sigh. Ascher already knew more about him than he would have liked; would it be any worse if Kristoph, and through him his benefactress, knew as well?

"I don't have the *sight*, though I can hear the dead, just as Sara can," he admitted. "And you are correct, there is more. I could have called the little girl's ghost to me, but I did not. I carried her away from that place."

"Physically carried her?"

"Yes."

"Alone?"

"No," Devon confessed. "My 'guardian' as you call her was with me. And you were right when you first said that she was strong. I am not sure I could have done what I did today without her."

"Her strength helped you?"

"Yes."

"And, you can touch the dead?"

"As though they were flesh and blood."

"Do they always do as you ask?"

"They do," Devon hinted, wondering how deep Kristoph's knowledge ran.

The look on the schoolmaster's face as realization broke was almost comical.

"You are…" But unlike Ascher, the schoolmaster stopped short of naming him for what he was out loud. "My friend, that is quite extraordinary! No wonder Ascher hired you!"

Devon could see the questions brimming up in Kristoph's face. Thankfully, he decided to take pity on Devon, leaving long before his curiosity had run its course. Which was good, because the sound of the waves lapping at the unseen shore were already calling him.

He blew out the lamp, and settled onto his pillow. The tickle of whiskers across his cheek followed him down into sleep.

CHAPTER XX

Gray Waves on Gray Sand

The sky above them was blacker than black and filled with stars. There was no moon to speak of, but Liam could still see the dark waves as they broke gently on the silvered shore. The girl next to him was little more than a silhouette, sifting the sand with her toes. A clean wind blew in from over the ocean, wandering through the sea oats so that they shushed and rattled around them. It was as though the house behind them did not exist, wrapped as they were in the soft night.

There was no denying that the past few days had been the oddest in Liam's life. Even now, all that had happened seemed more like something from a penny dreadful story than real life. But it had been real, every bit of it. And perhaps, that was the oddest thing of all.

And now here he was, sitting on Edith Island, watching as Sara buried and unburied her toes in the sand. He had been waiting for Sara to work up the courage to talk about whatever it was that had happened the day before. He had always made a point of not pushing, but he was beginning to think that might have been a bit of a mistake. He was gettting that itch that always came when trouble was brewing, and he needed to understand what that trouble might be. It was starting to look as if Sara might talk herself out of mentioning it at all, so he decided to.

"Did you hear that the old cracker house we went to burned down?" He asked her.

"It burned down?"

"Yep, went up in flames that very night, apparently. It was nothing but ash by morning."

"Does anyone know how it caught fire?"

He shook his head. "I haven't heard anyone say."

"But you think it too much of a coincidence for it not to have something to do with us being there?" She speculated.

"I do," he said. "I asked about a bit. Most people didn't remember there even being a house back there. Gertie was the only one and she said that it had been empty since the washerwoman who had lived there died, back when Gertie's mother was a girl. So, it makes sense that it burning down would have had something to do with what happened when we were there, whatever that was."

"What did it look like to you? I mean, what did it look like Devon and I were doing?"

It was harder to answer that question than Liam had expected. "To my eyes, it looked like you and your brother were just pantomiming. Pretending there was a person there that wasn't," he told her honestly.

Silence filled only by the sighing wind stretched out for a long time between them.

"You don't think that, do you?" She finally asked.

He could have teased her. Wanted to actually, hoping that it would make her blush like it usually did. Then he could laugh and she would blush more and try not to make a face at him and things would be as they had been this past month and a half or more. But he knew that what she needed was a straight answer.

"No, I don't."

"I wouldn't blame you if you did," she said softly.

He kicked sand over onto the little fairy's toes. "Don't be silly. I've always believed you." And that was the God's honest truth, though he couldn't deny that it was easier to believe in such things when you half-thought it was your imagination rather than when the reality of them was staring you in the face. Which was the opposite of how he would have thought it should be.

"But obviously I can't see what you see," he continued. "Can you tell me what it was that actually happened there, at that house?"

She was quiet for so long he had begun to wonder if she would answer at all. He leaned over and nudged her shoulder with his.

"Please."

"I want to tell you! Really, I do. I'm just not quite sure how," she confessed, then soldiered on. "There was a girl there, like I told you. To me she looked as solid as you do, a little girl in a red gingham dress sitting on the steps, crying. She sounded so sad and lost. She told me she wanted to leave, but something wouldn't let her. Thankfully Devon was able to help her; you were right when you said we needed him."

"So your brother, he can see spirits too?"

Sara shook her head. "No, he cannot see them, not unless he is holding my hand. But he can touch them, the same as I can touch you. And we can both hear them, and they can hear us."

"They can hear you? Can't they hear everyone?" He asked, a little puzzled. "From what you've told me, my *maman* has certainly heard everything I've said since she died."

"She has and they can, but they don't have to. Just like you don't really have to listen to a person when they are talking to you. You can ignore them if you want. But for Devon and I, the spirits can't not hear us. They have to hear us, I suppose you could say."

A cold feeling that had nothing to do with the wind sent goosebumps racing up his arms.

"So, you heard this little girl from all the way back at the schoolhouse..." Liam prompted.

"Yes. And when Devon got there, she couldn't come to him

even though she wanted to. That's why he picked her up and carried her, but the place didn't want to let her go."

The memory of bootprints a hand-span deep trailing down the path behind Devon came instantly to Liam's mind. As did the oddly shadowed trees and the river beyond, where the light had danced so sharply brilliant it had been hard to look at. "Why did he take her to the Shallows?"

"Because he hoped the running water would wash away whatever it was that had a hold on her," Sara explained, "allowing her to pass from this world to the next. Rivers can be symbolic that way."

He thought of Marie floating in the tree-lined ditch. It reminded him of other little things that he had noticed over the past month he had been working with Devon.

"That little girl, she wasn't the only thing your brother was carrying when he walked to the Shallows, was she?"

"No, she wasn't," Sara admitted. "How did you know?"

So he explained the unnatural dimpling he had seen walking up the wet fabric of Marie's dress, and how Sara's brother had seemed to be speaking to thin air when he had sent someone off to find Ascher.

"Ah, that would have probably been our companion. Or, I suppose you could call her our guardian, since she has been watching over us ever since Dev and I arrived here. She usually looks like a small cat, white as starched linen with rust-colored ears." Sara's voice, though still hushed, began to grow more excited. "Although, I'm sure she is much, much more. I'm just not sure what."

"Usually looks like a white cat?"

"Yes, but she changes shape. Sometimes she's a hound, some-times she's a horse..."

"And she was the one who I saw walking on Marie's dress?" Liam inserted.

"I believe so," Sara replied.

"Can all ghosts do things like that?" he asked though he had half-guessed the answer already. Had such a thing been possible, there were several people he had known in the past that his *maman* would have whipped bloody had she been able to.

"No, that is not something all spirits can do," Sara admitted. "But she seems to be unusually strong and very protective of me and Devon."

"Very protective?" Another thought popped into his head. "She was the one that bloodied up Tom, wasn't she?" he guessed.

"She was. She was also the reason the other boys ran off," Sara shivered and Liam didn't think it was because of the cold wind. "I feel like maybe she is here for a reason."

"Could it have something to do with what happened to Marie, do you think? Or why others have disappeared from the Bottoms?"

"People have disappeared from in the Bottoms?" Sara's eyes were so wide that Liam could see the whites of them, even in the dark.

"From what old Mr. Henry was telling me, there have been all sorts of things happening down there, angry ghosts and shadow men; people who have disappeared then reappeared but aren't the same as they were." There was something else that old Henry had said, something Liam had been meaning to ask about. "He also said your brother has the power. He called it magick. Is that how you and Devon do what you do? Is it magick?" Liam wondered if he had pushed too far.

Sara pulled her knees up to her chest and rested her chin on them. "It is and it isn't. When someone practices magick, they attempt to make things happen through rituals and incantations. They have to have a good understanding of what it is they are trying to do and what will be needed to achieve it. Magick, ritual magick, takes study, practice and sacrifice.

"Devon and I, what we are isn't quite the same. We were born with an affinity for the dead, the same as you were born with green eyes. We couldn't stop being what we are even if we tried, any more than you could stop being as tall as you are."

The darkness might have hidden her face, but it did not hide the loneliness in her words. Liam put an arm around her shoulders, uncaring as to whether anybody sitting on her aunt's porch behind them would take exception. The fierce feeling burning in his chest hardened into the solid promise that he would stand by her, the rest of the world and his own fears be damned.

Ruth had watched her visitors walk away that morning with the rising sun, her niece's hair like spun gold shining brightly in the frame of the two dark-headed men to either side of her. The need to know had invaded Ruth's heart the moment the shifting dunes had swallowed them up. She had recognized that need. It was like a drug in some ways, and she often closed her ears to it. But there was good reason to give in this time. Even though she was unsure if anything useful would come from whatever knowledge she might gain, she deemed the price worth it.

So, she had gathered up her needles, candle and salt. She had laid her cards out on the table to see what they could tell her. And when those had proven fruitless, she had delved deeper and asked those on the other planes to help her to see.

She saw nothing of the hunter from her earlier vision but when she looked at the paths of the dead, she saw two stars ascending. Around them, the other powers drew nearer; the dark queen and her knight, the golden sun and hers, and the old wolf whose roots ran through Ashwood.

Worlds, layered on worlds, layered on worlds, the past and future melding with the present. She could see the girl Devon had spoken of and the shadow writing that writhed under her skin. She could see the girl's present and past selves, but her future self was hidden. Behind her stretched a host of those who had been taken before, their spirits bound and tethered. And there were others offering up their hearts to be strung on black threads. There they dangled like flies in a spider's web, slowly

232

being consumed by darkness. But she could not follow the web to its center, to the bloated spider that waited there. Those that helped her see would not look at it for fear of being noticed.

Now, the rain was pattering against the window in short staccato bursts as she looked through them and watched the waves dash themselves against the shore. Gray waves on gray sand with a pewter sky above them. Murky shapes writhed in this gray world. Blind tentacles groped through the shadowscape. The glass chimes rang madly in the wind as they warned of a creeping abomination. An eater of souls, a drinker of magick.

If she could see Ashwood town, she was sure she would see the corruption lurking through its streets. She feared there was a reckoning coming but for what or whom was not clear.

She watched as shadows with the forms of men slipped over the dunes and wondered if she was the one they sought or if they searched for other, less suspecting prey. A bright light moved up the path from the beach, a shining golden beacon that anchored her to the plane of her natural existence. A man that walked up from the sea, holding his cap to his head in defiance of the wind. She wanted to warn him of the shadows, but there was no need. They slid around him and past him. He was untouchable to them. Like oil and water, they could not occupy the same space as he did. She remembered the other anchor, solid and steady, that Sara had brought to see her. And she hoped that he too could stand firm against the shadows that were closing in.

She heard the man come up the porch steps and the sharp knocking as he rapped his large knuckles against the door.

"Come in, Hugh," she said, though she knew her voice would not be loud enough for him to hear. That did not matter of course, he would come in anyway.

The squeak of the back door and a muffled curse when the wind tried to tear it out of the man's hands declared the truth of her prediction.

She made her way from the parlor to the kitchen where the clank of metal on metal gave birth to a second curse when the man realized that the stove was cold. Had she let it go out after her visitors had left, or had she forgotten to light it again today? Was it the same day as the morning of their leaving?

She found the man kneeling on the kitchen floor in front of the stove, trying to coax the fire to life.

"Thank you," she said, smiling at him as he grumbled.

He looked up from his task. His sea-blue eyes grew wide with shock when he saw her. "Lord's above, Ruth! What the devil happened to you?"

It was then she felt the ache of her belly and the tackiness of her dress. It seemed that it had not only been that morning that her visitors had left. She felt the world fold in on itself as she fell softly towards the floor. A smile pulled at her lips at the feel of Hugh's strong arms as he caught her. The words "Damn it, Ruth" followed her down into darkness.

CHAPTER XXI

Midwinter

Sara had found herself at something of a loose end that morning. It was Midwinter, the shortest day of the year (which was still a much longer day than it would have been back home in the North) and that meant Christmas was only a few days away. The whole thought of it had made her feel terribly homesick. So when Mrs. O'Toole said that she and some of the other boarders were going shopping, Sara decided to join them.

Her parents had sent her some money with their last letter, and when she had told Devon what she intended, he had given her a little more. The whole prospect had cheered her up considerably. Gift giving was always one of her favorite things about this time of year. Planning on what gifts to give and to whom was almost better to her mind than actually receiving them.

The whole group of them left right after lunch, and what a merry group they were as they walked down Market Street towards the shop district and the docks. There was Mrs. O'Toole, Miss Newkirk, Mrs. Madison, and Jeffery of course. Even Mr. O'Toole, home from the sea, had decided to join them. And they were not the only ones out and about; the streets were full of people shopping.

Not to mention, it was a glorious day! The air was just as chilly as it had been but not too damp, and the sun felt like a warm blanket. Most of the shops had their doors open, taking advantage of the lovely weather and the opportunity to entice people to come in.

They lost Miss Newkirk first, to the milliner's. Then Mr. O'Toole was sent off to the butcher's while Mrs. O'Toole went to the baker's across the way. Sara continued on with Mrs. Madison and the ghost of her husband until they stopped outside of a tiny shop whose front window was filled with books.

"I thought this might be a store you would be interested in," Mrs. Madison said as she opened the door and stepped in.

Sara was immediately enchanted. What a wondrous place! And right there near the front window was a book on penmanship that she wanted very much to buy for Liam, so she did. Though that, along with a slate and a slate pencil, took up a good half of her money. But she wasn't sorry for it, not in the least.

She found a book on the history of Ashwood that she knew papa would love, and a mystery she thought both her parents would enjoy. She had already made her purchases and had been on her way out the door when she spotted an adventure book on a stand near the front window, not far from where she had found the book on penmanship. She was not sure how she had missed it before. The cover was olive green and had the silhouette of an elephant embossed on it, and inside there were numerous illustrations.

"That looks like it would be interesting," Mrs. Madison commented from over Sara's shoulder.

Sara turned and smiled at her. "It does, doesn't it! I think it would be a wonderful book to read with Liam…" She glanced out through the window only to see the very person they were talking about walking down Market Street in their direction, as if her saying his name had conjured him.

Sara had set the book down, and was already taking a step in the direction of the door, when she remembered that she was carrying more than a few gifts for him in her arms. She stood there in a quandary.

The next thing she knew, Mrs. Madison, apparently having seen the same lanky figure that Sara had, was gathering the parcels from her arms. "Go," she said smiling. "I am sure he would be happy to walk with you while you finish your shopping."

"Oh! Thank you, Mrs. Madison! They are all paid for," she assured the woman as she rushed out the door to the sound of Mrs. Madison and Jeffery's gentle laughter.

"Liam!" she called out, waving to the boy who had already passed by the book shop in the time it had taken her to hand off her purchases. He turned when he heard his name.

"There you are! I was wondering," he said, lifting his hand in greeting.

"Are you on your way to a job?" Sara did not believe this to be the case, since normally at this time of day Liam would have still been working at the cemetery, but she did not want to assume.

"No, your brother let me go early. He said that you would be out and about shopping, and thought that you might be feeling a little bit homesick today."

Her eyes, silly things that they were, instantly began to tear up. "He's not wrong," she admitted.

In unspoken agreement, they turned and began to walk down Market Street towards the water and the docks.

"Why today, in particular?" Liam asked.

"Because today is always a busy day back home," she replied a little wistfully. "This is the morning when we would have woken up really early and headed out to find our evergreen tree for the season. It is much, much colder up there than it is here. But we would've been all bundled up to take the ferry across the narrows. Uncle John and his wife, Aunt Mary and her husband, and all our cousins would have met us on the other side.

"We all would have climbed into Mr. Poole's pony cart and ridden up to the hills. My mama is the best at finding trees that are just the right shape and size. It takes most of the morning. Then when we find them, we cut them down and load them up in the cart to bring home. We always stop in Jonesville on our way back to shop for Christmas presents. But it's when we arrive back home that everything really begins! Dev and Papa set the tree up in the parlor while mama and I make all sorts of food. My favorites are the apple cakes and gingerbread cookies, but mama also bakes loaves of bread. She puts together little bags of salt to go with them. We take out jars of honey and apple butter and the beeswax candles that mama and I would have spent all year dipping. We would put everything into baskets to give to our neighbors and those who have had a hard year. Any candles that are leftover, we put in lanterns that are set up around the house for later. Everything is ready by the time the sun starts to set, then we head out, pulling the little wagon filled with baskets behind us. By the time we have delivered them all, everyone is red-cheeked with the cold, but happy."

Sara's homesickness disappeared as she warmed to her subject. Bless her brother for being so thoughtful. Having someone there to share the memories with made her feel so much better, all the more so because it was a friend she was sharing them with.

"The first thing we do when we get back home is light all the lanterns in the house, so that their warm light will get us through the long dark and remind the sun to rise the next morning. We stay up all night decorating the tree with candle clips and ornaments of colored glass and little silver bells…" Sara looked over at Liam. He was smiling at her, but there was such a wistful sadness in Marguerite's eyes as she walked beside him that Sara's tongue froze.

Understanding dawned and she felt an utter nincompoop. It was doubtful that Liam and his mother ever had a fir tree to decorate, and had probably never had a Christmas like the one she had just described.

"What about your friends? Did you visit them as well?" Liam asked, not noticing her abrupt silence. Or perhaps he had become so used to her oddities that he was just politely ignoring them. "I imagine you miss them, your friends I mean."

"No," she hedged. "We live in a very small town so there aren't that many children. That's why Devon and I had to go across the narrows to school. But our closest neighbors are very nice and I miss my mother and father tremendously." What she was unwilling to admit was that there were no friends for her to miss.

238

She could not in all honesty put the blame on the other kids, not really. She had always felt so nervous, so scared that she would slip up and say something she shouldn't, that she had never really tried that hard to make friends. And of course, there were the times when she was younger; when she had tried to confide in the people that she had thought were her friends. Each time had been an absolute disaster. And yet, here she was, confiding in Liam, hoping things would be different. That this time, her dream of having a friend would be real and not pop like a soap bubble when she least expected it.

They found themselves at a broad avenue at the end of Market Street, which was funnily enough called Old Market.

Old Market ran along the edge of the docks and people always had stalls or carts set up there, where they would sell things right off the boats. It looked a little like what she had always imagined a Turkish bazaar would look like. There were people everywhere, and a good half of them dead.

One, an old woman, waved Sara over. Her skin was as dark as coffee beans, and the twists of her nearly white hair lay hidden beneath a sea-green kerchief. She was sitting on a stool, next to a much younger version of herself. In front of them, a plank of wood balanced between two old crates served as a table. It was covered with a brightly colored cloth and filled with all sorts of curiosities.

The young woman called out to Sara as the spirit next to her continued to beckon. "Miss, miss, come see what I have. Charms and trinkets only five cents apiece. You won't find anything else like them," she promised, holding up a small embroidered bag. "Put this under your pillow and you'll dream of your true love."

The older woman pursed her lips and scowled as she looked over at the young woman who was speaking. "Stupid girl, this isn't one of those you hoodwink," she huffed, reaching out to smack her in the back of the head. The younger woman's eyes rolled up 'til only the whites showed. She blinked and when they opened again, her eyes were silver. The ghost that had been sitting on the stool beside her was gone.

"Now missy, here's the things that are worth seeing," the young woman said with the old woman's voice. Reaching under the table, she pulled out a wooden box.

Sara glanced around to see who was near before turning a stern eye back to the young woman in front of her. "*Grandmother*, you know it isn't right what you are doing!" she admonished in a respectful, if disapproving, voice.

"*Tch*, no need to worry child. This one lends me her body often enough when they dance round the fire," the old woman cackled from the young woman's mouth.

"But she did not call you in this time," Sara pointed out.

"True, true, missy. But she well knows the price of the choices she's made." The woman held up a bracelet. The small blue enameled bird dangling from it looked as though it were about to take flight. "This one, for the sad woman to help her find happiness. And this one," she held up a battered ring, "for the young man next to you."

Sara's eye flew open wide, and she glanced over at Liam who was standing next to her. But he was not paying attention. His mother was at his side, pulling adamantly at his shirt sleeve and pointing to a bracelet with pretty blue stones.

"That one, *mon fils!* You should buy that one," she was whispering insistently in his ear though she knew he could not hear her.

Sara set her money down on the table and quickly scooped up the two pieces of jewelry. Half turning, she tucked them away in her pocket.

"Where to next?" Liam asked when she turned back towards him. He too had his hands in his pockets. Both he and his mother were smiling at her with identical smiles, like a pair of cats who had found the bowl of cream. Had he heard what the woman had said?

The ghost-ridden woman behind the table snorted in amusement at them. "You should go to see Joseph next," she advised. "He's just a few slips down. Got a shock of hair you can't miss. Tell him old Ezri sent you and he will show you the stuff worth seeing."

240

"Thank you, *grandmother*," Sara said with a nod of gratitude.

The young woman blinked. When her eyes opened, they had returned to the rich chocolaty brown they had been, and the old woman's spirit was back on the stool beside her.

"You take care, missy," the old woman said. "There's evil walking out and about today." Two pairs of eyes, one brown and one silver, looked back at Sara with the same concerned expression.

She thanked them both again before heading off further down the row.

"Back there, something happened with Clémence, didn't it?" Liam asked conversationally.

"It did," Sara confessed. "Do you know her?"

"In passing," Liam remarked. "She lives down here in the bird streets, between Old Market and Nightingale."

"How could you tell that there was something different?"

"Well for a moment it looked like she was having a fit. Then after that her eyes sort of clouded over."

"Oh! You saw when her eyes turned silver?" Sara nearly bounced with excitement. "I had wondered if you could. That's wonderful!"

"Silver? I suppose they could be called that. They looked a little like the eyes of a new corpse, to me."

"Well of course, they are the eyes of the dead after all," Sara declared enthusiastically. Her lips sealed shut immediately afterwards as her horrified mind realized what it was she had just said outloud.

"But Clémence isn't dead," Liam pointed out.

Sara looked over at him hesitantly.

He raised his eyebrows at her. "No need to keep it to yourself now. Not after all that happened last month."

He was right of course; the cat had already been well and truly let out of the bag.

"It wasn't just Clémence talking to us. In fact, it was really Ezri who was speaking with us. She was just using Clémence's body to do it."

"She was what!" Liam nearly shouted and Sara flinched. "Sorry," he said, lowering his voice. "But are you saying spirits can take over a living body?"

"Well, not just willy-nilly they can't!" Sara said adamantly, then lowered her voice. "But there are ways that it can happen. It is a form of possession where the spirit 'rides' the living, the 'ridden'. Some religions make a practice of it."

"Why would they do that?" he asked.

"To gain the spirit's wisdom. It is something of a bargain," she explained. "The spirit gives them the knowledge they seek and in exchange the spirit gets to use their body for an agreed amount of time. There are several books in my father's library on the subject."

"That must be some library," Liam said.

"It is! Our house is not as big as Mrs. O'Toole's, but my father's library takes up nearly half of it." She couldn't keep herself from gushing, just a little. "It would be wonderful if you could see it one day."

A little zing shot through Sara's heart as the words left her mouth, with it came a certainty that one day Liam would.

Old Ezri had been telling the truth when she said they wouldn't be able to miss Joseph. He was sitting on a crate whittling animals and figures from pieces of wood; a tall, raw-boned man with a head full of nearly pink hair. Strawberry blonde, her mama would have called it, but Sara had never seen it so brilliant! Even the man's eyebrows and lashes were the same unbelievable color.

"Evening, Liam," the tall man nodded in their direction. "Been a long while since I've seen ya."

"Evening, Joseph," Liam returned the man's greeting. "I've found steady work up at the cemetery, so I haven't needed to come look for it down on the docks as much."

The man turned his pale blue eyes on Sara. It was not an unkind look, but she did feel he was looking at her the same way he would have looked at a butterfly or an interesting bug.

"What brings you here now?" he asked, resuming his whittling though his eyes remained fixed on Sara.

"I am shopping for gifts," she answered. "And, Grandmother Ezri told us to come see you."

The man's eyebrows flew up into his rose-gold hair. "Did she now? Well, then…"

Setting down the wood he was carving and his knife, he turned and pulled a huge sea chest out to where they were standing. He slowly opened the lid as though he were revealing a secret trove of unimaginable wonders. And so he was! Everywhere Sara looked, she saw the unique and exotic. There were silk fans from the far-off east like she had seen the dancers use in the vaudeville show. Tiny figurines in porcelain and jade were nestled beside finely carved ebony wood boxes from India. Beneath their lids were piles of amber and ancient seashells long ago turned to opal from the very bottom of the world.

Sara bought two of those last, one for her mother and one for her Aunt Ruth. And for her last five pennies, Joseph put them into a silk coin purse for her. She thanked him and they left, heading back the way they had come.

While they walked, she fished her other purchases out of her pockets with the intention of adding them to those already inside the coin purse. But when she opened it up, she was surprised to find the tiny wooden figurine of a white horse inside next to the two opalized seashells. She showed it to Liam.

"Joseph must have not known it was in there," she said, turning to go back to where the man sat. She stopped mid-step, the figurine slipping from her fingers back into the purse. She snapped the purse closed and returned it to her pocket without thinking. Her attention riveted to the spot where she was sure she had just seen a flash of brilliant copper hair.

"What is it?" Liam asked.

"I thought I saw..." The crowd shifted and there she was; the woman Sara had last seen on the lane behind Miss Rose's, standing only a few stalls down from where they were.

"There, do you see her?" she asked, trying to show Liam where the woman was without being so crass as to point. But the crowd had closed in around them.

"I don't," Liam hesitated as he scanned the passersby.

Sara caught another glimpse of russet a little further ahead of where it had been. On an impulse, she grabbed Liam's hand and headed in that direction.

They made their way through the swirling mass of people. More than once, Sara was sure she had lost her entirely, only to catch a teasing glance of the woman at the next doorway, or down an alley. She couldn't even say why she felt compelled to follow the copper-haired woman. Except the memory of that old fear, of not being able to tell the living from the dead, had sprung up again at the sight of her. Sara needed to know for sure that the woman was not a ghost, or worse, just a figment of her imagination. And yet, she couldn't quite bring herself to ask Liam a second time if he could see her. Perhaps because she was half afraid of his answer.

They had just passed by a fairly questionable shop, when Liam finally asked her who they were following.

Sara paused, having lost sight of her again. "Do you remember on the first day we met, I asked if you had seen a woman standing near the redbud tree?"

Liam nodded. "Yes."

"Well, I'm sure I just saw her again," Sara said, though in truth she was not the least bit sure.

Liam stepped closer, leaning over her shoulder to look in the direction in which she was searching. "What does she look like?"

At that moment the crowd parted, giving them a clear view of the woman Sara had been following.

She looked like a model for a fashion plate with her violet

striped dress. Her hair was that brilliant copper that Sara remembered so vividly, like an autumn wood with rivers of gold running through it. Save this time, it was pinned up in a neat chignon and topped by a stylish hat.

For Sara, the whole scene stood frozen in time, like a daguerreotype photograph. Then the crowd passed between them, hiding the woman once again, like a cloud passing over the sun.

"I think I've seen her before," Liam said, his brow furrowed as though he were trying hard to remember something. "In fact, I'm sure I have. But, I can't for the life of me remember where."

Sara nearly wept with relief. She was not imagining things!

A flash of violet stripes set them off on their chase again. Marguerite followed after, murmuring worriedly in her native tongue all the while. But Sara was so caught up in the strangeness of why no one else seemed to notice the woman, who so obviously did not belong in that part of town, that she didn't pay the ghost much attention.

CHAPTER XXII

The Copper-haired Woman

They continued to follow the copper-haired woman, never losing sight of her for very long, but never seeming to draw any closer, either. Until finally she came to a stop in front of a two-story flophouse.

It was then that Sara realized just how close to evening it was. There were no street lamps where they were at, but the lantern at the flophouse's front door had already been lit. It was a sad-looking house with its unpainted sides and shuttered windows, nothing like Mrs. O'Toole's. And it was clearly not the upscale establishment one would expect a woman dressed like the one they were following to visit. Yet there she was, poised to walk up the front steps.

A large man suddenly passed in front of Sara, blocking her view so that she never saw if the woman went into the flophouse or not. His unexpected nearness startled her so that she looked up, then recoiled. She could not see the man's eyes, only a hungry darkness that filled their sockets. It flowed like tar down his cheeks in a parody of tears.

Her gaze shied away from his face, veering over to another man's. The darkness was there as well. Face, after face, after face; every one of them filled with the same oozing corruption. It spilled from their mouths and eyes, and dripped from their hands like blood. She tried to step away, but it was like fighting against a current. The flow of people seemed to have picked them up. It carried them along, dragging them closer to the flophouse regardless of their wishes, like leaves on a flood.

A well-dressed man stepped in their path, his features half-obscured in the fading light of the fast-retreating sun. Yet despite the growing gloom, his eyes shone brightly beneath the brim of his top hat.

"Why are you here?" he demanded in a voice cold enough to freeze her feet in place, though Sara felt sure the question was not directed at her. Liam took a half-step forward, squaring up to the man, a half-grown pup against a wolf.

"Be careful of this one, *mon fils*." Marguerite warned though the ghost knew her son could not hear her.

"I am the least of your worries, madam," the man replied and Sara realized with a start that he was speaking directly to Marguerite.

Liam and the man continued to eye each other as the creeping shadow of the flophouse fell over them all. They were standing much closer to it now. There was only a few feet between them and the bottom of the stairs that ran up the side of the building. Sara blinked twice at the familiar figure of Mr. Hegdus, who was even at that moment making his way down those very same stairs.

"Sara? What are you doing here?" His voice was filled with surprise and concern, but his features were thankfully free of the oozing miasma. She let out the breath she had not realized she had been holding, but next to her, Liam's shoulders tensed even more.

"Why did you bring her here?" The schoolmaster's voice was sharp with disapproval as he directed the question at Liam.

"You should look to your own queen before you give this boy grief on how he looks after his," the well-dressed man riposted with cool derision.

Movement from over the top of the schoolmaster's shoulder caught Sara's eye. The barbed comments flying between the stranger and Mr. Hegdus faded into the background as a figure stepped out from the door at the top of the stairs. Something about it made Sara's thumbs prickle. Shadow clung unnaturally to it, obscuring all its features save its face. Sara gaped as she watched that face fold in on itself over and over and over again in a nauseating kaleidoscope of flesh.

An instinctive revulsion filled her mouth with bile and her stomach gave an involuntary heave. She stepped away, somehow bumping into Liam as she did so. Mr. Hegdus, having noticed her reaction, turned to look behind him. What the schoolmaster actually saw, Sara didn't know. But he must have also felt the wrongness of it, because he swept back up the stairs, a knife suddenly appearing in his hand as he went.

The figure retreated before him, disappearing through a door at the top. It was not fleeing though; it was drawing the schoolmaster in. Just as they had been drawn in, Sara belatedly understood.

"Fool boy," the well-dressed man said from where he stood now behind them. Sara did not think he was talking about Liam.

The stream of people that had been flowing past the flophouse before had now turned into more of a pool. A growing mob, all of whom seemed to be ridden by the same weeping corruption she had seen in the crowd earlier.

"And see how neatly the trap closes," the well-dressed man said sardonically as he pulled the gloves off his hands and slid them somewhere inside his coat.

At that same moment, a sharp crash sounded from above as Mr. Hegdus burst back through the door at the top of the stairs. Lady Ana followed out on his heels. Her unveiled face turned in their direction, and Sara felt as though someone had punched her in the stomach.

The magnetic pull she had first felt that night at the vaudeville show was nothing compared to what she was feeling now. Suddenly she was not afraid any more, not of anything! And it seemed to make perfect sense that she should turn around and kiss Liam.

After all, it was something that she had thought about doing since she first met him. Or had in fact tried not to think about. And she should definitely tell Mr. Hegdus that she had always thought he was very handsome. Even though right now he mostly looked dangerous, lean and predatory, like a jungle cat, but a jungle cat she wanted to pet.

Undecided as to which thing to do first, she froze. Arms that she thought might belong to Liam wrapped protectively around her from behind. But they quickly fell away and a heavier hand came to rest gently on her shoulder. The voice that spoke over the top of her head however, was anything but gentle.

"Control yourself!" it commanded sharply. Sara could only conclude that it was the well-dressed man who was speaking from behind her because her eyes refused to look away from Lady Ana's unveiled face. But if the rebuke had been meant for her, it did nothing to lessen the euphoria and utter abandon that Sara was feeling.

"Keep a civil tongue in your mouth!" Mr. Hegdus barked, in a voice that did not sound at all like his own.

"Do not think to admonish me, boy. Certainly not at a time like this," the man behind her barked back.

"He was quite right to reprimand me, Kristoph," Lady Ana pointed out, nonplussed. "I was not being as mindful as I should be."

The feeling that had taken hold of Sara fell away then, and she was surprised to find herself nearly half way up the stairs with no memory of having climbed them. She would have been mortified if the fear she had been feeling before had not come back a hundredfold. And with it came a sound, a terrible keening that made her flesh crawl.

No one else seemed to notice, except for Marguerite who had moved closer, as if she would put herself between them and the danger that grew ever more quickly with the falling darkness.

"I do not know what is wrong with them!" Marguerite exclaimed as she watched the gathering dead. They drifted through the growing crowd, brighter and more real to Sara than the living in the evening gloom.

But there was something dreadfully wrong with them. They moved restlessly, gibbering and moaning as though they were in pain. There was no recognition, no thought behind their vacant expressions. An unreasoning fear snaked its way into Sara's belly. It was a fear she had never felt before, a fear of the dead. Suddenly, she desperately wanted Devon to be there.

"I don't know either," she admitted to the ghost beside her. She turned towards Liam, her cheeks burning at her earlier thoughts despite the intense fear roiling in her belly. "We need Devon," she told him.

He searched her face for a moment, then turned to look out at the dark shapes that moved in the twilight.

"Do you see a clear path, Mr. Ascher?" Lady Ana called down from where she stood on the stairs above.

"They would not easily let us pass," the man whom Sara now knew to be Serus Ascher replied. He turned his attention to Liam. "You however, they would take no notice of you at all."

"Doesn't matter if they would or wouldn't," Liam bristled. "I'm not leaving without Sara."

"If we need her brother, as Miss Amaris seems to believe, then you may not have a choice," the man remarked, proving that he had heard what Sara had said a moment ago. "If it is your intention to save her, that is."

"He does have a choice," Marguerite countered from where she stood. She smiled softly at her son and Sara. "He should be here with you. I will go find your brother."

"What if he is still in the cemetery?" Sara asked. Liam looked over at her, his lips parted as though he would answer. But he stopped himself as understanding dawned in his face.

"Having met him," Marguerite nodded in the direction of Mr. Ascher, "I believe I was mistaken to assume I could not enter there."

The man in question looked in the direction of Marguerite,

as if he could see her. A wash of emotions flitted across his face, surprise and sadness being among them.

"If you do, you will not be able to leave," he warned, his voice softer than it had been when he was talking to Liam.

"I know," said the ghost, her eyes never leaving Sara and her son.

"Sara, what is happening?" Liam asked her.

"I am not sure," Sara answered truthfully.

"There will be pain," Mr. Ascher continued, apparently ignoring the byplay between Sara and Liam. "Your body does not lie there."

"Pain is no stranger to me," Marguerite informed him.

"Is he talking to *maman?*" Liam asked. Sara nodded her head.

"Had I known…" Mr. Ascher began, but Marguerite turned her back on him.

"*Maman…*" Liam called out, but she had already faded.

"She's already left," Sara told him softly.

Sara thought for a moment that Liam was going to do something very rash, like grab Mr. Ascher and try to shake him. But it was just then that an overwhelming pressure descended on them and everything just stopped. The crowd who had up until that moment merely been milling about, froze. As one, they turned towards the stairs where Sara and the others were standing. It had grown so dark that Sara could barely see the living in the fitful light of the flophouse's lanterns, but the ghosts she could see quite clearly, as clear as if they stood in the noonday sun. Their faces were contorted in terror. Then almost as a single creature, the mass of bodies both corporeal and incorporeal began to move.

"Ascher?" Mr. Hegdus called down.

"I will hold here," the well-dressed man replied. "I assume there is no way out through the house?"

"None we would wish to take," the schoolmaster replied.

"Kristoph, give me one of your knives quickly," Sara heard Lady Ana say, though she couldn't bring herself to look up the stairs to where she stood. "And give this to Miss Sara's young man."

"I am not happy about this," the schoolmaster objected, but did as he was asked.

"I did not expect you to be," the lady replied as she took the knife from him, handing him something in return which he passed down to Liam.

It was a sap, about as long as Liam's forearm, which he took hold of as though he knew what to do with it. He slipped the attached loop over his wrist just as the mob of people, both living and dead, converged on the flophouse like a slow rolling wave. They crashed against the foot of the stairs where Serus Ascher stood, intent on making their way up them. Sara watched in horror as he met the onslaught with shocking violence, fear a metallic taste in her mouth.

The crowd itself though, was strangely silent. No one cursed or screamed or shouted out dire threats. There was only the thud of Ascher's cane against flesh and the insane murmur of the ghosts.

Inches away from Sara's feet, a face appeared at the bottom of the railing. For the eternity of a heartbeat, it stared at her, slack-jawed and white-eyed. Then the railing gave way and it fell back into the surging mob below. Another immediately replaced it, then another, as they tried to pull themselves up onto the stairs, climbing on those below, heedless of their well-being.

"What are they?" Liam asked as he brought the sap down on the wrists and clinging fingers of those trying to clamber up.

Sara did not have an answer for him. They were not alive, not truly; nor were they dead. Their bodies were just empty. Their spirits, bound in cords so tightly that their unearthly flesh bulged like a roast tied up in butcher's string, dragged behind them on silver leashes like some sort of grotesque child's toy. She had never seen such a thing before.

Another face fell as Liam brought his cudgel down, but more and more hands appeared, grasping onto the bottom of the broken railing. Feeling useless, Sara turned to look for something with which she could help Liam. White-eyed faces greeted her from high up on the walls, heads and limbs twisted in unnatural angles as their soulless bodies clung like spiders to the wood. Sara gasped and stepped back, almost into the reach of the ones trying to climb up behind her.

"They seem to feel no pain," Lady Ana remarked as she did something Sara did not quite catch. One of the figures on the wall fell away.

But that was not true. Sara could see their tortured spirits flinch and moan in pain as the bodies they were tethered to fell.

"What the devil are they?" Mr. Hegdus demanded, echoing Liam's earlier question.

"They are zombi," Ascher answered from where he was standing on the steps below them. His voice was no longer the coolly polished thing it had been. He tossed something in Sara's direction without looking. She reached out to catch it instinctively. "Throw that into their mouths if you can, Miss Amaris," he commanded as he continued to hold off the mob before him.

Sara looked down and found that she was holding a good sized bag of salt. Relief washed over her. Finally, something she understood, something she could help with! She made her way back and forth along the stairs, throwing small handfuls of salt into the slack mouths whenever they appeared. Each time she did, the bodies would fall to the ground, convulsing and moaning. She could see the bonds loosen, but the spirits and the bodies stayed stubbornly separated.

There seemed no end to them and even Sara could see that the battle they fought was a losing one.

The perverse quiet of the night was shattered by the sound of breaking glass. Flames quickly spread along the wall of the flophouse, feeding greedily on the dry wood. The mob retreated. But like a wave pulled back out to sea, Sara knew it was only a matter of time before they returned.

"The house is most certainly not an option, now," the schoolmaster declared as he and Lady Ana moved down the stairs, away from the spreading flames.

The heat from the fire licked at their skin. In its growing light, Sara could see the crowd nearest the flophouse had thinned. Many of the ones she had thrown salt at still lay on the ground, convulsing in jerky fits, but not all of them. A few were starting to rise to their feet again. And she could see more of them out in the darkness. Black on black figures that moved just beyond the reach of the fire's flickering light. And there were even darker things among them, things that her eyes refused to look at. She couldn't help but recognize that the odds of them being able to escape had not much improved. However, the option of them staying where they were was now no longer an option at all, if it ever really had been one. Her bag of salt seemed woefully inadequate for the task ahead.

"Choices are limited if we all want to make it through, Lady Károlyi," Mr. Ascher called back over his shoulder. "A frenzy may be in order."

An adamant "No" resounded from Mr. Hegdus's lips, followed closely by, "Absolutely not!"

"I can hold her if need be," Mr. Ascher assured the schoolmaster. A little prickle of fear danced over Sara's skin at his words as though someone had just walked over her grave.

"You presume much with that statement, Mr. Ascher," the lady herself retorted. "And such a course of action would leave many bodies on the ground. Perhaps too many."

"Better theirs than ours," Mr. Ascher pointed out, turning to look over his shoulder as he did so. The dapper gentleman of before was utterly gone. What looked back at them with glittering eyes was something savage and brutal, almost bestial.

"As you say," the lady agreed. "Stay close to Miss Amaris, Kristoph." The schoolmaster offered no further argument, merely bowed and moved to Sara's side.

Then they were moving down the stairs. Mr. Ascher led the way, with Liam, Mr. Hegdus and herself following closely behind him. As their feet left the bottom step, chaos erupted. Mr. Ascher met the rush with a speed and ferocity that Sara found hard to watch.

Confusion reigned in the darkness and flickering light, and it was hard for Sara to tell what was going on. Something wet splattered across her cheek, followed by a delighted laughter that rippled out into the night from behind her. The almost infectious sound of it smothered even the insane gibbering of the ghosts.

"Do not turn around," Mr. Hegdus said softly through gritted teeth, his hand coming to rest heavily on her shoulder.

The mob of living and dead around them seemed legion, though in the logical part of Sara's brain she knew they were not. There were most likely only a few dozen, but even so. Liam's hand came to rest firmly on the shoulder opposite the one Mr. Hegdus had hold of so that they kept her between them. That worked perfectly because it left her hands free to throw salt into the mouth of every zombi in their path.

Sara's world narrowed down to slack faces and increasingly smaller handfuls of salt, and carefully stepping around the bodies as they fell into fits on the ground. The three of them made their way slowly forward in Mr. Ascher's wake, but the burning house still remained so close that it seemed as if they were making no progress at all.

From one panting breath to the next, the air suddenly grew bitingly cold. Then came the wind, its sickle teeth raking through them. The ghosts fell silent as they flickered and vanished. The mob dissolved as those defiled by the oozing corruption fled before its ferocity, leaving only the empty shells of the zombi behind, their bound spirits pleading for release. Sara looked up into the punishing gale and found her brother only a few steps ahead of where they stood. He was mounted on the white horse like some sort of avenging angel, their eyes nearly incandescent with brilliant silver light.

Even after her brother slid from the phantom's back, the night did not hide him. He was as clear to Sara's eyes as all of the other spirits had been. She quailed as she considered what that could mean.

The white horse rippled and shrank, leaving the hound behind in its place. It let loose an eerie howl as it bounded away from Devon's side to chase after the ones that had fled. The lull that had come with their arrival was a short one. Many of the zombi that had been felled by the salt were already staggering back up to their feet.

Both Liam and Mr. Hegdus called after her when she shrugged them off and rushed to meet Devon. She grabbed his hand as soon as she reached him and sighed in relief when his warm fingers closed around hers. There was a small part of her that had been very afraid that she would not be able to take his hand. The eyes that looked down at her were a warm golden-hazel, just as they should be.

"Can you see them?" She asked, pointing at the nearest figure lurching to its feet.

"I can," her brother replied, just as the zombi launched itself at them. It did not make it far before coming up against the lean form of Mr. Hegdus, who did his best to keep it from reaching them.

"Can you hold it, Kris?" her brother asked as he stepped closer to the spirit that was tethered to the body of the man Mr. Hegdus was grappling with.

"Not for long," the schoolmaster grunted.

Keeping a tight hold of Sara, Devon worked the fingers of his free hand in between the cords and the spirit's flesh. They loosened at his touch, but refused to come away entirely. When he tried to snap them, they only grew tighter. The spirit whimpered in pain.

"Damn," he cursed. "I can't break them. These bindings are extremely strong."

"So is this creature," the schoolmaster said as he deftly spun his opponent to keep himself between them and it. "What do you need?"

Sara was trying to work out how she could throw salt and still keep hold of Devon's hand when she felt the bag being taken from her. It was immediately replaced by a smooth handle. She looked down at the glittering black knife in her hand.

"Here," Mr. Ascher's voice growled from behind her. The inhuman sound of it reached into her bones and froze her like a rabbit in a hawk's shadow. All except her pounding heart which was trying to escape from its cage whether her body had the good sense to move or not.

"Sara?" her brother looked back at her, breaking the spell. The presence behind her was gone, but the hairs on the back of her neck were still standing at full attention.

"Here," she went to give him the knife and instantly realized he had no free hand to take it with.

"Cut here," he instructed her, pulling harder at the cord he was holding.

She did as he told her, carefully slipping the knife underneath. The cord tensed against the knife's edge. Then with a pop, it split and melted away. The spirit, now free, dove back into its body which writhed violently for a moment, then slumped in the schoolmaster's arms. Mr. Hegdus lowered it to the ground where it lay still and unresponsive, but alive.

There was no time for her to take a breath though because soon another one was on them. Again, Mr. Hegdus stepped in, but he did not have to hold out so long this time. She and Devon made short work of the binding. They freed three more, then suddenly everything stopped. Like a hunting pack responding to its master's whistle, the remaining zombi turned as one and left. The night swallowed them up whole before anyone realized what was happening.

The queer silence that had prevailed through the entire affair was instantly replaced by the roar of the fire as it consumed the house behind them. The sharp crack of collapsing timber split the air.

"Shouldn't we do something?" Sara asked.

"Yes. We should leave," the voice of Mr. Ascher answered her from out of the night. "I can hear the bells ringing at the firehouse, so it will not be long before the fire brigade arrives, and it would be best if we were gone by then."

"I have a carriage waiting on Nightingale Street," Lady Ana offered. Her silhouette, still obscured in darkness, held something out in Mr. Hegdus's direction. "Kristoph, if you would please."

Whatever it was, the schoolmaster took it and handed something to her in return from his coat pocket. "Here you are, Mistress."

"Ah, yes. Thank you. I am afraid it will be ruined though once I am through with it."

The schoolmaster only nodded, then addressed the rest of them. "I'll show you to where the carriage is waiting," he said. They set off, following his lead.

CHAPTER XXIII

All the Threads Come Together

Mr. Hegdus led them quickly down the narrow, empty lanes. The ringing klaxon of the fire bell filled the night air but the houses they passed were silent and full of shadows. Sara's skin itched as they walked by them.

They finally came out on the dark side of downstreet Nightingale. The schoolmaster turned in the direction of a clarence that was waiting just a few steps up the road; its lanterns shone like beacons of hope on a far-off shore to Sara's eyes. The pale face of its driver seemed suspended in the darkness, wreathed by streamers of white pipe smoke. He looked up and saw them.

"'ello Kris, you're early. Where's her ladyship want… Lady Ana!" The driver exclaimed, having obviously only just then caught sight of the people following on Mr. Hegdus' coattails.

"Take us to Ascher House, if you would please, Logan," the lady said as she stepped up to where Mr. Hegdus was already holding the door of the carriage open, "Mr. Ascher, is that agreeable to you?"

"Yes. A sensible choice, Lady Károlyi," the gentleman replied from the tail end of their party.

Sara was the next one into the carriage. She sat herself beside Lady Ana, and the rest of their weary group climbed quickly in behind her.

Once everyone was settled, the carriage set off smoothly towards the Ascher estate. Sara could still hear the clamor of the fire bell, but it now seemed far away. The steady clop of the horses' hooves made everything feel strangely normal, almost serene. It was so at odds with all that they had just been through that she was finding it hard to reconcile the two into the same reality. The relentless mob, the conflagration, the fight to get clear, and the tense walk down dark streets; the feelings of terror and confusion that were already dulling, much to Sara's surprise. As if they had only been a dream and what was happening now was the only truth. She did not think feelings like that were supposed to fade so quickly. Whether they were or weren't, she did not fight against the blankness that wrapped itself around her like a warm blanket. Just floated in it until her brother's voice broke through her reverie.

"The people whose spirits were bound, the mindless ones, what were they?" he asked of the carriage's occupants at large.

"Zombi," the once-again polished voice of Mr. Ascher answered. "It is a practice somewhat unique to the region. Similar to revenants, though the ritual to create them is quite different."

"How so?" Devon asked.

"A revenant is created from a corpse that has been revived to haunt the living, while the flesh of a zombi is not actually dead, just made to think it is."

"This ritual, you have seen it done?" Lady Ana asked from where she sat beside Sara.

"I have, though it is not common," Mr. Ascher answered. "The body is made to believe that it sits on the brink of death. The practitioner then catches the spirit as it tries to flee its mortal shell, binds it, then leashes it to the flesh so that it can neither escape nor inhabit the body. The flesh becomes a puppet, mindless except for its master's wishes while the spirit remains a prisoner, powerless over the actions of its physical self. It takes an enormous toll on the person casting it even when the sacrifice is made willingly."

"Why would someone willingly do such a thing?" The question blurted out from Sara's mouth before she had a chance to stop it.

"It does seem extreme, doesn't it, Miss Amaris. But occasionally, when the debt owed is too high to pay back, a person will offer to enslave themselves in such a way for a set amount of time," he explained.

"That is…" She struggled for words as the understanding of what she had seen at the flophouse came into focus, "horrific."

"Some believe the alternatives would be more so."

Sara's mind refused to imagine what alternative could be worse than having one's own body perform acts they would never do while their spirit sat by powerless to stop it.

"But it can be performed on those who are unwilling?" Mr. Hegdus asked from where he was sitting on the other side of her.

"Indeed. However, the making of even one zombi is difficult. As I said, willing or not, the cost to the practitioner's own soul is very high. No single person could have made the numbers we saw this evening; their soul would have burned away entirely long before they had managed to make half that."

"And yet from what I saw, they were driven by a singular desire," Lady Ana remarked.

"Many people can have the same desire, Lady Károlyi."

"True, Mr. Ascher, but it manifests differently in each one. Every person may lust, but that lust is never truly the same. Just as twelve different bakers can make the same cake, but each one would still have its own unique flavor. These 'zombi' as you call them, would have had to have all been made by the same baker," the lady insisted.

"What a disturbing thought," Mr. Ascher said.

Sara was not sure if he was referencing the fact that a single practitioner had made all the zombi they had seen or that Lady Ana had likened them to cakes.

"But zombi were not the only things that were there," he continued. "Isn't that true, Miss Amaris?"

Goosebumps prickled up her arms at his question. A warm calloused hand, her brother's hand, came to rest on top of her own. The familiarity of it steadied her and she unclenched her fists from the fabric of her skirts. She did not know how Devon had known she was upset, but he obviously had. Perhaps it was something all big brothers just knew.

"No, they were not," she admitted quietly. Then she did her best to describe what it was that she had seen. How the corruption had filled people's eyes and spilled down their cheeks like black tarry tears. How great globs of it had oozed thickly from between their lips. The unclean feeling that had twisted in her belly when they had looked at her.

The darkness inside the carriage made it a little easier, but when she tried to talk about the grotesque wrongness that had been the figure at the top of the stairs, her lips sealed firmly shut. Even if she had been able to find the words, they would not have come out of her mouth. Instead, she concluded with, "And then there were the dead. The true dead, not the spirits still tied to their bodies. They were upset and not in their right minds."

"How so?"

"They were restless and incoherent like they were lost or in pain," she explained. "I could feel that they were there and did not want to be."

"Is that why you wished your brother to be there?" Lady Ana prompted gently, proving that she had heard the conversation on the stairs between Liam and Mr. Ascher.

Sara nodded, then realized they might not be able to see her in the dark. "Yes," she added aloud. "I knew he could help them if they wanted to leave but could… not." Her sentence came to a halting end as she realized somewhat belatedly that she had confessed a secret that was not really hers to share.

"Rest easy, Miss Amaris. Everyone here, with one possible exception, understands who and what you and your brother are," Mr. Ascher assured her.

Devon however remained silent, so she chose to follow his example.

"Well… I think it safe to say that there is still a great deal more left to discuss. So if everyone is agreeable, we can continue this conversation at the house, over dinner," the head of the Ascher family suggested.

"I, for one, would be glad to," Lady Ana volunteered. "Do you have some place where I might retire for a short while to… recuperate from my recent indulgences?"

"Of course. I have a room that I believe will suit your needs," Mr. Ascher assured her. "If you would have your coachman take the fork through the orange grove, we will come out on the main drive. I would rather not further incur my cook's wrath by bringing you all in past the kitchen. Since no doubt, she will already have plenty to say about five unexpected guests."

Mr. Hegdus relayed the message and in a very short time they were jostling along a much bumpier stretch of road. There was very little for Sara to see through the carriage's windows, save glimpses of moon-silvered trees still heavy with fruit. Even if the discussion had not been put on hold until dinner, it would have been hard to maintain without biting one's own tongue as they went over the teeth-snapping bumps.

But it soon smoothed out again, and not long after that they drew to a stop. Mr. Hegdus was first out, nearly before they had finished moving, and Mr. Ascher climbed out practically on his heels. Sara could hear him issuing orders to someone as soon as his feet hit the gravel.

First Devon, then Liam, followed quickly after. She was just about to make her way out as well when she felt a gloved hand cover her own where it still rested on the seat.

"Miss Amaris, a moment of your time, please," the carriage's last remaining occupant besides herself requested.

Sara settled back down into the seat, shifting slightly so that she faced the corner where Lady Ana sat. The absolute darkness hid the woman sitting there; not even her silhouette could be seen.

"I want to apologize," the lady said, withdrawing her hand from where it rested atop Sara's own. "I was careless with my power tonight. I promise you that it is not my habit to influence innocents and had not intended for you to have gotten caught up in it."

Sara's face flamed when she realized exactly what it was that Lady Ana referred to. She now had a much clearer understanding of Miss Newkirk's somewhat wanton behavior the night of the show, having felt it first-hand.

"It was…" Sara began but for the life of her, she couldn't think of what words to use. It was embarrassing? Exhilarating? Terrifying? Though to be fair, that last was more what she had felt afterward.

"The truth?" Lady Ana offered gently. For a moment, Sara thought the lady might actually be teasing her. "You should know Miss Amaris, that those feelings I bring out in people are never anything more than what they already want to do in their heart of hearts. There is no shame in it."

"Being embarrassed is not the same as being ashamed," Sara blushed even hotter and blessed the concealing night for keeping her secret.

"Very true, Miss Amaris, and very wise. Thank you for your understanding and refreshing lack of condemnation."

There was nothing that Sara could think to say to that, but she wondered just how much insight into a person's feelings Lady Ana's power gave her. Was it only their emotions that she sensed, or did it give her something deeper? Perhaps glimpses into what it was a person was thinking or about who. That possibility had Sara trembling, which only got worse when she found Mr. Hegdus waiting just outside the door to help her from the carriage. There was no way he could know what it was the lady had been referring to, even had he overheard their conversation. Still, she could not quite meet his eyes as she accepted his hand down.

She was not ashamed, not really. But she was sure that she would melt into a puddle if either one of the people who had been in her thoughts at that moment in time were ever to find out what it was she had been thinking.

Mr. Ascher was already mounting the stairs of the grand house they had come to; a tall, pale man following along at his side. Mr. Hegdus offered his arm to Lady Ana, and they moved in the same direction. An arm fell across Sara's shoulders; she turned her head to look up into her brother's reassuringly familiar face.

He did not say anything, just smiled and gave her shoulders a quick squeeze. Together they set off after the others, Liam falling into step on the other side of her, hands in his pockets.

She itched to ask Devon if he was okay. A worm of worry wriggled in her belly at the memory of him stepping from the paths of the dead, eyes awash in silver. But for once, she kept her questions behind her teeth. Now was not the right time to ask them, but she leaned hard into him. He hugged her shoulders all the tighter as they made their way towards the warm glow that beckoned through the stained-glass of the transom window. They followed the others through the front door beneath it, into a quiet foyer. Once they were all inside, Ascher turned and addressed the pale man who was closing the door behind them.

"Jonas, please show the gentlemen to a place where they can wash up. Lucy," he turned his attention to a young woman wearing a practical-looking gray dress. "Please show Miss Amaris to a room where she can do the same. Someone will come around to let all of you know when dinner is ready. Lady Károlyi, if you will follow me, I will take you to the room that I believe will suit your needs."

Lady Ana followed the head of the Ascher family towards a spiral staircase that rose from one side of the room while the tall pale man, Jonas, led Mr. Hegdus to a staircase on the other side. Devon squeezed her shoulders again and kissed the top of her head, then left to follow after them. Liam gave her a wink and a half-hearted grin before bringing up the rear.

The young maid, Lucy, beckoned to her. "This way, miss."

She led Sara up the same staircase as the men had gone, but turned in the opposite direction from them when she reached the landing. The maid continued up another short flight of stairs to a hallway lined with doors. She opened the first one they came to.

On the other side of it was a cozy room with several windows and a door that led out onto a balcony. Even in the dim of the evening, Sara could tell it was a room made for the morning sun. The maid turned up the lamps so that the light shimmered over the silk-papered walls.

"I'll bring up some warm water and a brush, miss. And if you'll give me your frock, I'll see if I can freshen it up some."

Feeling awkward, Sara thanked the young woman as she removed her dress and handed it to her. She had never had someone wait on her before unless she was sick.

Lucy took the dress and draped it over her arm then turned towards the door. She stopped after only a couple of steps, and patted at the fabric. Reaching into one of the pockets, she took out the things that Sara had purchased in Old Market only a few hours earlier.

"I'll just leave these on the dresser, if that's alright with ya miss," she said, then left promising to return shortly.

Standing there in only her smalls, Sara took a deep breath. Then she took another, surprised at how it shuddered out of her body. In fact, her whole body had started to shake, then tears began to pour out her eyes without stopping as the day's events hit her all at once. She sat on the edge of the bed, crying, and wondering why the thought forefront in her mind was that she was glad she had sent Liam's present home with Mrs. Madison.

Liam was not happy to see how red Sara's eyes were when she joined them at the table. He certainly understood though; as soon as he had been left alone, his hands had started shaking and hadn't wanted to stop.

She sat down next to him. He smiled over at her, and she smiled back just as Mabel started to bring in dinner. The woman didn't say a thing when she saw Liam sitting at the table, but her eyebrows did. They jumped up so high they all but disappeared into the white cap she was wearing on her head.

"I am sorry, Mr. Ascher. I didn't know you had guests coming so I had to make do." Mabel did not sound sorry at all as far as Liam could tell.

"And you made do admirably, Mabel," Ascher said as the woman slid a small stack of hoe cakes onto his plate, either not noticing or choosing not to notice his cook's annoyance. "In fact, bring all the dishes out if you would, then you can head home for the evening. We can serve ourselves."

"As you like it, Mr. Ascher," the cook said, eyeing Liam all the while with a look that said he better fill her in later on anything she missed.

Liam gave her a little smile and winked, as though to say he would. Though he doubted that whatever was discussed in this room was something he would be able to explain to someone else no matter how hard he tried.

Mabel left the plate of hoe cakes, and in short order brought out a ham and a pot of black-eyed peas that were probably left over from an earlier meal.

"Please help yourselves," Ascher said as he put a slice of ham on his plate.

Everyone followed his example though Liam noticed no one touched the food once it was on their plates. Liam's belly, despite what had happened, was not inclined to wait when food was right there in front of them. It kicked his backbone hard and growled loud enough that all eyes turned in his direction. Well, there was nothing for it now; he cut a slice of ham and put it in his mouth.

Ascher's lips quirked up and he gave a snort of a chuckle before turning his attention back to the table at large. "No need for us to stand on ceremony. We can just as easily continue our earlier conversation while we eat. Lady Károlyi, you said before that you believe a single practitioner was responsible for all of the zombi we saw tonight. Is it also your belief that the mob we encountered was controlled by the same person?"

"Of that, I am less sure. Although as you know Mr. Ascher, influencing a large group of people is certainly possible. But that person has to be very practiced in the arts. Personally, I would think it beyond any single human's ability to have accomplished the magnitude of influence and control we witnessed this evening. Perhaps a powerful enough cabal, or a denizen from another plane, could have managed it, but a single practitioner seems doubtful."

At the word "control" Liam's stomach clenched as the memory of that moment on the stair washed over him. He kept his eyes fixed on his plate, not sure how much of his desire to protect the holly-blue eyed girl next to him was being "influenced" by the lady on the other side of the table.

"That such a powerful practitioner, or group of practitioners as it may be, are in your territory without your knowing of them, Mr. Ascher, is a bit surprising." The schoolmaster's suspiciously bland comment had Liam believing that he was not the only person who Ascher rubbed the wrong way. It almost made him feel better inclined towards the schoolmaster.

"You may believe me to be omniscient if you wish to, Mr. Hegdus," Ascher replied drolly. "And to be completely forthcoming, I have known ever since Mr. Amaris first brought the girl Marie to my doorstep that someone of not-inconsiderate-skill has been practicing in Ashwood. I assume, Lady Károlyi, that you are familiar with what happened to the girl of whom I am speaking?"

"I am."

At this, Liam looked up and over at Devon, but the man did not seem at all surprised at this revelation. Apparently, Sara's brother did not harbor the same distrust of the schoolmaster that Liam did. And the schoolmaster must have been the one to have told his mistress, or how else could the woman have learned about Marie? Unless of course, she, herself, was involved. An idea that Liam was certainly willing to consider.

"I have been able to learn nothing from her," the man at the head of the table continued. "Nor did I learn much from the old washerwoman's house down near the river. It has been an empty hunt thus far. Whoever they are, they have proven elusive."

"The old cracker house near the river? The one that burned to the ground?" Devon asked.

"One and the same," replied Ascher. "Freeing whatever spirit that had been trapped there was quite a feat, by the way Mr. Amaris. One I am not sure I could have accomplished unaided."

"You were there?" the schoolmaster asked. "And yet I did not see you make an offer to help."

"Things looked to be mostly well in hand, and I had the house to look into. You must be stronger than you look, Mr. Hegdus, to have supported Mr. Amaris's weight as far as you did before the carriage arrived." Ascher's statement left little doubt in Liam's mind as to who had sent the carriage.

The schoolmaster ignored the jab. "But the house told you nothing?" he prompted instead.

"Very little," Ascher admitted.

"So you burnt it to the ground?" said the schoolmaster. "A fit of pique?"

"The removal of a trap that had already been sprung," Ascher answered, apparently unfazed by the schoolmaster's return salvo. "Did you have help springing that trap, Mr. Amaris?"

"I did," Devon nodded.

The lady, who had been mostly quiet till then, spoke up. "And did you also have help in coming so quickly to our aid this evening?" she asked.

"Yes."

"How was that managed, Mr. Amaris?"

"I suspect you have an inkling, Lady Károlyi. Is there a reason you want me to say it out loud?"

"I would prefer not to make assumptions," she said.

"I was carried there as I believe you have guessed."

"By your guardian?"

"Yes."

A heavy silence fell on the room, and Liam knew that he was missing something that all the others understood. He had been too busy cudgeling anyone who came close to them to have seen when Devon had arrived. The wind came howling through and then all of a sudden the man had just been there. But it seemed there was more to it.

Several heartbeats passed before the lady continued. "I have met your guardian before, but I suddenly find myself extremely interested in meeting her again. She was the one who routed the mob who was attacking us, wasn't she? Were you aware that was something she was capable of?"

"I knew," Sara volunteered. Liam looked over at her, but she was looking at Devon. Her brother gave a small nod.

Liam listened as Sara told everyone about the day she had first met him. It was a bit of something to hear her tell it, to realize how much had been happening while he had been fighting with Tom that he'd had no notion of.

She left a few things out, namely that Tom and his crew had been offering to train her up as a dove. Which was probably lucky for Tom, because Liam was sure that if Sara's brother ever learned about that, Tom would be getting something a lot worse than the beating Liam had given him. Liam was tempted to mention it to Devon later.

"Has your guardian always been with you, Miss Amaris?" Ascher asked, breaking his silence.

"Only since we came to Ashwood," Sara replied.

"Now I am curious as well, Lady Károlyi," Ascher confessed. "It would be interesting to learn if there is a connection between the Amaris's guardian and the one behind tonight's events. After all, it does seem an unlikely coincidence that two such powerful influences would have converged at the same place and time for no reason. So, what do you say Miss Amaris, would you be willing to ask her?"

"A… ask her?" Sara stammered.

"She speaks to you, doesn't she?"

"Not… precisely. Not in words anyways. But I have always felt that she would if she could. Maybe in the right setting…"

"Such as a seance?" Ascher suggested.

"Yes, a seance might work perfectly!" Sara agreed.

"Have you conducted a seance before, Miss Amaris?" the Lady Ana queried.

"Me!" Sara squeaked. Liam watched her cheeks go from pale to pink in a flash at the realization that she would be the one expected to perform whatever it was they were suggesting. "I have never done one, not a proper one anyway," Sara admitted. "But from what I have read, it is only a more formal way of inviting a spirit to come speak with you, isn't it? Like calling someone on the telephone." she sounded a little hesitant when she added the last.

An explosion of musical laughter caused Liam's eyes to snap over to the lady Ana's face before he could stop them. He was gobsmacked by the beatific smile that beamed there.

"For you, my dear Miss Amaris, that very well may be the case," the lady said still smiling.

There was a little more back and forth, but it seemed that whatever decisions there were to be made, had been. In truth, it had only left Liam with more questions. But he wasn't going to ask those questions here; better that he find Sara later.

Ascher rang a bell and the pale man from before appeared at his elbow as if by magic. A few whispered instructions later, and the man left while Ascher informed everyone that they would gather in the drawing room after dinner.

From that point, most people set to finishing their food which had grown cold. All save Liam, who had finished what was on his plate some time ago (not that he had tasted it), and Sara, whose eyes seemed to be drilling holes into hers.

He nudged her foot under the table. Her gray-blue eyes were a little wild when she looked over at him, but not nearly as red as they had been at the start of dinner. He flashed her a grin and a wink, and a blush flooded her cheeks just as he had hoped. When he looked back at the rest of the table, he found several hawk-like gazes watching him speculatively. But since none of them belonged to Sara's brother, he ignored them and stole a hoecake from her plate.

It wasn't long before the man Jonas had returned with the steward Nathan, who began to gather up the empty dishes. Everyone stood, and Ascher suggested that they follow the pale man to the drawing room.

"Liam, a moment if you would," Ascher said as Liam made to stand with the others. "Do not wait Jonas, we will follow you shortly."

Liam settled himself back down in his seat.

"Am I correct in assuming that you cannot see spirits?" he asked Liam once the others had left.

Liam shook his head. "No, I can't."

"So you only know them through Miss Amaris." It was not phrased as a question, so Liam did not answer. "But you believe in them and understand that there are things beyond what can be seen and felt on this plane of existence?"

Again Liam did not answer him, but he did not deny it either. He wasn't sure where the man's questions were leading.

"Do you know there is a woman who has been haunting you?"

"Haunting me?" Liam said.

"Yes, it is a term often used when a spirit has attached itself to a particular place or person," Ascher replied. "There is no need to be coy, I am sure you know of her. What is she to you?"

"Why do you want to know?"

"Curiosity, mostly," the man replied, surprisingly not seeming to take offense from Liam's dodging of his questions. "She seemed very concerned for your welfare."

"She is my *maman*," Liam finally confessed.

Ascher nodded his head, like Liam had just confirmed something he had already guessed for himself. "What was her name?"

"Marguerite," answered Liam.

"And her last name?"

"Adeline, the same as mine."

"Adeline? Was that her mother's name?"

There was a little twist of emptiness in Liam's gut. "I wouldn't know. I never met my *grand-mère*."

"Did your *maman* never speak of her?"

"She hardly had time to. I was six when she died."

"And your father?"

Liam shrugged. His *maman* had never mentioned him, not once. Liam only knew that he had been born not long before she had come to Miss Rose's "Why all these questions about my *maman?*"

"I was curious as to why she was willing to make the sacrifice she did in order to keep you with Miss Amaris. Whether it was the young lady's welfare or your own she was most concerned with. I am still curious, but at least I understand why it was important for her to save you."

A cold fist punched Liam in the chest. "Sacrifice? What sacrifice?"

"She chose to go into the family's cemetery knowing she would not be able to leave. She also knew that it would be painful for her there since her bones do not lie in that hallowed ground."

Painful for her there. Ascher's words echoed through Liam's head, joining all the other questions that had started buzzing like bees between his ears. He was sure the man in front of him had the answers, and yet he couldn't seem to bring himself to ask. It didn't seem to matter, because the man appeared set on giving him some of those answers anyway.

"There is something that it is very important that you understand; all magick requires sacrifice," Ascher informed him. "A sacrifice of one's self, the sacrifice of another. Sometimes they are willing sacrifices like your *maman's*. Sometimes they are not, like the girl Marie's. This allows us to tap into forces beyond what you can see or hear or touch. They are not make-believe, in fact they can have profound effects on our reality whether you believe in them or not. There are things that defy rational explanation; ghosts, spirits, demons, magick. They are all just as real as the people you pass by every day on the street, a whole other world next door to ours that most are unaware of. And you made yourself a part of that world the very moment you chose to stand by Miss Amaris.

"So I have a proposal. Ascher House is currently without an heir. Move here, assume that role, and we will move your mother's bones to the family cemetery so that she can have peace."

Liam was gobsmacked for nearly a full minute, then his jaw clenched. "Are you saying that you will not move her bones if I don't take your offer?"

The man flashed Liam a smile, as if he had just done something unexpectedly interesting. "No, I would move them regardless. Unless you had some compelling reason to leave her soul in pain?"

"If that is the case, then why make the offer?" Liam scoffed. "You're young enough, go make some more heirs."

Ascher laughed. It was the most real emotion that Liam had seen from the man yet, and it was terrifying.

"You could say I've lost the stomach for it. Think about my offer and what having such means at your disposal would allow you to do for the ones you care about." The man stood then, gesturing towards the dining room door. "Now, I believe the others are waiting for us."

Numbly, Liam stood up to follow. Well, it seemed that Old Henry had been right when he said the new head of the Ascher family was a magick man.

CHAPTER XXIV

Aisling

The scents of warm beeswax and tobacco filled the drawing room. Devon breathed them in. The faces of those around him hovered disembodied in the darkness, lit only by the glow of a single candle set in the center of the table around which they all sat.

Sara's nerves were made obvious in how tightly she squeezed his hand. Talking to the dead was second nature to them both, so she had never needed trappings like the ones that surrounded them now. They added an unexpected gravity to something that for his sister and himself was a very ordinary, commonplace occurrence.

And yet, his heart beat a little faster as his sister's voice filled the silence; sounding so grown up as she spoke the ritual phrase suggested by Ascher.

"Spirits who have gone before, listen! We seek one who has the answers to our questions. We call her here before us. Come…" There was a pause at the end where the spirit's name would usually reside, but of course they had none to call out.

He added his voice to hers when she repeated the summoning a second time, and the others around the table soon joined in. With each repetition, Devon could feel the spirits gathering. Drawn there, it seemed, by his and his sister's presence; like a crowd gathered to see the newest display in a department xtore window.

The salty taste of a sea wind had settled on Devon's lips the first time he had spoken the incantation. By the third, they were

276

buzzing. An unspoken name danced on the tip of his tongue, teasing his lips to form its shape.

"Spirits who have gone before, listen! We seek one who has the answers to our questions. We call her here before us. Come…" they intoned together, but it was his voice alone in the end that whispered… "Aisling."

He blinked and the white cat blinked back at him from the center of their circle, the candle lighting her up from within like the sun caught in milky glass. A muffled curse from the other side of Sara told Devon that even Liam could see their visitor.

The white cat seemed to unfold in front of him and the figure of a woman sitting tailor fashion took its place. A dark-haired woman whom Devon had met many times at the edge of an unknown sea, with eyes like twin moonbeams captured in a jar.

His lips caressed her name again, "Aisling."

Aisling looked at the man in front of her and smiled. He knew her, she could see it in his eyes as they shined back at her like two gold coins.

She turned her head this way and that to see the other faces that watched her from around the table. Given their various expressions, they all could see her in some fashion. Even Sara's young gallant who was at that moment sitting next to Sara with his eyes as big as saucers, and his mouth hanging open like a fish. It took a lot for her to resist the temptation to reach across and close it for him.

"Oh. Oh!" Sara exclaimed. "This was what you were trying to show me that day on Market Street!"

"Yes, it was," she nodded. "But it has been so long since I've worn this form that I had forgotten how it went. In the end, it was probably for the best."

"Why has it been so long? And why would it be for the best?"

Sara asked, and Aisling could almost see the questions building up behind the girl's teeth like water behind a dike. They would come spilling out in a deluge here soon.

A smile tugged fondly at Aisling's lips as she looked at the golden-haired sylph in front of her. "I'll be happy to answer all your questions, little sister. But if you want anyone other than yourself and your brother to hear the answers, you'll have to let me speak through you. Though the *werwulf* over there also has ears to hear the dead, I do not know if he can understand me." She gestured with her chin over to where the powerful magician sat, the one that smelt of earth and old bone. "Unless you would rather me speak through another?"

"Speak through me," the girl's brother suggested.

Aisling couldn't stop herself from leaning forward and running her knuckles along his jaw, as she had done her whiskered cheek so many times before. "Yes, that seems right," she agreed.

She slid into his body like a hand into a glove. It had been many, many, many lifetimes since she had last felt breath in her chest; the warmth of blood rushing through her veins. She breathed in deep, closing his eyes as the sensations washed over her. When she opened them again, she was looking across the table into the green eyes of the *werwulf.*

"Who do you serve?" he asked, direct and to the point. His beast was in ascendance, discarding the human dance of social niceties like so much rotten meat.

"I serve no one," she scoffed lightly.

"Are you saying you have no master then?" he pressed. "No one set you to act as guardian for these two?"

She laughed at the idea, then someone squeezed their hand. She looked over at the girl who held it. Their sister looked so much duller through these mortal eyes. The brilliance of her aura hidden from their sight on this plane.

"Why do you protect us then?" Sara asked.

The girl's emotions were all tangled up in her eyes. The other

278

soul within them made their body lean over and kiss the top of the girl's head. But it was her words that answered the girl's question.

"Because you have gifts that touch the other planes, and it is a surety that what I hunt will seek you out eventually." She could feel the slight untruth in her words. What had started out as a means to an end had become so much more. But she could not tell them that here, so she continued on as she had begun. "You are as a flame to a moth for it, unclean horror that it is. Squatting like a toad behind the mask of a kind face while it whispers honeyed poison into the ears of those around it. Leading them to do heinous things while the soul of the one it rides bears the price of the unwilling sacrifices it takes." Their lips twisted in disgust at the thought of that which she hunted.

The *werwulf's* face remained impassive, but his eyes betrayed him. He was disturbed by what she had just said, as was the dark queen and her knight. And so they should be.

"Are you saying we have a demon in our midst?"

"Several, from what I saw," she replied, "riding their hosts for all they're worth like jockeys at a fair. But the one I seek is no demon, better if it were. At least a demon has a contract and rules it must abide by. There are no rules this one need follow, no limitation to its time here. It needs no summoner to call it nor an anchor to keep it on this plane because it, itself, is natural to it."

"Are you saying that it is mortal? A living human, not one of the dead?"

"It is older than I and I don't know the whole of its story," she shrugged. "Its spirit walks freely on both planes, neither living nor dead. But the fate of its body, who knows? Encased in crystal or hidden inside a needle, inside an egg, inside a duck, inside a hare, inside a chest long buried, as the old tales say."

"Be clearer, if you can," the *werwulf* said.

But she saw him tense and was sure he had an inkling about that of which she spoke. "The creature's body still resides on the mortal plane, suspended in time somehow. It is an abomination that has learned a way to circumvent the rules of sacrifice, eluding the price owed by its soul as it gathers power through the actions of others. It takes great pleasure in perverting that which should be good and holy; revels in taking the virtuous intentions of its followers and twisting them into mockeries of what they were. All the while it feeds off their corruption, telling them they're walking the path of the angels as they drink the blood of innocents."

She felt the moment when the other soul recognized the dreams she had shared with him for the memories they were.

"I hunt it now as it once hunted me, hounding it as it moves from place to place. But it continues to elude me." The frustration of that burned her, tempering her resolve as it always did.

"You believe this 'abomination' as you name it is responsible for laying the trap we encountered earlier?" This question from the dark queen's knight. There was a curiosity in it which echoed that often heard in Sara's questions. But would that curiosity prove to be useful or a concern?

"Most certainly. Though whether the trap was general in nature or set specifically for the prey it caught, I cannot be certain," she admitted.

"How long have you been hunting it?" he asked, and she could tell he was trying to weave together a picture from the truths that he knew.

"Many, many of your lifetimes."

"Not many of my lifetimes," his mistress rightly said. "If this 'abomination' has been among us for so long, why have I not heard mention of it?"

"Because it is an insidious thing that hides behind the faces of others, then leaves them to their fate when it is done," she spat. "And though you may not have heard of it, you have seen its work before. It was the spark that ignited the tinder which led to the Burning Times, as you call them. And the blame for the holy wars before that could be laid at its feet as well. Not to mention all the lesser-known evils it has visited on this world,

280

which I have lost count of. Though there is one such evil which touched you not so long ago."

"My homeland?"

Aisling nodded.

She saw the anger rise in the dark queen, felt it ripple out through the others for a breath before it was ruthlessly drawn back. Aisling doubted anyone else there knew who it was that sat among them, not even the knight who sat loyally at her side. Perhaps the *werwulf* knew, for his knowledge ran deep, but she wasn't certain.

Liam finally spoke up, looping back around to the answer she had given to Sara's question at the beginning. "So you are using these two as bait?"

They liked this young man who had attached himself like a stray cat to Sara. They smiled at him.

"No, I am protecting those for whom it will inevitably come," she replied. "But this time there will be an end to my hunt."

The other one within their body understood. Knowledge rippled through them as both souls, hers and Devon's came to a harmony of realization. There was no need for explanations, no possibility of misunderstandings. Only the rapture of not being alone and the warmth of touching completely, with no barriers between them. Why leave when they were so complete? That temptation was the hardest to deny, but denied it must be.

On the next breath she left their body, Devon's body, with the promise that she would meet him later at the edge of the endless sea.

Devon blinked. "She is gone."

CHAPTER XXV

Overheard Conversations

Liam padded barefoot along the second-floor balcony until he reached the door that led to the bedroom where Sara was staying. The rest of the house was dark for the most part, and he had promised himself that if she did not answer at the first knock, he wouldn't knock a second time.

His knuckles had barely tapped the glass when her face appeared on the other side of it. She smiled and slipped out the door to join him.

"Were you asleep?" he asked, though it was patently obvious that she had not been.

"Not at all," she replied, pulling a robe that looked to be at least two sizes too big closer around her. "In fact, I was thinking of tapping on your door, but I was not sure which room you were in."

"My *maman* didn't tell you?" he teased, hoping that Ascher would prove to be a liar. When her smile faltered, he knew his hopes had been in vain.

"I haven't seen her since she left to find Devon," Sara admitted, the darkness hiding the soft expression that her voice hinted at. "I'm sure you have loads of questions after everything that has happened. If you want to sit and talk, there's a bench swing just over this way…" She reached out as though she was going to

282

take his hand, then stopped herself. There was an awkwardness between them that hadn't been there before.

The jumble of emotions he had felt earlier came back in a rush. He was honest enough with himself to recognize them for what they were. He was also smart enough to know things came about in their own time, and that time wasn't now.

It didn't stop him from reaching out to take her hand anyway, because he knew if he didn't, she would think there was something wrong. And he was not willing to give up their friendship just because whatever had happened at the flophouse had spun his head around. He had no doubts that the Lady Károlyi had something to do with that. In fact, that was one of those 'loads of questions' he had that Sara had just mentioned, but he was pretty sure it was one that he wasn't going to be able to bring himself to ask.

They turned the corner and sure enough, at the end of the porch there was a bench swing. The grove of orange trees they had driven through was spread out below them, awash in silver light from the rising moon.

They sat at the same time and made themselves comfortable. There were no windows nearby, so it was private. Still, they spoke quietly as they set the swing softly swaying, the night air being notorious for sharing secrets.

"I'm sorry, by the way, for bringing you into this," Sara said as she pushed her toes gently against the floor's wooden planks. "All of this, not just what happened tonight."

"Don't be a goose, there's no reason for you to apologize," he admonished, and he meant it. Even after everything, even with the uncertainty of what may have happened with his *maman*, he meant it. "It's true though, isn't it, about my *maman* not being able to leave the cemetery?"

He felt her shrug her shoulders. "I think so? Though I am still unsure how she was able to enter at all."

Liam thought of the one-sided conversation he had heard on the stairs between Ascher and the empty air. He also remembered

Sara telling him when he first started working with her brother that his *maman* was not completely happy about it because she wouldn't be able to follow him into the cemetery. One did not equal the other. He hoped Sara would be able to clear a few things up.

"Can you tell me, what did my *maman* say when she offered to find Devon, the exact words?"

"When I asked 'What if he is still in the cemetery'? She said 'Having seen him, I believe I was mistaken to assume I could not enter there.' She was talking about Mr. Ascher. Spirits see many things we cannot and she must have seen something that made her think she would be able to enter into Ascher cemetery despite it being consecrated ground."

"You've called it that before, consecrated ground. Is that the same as 'hallowed ground'? Does that mean that it has been blessed or something?"

"Yes, in a way. It often means that the place has been blessed by a priest or a holy person, but another way to look at it is that the land has been promised for a particular purpose. So, a practitioner might perform a ritual promising that part of the land to a specific purpose. That then becomes a protected place, and only certain spirits can be there," she explained. "The only spirits allowed in Ascher cemetery are those related to the family by either blood or marriage. Your maman did say after having seen Mr. Ascher that she believed that she could enter the cemetery, so she must have thought that there was a blood connection of some kind. And, for his part, Mr. Ascher did not deny it."

Liam frowned. "It would explain why he was so interested in my *maman* and my *grand-mère's* names, though it beats me what he thought to gain from knowing them. Did you know he spoke to me after dinner?"

"No," she hesitated, curiosity warring with manners, no doubt. Curiosity must have won in the end because she asked, "What did he have to say?"

"He offered to move my *maman's* bones to Ascher cemetery.

284

In return, he wanted me to become the Ascher family's heir, whatever that means."

"Oh. Oh my…"

On top of everything else that had happened in the past few hours, the thought of him actually being a blood relation to the somewhat suspect (at least in his mind) Mr. Ascher hit him full in the face. A sigh exploded out of him as his head thudded against the back of the seat. The whole bench swung hard enough to make the beam above them creak. His gaze fixed on the ceiling and the deep shadows that obscured it.

"Ghosts, sacrifices, demons, magick, zombi… your little phantom cat which isn't a cat at all. The world has turned upside down, *ma fée*." He felt the swing give a little jerk. He rolled his head to the side and saw Sara's slumped shoulders. "I'm sorry. I'm not meaning to put any blame on you."

"No, I know. That isn't it," she sighed. "It's that I think we have just been tattled on."

"Tattled on?"

"Yes. I think that Aisling just went to tell on us."

"She did," Devon confirmed as he walked around the corner, the dark-coated schoolmaster a shadow at his side. "But I suppose after a day like today, I'm not surprised to find the two of you out here instead of in your beds."

Sara looked at her brother contritely. "I knew Liam would have some questions."

"I can imagine he does," her brother said. "But first I have one of my own. How is it pet, that you and Liam ended up at a flophouse down in the bird streets?

Devon sounded mostly amused, but there was a bit of steel underlying his words.

"Well, that wasn't where we intended to go," she answered, managing to sound both exasperated and sheepish at the same time. "We were shopping for Midwinter gifts down in Old Market when I saw someone… Do you remember me telling you about the day

I first met Liam? How I had gotten myself a little turned around? The reason I ended up where I did was because I saw a woman and I thought I would ask her for directions…"

Sara's words trailed off into silence. When she continued her voice was even quieter than it had been, nearly a whisper, as though she didn't want to admit what she was about to admit, even to herself. "I had been positive that she was an apparition. But then I saw her reach out and pick a leaf from a tree and I realized she was not. That I was mistaken shook me so much that I didn't see the group of boys, the ones I told you about, standing off to the side of the road. Then after the white cat came through like she did and they had all run away, I looked around for the woman, but she had already disappeared."

Liam remembered her stopping under the redbud tree; looking up at the branches as if something there had the answers she needed. The question she had asked him then made a lot more sense now.

"And she is the one you thought you saw in Old Market? You are sure?" The schoolmaster asked.

"Perfectly sure!" Sara insisted. "It would have been hard to mistake her. She had the brightest copper hair, like autumn leaves run through with rivers of gold."

That same tickle that Liam had gotten earlier, when they had first started following the copper-haired woman, returned.

"So you followed her because you wanted to know for sure that she was not an apparition?" her brother asked, his tone knowing and gentle. It made Liam wonder if such mistakes had been a concern before.

"Yes, exactly," Sara confirmed. "Oh Devon, I cannot tell you how happy I was when Liam said he could see her also! I nearly fainted."

"Today isn't the first time I had seen her either," Liam recalled the memory of Halloween night under Sara's window suddenly clear in his mind, like a soldier presenting itself for inspection. "She was in the alley next to Mrs. O'Toole's on Halloween."

286

"I thought it was a man you saw?" Devon questioned.

"It was," Liam confirmed. "Turns out that it was Ascher. But before him, a woman had stopped and stood under the old oak growing over Mrs. O'Toole's garden fence. She left just as he was coming down the alley."

"Ho ho," the schoolmaster chortled softly, reminding Liam of his presence. "So Ascher was the Riverview man you saw! I wonder what himself would think about being lumped in with new money. Well, boy; you were certainly right when you said he was dangerous. But how come you did not mention the woman when we questioned you that night?"

The schoolmaster's questions didn't make Liam bristle as much as they had done in the past. Perhaps because it was one that he wanted an answer to as well.

"I didn't remember it until just this moment. Which is odd because the woman's hair was as bright as new pennies, just as Sara said. She's someone who should stand out. But it didn't come to me that I had seen her before even when we were following her through Old Market, and I have no good reason as to why it didn't."

"I noticed something odd too!" Sara exclaimed. "All the way through Old Market, no one seemed to notice her except for us. Which was not what I would have expected since she stuck out like a swan amongst geese in that crowd, with her fashion-plate dress and hat. I almost asked Liam again if he was sure that he could see her because of how no one else paid her any mind."

"And that is the woman you followed to the flophouse," the schoolmaster said. "Hmm, I wonder, was she an innocent bystander or bait for the trap? And if she was bait, then for whom was the trap intended? I know what your guardian said, but I am inclined to say it was for the two of you. But that may be me jumping to a hasty conclusion since all of us ended up at the same place in the end. Even you, my friend," he said, directing the last comment at Devon. "That was quite the entrance, by the by. Though I would urge you not to travel in such a way again if it can be avoided."

"Yes, Devon please never do that again if you can possibly help it," Sara added emphatically. "I was so scared when I saw you standing there looking as though you were an apparition yourself."

"Did he really?" the schoolmaster asked eagerly, sounding almost as excited as Sara did when she and Liam were in the middle of their reading lessons. It was a bit of a revelation for Liam. "When I first noticed him, you already had a hold of his hand, after that stinging gale came through and you suddenly ran off. Tell me, when did you first see him?"

There was a slight tremble in Sara's voice when she answered. "When he rode from the paths of the dead on the back of the white horse. They were shadowless as most spirits are, but unlike the others they shone with a brilliant light. It was both beautiful and terrible at the same time." She added the last softly.

"And the white horse, that was also your guardian?"

Sara's gaze seemed to shift past the schoolmaster to a portion of railing that was bathed in moonlight. "It was."

"When she spoke to you in the seance, you could understand her words? Before she took possession of Devon's body I mean." The schoolmaster pressed.

"Yes, of course. The same as I am speaking to you now," Sara replied, looking back at the schoolmaster. "You did not understand them?"

"No, I cannot understand the language of angels," the schoolmaster replied softly, maybe even wistfully if Liam were to say, like a man at a shop window dreaming of something he knew he could not afford.

Sara's eyes went back to the moonlit railing. "Is that what you are then," she asked the apparition that only she could see at the moment, "an angel?"

Liam felt a feral grin split his face as his gaze followed hers. "If she is, then she is an avenging one."

Devon soon deemed it too late for more questions. Though Liam wondered if that was his way of ending the increasingly boisterous conversation between Sara and the schoolmaster. Even in that short time, they managed to go over what it was that Sara had seen both before and after the attack, as well as at the old cracker house down by the river, in minute detail. It had been eye-opening, to say the least.

The two men walked with them back to their rooms. They reached Sara's door first, then after wishing her a good night, they followed Liam to his. As he reached out to grasp the doorknob, he felt Devon's hand come to rest gently on his shoulder. He turned to face the man who had done a lot of good by him.

"Thank you, Liam." The simple words were said in such a way as to hold a mile's worth of meaning.

Liam gave a nod and smiled. That was the nice thing about a man like Devon; words were not always expected or needed. However, Liam still had one question whose answer he wanted to know for certain. "My mother, did she come to the cemetery to find you?"

"She did."

"And is she still there?"

"She is," Devon squeezed his shoulder. "We will make it right, soon. My word on it. Now try to get some sleep, and we will see what can be done in the morning."

Liam nodded again and quickly went in the door, closing it behind him. His breath was coming hard. The look on Devon's face had confirmed all that Ascher had told him, his *maman's* spirit was in pain. That understanding banged about in his head as he sat himself down on a chair in the corner of the room. He wasn't quite ready to stretch out in the bed, restless and not knowing what dreams might await him there.

Despite the closed door, he could still hear the two men as they moved off down the porch. Their footsteps went on for a ways, then stopped. The creak of the wooden railing as they leaned against it drifted back to him as plain as if they were standing right outside his door. He heard the strike of a match. For a moment there was only silence, which was eventually followed by a long exhale.

"Well, after hearing everything I have heard tonight, I feel the need to take back most of my uncharitable thoughts towards your assistant," the schoolmaster's tenor voice admitted wryly.

There was a snort, then Devon's deeper baritone answered, "How generous of you, Kris."

Another long exhalation. "Can you blame me for being wary? I've grown to like this place and the company. I am not inclined to leave, and I am afraid we may have to. This growing feeling of darkness, the hidden canker eating away at respectable people, everything we learned in the seance, it is all too familiar to me."

"You think the same thing is happening here as happened in your homeland?"

"Your guardian angel practically confirmed it. Although at least now I know that there is a force behind it, a singular entity that can be found and destroyed."

"It seems that you and my guardian angel are of a similar mind."

There was another drawn-out pause. The smell of pipe smoke inveigled its way into Liam's room, soon followed by Devon's voice.

"My guardian angel," his voice had grown thoughtful. "How did you know that she spoke the language of angels?"

"I have a great interest in such things. As I have mentioned many times before, much to your not-always-well-hidden dismay."

"I was not dismayed by your interest. I am just not in the habit of speaking to others about such things," Devon scoffed lightly.

"For reasons I am sure you can guess. Though I suppose that you having such an interest would only be natural, your benefactress being what she is and all."

The schoolmaster cleared his throat. "Well… strictly speaking, I am walking a fine line in such knowledge. As retainers of the Lady's house, my family is actually forbidden to study the deeper mysteries. And yet, I am drawn to them like a moth to a flame. Worse yet, a moth who knows better. I envy you the household you grew up in; having a mother and father dedicated to understanding such knowledge must have been something extraordinary."

"Although Sara shares his love of learning, those studies are really my father's passion. For my mother such things come naturally, as they do for Sara and myself."

There was a long pause. Long enough that Liam wondered if perhaps they had left, then he heard a quiet bark of laughter.

"You'll catch flies with your mouth open the way it is, my friend," Devon chuckled.

"My apologies! But I never… I always assumed that your father was a practitioner and that yours and Sara's gifts had come as a result of his efforts. I never dreamed that the two of you had been born to it. Good heavens, natural born! Truly!"

"You say that with such incredulity."

"Again, I apologize, but you can hardly blame me. People who can set fires with a look or change their shape at will or even move objects without touching them, is it any surprise that I half-believed them myths?" the schoolmaster reasoned. "Though I suppose that solves the mystery of how someone such as yourself could be surrounded by magick but have so little understanding of its workings."

"It's true that I have felt little need to learn much beyond the old lore of running water, salt, and thresholds. And there is certainly no blame on you for thinking us little more than a myth, since you are not far wrong. Most families were hunted to extinction generations ago. But as you've said before, we are now living in the 'age of enlightenment'. Such fears should be behind us." Devon's voice was neutral, so Liam could not tell if there was mockery behind the man's words or if he truly believed what he was saying. "Ah, yes. The 'age of enlightenment'." The derision in the schoolmaster's voice however was quite clear before it grew heavy with concern. "You need to take great care, Devon. Your guardian may be powerful, but who can say if her power alone will be sufficient?

"My loyalties must always lie with my mistress's house first; however, I pledge to support and protect both you and Sara by whatever means I can." Liam could almost feel the deep commitment of the man's words.

"That is quite a pledge, Kris."

"I would offer more if I could."

"Thank you. Your friendship is all I could ask for and more than enough."

"I pray that proves true," the schoolmaster gave a final long exhalation. "Good night, Devon."

"Good night, Kris."

Liam continued to sit in the dark while the sound of footsteps faded away, mulling over the conversation that he had just overheard. A softer sound caught his ear, the brush of a skirt against wood. It gave him pause. It seemed that he had not been the only one eavesdropping, though when he went to look he found no one there.

He finally allowed himself to crawl into bed. The soft mattress nearly swallowed him whole, though if his mind hadn't been so preoccupied, he might have actually enjoyed it. As it was, he found himself feeling surprisingly of the same mind as the schoolmaster. But how could he protect anyone when he knew so little about what he would need to protect them from? And then there was his *maman*… There was nothing for it, he would have to take Ascher up on his offer, tying himself to the Ascher family and a man who made his teeth itch, damn him.

He wondered if his beautiful, strong-minded, somewhat devious *maman* hadn't already considered this might happen when she made her offer to find Devon.

EPILOGUE

Where Her Bones Lie

Liam stood at the prow of a flatboat watching as the dark trees drew closer, the angel's pale figure glimmering in their shadows. Her up-swept wings beckoned to him, calling him back to collect the bones he had left there.

The End

THANK YOUS

Thank yous are most definitely in order.

Thank you Jenni for reading a very early version of this story. You are a fantastic friend and it was your enthusiasm that gave this story the legs it needed to continue.

Thank you Erick and Darke for taking the time to beta-read and share all of your insights with me. They made a difference. And a huge thank you to my husband, Chris, whose constructive criticism was invaluable and who, unlike my other beta readers, did not have the option to escape.

Thank you Kath for being a gem of an editor. I have said it before and I'll say it again, I was very lucky to have found you.

A second thank you to my husband, and to my mother and daughter, for giving me the thing all writers seem to need in abundance; emotional support.

And finally, thank you, reader, for allowing me to share my stories with you.

AUTHOR'S NOTES

Often gas lamp fantasy stories are set in places like Victorian London or New York or a similarly industrious city, or perhaps the fantasy equivalent of them. But for Ashwood town and the land around it, my inspirations came from places a little closer to home.

I grew up on the southeast coast of Florida. And although that may not be the first place that comes to mind when you think about the turn of the 20th century, there was a great deal of history being made here at that time. Henry Flagler was bringing down the railroad and with it change and an interesting mix of old and new. The old settler families who had long been here trying to carve a living out of the sand and swamp would find themselves now side by side with the extremely rich who were moving down to build their mansions and enjoy the milder winters.

Like any storyteller, I took little bits of this history and wove it in with my memories of growing up here. I wanted to share a part of Florida that not everyone sees, but that I had the luck to grow up running wild through.

Interesting Tidbits

The original inspiration for Ashwood town came from the city of St. Augustine on the far northeastern coast of Florida. The city was founded in 1565 and is the oldest continuously occupied settlement of European and African-American origin in the United States. Ashwood soon became its own place, of course, so that by the time everything was said and done there was not a great deal of "the oldest city" left in it. Still, much of the flavor of my late-night rambles past the Huguenot cemetery, through the old city gates, and down the narrow streets in the historic district lingers in the Bottoms and the streets of Ashwood.

The Ascher family cemetery grew from my visits to St. Augustine's Huguenot and Tolomato cemeteries, and the cemetery at the shrine of Our Lady of La Leche. Only the Ascher's cemetery is much larger and much, much more overgrown. Whether it is more lively than its inspirations I can't say; I guess you'll have to visit St. Augustine to find out.

What is that?

It was pointed out to me that not everyone will know what an oak hammock, coquina, or a tidewater house are. So, I thought why not include a few short descriptions? It was interesting to put words to things I have seen my whole life. I hope you enjoy them also, either as satisfying little bites or doors that send you down rabbit holes.

Coquina is a sedimentary rock made up of layers and layers of tiny shell fragments and quartz grains, all held together by calcium carbonate. Native to Florida, it is soft and easily cut from the ground but hardens once it's exposed to air. It was used extensively for construction in early settlements, sugar mills, and plantations across Florida. The Castillo de San Marcos in St. Augustine which is 450 years old is built from coquina, as were the city gates. You can still see many other standing walls of this beautiful, unique stone throughout the old city.

Another building material that isn't mentioned in this book was tabby concrete. It was also used extensively in early settlement construction. Oyster shells were burned to make lime, which was then mixed with sand, water, and more broken oyster shells to make, in essence, a man-made version of coquina.

The term "Cracker" was used for the descendants of Florida's (and Georgia's) early English settlers. *Cracker houses* were simple structures out of necessity since the settlers had little money or building materials to work with, other than what they could find right there. They were built up on pilings made of oyster shell, coquina, or clay brick, with plenty of windows and a deep front porch to help manage the extreme heat of Florida. They only had one room and had steep roofs covered in cypress shingles to shed the rain quickly. Made of wood (cypress or pine usually), they sometimes had a stone or brick chimney at one end, though not always.

Houses built in the *Queen Anne Victorian style* have always reminded me of fairytale castles with their turrets, towers, and balconies dressed in gingerbread trim. Whimsical and unique, they often sported windows of leaded or colored glass and wrap-around porches. Multi-storied affairs with dormers and gabled roofs, they were the epitome of decorative excess. But very beautiful nonetheless.

Tidewater houses, which can be found all over the South, are wooden houses built with coastal or seasonal flooding in mind. Often two stories high themselves, they were also built up on stilts or pilings, sometimes a full story high up in the air, with the main entrance and living spaces on the upper levels. Both stories commonly had expansive wrap-around porches with a low-hipped roof line that extended over the porch and wide eaves. They had numerous windows set up to catch the cross breezes that might bring some relief in the intense heat of Florida summers. They are also sometimes called Low Country houses because of the areas where they were built.

You can still see examples of *Spanish colonial architecture* in St. Augustine today. Houses built in this style had thick walls, usually made of adobe or brick, or in the case of those built in Florida, coquina or tabby concrete covered in stucco or lime wash. The earliest versions were often one story with flat roofs, but those built later stood two or two and a half stories high. They were inward-facing houses with loggias, courtyards, and balconies mostly encompassed by the mass of the house. Though shorter, exterior balconies built to overhang the streets the houses were on would sometimes be included. Shutters or bars made of wood or iron were common features, as were gardens and garden walls. There are several interesting books on the architecture of St. Augustine, including Houses of St. Augustine, 1565 - 1821 by Albert Manucy, which is well worth checking out if your interests lie in that direction.

In this book, the architecture of the original Ascher homestead fell more along the lines of Spanish colonial, while the newer Ascher house was of the Queen Anne style.

Florida has many wonderful, interesting habitats, and it was hard not to try to include all of them here (many a day was spent down the rabbit hole on this one) But, I've decided to stick to the ones you see in and around Ashwood, or run the risk of doubling the size of this book.

Mesic pine flatwoods have sandy, acidic soil with very little organic matter. A few feet below that is usually a layer of hardpan or marl. The canopy is made up of slash or longleaf pine and saw palmetto is the dominant understory plant. They are an open kind of wood. Their beauty is subtle and as unforgettable as the sweet ephemeral fragrance of the tarflower that grows there.

Oak Hammocks often occur as little "islands" of high ground in surrounding wetlands. Live and Laurel Oaks interspersed with Sabal Palm usually form a heavy, closed canopy, and it is not uncommon to find their limbs covered in Resurrection Fern and draped in Spanish Moss. The understory tends to be shrubby and is often made up of Saw Palmetto, American Holly, Hog Plum, and Wax Myrtle. There is a timeless quality to the air in a hammock, a glimpse of old Florida.

"The sand dunes were the closest thing to hills this area had. And yet, Ascher house sat up on high, atop a rise in the land made by the discarded shells of a long-dead people."

Shell Mounds or *Shell Middens* are exactly that, huge mounds of discarded shells. For thousands of years, the early peoples of Florida lived on the bounty of its extensive rivers and waterways, and these shell mounds were a result. They can be found throughout Florida, though many are gone now, having been used for construction and early roadworks. There is one in my hometown of Jupiter, in fact. It was, and still is, 20 feet high, but once measured 600 feet in length but now it only measures around 90 feet. It was made by the Jeaga (hay-gwa) tribe that once inhabited the area.

Today, the Dubois Pioneer House sits at the top. Built in 1898 it is the second oldest house still standing in Palm Beach County. Although as you now know, the mound it sits on is much, much older still.

The natural springs of Florida are beautiful places where the water is always cool, crystal clear, and often the most amazing shade of aqua or green. They are surrounded by hardwood forests and their bottoms are often covered in white sand and seagrass. They are a favorite spot for manatees. Is it any wonder that these magical places were the inspiration for the Shallows at the end of Washboard Lane?

Barrier islands line Florida's coasts, some 700 miles of its coasts in fact. They often begin in one of two ways, as simple sandbars or emerged shoals that grow over time into more substantial islands separated from the mainland by tidal creeks, bays, and lagoons. Beaches and sand dunes covered with deep-rooted grasses form on the side of the barrier island facing the ocean while the side facing the shore often develops into marshes, tidal flats, or maritime forests.

The barrier islands I am most familiar with were covered

in coastal scrub and maritime forests made up of mangroves, sea grape, and gumbo limbo trees. I often visited Jupiter Island when I was younger, walking along the beach from Coral Cove to Blowing Rocks Preserve. Australian pines grew there then, and the sound the wind made through their long needles was like nothing else in the world. I used to sit there on limestone rocks worn smooth by the waves and listen to the pines whispering and watch the osprey or sea birds flying overhead. Talk about a wonderful place to daydream! The Australian pines are gone now. I know it had to be because sadly they are an invasive species, but I miss their voices.

From what I have found, the French language has a near-endless list of endearments. There are a number of French phrases throughout this book, courtesy of Marguerite. And if you had been wondering what exactly it was that she was saying, fear not, I have included a list of meanings below.

ma fée - my fairy

mon poussin - my chick (as in baby chicken)

Bonjour - Hello, Hi, or good morning

Bonsoir - Good evening (or bonne soirée)

mon fils - my son

maman - mother

Gobemoucheron gris-bleu - Blue-grey gnatcatchers (adorable tiny birds)

ce serait merveilleux - that would be wonderful!

ma cherie - my dear

ma belle - beautiful

Que dis-tu – What do you say?

A sap is a leather-wrapped iron rod or shot, usually about 8 to 12 inches long, sometimes with a loop on the end of it. They are sometimes called slapjacks, blackjacks, or slappers.

The book Sara used to start Liam off on his letters is a real book, Fairyland ABC by Grace C. Floyd, published in 1890 by Raphael Tuck & Sons.

Join the reader newsletter for more authors that have taken a stand against the use of AI-generated content: https://www.authenticityinitiative.com/for-readers